The
CHRONICLES of IONA:
PROPHET

The
CHRONICLES of IONA:
PROPHET

by

Paula de Fougerolles

ISBN-10: 0615753361
ISBN-13: 9780615753362

Library of Congress Control Number: 2012917397
Careswell Press, Brookline, MA

Careswell Press
P.O. Box 1699
Brookline, MA 02446

Cover Art: *Scotiae Tabula*, from the atlas *Theatrum Orbis Terrarum* (1592-1606) by Abraham Ortelius. Property of the author.

Also by Paula de Fougerolles:

The Chronicles of Iona:
Exile

For my mother,
Joyce M. Charland

Many credit the foundation of the nation of Scotland to the efforts of two men, an Irish saint, Columba, and a Scottish warlord, Áedán mac nGabráin.

This is their story.

There was a man of venerable life and blessed memory, the father and founder of monasteries, whose name was the same as the prophet Jonah's. For though the sound is different in three different languages, in Hebrew *Jona*, in Greek *Peristera*, in Latin *Columba*, the meaning is the same, 'dove'. So great a name cannot have been given to the man of God but by divine providence ... The reader should also be reminded of this, that many things worth recording about the man of blessed memory are left out here for the sake of brevity, and only a few things out of many are written down so as not to try the patience of those who will read them.

Adomnán of Iona, <u>Vita Columbae</u>, (<u>c</u>. 690 A.D.)

A son of the clan of the Shadow
will take the kingdom of Alba by force of strength,
a man who will feed ravens, who will conquer in battle:
Ferbasach will be his name.
Alas for the Picts to whom he will go eastward,
the distressed traveler, the red flame that awakens war.
With grey men, the rider of the swift horse
will cast the Picts into insignificance
and will seek Hibernia in one day.
After the slaughter of Picts,
after the harassing of Foreigners,
many years in the sovereignty of Alba.
He will not be king
at the time of his death, on a Thursday, in Cendtire.

<u>The Prophecy of Berchan</u> (1165 × 1169 A.D.)

I would like to thank the following, without whom this book would never have come to pass: Tony de Fougerolles, Mila de Fougerolles, and Simon de Fougerolles, as always; Joyce Charland; Lida de Fougerolles and Robert de Fougerolles; Maria Němcová Banerjee and Ron D.K. Banerjee; Simon Young; Camille White, Frank Charland, Karen Green, Jean de Fougerolles, and Justine Recordon; Marc Anderson and Melanie Anderson; Anne Pomerleau and Humphrey Gardner; Heather Neal; Kristina Lumsden; Susan Whoriskey and Máirtín Ó Muilleoir for helping *Exile* find its Irish audience; The Venerable M. Edward Simonton OGS; Professor David N. Dumville and my other colleagues at the Department of Anglo-Saxon, Norse and Celtic, University of Cambridge; The Wednesday Wits (John Amiard, Kitty Beer, Jackie Fenn, E. Jeanne Harnois, Terry Kitchen, and Marty Levin) and my other talented and dedicated readers: Michelle Muhlbaum-Aviksis, Muriel Barnes, Karyn Wang, Bonnie Gilbert, and Dixon Bain; and my friend Kim Kennedy (†2011) for the photograph.

· CONTENTS ·

Part Three:

CALEDONII

CALEDONIA

MIATHI

GODODDIN

BERNICIA

STRAT CLUT

DALRIATA

AERON

GALLOWAY

NORTHERN UI NEILL

DAL RIATA

RHEGED

DEIRA

ULAID

MARE HIBERNIÆ

BREIFNE

AIRGIALLA

MANAU

ELMET

CONNACHT

LINDSEY

SOUTHERN UI NEILL

LAIGIN

GUINED

HIBERNIA

MERCIA

MUMU

POUIS

BRITANNIA

DEMETIA

MUIR NICHT

GAUL

NEUSTRIA

HIBERNIA

Rechra
Dún Sobairche
DÁL RIATA
The Flagstone
Daire
Grianan of Ailech
CENÉL CONAILL
NORTHERN UÍ NÉILL
DÁL nARAIDE
Bancher
ULAID
Emain Macha
Dún Echdach
DÁL FIATACH
Cúl Dreimne
BREIFNE
AIRGIALLA
Teilte
CONNAUGHT
UISNECH
SOUTHERN UÍ NÉILL
Temair
Cluain Moccu Nóis
Cluain-Erard
Cill Dara
LAIGIN
Birr
Glendalocha
MUMU

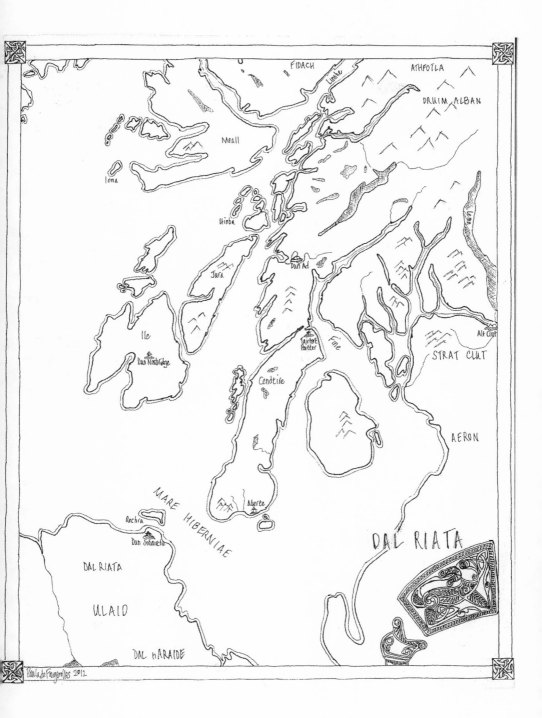

FIDACH · Linnhe · ATHFOTLA

DRUIM ALBAN

Meall

Iona

Hinba

Dun Ad

Jura

Tairbert Boitter

Fine

Ile

Dun Nosbridge

Cendtire

Loam

Ale Clut

STRAT CLUT

AERON

Aberte

MARE HIBERNIAE

Rechra

Dun Sobairche

DAL RIATA

ULAID

DAL nARAIDE

DAL RIATA

Paula de Fougerolles 2012

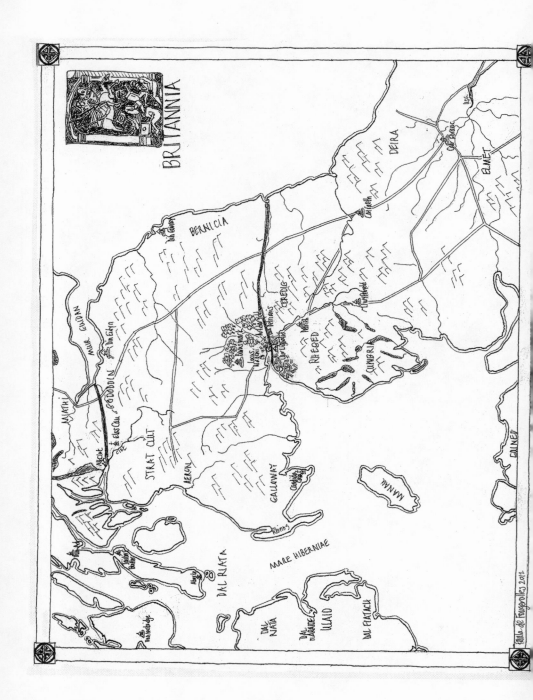

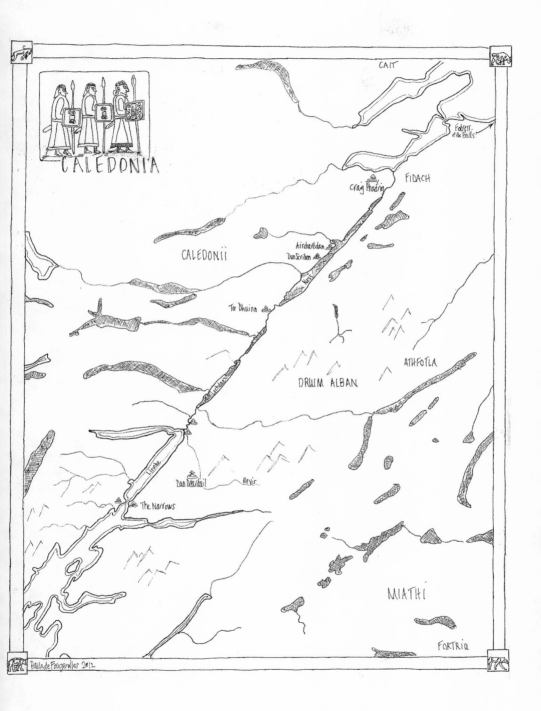

CAIT

Forest of the Bulls

CALEDONIA

Craig Phadrig

FIDACH

CALEDONII

Airchartdan
Dun Scriben

Ness

Tor Dhuinn

DRUIM ALBAN

ATHFOTLA

Arcaibh

Linnhe

Dun Deardail

Nevis

The Narrows

MIATHI

FORTRIU

Paula de Fougerolles 2012

xxi

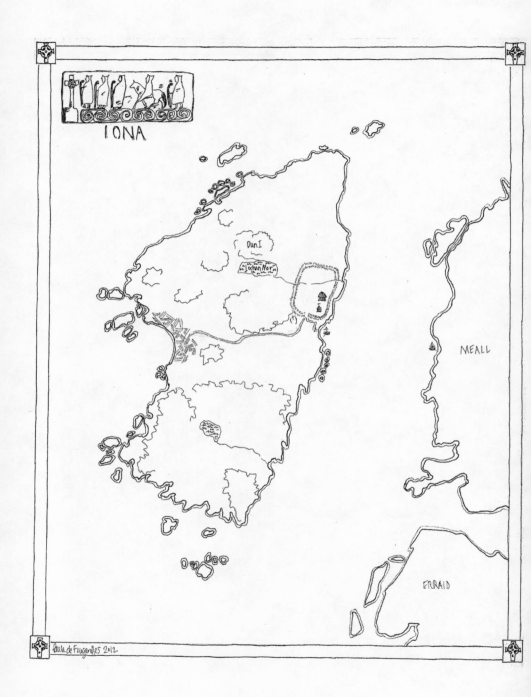

IONA

Dun I

Lochan Mor

MEALL

ERRAID

Paula de Fougerolles 2012

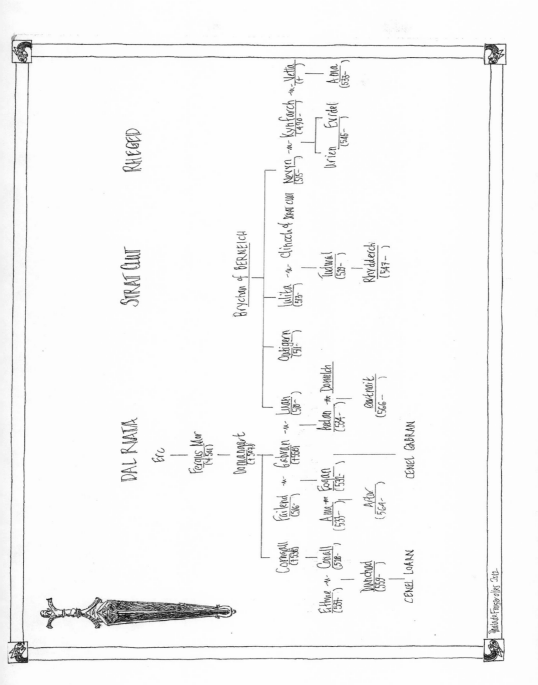

· PREFACE ·

Iona, June, 567

"I wish you wouldn't go, *Abba*. Not now. Storm's coming."

The shingle of the shore shifted uncertainly underfoot as Columba turned to eye the sound, awash with the first rays of a fitful sun, then back to Baithene, worriedly holding the small, leather-clad *curragh* which would bear Columba to the mainland. "Conall has summoned me," he told his cousin. "You know I must go."

"There was a time you would disobey kings gleefully. I liked you very much then."

Columba laughed, a rich, booming sound. Aye! And look where that had got him. He shaded his eyes, studying the skies. Dawn had unveiled itself shyly, peeking over the looming mountains of the island of Meall and the mainland beyond with a mild pink blush. But now the clouds were leaking red. Storm threatened, coming from the west. He would be sailing before it. With luck, using the following winds, he might just outrun it. But the broad sea-loch in the fretted coastline which kept the king's hillfort of Dun Ad safe was still a full-day's sail away.

He turned back to his cousin with a sigh. "If I were to do so now, what would become of all of you?"

"Alone though? Take one of us with you, at the least."

"No. Your brother is still out."

"He knows what he's doing."

"Aye. But watch for him anyway. He may need help getting back in."

Together, they launched the *curragh* into the waves. Columba sprang abroad, took an oar, then picked his way carefully through the treacherous shoals which guarded his island of Iona. The burgeoning wind beat his face and ran questing fingers through his hair. Once safely in the tide-race, he breathed in deeply of the briny air to dispel his unease. Cobthach, the monastery's best fisherman, had not returned from Erraid yesterday as expected. The big monk was a skilled sailor: he would also have sensed the storm. Had he passed the night on the rock, amongst the seals? Or waited until the falling tide uncovered the strand linking Erraid to shore, and then retreated to the safety of Meall?

Wrapping his cloak more tightly about himself, hunching into its warmth, Columba turned to look back at Iona, tiny, hardly a bump on the horizon behind him now as the island rapidly receded from view. For a moment his concern and the waves and the coming storm faded away. His island. Squinting through the grey veil of drizzle which had begun to fall, he could just make out her turquoise waters darkening as the churn of surf, the advance-guard of the storm, began to hurtle itself against the white-shell beaches. There, farther up the shore, black against the rain-haze, smoke was rising from the fire in the *magna domus*, the great house, lit to keep the monks warm. Huddled alongside it was Iona's little wooden church.

His Iona. A beloved, beautiful gift. A bounty, unexpected. Here in Dal Riata of the Scots, this harsh, unwanted land of exile.

As his little boat heaved through the choppy waves, the wind inciting the swell, rain spitting into his face, a new hymn came to Columba: *I beg that me, a little man, trembling and most wretched, rowing through the infinite storm of this age, Christ may draw after Him to the lofty, most beautiful haven of life.*

He hummed this hymn over and over again, summoning heaven's protection as the day lengthened and, cackling her own ditty of malice and glee, the sea rolled monstrously beneath him; as, like an insect in the curl of a leaf on a rip-tide, he sailed through the heart of the storm.

· PART ONE ·

Selkirkshire orans figure (National Museums of Scotland, 400-700 A.D.)

· 1 ·
THE MOUNTH

The toes of his boots peering over the precipice, Aedan mac Gabran was pondering the rippling waters of the loch below, so distant, so dark, his thoughts far, far away, when a sound he had not heard in many long weeks caused him to snap instantly alert: the sigh of wood winging through air.

This caught him by surprise. Few things did. Wilderness, this heartland of the Caledonian Picts, stretched vastly around him, unkind and menacing. He had climbed to the woods which cloaked the hillside above this grey loch to find the most isolated spot to brood with his memories, of her, and of the babe and his kin, and he thought that he was quite alone.

But, after countless years on the battlefield, he knew this sound: a spear splitting the air. As soon as his quick mind recognized the threat, he was spinning around. It was indeed a spear, hurled by a Pictish horseman lurking in the safety of the tree-cover. The weapon arced for his throat, vulnerable between breast-plate and helmet.

Aedan cursed. He was a fool to have let down his guard, here, deep in Caledonian territory where no other Scot dared to go, with his back now to the precipice and his only haven the dark water of the loch too far below. He thrust out his shield just in time. The Pict's spear-point deflected off the toughened wood, then skittered along the stony ground before kicking up and tumbling over the cliff's edge a hundred or more feet to the awaiting water.

Nearby a hound was barking frantically—Aedan's wolf-hound, Ceo. Ceo! Where was she? This was odd: she was never too far away. Snapping down his visor, Aedan grabbed for his own spear, sunk into the thin soil beside him. But the Pict, who had kicked his excited horse into a gallop, was already hurling his heavy axe. Aedan thrust his shield up again and, as the axe embedded with a *thunk*, the muscles of his shoulder reverberated, absorbing the energy of the blow. The axe hung from the shield, weighing it down, rendering it useless. With another curse, Aedan flung it to the ground before him—anything that might buy him some time. With luck it would trip up the Pict's mount.

He hoisted his spear, studying the Pict sourly. He was fit, young, about Aedan's own age, wild brown hair flying freely, his teeth, sharpened to points, a grimace over the horse's rippling mane as he wheeled it about. His face and limbs swirled with the fantastic, be-magicked symbols of the Picts. Able to read the blue tattoos, Aedan scowled. He knew his attacker: it was Drust, son of Bridei, king of the Caledonii—Aedan's brother-in-law.

Aedan smiled at the long, ugly scar which rippled across Drust's forehead: it was a wound he had put there himself, many years ago now, back at home in Dal Riata; and then he steadied himself.

Drust had caught him unawares, it was true, but he was ready now. Waiting until Drust galloped within range again, he hurled his spear with a grunt. But Drust's shield came up, deflecting the missile easily. Drust grinned, a flash of white on a blue-tattooed face. He was enjoying himself. Bastard. His sword drawn overhead, Drust continued his charge, whooping.

Panting in anticipation, Aedan crouched, waiting it out, diving to the side at the last possible moment, just as the horse was bearing down on him. His brother-in-law's triumphant sword-swipe cut only air.

With a roll, Aedan came to his feet. His helmet tilted, momentarily obscuring his vision. With another muffled oath he righted it. The damned thing needed adjustment. It was a hazard. He was a fool not to have taken care of it sooner.

The horse wheeled, its hooves scattering rock and clumps of dirt over the cliff's drop as Drust circled Aedan, backing him up step-by-step, herding him back to the edge. Feet from the precipice, Aedan stumbled, landing heavily on the stony soil. Down snapped his visor again. As he righted it, he judged the distance left between them. He would not be able get to his feet in time to repel the next charge.

He did the only thing he could: he stayed down. Anything else would have been suicide. Seeing this, grinning that damn grin again, Drust dismounted in full gallop. He hit the ground at a run and leapt over the discarded shield, sword held high in both hands, whooping in triumph.

Aedan gave his own grim smile. Although a beautiful display of his brother-in-law's horsemanship, among the best Aedan had ever encountered, Drust had just made a mortal miscalculation. There was little Aedan, or anyone, could do against a mounted warrior, but in hand-to-hand combat Aedan had yet to meet his match, even when arse-down in the dirt. Drust should have remained on his horse until he had driven him over the edge. So Aedan let him charge, leaving his chest unprotected to entice him even closer. When the sword slashed down, Aedan grabbed Drust's arm and, using his own momentum against him, heaved him over his shoulder. Drust slammed into the ground, grunting in shock.

Aedan twisted and on bent knee jabbed the point of his sword at his brother-in-law's throat.

Breath heaving, Drust gaped up at him, brown eyes wide, the tattoos of the elaborate sunbursts inked onto his face elongating with his surprise at being bested. His sword clattered to the ground. Hands raised in defeat, he panted in a heavily accented version of Aedan's own speech, "I concede!"

"Damn right you do," Aedan growled, pressing the point of his sword into the center of a sun on one of Drust's cheeks.

"If you cut me," Drust warned, "my sister will have your head. Once was enough."

Drust's sister. Aedan's wife, Domelch. The mother of his son. The thought of her brought a wry smile to his face. "She would, wouldn't she?"

Offering a hand to his brother-in-law, he hauled him to his feet. The two men stood companionably, Drust with his hands on his hips, his face flushed with the thrill of the contest. "You have to admit, this time I almost had you."

"No, you didn't," Aedan scoffed.

"You fell!"

"On purpose, you idiot."

Drust's eyes narrowed in disbelief.

"And I stayed down," Aedan added cuttingly, "to lure you off your horse. And you fell for it. You always do. You're always too eager to finish the job, Drust. You take too many risks. It'll get you killed some day."

"But not by you."

"I hope not. But here, if you had stayed on your horse, you would have had me." He waved vaguely at the cliff drop only feet away.

Understanding, Drust's face fell. But then, just as quickly, his grin returned. He bent for his sword, sparing a regretful glance over the edge at the waters of the loch below into which his spear had disappeared. "This makes us even, yes?"

"No."

"Then you miscount—in your favor. Again. And, by the way, if you are looking for the cause of your own death, look no further than that stupid helmet." He banged on Aedan's simple metal helmet with the butt of his sword.

The din was deafening. "Ow!" Aedan protested, ripping it off.

"How many times must I say it?" Drust sniffed. "It is unmanly to wear a helmet."

"Yes. I know: *A bare-headed horseman is a king.* By all means, do as you see fit, but I am no king, am I? I've got to protect what little I've got." He rapped on his helmet with the flat of his own sword. "Especially with bloodthirsty Picts lurking behind every tree."

Drust whistled for his horse. It came at a trot, then the two men trudged side-by-side through the springy turf, equal parts exposed rock and bushy heather, high mountains all around. They were traveling along the winding river glens north of the Mounth, the mountain barrier which kept the Caledonii from the Miathi. There was something along this route that Domelch insisted he see.

"So how do you do it?" Aedan asked. "How do you keep your seat?"

"Keep my seat?" Drust twisted around to look bemusedly at his own backside.

"Don't be an ass. You know what I mean. You ride bareback, at a gallop, with no hands on the reins. You hold both shield and spear—all without being able to brace your legs. All that, and you manage to hit the target—*me*—nearly every time. It should be physically impossibile."

"Yes." Drust's chest swelled with pride.

"Well?" Aedan prompted again after a moment.

"Well what?"

"How do you do it?"

Drust's brown eyes were shrewd. He studied Aedan a long time before saying, "It is not enough that we have let you live, and that you have my sister. You're after more of our secrets, aren't you?"

In his three years amongst the Picts, his avowed enemies, and now his kin, Aedan had mastered their tongue, their customs, and their ways. He had visited all three divisions of the Caledonii, openly as the king's son when he could, disguised as an insignificant traveler when he could not. He had learned the location and the strength and the weaknesses of their strongholds, and the passes through their mountains, both those known and those secret. And everywhere with him had gone his wife, the daughter of the king and, lately, their son. And everywhere with him had gone his great hound Ceo, and the Caledonii had begun to marvel, seeing in his awe-inspiring animal-companion an echo of the attendants of the gods. But the Picts' legendary horsemanship, the one thing which gave them supremacy in battle over his own sea-faring people, at least on land? Aedan was still trying to dismantle that, piece by piece.

There was no need to prevaricate now. Though he bore no love for the Picts, Aedan had long ago decided that he would never consciously betray his newfound family. But no matter how much time passed, much of it peacefully, even pleasantly, Aedan was still, in essence, their captive, and a Scot. He knew where his loyalties lay.

He was indeed after their secrets. Every one of them. "Yes," he replied simply.

He was startled to see what looked like disappointment in his brother-in-law's eyes. Or was it regret? "You still do not consider yourself one of us, do you?" Drust asked.

Aedan felt a flash of anger. This was undeserved. Though he had lived amongst them all this time, honoring the contract between them, it was only last summer that King Bridei had called off the guards by which he had kept Aedan constantly under watch, shadowing his every move. A year ago, when Gartnait was born. Aedan would still be under watch, he was certain, except that he had not yet made it a point to demand that Bridei honor their agreement and allow him to return to Dal Riata. Somehow he knew that when he did, the king's answer would be a resounding *no*.

"If I were truly one of you, there would be no secrets between us," Aedan answered.

Drust studied his boots as he trudged through the turf. Just when Aedan had decided that Drust would not answer, his brother-in-law surprised him by nodding curtly. "Alright. I suppose you have earned it."

Drust stopped in his tracks. He released his horse which bent its head gratefully to pick at the turf. "You rein the horse back to steady your throw," he said, pulling the imaginary reins of an imaginary mount to illustrate his point.

"Impossible. You're at a full gallop."

Drust grinned. "Yes! Yes! That is the art of it! You have to hold to your charge—puts the fear of the gods into your enemy ... "

"No—not fear," Aedan said, recalling Drust's unexpected attack and his own response, which he had thought admirably clear-headed.

Drust rolled his eyes. "Listen. You asked, and I am telling you. You must rein in, otherwise you cannot throw. But the throw is your own moment of weakness, so rein in as little as possible. Control the horse, like this, with your knees. That is the secret: your knees; your thighs. Raise your shield. Protect your chest. Out in front of you like this, slightly to the side, the shield will also counterbalance your throw, helping you keep your seat. Then hurl the spear, as quickly as you can. Get rid of it. Let it go. Let it fly. We practice this endlessly when we are children until it becomes second-nature, rather like breathing. Or screwing." A quick grin. "And then get the next weapon in hand—axe, sword, whatever you've got. Hurl it. Quickly, quickly, quickly. Kill them. Kill them. Kill them."

His eyes gleamed, recalling former victories. That many of those former victories had been at the expense of Aedan's own people, Aedan decided, for the moment, to ignore. Then Drust's arms came down, the lesson finished. He headed off again in the direction of the smoke plume rising from the vale below them. "Most of the time the spear has done the trick and has skewered the bastard. But, bastard or no, you're better than most, I'll give you that."

Aedan was careful to hide his amusement. In the past three years, Drust had yet to win any of their mock contests—which is not to say that his brother-in-law, delighted to have turned from Aedan's captive to his captor, had not continued to try.

"I will show you how it is done. Next time."

Aedan nodded his thanks. But then they were cresting the little rise and could see in the sheltered hollow below the small, dark woman, the little boy at her side poking the fire with a stick, sending up sparks, and Aedan's wolf-hound, Ceo, whose spiked, iron great-collar the woman released so that it could speed towards the approaching men with a relieved *woof*.

The hound planted her massive paws on Aedan's chest. Eye-to-eye, she lathered his face joyfully, her tail wagging the back-half of her massive brindled body. "Ah! My love!" Aedan praised, rubbing her smoke-grey ears. "Where were you when I needed you, you big furry beast?" But then his son was toddling up the uneven slope to him on his little legs so determinedly that Aedan would have found it comical if he hadn't adored the boy so much. At the fire, Domelch stood, a hand on her hip, a palm up to shield her eyes against the sun, blinding behind them.

"Da! Da!" Gartnait cried, arms raised expectantly.

Shifting his weapons, Aedan lifted his son, set him, squealing, on his shoulders and headed down the slope. At the camp, he reached up, took the boy by the hips and somersaulted him back to the ground where he placed him gently on his feet. Gartnait shrieked in delight.

Domelch's dark eyes met his. "Still alive," she observed, the expression on her tidy, clever face, as hopeful and as guarded as ever.

When he shrugged, she *tsked* her disappointment to her brother. "Drust, are you quite certain you're trying hard enough?"

"If you think it so easy, Sister, have a go!" Drust's arm swept towards Aedan in exasperation. "He's all yours!"

Domelch smiled, but her expression was in no way jesting. Rather, it was hot and possessive. *Yes*, it said. *He is.*

That look was for Aedan alone. What she said to both men was, "Come and have some supper then".

· 2 ·
DUN AD

On most days Ama mac Gabran had the sense that he might still be alive. When she permitted herself a moment of stillness in her mind, she could feel him with her, present and watchful, as if he were breathing just over her shoulder, raising the sensitive hair on the back of her neck, observing with a wry smile what her life had become without him. Just the thought of him—solid and warm and whole—anchored her, just his name: Aedan. On those days, the memory of him cleared away her stormy thoughts like a stiff, fresh breeze. His memory was the thing that made her feel palpable.

Then there were days in which she struggled to sense him, as if he were shifting between this world and some other realm, shapeless, leeched of lifeblood, of emotion, as insubstantial as mist, unable, in the Otherworld which had stolen him away, to answer her call. On those days she felt adrift. Rudderless. Unreal and untied to the world.

Today was a day like that. They had been summoned to Dun Ad's Great Hall for no other reason she could discern than that Conall could spar with her husband Eogan over the prospect of war. With all her being, this was the last place she wanted to be. By the gods, her head hurt—the tightness behind the bridge of her nose threatened to squeeze the very reason from her brain. But Ama fought against it. She needed to be alert, now more than ever. The hall's massive wooden doors had been shut tight against the summer storm, the heat of the great fire inside oppressive. Need it be stoked so high? Thick smoke glomerated at the rafters, unable to escape through the roof's central hole against the rain which was pouring in. The heavy, dirty tapestries which lined the walls collected the reek; the rushes underfoot were unclean too, strewn with the half-eaten remnants of the previous week's feasts. Irritably, she kicked away the glistening pork hock which was unbalancing the sole of her boot.

Dun Ad. Fortress of Kings. Rising on its rock, vast marsh reeking all around, isolating it, protecting it, this famed capitol of the Scots was impregnable. Safe, it was supposed to be; never taken by an enemy. But she had never felt safe here. She hated this place. It was not the threat from without that kept her on edge: not the Picts, menacing from the mountain fastnesses to the north. Nor was it the risk posed to the Scots by her own people, the Britons, whose kingdoms spread southwards, inviting her home. No. These things did not frighten her. What did was the threat from within.

Unwillingly, her gaze met the queen's. Eithne was waiting petulantly for a response to a question which Ama, distracted, had failed to hear. Wheaten hair artfully falling, blue eyes cold as the sea, Eithne was frosty and untouchable, both impeccably attired and remote in her beauty. She was the one faultless thing in the hall, untouched by struggle, which amazed Ama. Couldn't Eithne also sense the pervasive tension, brittle as spring-ice on a frozen pond? Didn't she care that her husband willingly led their whole people to war?

Ama longed to rebuke her, to re-call Eithne to her senses, but she bit her tongue. She had more pressing concerns. Conall and Eogan were at the fire, flagons of wine in hand, flanked by their respective retinues: Conall's men drinking as heavily as the king, swearing, gaming, ready at a moment's notice to launch themselves between their *ruiri* and an enemy which this evening lurked only in the prickly king's imagination; Eogan's guardedly watching. Mutual disgust stained the two men's faces. Conall's flaming red hair, his crimson cloak, his ruddy face did little to distract from the fact that his features, normally even and pleasing, were wan, drawn, and used. His eyes were bloodshot, the skin below them puffy and grey as if he had yet again foregone a good night's rest for the false friendship of the wineskin. He looked altogether ready to pounce.

An edgy exhaustion seemed to leak from her husband too, who was usually a study in artifice and diplomacy. Eogan's black eyes were dull, weeks of his own uneven sleep had etched weary lines into his comely face, so much so that he had begun to look gaunt. He hunched, the long lines of his body folding wearily towards his cousin, the man who by capricious fate had become his overlord. His fears were keeping dreams from him, Eogan said. Late into the evening he would still be stirring, devising new and clever ways to forestall the civil war which was brewing between Conall and the third kindred of the Scots, the Cenel Oengussa. Such a war would engulf their *cenel* too. Then he would turn to her in the night, to talk, to be held, asking for the fleeting oblivion which her body could give him. She did what she could—she did care for him; it was not he who had betrayed her by selling her into this marriage but her own stepfather—but the constant effort of it all, the time, the care, Eogan's unremitting need, depleted her too. And it was all because of this king.

And because of Aedan; her husband's brother, her love, taken by the Picts.

The pounding behind her eyes intensified. Something old roasted on the fire's spit, greasing the air, making her stomach roil. It was as if lightening was brewing here, inside the hall. It did not help that the boys were playing boisterously at her feet: Dunchad, the queen's son, scampering in the filthy rushes with his little dog; her own son Artur, delighted by the older boy and his pet but unsure how to join their game, scrambling onto and off her lap. "Mama! Mama! Look! Look!" Artur trilled, enchanted by Dunchad who with sharp jabs with a stick to its hindquarters was making his yipping dog do clever tricks.

It all made it so difficult to hear the men's heated conversation. Across the hall, her husband's spine was stiffening. "Will you meet their terms?" he asked Conall irritably.

Yes. This is what they needed to know. Would he? Would Conall finally make redress to the Cenel Oengussa for the raid? If the king wished it, it could be a simple enough matter. A few cattle exchanged, their loss of face restored, and with it peace. But Ama thought not. Conall hunted, he feasted, by the way he leered at her when he thought Eithne was not watching, she had no doubt that he whored. She feared that Conall would think only of himself and avoid the prosecution of the suit which the Cenel Oengussa had brought against him for hacking off the sword-hand of their king. Because he liked a fight; at the slightest hint of insult, he bristled like a boar. Indeed, he was garrisoning all the fortlets within sight of Dun Ad and refitting his warships for active duty. He would not negotiate, and she had told Eogan this. Rather, he would retaliate against the Cenel Oengussa, and soon, which would mean that he would call up for the hosting her husband's men, the men of the Cenel Gabran—a situation which both she and Eogan wished desperately to avoid. But how? Eogan thought it worth another try. She thought not, but here they were.

"No, you *will*. You *will* go to Alt Clut," the king bellowed. "You *will* pay my render."

Everyone stilled: the king's retinue, her husband's, the boys, even Dunchad's dog. Alt Clut, the chief citadel of the Britons of

Strat Clut? Her blood rose, got very hot. Conall would make Eogan go to the Oenach to pay those Britons his tribute because he was too proud to do it himself? He would make her husband, her *kingly* husband, beg for good terms like a dog for scraps?

Never. She had had enough—of her own impotency, of the stupidity of kings, of the nagging suspicion that she was living a life which was not her own. She was springing from her chair to go to her husband's side—she was a lady of Rheged, after all, the stepdaughter of its mighty king, who higher?, a lord to whom the Scots paid a withering tribute; Eogan was a king in his own right; and shouldn't Conall bear this in mind when he dared to speak to him this way?—when she was suddenly yanked back by a talon-like grip on her arm.

It was the queen. "Don't," Eithne said.

Ama shook her off. "Your husband leads us to war!"

"You are a woman," Eithne replied coldly. "Conall would rather bend you over a table and skive you from behind than listen to a word you had to say. And, because you're a Briton, he'd do it until you bled."

Ama was struggling to find a suitable retort when the doors of the Great Hall burst open with a bang. The storm's roar was huge, and in with a shout came more of the king's men, ushering into the hall a stranger they swirled around suspiciously. The man was large, with heavyset features and a graceful, polished manner. He thrust off his heavy cloak, rain sluicing as it fell to the floor. Underneath, jewels glittered. A gold cross of the Christians bumped up and down on a great gold chain as he approached, cushioned by his sumptuous, fur-trimmed robes. He was a cleric clearly, but not a monk since his scalp was unshorn. He could be a priest but, in all the years of Ama's childhood at the Christian court of Rheged, she had never once seen a priest so bedecked in splendor. No. This was a bishop, a pawn of kings.

"Who the devil are you?" Conall demanded, his retinue closing around him protectively.

The stranger flourished meaty hands in greeting. "A friend, my lord! A friend, with a common enemy, and a mutual need!" Though he decorated his face with a broad smile, underneath it was cold calculation. "I am Bishop Budic, my good lord. Bishop of the court of the highking, Dermot mac Cerball." There was pride in the bishop's tone.

Conall frowned. "You were the bishop to the *former ard-ri* of Hibernia?"

"The very one." Budic's chin lifted, as if that association had been his finest, and his highest.

"But not to the *current ard-ri?*"

"Indeed not, my lord." The bishop's tone now spoke insult.

This, interesting: Budic wished it known that he was no friend of the current high-king, Ainmire mac Setna. Neither, in fact, was Conall. The Northern half of Hibernia, of which Ainmire was still overlord, contained within it the other division of Dal Riata, a territory which Conall also ruled, in name at least. And, for the Scots' ancestral homeland, from which many years ago they had fled, seeking refuge in this benighted new land, Conall wished to submit to no one.

"So you are bishop of nothing," Conall replied.

Budic's hands fisted at his sides. He studied the king for a long moment under heavily lidded eyes. Finally, in a surprisingly placating tone, he said, "My lord. It is true that my former lord, Dermot, is dead, God rest his soul! But I minister to his son now, Colman Bec. It is on his behalf that I am here. Indeed, he offers you his friendship. But first, my lord, do you not remember my name? We corresponded once, you and I, many years ago. About the abbot Columba".

At mention of Columba's name on the bishop's pouty lips, Conall spluttered and his ruddy face flushed an even deeper shade of red.

"No! No!" Budic quickly assured him. "Please do not misconstrue! I am no friend of Columba's! In fact, I have come to Dal Riata to destroy him."

For the first time, Conall smiled, as if the king had discovered, inadvertently and at the last possible second, a way to avoid an unwanted path. And then Conall took Budic aside, carefully out of earshot, where, after intense discussion, he clapped a hand on the bishop's shoulder, sealing some sort of bargain which, by his delighted grin, Conall was thinking was entirely in his favor. And, before Ama knew it, Budic was making an oath of fidelity to Conall and had become the king's client and, indeed (preposterously, since Conall was as far from Christian as it was possible to be) Dun Ad's bishop. Then, as her head pounded and Artur fidgeted and Eogan shifted from foot to foot, struggling, as she did, with what this all might mean, the hall's doors banged opened a second time and in strode the man himself, the abbot Columba.

Ama had not seen him in years, but time had not seemed to touch him. He was tall, he was lean, he was fit, hardened by the relentless physical labor required of life on his nearly inhospitable island of Iona. His nose was long and his grey eyes were sharp, lending him a rather imperious air. A cap of grey hair fit his scalp from his ear-line backwards, leaving bare his forehead and the front half of his pate, the tonsure of a Hibernian monk. He wore a thick woolen travel cloak over a white abbatial tunic, and was carrying a crook-headed staff in a manner which suggested to her that that same hand might at some point have known a sword. But, unlike Bishop Budic, the Christian cross dangling over his chest was a simple thing, a symbol of faith proclaimed in weather-beaten leather and wood.

Strangely, Conall did not seem surprised by Columba's sudden arrival. Rather, the king clapped his hands sharply, saying, "Ah! Columba! Come! Greet an old friend!"

Columba, who had been striding towards them all confidently, pulled up short at the sight of the burly bishop. Even in the dim light Ama could see him blanch. It was true then—Columba had something to fear from Budic. But Columba composed himself quickly, saying, "Budic! Ainmire has thrown you out at last! Good for him!"

Budic *tsked* coldly. "Careful, Columba. That is no way to speak to your new bishop."

Columba's lean face hardened. He stared at Budic for a moment but then turned to the king. "If this is true, my lord, we have cause for celebration."

Conall cocked his head quizzically.

"You have finally converted to the true faith."

Conall scoffed. Columba, grey eyes flashing, nodded curtly. "I thought not," he said. "Tell me, then, Budic: do you come to Dal Riata to enrich and to receive? Or to control and to despoil?"

"The Lord strike you down for your arrogance!" Budic roared. "You speak of despoiling as if you yourself had never taken a life! But you have! You have! You have killed a man! You have killed a great many men! And I have come to Dal Riata to see that you pay for it!"

Ah, yes. The rumors had been hard to avoid: a battle waged between Columba's cousin Ainmire and the now-dead Dermot for the high-kingship—a battle in which Columba had assisted, which, perhaps, he had even instigated. A battle in which it was believed that Columba had slain at least one man.

Inwardly, Ama shrugged. Columba killed a man? Who amongst the men here had not? Yet Columba was a monk. Not just a follower of the Christ god, not just a priest or a bishop, but a monk—the new god's most fervent devotee. She thought she knew what that meant. She had been Christian once; her mother had remained one—her adopted home, the kingdom of Rheged, kept that faith. A monk revered life, he did not take it. It was a guiding precept: the Christ was against such things.

"Have you completed your penance, brother?" Budic demanded. "Have you even consented to undertake it?"

She was astonished when Columba threw back his head and laughed. It was a harsh sound. "My *penance*? What more do you require? I am exiled from my people. You saw to that. What other penance I may or may not perform is a matter for me and my Lord; certainly not for you." Columba's chin came up. "I have been forgiven."

Budic snorted in disbelief, his big body convulsing, his cross jangling on its chain. "You truly believe that our Lord has forgiven you?"

"I do."

"Impossible. How? When? What is your proof?"

For a moment, it looked as if Columba would not respond. His head tilted to one side, then the other. Finally, he drew a deep breath and replied evenly, as if only under duress did he reveal such a private matter, "Through me, He raised a boy from the dead".

This was met by silence, though Eogan, Eithne, Budic, the king, leaned in as if to better take in what the abbot had just said. This was another preposterous tale which Ama had heard being bandied about as truth—that deep within Pictish territory, a boy, a Caledonian boy, lay dead and, with Aedan's life in the balance, and his own, Columba had prayed and the boy had risen, alive. That the boy still lived, proof of the awesome power of Columba's god. Indeed, that because of that so-called miracle, some of the Caledonii had begun to revere Columba as a holy man, greater than their mages. For who can raise the dead?

Budic drew back, his chest swelling with indignation. "Pictish tales are not to be believed. They are witchcraft. Devilry."

Columba shrugged. "Perhaps. But the boy was dead. And now he lives. And there was no god in that hut when it happened but my God—the one you also purport to worship."

Ama did not know what to make of it. Columba's level tone was intriguing, encouraging her to entertain the thought that the tale told about the boy might actually be true. Had Columba really done it? Was he so powerful as to have brought someone back to life? But there would be no time to pursue this for the king pushed himself between the clerics, crying, "Enough! You bicker like old women! Columba! When you made your oath of clientship to me, you also promised fealty for your men, did you not?"

"I did," Columba replied, his confusion clear on his face. "I do."

"Then answer for this." The king snapped his fingers at his men. They ran out of the hall. They returned moments later, dragging between them an enormous, lumbering, monk, larger even than the bishop. His wrists had been bound, his grey tunic was torn and filthy. Blood caked about his nose and mouth, his nose crooking horribly to the side, broken. Ama's heart went out to him: big as he was, the poor thing was crying.

Columba rushed to the monk. "Cobthach! Where have you been? Who beat you?" He touched the monk's face tenderly, feeling for other damage.

Cobthach, holding himself very still under Columba's gentle exploration, gasped, "I am sorry, *Abba*. I am sorry".

"Sorry for what?"

"He is dead."

"Who is dead?" Columba asked, but the big monk only shook his head in misery. "You have nothing to fear from me," Columba said as he held Cobthach by the shoulders and looked him in the eye. "Tell me."

Cobthach took a deep, shuddering breath, looked worriedly at the king and then back again. "I rowed out to Erraid, as you asked. I let be the mother seals and pups. I took a bull. Only one, just as you asked." He faltered. He made an anguished sound and his face fell. Columba dipped his own chin until he met the monk's gaze. "Tell me," he encouraged again.

"I was worried. The sea was rough. You know how the currents mix there. How they swirl. Big waves. Storm coming. I was on my way back when another *curragh* appeared in the water right in front of me. It wasn't there, and then it was; below the swell, then on it. I couldn't help but run into it. There was a man in the boat, and blood everywhere—seal pups. *Our* seal pups, their skulls caved in."

Columba hissed. Cobthach shuddered again but he continued to speak, eyes unfocussed, as if seeing the man in the boat, the destroyed pups, and not his abbot before him. "He shouted and swung his oar at me ... "

"Is that how you broke it?" Columba probed the monk's nose again, the pain of which Cobthach pulled back to avoid.

"No," Cobthach replied, looking away from Conall's guards pointedly. Columba caught the gesture, glared at the men accusingly, but Cobthach was continuing his tale. "He swung again but missed me. He was terrible angry. Didn't want to get caught. I tried to get away, but the boats were tight close, right up against each other. *Abba*! My oar ... my oar... it tangled up with his. It struck him in the face. There was a ... a *crunch*. It broke something but I don't know what. His eyes rolled back and he fell into the water. He slipped right under, and I was afraid I wouldn't be able to reach him, but I did. I did! Before the sea could take him I grabbed his cloak and hauled him into my *curragh*."

Rough seas, a small boat tipping, and the monk was able to haul an unconscious man into it? This was deeply impressive, on two counts: Cobthach's impulse to help a thief who had tried to harm him; and his sheer physical strength. And, what was frankly more astounding: that he had not let the man go to the deep, the sea swallowing all evidence of his death and the manner by which it was achieved. Ama knew many men who would have done just that, and thanked the gods afterwards for their extraordinary luck.

"And?" Columba prompted.

Cobthach's answer was issued as a whisper. "He had no breath. I tried to breathe the life back into him. I tried and tried. But, but *Abba ... He was gone*."

"Yes," the king interjected coldly. "He is well and truly dead."

Columba and Cobthach stared at one other, the one comforting, the other stricken. When Cobthach began to weep again in earnest, Columba wrapped his arms around him and whispered soothing words in his ear, only letting go when the monk's agitations ceased.

23

Then, breathing deeply, his shoulders expanding and contracting as if to steady himself, Columba turned to confront the king.

"Who is dead?" he asked. "Who is gone?"

"*My kin*," Conall replied, his voice oily and, to Ama's ears, devoid of any grief.

"What was his name?"

"Does it matter?"

Columba became very still. When he spoke again, his voice was steely. "You gave us that seal colony, with Iona. That man—*your kin*—was poaching."

The king shrugged, his mouth a little pout, the point inconsequential.

"He was a thief," Columba said.

"He is dead."

"Since it appears that he has already paid the most grievous penalty, I am prepared to forgive him his theft."

"How very generous of you. Still, the point remains: he is dead."

"We shall pray for him."

"You shall do more than pray. Your monk killed him."

"Your man attacked mine. Mine was attempting to get away."

"So he says. What proof have we? All we know is that your monk was found floundered on our shore with my dead kin in his boat."

"Our proof is his word."

The king scoffed. "Any man would lie at a time like this. If he is innocent, why does he weep?"

"He weeps with sorrow that a man's life has been lost."

"He weeps because he took it."

"No. You are wrong. Nevertheless, since there are no witnesses to over-swear for either of our men, let us, their lords, settle this. Surely that is why you summoned me here today? I will pay your man's honor-price, on Cobthach's behalf. To whom do I make redress?"

"You make redress to *me*," Conall said with a thin, slick smile. He expressed no grief, only an emotion which seemed to Ama like triumph. He would not allow this to be a simple matter of reparation. The king brooked no opposition, he permitted no equals at his court and, in terms of status, Columba, the cousin to Hibernia's *ard-ri*, befriended by the king of the Picts—and, if the tales were to be believed, a raiser of the dead—was a far greater man than the king.

Dipping his chin to the king, Columba said coolly, "As you like. What do I owe *you*? What was the man's worth?"

"Come, now. It's not that simple. You know that. You owe me fealty. As do your men. Do you remember the oath you made when you became my client and I gave you Iona? Do you? I do. *If ever I, or my men, harm you or your own, in word or in deed, then we forfeit your protection*. That part bears repeating: *we forfeit your protection*." Conall smiled maliciously. "Your man harmed mine. Therefore— yes that's right; you begin to see—he has *forfeited my protection*. He has forfeited *his life*."

At the words, Cobthach moaned, a cry of distress ripped from the belly. But Columba only stood truer and straighter. Ama felt a thrill, something like exhilaration. Not even her husband, a king in his own right, dared to confront Conall this way, head-on and fearlessly.

"If you harm this monk, you offend me," Columba declared. "If you offend me, you offend Ainmire mac Setna."

"The *ard-ri*?" Conall's head tilted as if this had somehow confused him. "How would it offend him, precisely?"

"My cousin is your overlord. As he is mine. As he is *his*." Columba pointed decisively at the shaking Cobthach. "He is also, in case you did not know, his *kin*."

Yes, Ama thought. *Yes*. Columba had the king there. Conall would not risk offending the *ard-ri* over such a trifle as the life of a man he refused to even name.

25

But Conall was not dissuaded. "On the contrary. I have yet to make my submission to your cousin. Until I do, he is *not* my overlord. There is nothing that I owe him. Nothing that I owe *you*. Nothing at all. In fact, I shall be taking Iona back."

His expression hardening, Columba inhaled sharply then, pounding the floor with the butt of his staff so that his every word was punctuated, said, "You gave me Iona. As fief. *You cannot take her back.*"

"I can," the king said. "Of course I can. Or ... "

"Or?"

"You can accept Budic's jurisdiction over Iona."

"Budic? Iona?"

"You cannot discipline your men. That much is clear. They run amuck, murdering innocent fisherman. A bishop should do the trick."

"No."

"I was afraid you would say that. And with your monk's life in the balance too. I had thought better of you, to be honest."

"Cobthach's life is in the balance?"

"You heard me."

For the first time Ama saw doubt cross Columba's face. "It is Cobthach's life, or Budic as head of Iona?" he asked.

The king shrugged *yes*.

And Ama suddenly had to know. What kind of man was Columba? What kind of man dared to thwart Conall so openly? Was he a fool, still drunk on his former power in Hibernia, where he had been as eligible for the high-kingship as his cousin? Or was he a sage, and a saint, as the Picts would have it be believed? What kind of man was an abbot, and an exile, and a prince of incalculable power, and a killer of men, all at the same time?

She had her answer more quickly than she expected. Columba spared his monk only a glance, and Budic and the king none at all, before he snapped through gritted teeth, *"Let him take her then"*.

"Ah, excellent! Excellent!" The king clapped his hands, pounded the bishop on the back. "Iona is yours, Budic. I wish you luck with it; you will need it. Now, as to the question of Cobthach's life ... "

"*You said he would be spared!*" Columba roared, shaking his staff, rushing at the king. The king's retinue, drawing weapons, answered in kind.

"Did I? Did I really? Well, think it through. In giving Budic Iona, you have given him jurisdiction over its monks. Is that not how it works? He is the one who must decide. What say you, Budic? Shall the murdering monk be allowed to live?"

The bishop seized upon the unexpected gift. His fingers steepled to his lips, he hemmed and he hawed, he even closed his eyes as if praying for guidance from his god, but it was clear to Ama that he savored every second of his newfound power over the abbot. He had come to Dal Riata to have it, and here it was, so speedily.

Her blood rose. She had to do something, anything, but Eogan yanked violently on her hand to keep her in place. She was shaking him off when Columba lunged at Budic. The bishop reeled back, hands up in self-defense, but Columba, letting go his staff which clattered to the floor, had only made a supplicant grab for Budic's fur-lined sleeve. "Please!" he cried.

Budic flinched as if the abbot's touch seared him, which was odd. Odder still: he made no attempt to pull away. He was staring down at Columba's hands, transfixed, as if Columba's touch had a power over him which he could not deny.

No. That he had no *wish* to deny. Ama could see it in his face. The sickly, sweet absorption.

"Please!" Columba cried again. "I know that you harbor no love for me ... "

He's wrong. She was certain of it. It *was* love. Couldn't they all see? But only Eithne, her exquisite face puzzled, seemed to be seeing what was truly being conveyed beneath the clerics' exchange.

"Please, please spare him!" Columba implored.

27

Budic's cheeks stained red, but he did not reply.

"I beg you. For the love of God!"

Budic finally looked up from his rapt contemplation of Columba's grasp. His words came haltingly and from far away. "Your lord has made me his bishop. My will must now be his own." He turned to the king. "Will you spare the monk?" he asked.

Hands on hips, every inch a king about to dispense justice, Conall regarded Columba, Budic, even Eogan, but not, Ama was enraged to witness, Cobthach, whose life it was his to decide. Then his lips curled slowly upwards.

"I think not," he said.

With a snap of his fingers his retinue closed on Cobthach, daggers drawn. There was turmoil as the rest of them sprang into action, Columba to throw himself over the gasping monk, Eithne, hands up, away from it all, Budic towards Columba and then back uncertainly to the king.

Ama and Eogan had the same reaction, the same fear—he launched himself between her and Conall's men even as she was sweeping up their son to bury his face in her neck. She turned to flee that cursed hall, but not quickly enough to prevent Artur seeing Cobthach's head yanked back by its fringe of hair, a dagger at his throat, and Columba reaching ineffectually to disrupt it. The blade sliced, skin parted quickly, efficiently, Cobthach *oomphed* his surprise, blood jettisoned, drenching Columba's white tunic a shocking red, spraying bright droplets onto her boots, onto her hands, into Artur's hair, and the big monk toppled to the floor.

Blood globbing in her son's black hair, tainting his cheek, his neck. Cobthach jerking on the floor, blood gurgling from the gape, the dagger-slice so deep his head listed to the side. Everyone rendered dumb by surprise. In a kind of a daze, she was frantically wiping the mess from her son when she heard moaning. Deep, wrenching moans. But from where? Artur had smashed his face into the crook of her neck, his arms strangling her, but he was whimpering, the sound he would make just before he vomited. Columba was cradling

Cobthach's body in his arms. The monk no longer twitched, his blood seeped out. The bishop was hulking mutely over the pair. Eithne stood stiffly at a distance, her stony face determinedly turned away as if, in not looking directly at it, the monstrous act had not occurred. Dunchad's dog tracked through gore to the entwined bodies on the floor. It bent its head, snuffled the blood, and began to lap it up. The king's son, Dunchad, watching it all remotely, did not call the dog off. Ama gasped her disbelief. Why didn't Eithne make the boy call it off? Why didn't the king?

The king? The king, thumbs hooked in his rich sword-belt, was rocking back and forth on his heels, smiling in a self-satisfied way and nodding.

And underneath it all, like rollers breaking on the shore again and again, was that undercurrent of sound. That moaning. Ama did not need to search any longer to know from whom it issued. She knew him, now; and what kind of a man he was.

It was Columba.

· 3 ·
IONA

"No," Ama whispered, pulling Eogan back into the chamber. "Not yet. Stay."

She glanced down at Artur on his pallet. A small hand curled in the furs under his cheek, breath issuing through red lips. Their son had only just settled to sleep, sung there in tender tones by Eogan, dear, dear man! as, Artur's face buried in her neck, her palm on his bloody hair, she had rocked him. How the raucous laughter coming from just outside was not waking him, she did not know: the king's men continued to celebrate with whatever intoxicating liquid or woman they could get to hand. It was a nightly ritual; any occasion for feasting sufficed: tonight it just happened to be Conall's victory over the monks.

Black eyes haunted, dark brown hair throwing the lines of his lean face into shadow, Eogan leaned wearily against the flimsy wattle partition, the only thing separating the three of them from the mayhem. Eogan was expected to return, she not: the main chamber of the Great Hall was no longer a safe place for an unwilling woman to be. And, indeed, she wanted him to go. But first, he had to be made to see. "You must obey him," she told him urgently. "You must go to Alt Clut."

He snapped alert. "Ama! Render his tribute for him? It demeans me!"

"Yes, it does."

He pulled back, affronted. "Where is your pride?"

"My pride is here," she said, pulling his hand to her heart. "You are my pride."

"I don't understand."

"I shall go with you to the Oenach," she told him. "It is high time you began to profit from me." When he looked at her as if she had spoken gibberish, she said, "You chose me because I am a lady of Rheged, correct?"

"*What?*"

There was no time for this. Couldn't he see? "Because of Kynfarch."

He winced. "*Ama*. I wanted—I *want*—you. Your stepfather ..." He took hold of her other hand. "It is mere happenstance that he rules Rheged."

She pulled him closer. There was neither time nor need for these kind of niceties. She could set aside the fact that in marrying her he had thought to benefit from an alliance with her family. She was also willing at the moment to overlook that, in his doing so, she had been denied his brother Aedan. Because now she was Eogan's queen, and the Cenel Gabran were her people, and the monk's blood was only just drying in Artur's hair.

"Yes. You love me. I know," she said. "But you must admit that your choice of me was made the easier because Kynfarch is the most powerful of the *combrogi*."

His expression pained, he did not contradict her. He did not have to. "I shall send a message to my stepfather," she pressed. "Let him know that we shall be at the Oenach, that we would like an audience with him. Let us make alliances of our own—mightier alliances, with the Britons. Do as Conall commands. Render his tribute to Tudwal, and then give Tudwal some of our own, on behalf of the Cenel Gabran; renew your relationship with Strat Clut, but make it clear that it is one that does not derive through Conall. Tudwal must respond favorably. He is our foster-brother. Make him remember that we, the three of us—you, me, him—were playmates together on Alt Clut."

Eogan drew back, but she did not let go. "Yes. I know you find this sort of thing repellant. But we must rise to the occasion, profit from this—for it is an opportunity. You treat with Tudwal. Get Strat Clut. I shall speak with Kynfarch—or you can do it, or we'll do it together—and we shall have Rheged too."

She took his face in her hands so that he had to look her squarely in the eye. For the moment she ignored the signs of his exhaustion: he had always been a handsome man, but lately his skin had taken on a worrying pall. "This dispute with the Cenel Oengussa, it will hurt us," she said. "You would stop Conall if you could. But you cannot. It is simple arithmetic. We don't have enough men. But what if we *were* strong enough to resist him? What if we were not solely reliant upon his favor, what if we had the support of other lords, lords more powerful than he is? So that he cannot force our hand without involving them too?"

Eogan's dark eyes were narrowing, his clever mind working swiftly through the ramifications of her words.

"If Conall makes war against the Cenel Oengussa and cannot count our *cenel* as an ally, then he stands alone. *He stands alone.*" She whispered this because what she proposed was tantamount to treason, and Conall's men caroused not too far away on the other side of the screen. While he remained Conall's client, Eogan was not permitted to swear fealty to overlords more powerful than he was. Yet, would Eogan consider it?

"No man goes to war alone, Eogan," she said. "By isolating Conall, we may prevent war altogether."

His mouth hardened into a grim line. Had she gone too far? She wasn't certain.

But then he drew her fully into his arms and kissed her hard. She let herself be embraced. "The king has made a critical error," he said.

"What?"

"He has forgotten that I am married to *you*."

Budic put the thought of the murdered monk from his mind. Filled it instead with the knowledge that he had at last achieved it. What had begun so many years ago, on a high summer day in his youth. They had been at work in the schoolroom in the shady glen beneath the trees that shrouded the great monastic school of Cluan-Erard. Sunlight streamed through the windows, fresh and lulling. Outside, breeze ruffled the oak leaves; sparrows twittered and blue sky beckoned. It was a lazy day and Budic longed to be out at play, or asleep in the shade of one of the ancient oaks. Instead, he was at work with the rest of the novices, their heads bent over their books, copying the gospels. All around, styli scratched fitfully on the surfaces of writing tablets. They were many years away from using vellum, so costly to make that it was reserved for the master copyists and the school's finest works; instead they practiced on wax. Bishop Finnian, their stern taskmaster, a man whom Budic would never love, skulked over them, watching their every move— their every mistake, in Budic's case. Try as he might, the Latin made no sense to him. The examplar's black-ink scribblings swam before his face like little fishes at play in a stream, making his head reel. He couldn't catch hold of them, so slippery were their forms and meanings.

Yet, day after day, he bent himself to his task, determined to succeed for, as his father had said, over and over again (even now, Budic could hear his plaintive reprimands echoing in his head): what choice had he? Who would care for his mother, once his father was gone, if not he? Who, his idiot brother? Fearful for his family, unsure where Budic's talents lay, unsure whether Budic had any talents at all, his father had looked to the new church of Christ. There, he saw that men, lowly men, men with very few prospects, men like Budic, could rise to wealth and power. There, it did not matter who a man was: Christ loved, Christ promoted, all.

So, "Don't fail, Budic," his father had pleaded. "Do this right. You must do at least this one thing right." And Budic loved his father. But Budic was not made for the mastering of the intricacies of language. His talents lay in the management of men, as he now knew. No matter how often he stayed up late, after all the boys were abed, scratching his approximation of the letters on the earthern floor of their dormitory with the tip of an oak branch he had sharpened to a point, practicing in the moonlight, the Church Latin continued to elude him. And that day, as the sun and the birds and the summer breeze all conspired to call him outside, was no different.

Then, in the midst of his frustrations, a soft singing came to him. It was a beautiful sound—but also one which was forbidden in the schoolroom. Scandalized, he looked around until he spied Columba bent over his own tablet: Columba, of the Cenel Conall Gulban. Prince. The older boy was singing sweetly under his breath and rocking happily back and forth. Columba! From the first day, Columba had taken to his studies like he was born to the Life: no lesson was too difficult, no rhetoric too convoluted, no theological doctrine too subtle. And he had an equally smooth bodily grace, as they quickly discovered when their studies switched to games and play. It was enough to fuel anyone's childhood admiration, and the younger boys worshipped him. Budic certainly did, desire and envy twisting in his gut.

That day, Columba's face was transfixed with wonder as he worked, his wide-set mouth smiling around his song, his bright grey eyes shining. His stylus seemed to fly over the tablet, as if propelled by his song. And all about him was a golden glow so that the air itself looked to be on fire. Even then there had been something holy about Columba. Their people had an expression for this: *the nimbus of nobility*.

Fascinated and aghast, Budic waited for Master Finnian to intervene, to make him stop. Singing was forbidden during lessons, everyone knew that. Yet, even as it irritated him, Columba's quiet song began to soothe Budic, washing over him, making him feel somehow lighter. Happier. Budic took a deep breath. The exemplar caught his eye. And he couldn't believe what he saw. The spindly black strokes of the letters, those slippery fishes, had somehow ordered themselves on the page. The letters seemed to jump together just as his eye reached them. They made sense to him; he could see their logic, feel their rhythym. Budic could *read the Latin*. Amazed, he flipped ahead through the manuscript, flying ahead through the text. He could, indeed, *read*.

How wonderful! How truly wonderful! With renewed vigor and a huge surge of hope, he set to work, eager to copy what he was reading, fearful lest he lose his newfound skill.

His happiness was short-lived. Out of the corner of his eye, Budic saw the impeccable hem of Finnian's robe swish about his well-worn sandals as the master bustled up. With a sinking heart, Budic realized that he, and not Columba, was about to be rebuked. Again. Still, Budic did not break from his task. His ability to read so astounded and delighted him that he refused to be parted from it: with sudden insight he understood why Columba sang. He felt like singing too. What had been so difficult had become beautiful, easy; a joy. With a sense of calm utterly unlike him, he waited for the master's reprimand. It would be thick with disappointment, Budic was sure. It usually was. *Shame, that it comes now when I least deserve it*, he had thought sadly.

"Columba," Finnian said instead. "Come."

Budic's head snapped up. All the boys gaped as Finnian led Columba outside. They scrambled to the windows to spy on the pair in the clearing, but were too far away to hear what passed between them. Spellbound and with a sort of glee, Budic watched the old abbot set a well-lined hand, browned by years in the sun, upon Columba's shoulder. It was coming—Columba's well-deserved set-down. Their strange schoolmate was about to be punished for the first time that any of them could remember. Guilty pleasure washed over Budic. But then Finnian gazed upon Columba with what Budic could only interpret as affection and approval—emotions, since they had been so rarely directed at him, which were as unfamiliar to Budic as his Latin letters. Columba beamed back at the master, his face leaking delight. Whatever the abbot had said to Columba—and it certainly was not the rebuke the boys had expected—had pleased him. Budic had felt both incredulous and horribly, horribly, cheated: *this Columba inspires love in whomever he meets!*

I want that. The force of the emotion had slammed into Budic's heart. *I want that. I want that. I want that.* He feared he might burst from the strength of his longing.

I shall have it, had come the answer.

It was then that the plan had crept into Budic's heart, the insidious plan, unbidden and vigorous, like a vine breaking ground as it reaches for the light. Such a sweet simple thing, not yet rampant or desperate. On that glorious summer afternoon, his scheme had a sort of purity: the true desire of a heart. One day Budic would bring Columba low. One day Columba would know Budic's pain. Time had not diminished Budic's craving for this, even as it had deformed it. Fed on an unending stream of Columban successes (the accolades; the adulation; the renown; his monastery; his high friendships), Budic's need had swelled to become a sort of lust such as he had never felt for any creature, woman or man, before or since. More than his ambition for power, more than his love for his Church or his family, more than any other imperative he had ever obeyed, Budic's need to see Columba humbled had become the overriding impulse of his adult life.

Which made today rather extraordinary. For today he had finally achieved it.

Over and over again Columba punched the shovel into the soil, heaving dirt from the ditch and swinging it over his shoulder to mound on the bank behind. The sun beat down. Sweat sluiced from his brow. His work-tunic stuck to his skin and his palms had begun to blister, but he gladly gave himself over to the work. In fact, he welcomed it. With his back to the shovel, aware of nothing but his body's discomfort, he did not have to think, or recall, or ruminate. Stillness only brought back the horrifying memory of Cobthach's stupefaction as his throat was cut.

Columba cursed. He would work all day and night if need be, building the monastery's boundary-bank; single-handedly, if he had to. It was a kind of penance. Inside the *vallum monasterii* was everything he loved. Inside were his brothers. Inside, he would wall them in, keep them safe; keep everyone else out.

He could hardly bear to think of it, the sorrow that had been when his *curragh* made landing and his brothers had come running to welcome him, only to find that he bore Cobthach's shrouded body back to Iona for burial. How they grieved! Especially Baithene, for Cobthach had also been his brother by blood. A week had passed, Columba railing against the king, against Budic, against his own shocking inability to save his friend. He questioned his purpose, here in Dal Riata, even though there, on the summit of Dun Mor, farther up the island, where now a beacon tower had been built to communicate with the hillfort of Dun Ad, he had long ago been shown that his God did indeed have a plan for him, was guiding his mission in this new world. A vision granted him after all the astounding things that had occurred on his journey to the Picts, both those he had made manifest and those he had simply survived—the demon driven from the poisoned well; the loch-monster; Bred, the Pictish boy, brought back to life—causing him to marvel anew at how powerful was the God that had chosen him for His devotion.

But now Cobthach was murdered. And his old adversary Budic had been given Iona. And they were all at the mercy of a very deranged king. How could he continue his mission, here in Dal Riata, if he could not keep them safe?

Throwing down the shovel in disgust, Columba clambered up the bank. His gaze traveled over the island, taking in the well-known sights. Wind was whistling, and waves beat rhythmically upon the shore, two sounds to which he awoke every morning and fell asleep every night. The sky stretched endlessly, broken by the occasional cloud, the great storm-wind over. Islands and islets sat on every horizon, some near, many far; the island of Meall rising to the east, just across a very narrow sound, and then, behind it, the mainland towering. The colors of everything beautiful: turquoise, white, teal, dun. Elsewhere, Iona's coast was rocky, fully exposed to the pitiless force of the Mare Hiberniae, but, just below him, being enclosed now within this new *vallum monasterii*, a long flat plain which seemed to have been created just for them, for their increase and pleasure. Sheltered from the prevailing winds coming off the west by rugged little inland cliffs, the plain sloped down to the shore to the east, an apron, open for their industry. Upon it, they had begun all the buildings of their monastery. There, the largest, the *magna domus*, their refectory, their dormitory, their scriptorium all in one. The church next to it, its back to the sound; not large, but sweet, sufficient. In vile weather, they all fit snugly inside, spilling out again when that weather cleared to hear the gospels read in the open air, the Lord's words carrying on the wind to be scattered like seeds, for who knew where they might fall, where take root?

Men moved below him, his monks at their tasks, his anxious eyes locating, accounting for each one. Some were in the grassy *machair* at the sea's edge to the west, tending the crops, others in the north pasture with the livestock. Here came Baithene now, Columba's second-in-command, back down the path from the pasture. Columba checked the position of the sun: it was nearly *none*. Baithene was heading for the church to ring the bell to gather the men for prayer, his cattle prod not swinging in its customary fashion, side-to-side, keeping time with whatever he happened to be singing, but still today, stiff with deep grief. Yes: no song today unless it be a dirge.

Baithene passed, the door of the *magna domus* banged open and Diarmait, Columba's young servant, hustled out. Shading his eyes from the sun, he looked around, found Columba prominently on the bank. He waved tentatively (Columba had been short-tempered this week, quite unforgivably) but when Columba answered in kind, Diarmait smiled broadly and with a renewed spring in his step, headed around the back of the building. He returned shortly, a load of peat bricks balanced in his arms. Back into the *magna domus* he went and moments later sparks shot from the hole in the roof as he added the bricks to the fire which burned steadily inside.

Columba breathed in deeply, full of melancholy. He loved the tang of smoldering peat; it usually meant that all was well. Today, it merely meant that all eleven were accounted for. Twelve, if he were to include Cobthach in his cold patch of ground in the new cemetery beyond the *vallum*. They had had to dig it out for him; they did not have a cemetery before.

Cobthach! Dear, dim, steadfast, loyal Cobthach. Columba averted his gaze: his dear friend's final resting place was the one place on his island at which he would not permit himself to look.

Iona was a good home. He had to believe that. Consider what they had achieved in only three years. Exiled to Dal Riata, so perilously close to the Picts! Nobody had thought it could be done—for nobody had ever before achieved it. But here they were. Indeed, some days, amidst the sweat and back-break and honest effort of their toils, he could even forget for a time how much he still longed for home, for Hibernia. His men were happy here. If left in peace, they might even prosper.

But Iona had been given to Budic. Budic—who wished for nothing more than to destroy him. And Conall was a madman.

Just then, a shout from young Tochannu, on lookout today, and, out of the corner of Columba's eye, something stirred. Columba swung about on the bank, alert for danger, saw the boat, lowering its sails, approaching the sandy bay which served as their harbor. It was a four-bencher, twice the size of Iona's main *curragh* but half that of a warship. He let out a sigh of relief, its flag telling him it was not a Pictish slaver nor indeed King Conall's ship. Neither was it Budic come to claim his prize. The white sea-eagle rippling on the black cloth was that of the Cenel Gabran. The vessel set anchor, and a lone man climbed up onto the rail, balanced there a moment and then jumped into the knee-deep surf with a splash. Wading to shore, he started up the path which curved along the foreshore. By his loping gait and dark mien Columba knew him at once: Eogan.

The young king was a frequent visitor to Iona, intrigued by the progress the monastery was making, he claimed—intrigued, Columba suspected, by Christianity itself, though Eogan had yet to come to this realization on his own. By the cloudy look of him today, however, and by his purposeful stride, Columba doubted that the matters to be discussed would include the formation of Latin letters on parchment or the secrets the words formed there.

Clambering down the bank and crossing back over the wide plank which breached the ditch, Columba met him half-way. Nodding once in greeting, Eogan launched into his purpose: "What did you say to him?"

The young man's manner was uncharacteristically awkward: he shifted restlessly from foot to foot, his wet boots squelching on the turf, his long black hair swinging, his left hand gripping the pommel of his sword (though why he still thought it necessary to bear arms when coming to a monastery Columba did not know), his right thumb hooking in his sword belt, as if he did not know where better to put it. "I'm sorry—what did I say to whom?" Columba asked.

"To Conall." Out shot a hand to point in disgust back at the mainland where, Columba had to presume, Conall gloated, still drunk, in his hillfort. "When you came back from the Picts,"

Eogan said. "What did you say to Conall? There has to have been something, something I have missed."

"I don't understand."

Eogan threw up his hands in exasperation. "Something has changed him. He is not the man he was. I mean, when we were boys, he was always rash, always hot-headed, a flat-out bully, if you must know. But that's not so very uncommon. He was only mimicking the older men. And, oh! How Aedan loved to put him in his place! And his father, the old king, was a good man; my father too, who looked after him after his own father was killed. It all seemed to do the trick: he matured a bit over the years to the point where it wasn't quite as awful as it could have been when it was he who was acclaimed king and not some other; he had learned to temper his aggression with some thought first. But now? I don't know. I can't account for it. A sort of madness has taken him, and not only because of what he did to your poor monk."

His poor monk. A mournful glance back at the bank and the men Columba could no longer, from this angle, see.

Eogan nodded in sympathy. "I am sorry. I am. I wish ... I wish I could have stopped him. But this is only Conall's most recent depravity. He is haunted. Since it seems to have something to do with you—most things around these parts do, these days; you are like the crane driven in flight before the storm-wind—I need to know: *what did you say to him?*"

The crane driven in flight. The long-legged marsh bird the *druidi* equated with ill omen, with unwanted change. Comprehension came with a flash. But first, Columba spat into the dirt, trying his best to bring his hatred under control, his consuming desire for revenge against this king; managed it somewhat, could say to Eogan, "I know his secrets. As does your brother. As do you, now. In sending Aedan and me north into Glen Mor, your cousin had hoped to have us killed; you know that. But it didn't quite work out the way he expected, did it? Because Bridei turned against Conall, his old, secret, ally, and befriended us: gave me a holy island,

42

and Aedan his daughter. That has got to rankle Conall. Indeed, I hope it does! I hope it befouls his sleep. But now Conall wants us dead more than ever. He cannot kill me outright, with my very own cousin high-king. It wouldn't be prudent. You, he toys with, for the moment, because you have your uses. Aedan? Aedan is out of reach."

Eogan was taking it all in silently, a nod of agreement here and there. "You know, Ainmire is the key here," Columba said. "He has Hibernia—all of it. Including your Dal Riata, there. The division you say you have never seen. What does Conall have, what does he rule?" Columba swept his arm out expansively, taking in all the islands that could be seen, and the inhospitable arms of the mainland to which the Scots precariously clung. "Forgive me, you know that I have come to love this place and your people, but what is Dal Riata, really? The smallest, the poorest, the most insignificant of all of Hibernia's colonies, surrounded by enemies who wish to consume her and with no allies back home in Hibernia who might come to her aid. Conall should ally himself with Ainmire, but it would require that he submit himself, and that Conall is too proud to do. Your cousin has made it a habit, a policy almost, to squander, or betray, all his allies. In fact, if he truly thinks of Budic as trustworthy then he can no longer distinguish his enemies from his friends."

"Tell me," Eogan said. "Did you not say that, once my brother had fathered a son on his Pictish wife, he would be free to come home?"

"I did."

"Well, surely he has done that by now," Eogan said, turning bleak eyes towards the mainland into whose mountainous wilds his brother had disappeared, as if he had been swallowed whole. "He has had three years to get the Pictess with child. Why hasn't he come home?" The young man looked back, fear in his dark eyes. "Do you think he may be dead? That the Picts have not kept their word?"

Columba shook his head; he did not think it so. The Picts did stubbornly cling to the Old Ways, but in his brief, momentous, time with them Columba had found them to be honorable, in their way. He offered Eogan the only reassurance he could. "Aedan may yet be alive."

Unsatisfied, Eogan nevertheless nodded. "Conall sends me to the Oenach at Alt Clut to render his tribute to Tudwal Tutclyt."

"Really? He doesn't go himself?"

"No. He hates the Britons."

"So?"

Eogan shrugged.

"Do you mean to say that you are going?" Columba asked.

"It is not as if I can refuse. But now ... Ama ... " And, eyes alight with cunning, Eogan told him. As the waves bathed the shore and Eogan's trews, drying in the heat of the sun, smoked, Columba listened with great interest to the young man's plan, admiring both the logic of it and Eogan's pluck, none of it explaining Eogan's purpose there, however, until Eogan said eagerly, "If you were to come to Alt Clut with me, Columba, I could introduce you to the Britons as my friend and ally. They are Christian. I should think they'd be inclined to support your efforts here on Iona. That is, you are who you are. You are a most desirable ally—Conall's inability to see this notwithstanding. So, please. Come with me! It is there that we should look for support, Columba."

Wonder, hope, excitement reared up so violently in Columba's chest that it hurt just below his breastbone, rendering him momentarily breathless. All day, all week, he had been wondering at his Lord's will, certain that He had a will for them, but despairing his own inability to see it. Was this it?

"But we need Aedan," Eogan was adding firmly.

"Aedan?"

"Ama and I can negotiate with Strat Clut and Rheged. But Aedan is the best one to deal with Gododdin—he may hate them, but they fostered him. That counts for ... well, everything."

"Aedan?" Columba repeated dumbly. How unexpected.

"Yes. Of course. Think it through. His ties with the Gododdin are reason enough to bring him home. But there is another. What better proof is there that we—not any of the Men of the North, but us!—have managed to befriend the Picts, than my brother alive and well and married to Bridei's daughter?" Eogan shook his head in amazement. "Imagine it! A Scot living amongst the scourge of the North! Bedding their princess! It has never before been done! Never! But *we* did it." He pounded his chest. "The Cenel Gabran. Not any of the Britons. Not Conall. *Us.*"

"*Aedan* did it," Columba pointed out with a sudden surge of loyalty for the young man whom he dearly hoped was still outwitting death somewhere in Caledonia.

"'Tis the same thing."

It was not, but Columba did not contradict Eogan a second time. "Have you sent a messenger to retrieve him?" he asked.

The look which Eogan gave him was disarmingly direct. "Any man I sent would be skewered. *I* would be skewered if I were to go, and I am a king. No. There is only one person I know whom they may let through to the Craig—a man they think of as holier and more powerful than even their mages. *A man who has raised from the dead one of their own.*"

A man who has raised the dead?

The true reason for Eogan's visit became startlingly clear. "That's why you're here? You wish *me* to go all the way back to Caledonia to find him?"

"Yes."

His mind in turmoil, Columba thought about what that would mean. Leave his men again now, having just lost one of them, and go back into the Glen? Who would protect them? Expose himself a second time to the murderous whims of the Picts? Retrieve Aedan and haul him home again? It was unthinkable.

And yet ... And yet ...

45

A bee buzzed by Columba's ear. A gull winged silently overhead, starkly white against the blue sky. In the northern pasture a heifer lowed. And his men, his men ... Their muted conversations came to him from the other side of the *vallum* as they assembled for *none*.

It was something he could do for them. If it meant securing their greater safety, indeed he ought to. The secondary benefits were not lost on him either. He might subvert Conall. Render Budic impotent. Strengthen his own hold over Iona—perhaps even extend his ministry into Britannia. Yes. It was something he could do.

But Eogan had to be made to understand. "If I go, you must give me your oath that you will protect my men while I'm gone."

"I give you my word. If they light the signal fire—once, then out, then once again—I shall come."

A second thought occurred, perhaps more on-point: "Aedan might not wish to come home," Columba said.

"What would keep him from us? We are his kin. This is his home. But," Eogan added with a firm shake of his head, "in one thing you are quite correct. He cannot come home—that is, he cannot come here, to Dal Riata. At least, not yet. He has been beyond Conall's reach for too long, as you rightly say. Conall is very angry with him. If and when Aedan does return, if Conall doesn't just kill him then and there, he will make him renew his duties as *fennid* with a vengeance—Murchad is pathetic at it and while there is no question that Conall is a good-enough swordsman to do the job himself, it is frankly much easier to have someone else mete out your justice; and Aedan is so very good at what he does. No. Bring Aedan with you to the Oenach. If you leave soon, you will have the better part of the month to find him. Meet me at Alt Clut at Lughnasadh."

Columba should have added, *And if your brother is dead?* But he didn't, not wanting to court Eogan's pain; wanting to move on from his own. Instead: "And if Aedan refuses to come with me?"

"He will not refuse."

Columba's only response was to raise an eyebrow.

"Very well," Eogan said. "If by some unimaginable chance my brother does wish to remain with the Picts, tell him that, as his brother, as his king, I command that he come home. Tell him that I never gave him permission to stay there in the first place. Tell him that we cannot do without him. That his duty lies with us."

· 4 ·
DUN DEAR DUIL

Leaving their camp behind, the small party crossed wide loch Linnhe by logboat, their horses, tethered, swimming alongside and, coming upon the river at the loch's mouth, followed the trackway carved along its northern bank. They were headed for the far northern coast of Caledonia, for the Fortress of the Bulls, the great naval base from which the Caledonii had launched their terrifying sea-borne attacks against Roman Britannia, and then Hibernia and now Dal Riata—another of their secrets which Aedan had not, until this point in his captivity, been permitted to see.

In the gentle northern summer, the light lingers long. At leisure, late into the evening, they followed the gurgling river, Ceo hunting happily, Aedan trailing the pair of Picts, their long, sleeveless, hooded riding cloaks brightly colored in the gleam. Since they traveled through Caledonian territory, they had no need for additional escort, no need for weapons of defense, for his customary state of watchfulness. Aedan rode in a kind of daze, his thoughts neither here nor there, but touching lightly upon all things and then nothing and then back again. As it tended to when he was at ease, his mind strayed homeward. It winged along the silvery waterways, retracing his own steps, southwards over the lochs, vast, indifferent mountains looming, until out it was blown, over the ocean, her isles, islets, shoals, shingles, skerries, to fair Cendtire, his boyhood home and, now, hers.

Ama. On her he would gladly gaze; he would give the bright world, all of it, all of it, though it be an unequal bargain.

Three years ago he had not known how to bear the loss of her to his brother. Now, the truth was that he had grown, if not content, then at least less consumed by the macabre turns of fate which had landed him here with these Picts. And, if, in the first year, his mind had turned ceaselessly to her and their dark-haired babe on a distant rock-stack beside a small loch on its way to the sea, to Tairbert Boitter, his home, then, when in the second year Domelch, the daughter of his greatest enemy, conceived, it had drifted a little less. Until, in due time, after the slow passage of many seasons, it was fair to say that it strayed but once each hour of the day. Aedan had only to look at his son swaying side-to-side in his sling on his mother's back to know the reason why.

It was as if these days he were in a sort of dream—not an unpleasant one, thankfully, not a night-terror to which he was prone, but one curious and puzzling, peopled by figures not quite human, like those now leading him on past water's fall and slide, and by spectral landscapes. It was a lulling dream, an early-morning dream, the kind that comes just before sunrise. And so he was unprepared when, issuing out of a mountain pass, he realized with a start that he knew the long, starkly beautiful, curving glen unfolding below them.

His wife and brother-in-law had halted on the track. They watched him with knowing eyes. The sense of betrayal which shot through him stole away his breath.

"Why have you brought me *here?*" he hissed.

The glen they had entered cradled the dark water of the river Nevis. The valley was overlooked on the one side by a bulky, massive ben, the highest mountain that Aedan had ever seen; and on the other by Dun Dear Duil, a squat Caledonian hillfort which Aedan knew well, as did they—under its malevolent eye their father Bridei had slaughtered Aedan's father, Gabran. With Drust present.

It was a cursed place which Aedan had hoped with all his heart never to have to see again.

Unbidden, he was there all over again in his mind, no time having passed, at the head of his father's army, a much younger man, proud, untested, teeming with a boundless, joyful vitality and a hatred which had an unquestioned focus: the Picts who, for as many years as he had been alive, had preyed with abandon and a cruel delight upon his people. His father, Gabran, assembling the greatest army Dal Riata had ever hosted, had lead them to this glen, here, to march their way to the Craig, fortress of Bridei, king of the Caledonii, to annihilate him. How proud Aedan had been to ride at his father's side! Except that they had been betrayed by Aedan's own cousin, Conall. His own cousin! Raised by Gabran as if his own son.

Bridei, joining forces with his enemy Galam Cennalath, the overlord of the Miathian Picts, had routed the Scots, scattering them from the glen. And had taken Aedan's father's head.

Domelch's gentle voice intruded upon his crippling memories. "What hold has this place over you? You could not have saved your father. You know that."

So Bridei had claimed. Still, Aedan was tight and angry and would not look at his wife or her brother.

"You are not the only one who suffers because of that day," Drust chided cryptically. "Not the only one who yearns for revenge."

Not the only one? Whatever could he mean? But Drust's face was heavily guarded, as if he struggled to protect a well-defended secret. Domelch's face, on the other hand, was rigid with hatred.

Aedan shook his head. He was certain that there was no secret which could surpass the horror of witnessing one's father's decapitation. "Then why are we here?" he demanded.

Domelch wheeled her mount to look down the deep, bowl-shaped glen. Below, the blue-grey river wended widely, the valley flattening out either side for some distance before giving way to steep, seemingly endless mountains, their wooded sides pockmarked with dark crevices and caves. "These hills are the haunt of the *sidhe*, the fairy folk," she said. "They have always been sacred to our people. A god presides over them, the god of the ben, who would never have allowed your father to triumph over ours, not here. Your father could not have known it, but his efforts to hurt us here, of all places, were doomed from the start."

When Domelch turned back, her eyes were steely. "There is a place in this glen about which *The Shadowed One* must know."

The Shadowed One. At mention of that preposterous prophecy Aedan could only gape. His horse, sensing his anger, shied. It was a prophecy which foretold that one man, *The Ferbasach*, or *The Shadowed One*, would unite and rule the Picts and the Scots. A prophecy which, because it happened to have been uttered at the occasion of his birth, everyone believed, quite absurdly, to be about him. And he heard it incanted in his head again, as the hag had incanted it, all those years ago at Sillan's dun in Cendtire, when Ama had been at his side:

> The sun!—it rises in the west!
> Upon the east a shadow falls.
> It casts in crownless twilight
> All whom its terror calls.
> And ravens feed upon the rest!
>
> Alas and woe whom Shadow knows!
> Alas and woe!

A son of the clan of the Shadow
will take the kingdom of Alba by force of strength,
a man who will feed ravens, who will conquer in battle:
Ferbasach will be his name.

Alas for the Picts to whom he will go eastward,
the distressed traveler, the red flame that awakens war.
With grey men, the rider of the swift horse
will cast the Picts into insignificance
and will seek Hibernia in one day.

After the slaughter of Picts,
after the harassing of Foreigners,
many years in the sovereignty of Alba.

He will not be king
at the time of his death,
on a Thursday, in Cendtire.

Bridei's faith that this prophecy spoke of him, or, more precisely, that it spoke either of the man he had yet to become or the son he would father, was the reason that the king had given him not to the Cauldron of Rebirth as a sacrifice but to his own daughter. They awaited a *Ferbasach* to deliver their people from oppression, to unite and to rule the Picts. But, truth be told, these events had transpired so many months ago that Aedan had secretly begun to hope that he might finally have put it all behind him.

Apparently not. Domelch was glaring at him defiantly. He seethed. How dare she? How dare they? Why now, here, after all this time? "Damn it! *How many times must I tell you? It is not me.*"

"You search out our secrets," Domelch replied, her knowing gaze holding his unrelentingly. "The place in this glen is one of them."

And before he could formulate a suitably scathing reply, something slammed into the back of his skull with such force that, stunned, Ceo barking, he was sliding off his horse even as all went dark.

He caught her scent first, her musk, and the honey on her breath. He was lying on hard stone somewhere cold and dark and damp, but then something else that was silky was caressing his cheek: her hair, which he knew without having to open his eyes was the same shade as the raven's wing. Tenderly she kissed his mouth, and he wanted to return the kiss but there was a blinding, wrenching ache in his head.

An ache in his head. It came back in a rush: their betrayal, Drust attacking from behind.

He tried to spring to his feet but his arms and legs were leaden and would not obey. Groggy, he pushed himself up onto his elbows and wrested open bleary eyes. Everything wavering and his stomach somersaulting violently from the pain of moving his head, he blinked until she came into focus, a small, determined figure with her back to a stout, oak door.

But before he could regain his feet, she stepped out that door and, with a resolute look, slammed it shut. He sprang at it clumsily, but the bolt shot home with a clang, walling him in darkness.

He pounded on the door for a long time. He called out until he was hoarse. Eventually he came to the realization that if they were going to let him out again—and they were; weren't they?—it would not be until they were ready. So he slumped down against the cold, slimy stone to stew over their betrayal and to wait.

His prison was a bare cave in the hillside, damp, mossy and lichened. He could stand up, he could pace—twelve paces end-to-end—but there was no means of escape other than the door. Rivulets of water ran down the cave's sides, pocketing in holes in the floor. The cave sloped downwards, a silvery pool of water gathering at its far end, deeper into the hillside. Slowly but steadily, the daylight leaking through the stout door's cracks began to dwindle. Then there was no more light and his only companions were his fury and the steady drip of water down the walls.

Head against the cold stone, he rested. He did not sleep, but nonetheless a short time later it was as if he awoke again, to the sound of bells tinkling; sweet bells, muffled, like those on the harness of a horse trotting through snowfall. Hand pressed against the wall to guide himself, he worked his way to the door and listened. But the sound was not coming from outside. It was coming from behind him, from the pool of water at the cave's end.

As his eyes adjusted to the deeper darkness at the back of the hollow, the pool suddenly shone with light. Like the sound of the bells themselves, the emanation of light was gentle and diffuse, like a full moon's glow behind cloud about to part. It was calling to him. Haltingly, but curiously without fear, he made his way to the pool and, on hands and knees, gazed within.

From the flat, silvery surface, first the reflection of his own face, diminishing. Then his father looking back at him.

Startled, Aedan shot back on his heels. There was no mistaking it—he had seen his father's face, dark, kind, weathered, clever, very much as it had looked the last day he had gazed upon it, before the battle and the bloodshed and Aedan's loss of innocence.

Hesitantly, his heart in his throat, he looked within the pool again—and there was his father. His father! His beloved, fallen father. "Father!" he gasped.

But Gabran no longer gazed back. He was galloping headlong on a fine silver stallion at the head of a hunt through light-dappled glades, surrounded by baying hounds with a stag on the run. His father was carefree and ebullient, laughing out loud with the joy of it. Leaves floated from the trees to carpet the forest floor with autumn's hues: sun-burnt ochre, faded green, mellow red. Woodland flowers glowed golden. Acorns, fruit of the oak, sprinkled the loam, mast for the woodland creatures. There were others with his father, men and women oblivious to Aedan's ghostly presence, and all of them were laughing.

Aedan watched, spellbound. The horses' hooves thudded over bright leaf-gloam, kicking up the leaves. The horn of the hunt blazed brassily. Little silver bells, mounted on horse-harness, sang. The hounds bayed and the riders called to one another, their voices bright and full of cheer. On through the autumnal forest the hunt twisted and leapt, and Aedan's breath twisted and leapt; the riders exulted, and he exulted. When the stag was brought down by the hounds, its belly shredded, its innards spilling, Aedan died too, and was happy. He hunted with that ethereal retinue for a long time, as the hunter, as the hunted, as all things. Eventually, cheek against the cold stone floor of the cave, one hand outstretched in the silvery water in search of his father's hand, he slept, more soundly than he had in years. And his dreams were of the hunt.

When the oak door at last opened, it was to emit the strong light of day.

Aedan stalked past his wife without looking at her. Without word, she followed.

He strode out of his erstwhile prison and blinked in the light. They were in the sloping cliff-face directly below the fort of Dun Dear Duil; the river rippling blue-grey below; Ben Nevis hulking higher up the glen. He rounded on his wife, but at sight of the dark circles under her eyes, the sharpest part of his ire melted away—she had spent a fitful night, worrying for him.

"What must I know?" he demanded.

She nodded solemnly. "Come. Eat," she said. "And I shall tell you."

She led him down the slope to the camp they had made in his absence. Ceo came at once, overjoyed to be with him again. Drust grunted in welcome but kept his distance. Gartnait seemed to sense his anger and with a shy wave kept to his games on the far side of the fire. Only after Aedan was full of roast deer and a heady, honey ale which slid down his throat with welcome ease did Domelch ask, "What did you see?"

What did I see? What did I see?

The dead. The dead. Alive.

Aedan curtly shook his head. He would not tell her. He was not yet certain if he trusted her; he was not certain that either of these Picts deserved to even hear him speak his father's name.

"Did you see it?" she asked. "Did you see the veil and, through it, the world in which the dead dwell? The Otherworld?"

The world in which the dead dwell. His people knew it as Tir na nOg, the Land of Youth. His father had told him that it is a peaceful place, achingly beautiful, and that time passes there without effect, vanquishing the dominion of decay. That there, there is no time. Until today, Aedan had given the stories absolutely no credence. He believed in neither Tir na nOg, nor the Otherworld of which Domelch was speaking, nor Heaven, the Christians' desired final realm. From the day his father's head had been hacked from his shoulders, here, in this very glen, Aedan had believed in nothing save the merciless grace and power of his own sword.

On the far side of the fire, Domelch's gaze had misted as if catching sight of a loved one too far away to hear one's call. "The Otherworld coexists with ours," she said dreamily. "It travels alongside. There is a veil separating us, thin but existent. From that other realm the dead can look back out upon us, their kinfolk, still warm with life. They see us at the hearth, singing and drinking, or in the fields. They yearn for us, their living ones, but they cannot pass back into life except at certain junctures of the year, festivals which we, the living, hedge about with ritual and sacrifice lest other things cross the divide, things dark and unclean, things which do not wish us well."

His people believed this too, that at the festivals, quarter, cross-quarter, all of them, the dead and the living traveled side-by-side more closely than on any other days of the year. This coming festival, Lughnasadh, Lugh's feast, was one of those times, and for it they traveled to the Fortress of the Bulls. What rituals Aedan might witness there he did not know—he only hoped that the existence of his son, Gartnait, which proved his fidelity if not to the Picts then at least to the contract he had forged with them, would ensure that he would not become one of the sacred day's sacrifices.

"The dead can also cross at certain places," Domelch added. "Certain *sacred* places. And this they can do at any time."

Drust was nodding his agreement. Gartnait, who had nestled himself in Drust's lap to hear his mother's story, was absorbing it all with wide, uncomprehending eyes.

"This is one of those places," she said, gesturing back up the slope towards the cave. She sat forward eagerly. "Do you understand? Do you understand that the soul migrates from one body to another? That the body we know dies, but in another guise the soul travels from this life to the great realm of souls and can be embodied again, if it so desires? That death is, in essence, the middle of a long life—an endless life?"

She sat back on her heels. "Forget what you think you know," she declared passionately. "The dead are not dead. There is no death."

No death? Aedan scoffed. He had caused enough death in his short life to know the thing when he saw it. Everything that ever lived had died and would die. But he did not attempt to contradict her. He wasn't entirely certain that he believed what she was telling him, but no longer did he fully disbelieve it—not after having spent the long blissful evening with his father, deceased for the better part of a decade.

"Husband," she said, "you do not have to tell me what it was you saw, but I trust—I hope—that you saw that life continues after this mortal body is shed. The life-spirit is not extinguished. It cannot be destroyed. How can it be? It is the same as the earth's spirit, the same as any creature's. We eat the flesh of this roe deer, but do not be deceived that we have consumed what truly made, what continues to make, her alive. She bounds through woodlands, just as she did before, but in a different form—as an inviolable essence, a sort of a wind perhaps, undetectable by our eyes, but not *gone*."

A log settled noisily on the fire, making it hiss. While she tended it, he ruminated over her words fruitlessly. When she met his gaze again, it seemed to him that she did so reluctantly. "Forgive our deception," she said with uncharacteristic apology. "But *The Shadowed One* must know these things."

"Why?" he asked, now more curious than angry. He was not *The Shadowed One*, but still he wished to know.

"If his reign is to be strong and prosperous—if it is to be beneficial for those he rules—he must not fear death. The fear of death makes one weak. And weakness makes one cruel."

"You *are The Shadowed One*," she said. "For the good for my people—and for yours—you must shed all weakness."

He again slept for a long time. But in the brief, soft glow between sundown and sunrise Aedan was awakened by a sense that he was being watched. Drust slumbered soundly; Gartnait, curled in his cloak next to his mother, twitched in dream. It was Domelch, also awake and looking at him over the fold in her own bright cloak. Her dark gaze glittered hotly in the low light.

Aedan threw off his own cloak, rose silently and, taking Domelch by the hand, led her to a bed of moss on the verge of the field, near where spear-thistle crept.

He did not speak. Smoothing raven hair away from her face, he covered her lips with his. It was a rough kiss, but he tried to fill it with forgiveness. When her arms encircled his waist, he knew that she understood, and had already moved beyond it: in her glittery black eyes he read a challenge which he was entirely ready to meet. He unpinned the brooch at her breast, a beautifully carved silver bull, the emblem of her family, which glimmered in the low light, and her cloak fell away. He drew her tunic over her head, then slipped her riding trews down over her slim hips, until she was fully revealed to him.

Her tattoos swirled deep blue like the night sky. No part of her skin was unadorned by art. He had always found the sight mesmerizing; in the shy light of the coming dawn, still reeling from his vision, it bewitched him. Though he knew her body well, he felt suddenly that there were even more secrets here, secrets which he must uncover— that she was an unknown language he had yet to master, and that until this moment he had been mouthing the words without truly comprehending any of their deeper, more true, meanings.

He tugged her down onto the moss beside him. Slowly, he began to trace the images which, under his determined fingers, were emerging from the elaborate interlace of ink on her skin. In the firm, flat plane between her shoulder, collar, and breast bone, a fletched arrow lay broken over the curve of a shield. He traced the arrow's vee, the shield's bulge, before kissing the mark, the sign of the fallen archer.

She inhaled sharply, her breast rising, its tip brushing his cheek, tempting him. "Tell me again," he whispered.

"My first kill," she breathed in his ear.

He took the peak of her breast in his mouth and suckled until she began to pant and squirm. All the while his gentle hands continued their exploration, tracing her skin, re-learning her language. Just under her breastbone, there emerged from her life's pattern a double-sided comb. Leaving aside her breast with regret, his mouth trailed to kiss that image too. "When I became a woman," she told him, sighing. "When I first bled."

Down her belly he nuzzled and kissed, his hands wandering leisurely, caressing, back up to breasts, over to the swell of her backside where they uncovered, on her hip, overlaid on pre-existing lines, a strange aquatic creature, half-porpoise, half-fish, which her people called a water-horse. "Gartnait, as you know," she told him.

Resting his head on her belly, her fingers entwined in his hair, he explored the length of her legs. There, high on the creamy inside of a thigh, at the junction of leg and womanhood, he discovered a stern sea-eagle, wing-feathers ruffled in flight and talons ready, poised to dive to ocean's kill.

His fingers stilled on her thigh; hers tightened in his hair. This tattoo was new. He raised his head and looked at her. "My love," she said, meeting his gaze boldly.

The sea-eagle. The totem of his *cenel*, the Cenel Gabran.

He looked away quickly. He was no coward but, despite his lazy, exploratory mood, this was too intimate an admission. He wanted this woman's trust and companionship; he could not return her love.

But he could give her pleasure. Twisting on the soft moss, he pulled her back to fit against him. Purring, she pushed her bottom against his arousal and wound an arm about his neck to pull him down for a kiss. While he adored her sensitive breasts with a palm and with long, patient fingers stroked the wet nub of her pleasure, she freed him from his trews.

With his mouth, he traced the images inked on her back, feeling beneath his lips angry lines of mottled, raised skin where she had been whipped while a captive of Galam of the Miathi. He took care with these at first—he, too, had been flogged, by his cousin, Conall, though the scars from it were not external—but then, as she squirmed in his arms, he bit down on a scarred ridge of flesh, just hard enough for the pain to be sweet.

She gasped and her bottom ground against him. Squeezing him gently in her hand, she looked at him over her shoulder, inviting him to take her from behind. But he wanted to see her, so he turned her to lay her face-up beneath him. Her thighs fell open, she sighed, hands thrown out to either side, upturned on the moss. Taking her hips in his hands, he entered her with a sharp thrust and then rode her the way she liked it, hard and smooth, until she cried out, raven hair in the moss, face bathed in new light.

He went where she went, his own eyes wide open, his head and heart filled with thoughts of death and of life.

When the morning was full and they turned to the north, Aedan still carried the dead with him, just differently than he had before.

· 5 ·
BELOW THE CRAIG

"**A**re you that man?"

The voice trickled down. Columba, who had finally nodded off, started awake. He had been dreaming of Hibernia, of running through bright green fields as a boy, clouds reeling overhead, his hound alongside. Now, in the pitiless darkness he could make out nothing except that the voice was coming from above, from the other side of the rock slab of his prison door.

He rolled onto his back so that he could look up at the slab, ignoring the agonizing stab of pain as blood flooded through his bound wrists, crushed beneath him. He had been trussed and then stuffed into this hole in the ground, the kind of narrow fissure into which, to escape the heat, his people believed the Picts would wriggle like dark throngs of worms when the sun shone too brightly in the heavens. But after a dark day of captivity, Columba could put those scurrilous rumors to rest: his prison was no worm-hole but a stone-lined underground chamber hardly bigger than a human body. It fit him like a glove—there was no room to move save from side-to-side, which he did often, rolling onto either shoulder to relieve the unbearable pressure on his bound arms.

His people were fools to have believed the tales: no Pict would willingly entomb themselves this way, even to escape a relentless sun. It was in every respect a crypt, save that he was still alive.

He had crept up Glen Mor. The way to the Craig of the King was known to him. Unwilling to endanger any of his monks, Columba had hired two Caledonii from the island of Meall to help with his *curragh* and provisions. They had served him admirably enough, moving quickly and stealthily up the interconnecting lochs and rivers of the Great Glen until, a week into their journey, catching sight of the king's warriors short of the Craig, they had deserted him, melting into the mist of the hillsides. The king's men, spooked and unsure how to deal with him, had wasted no time in stuffing him into this horrible hole. He did not know for whom, or for what directives, his captors waited, why indeed he was permitted to live. He waited, catching water-drops from the ceiling on his tongue, he was so thirsty, and trying his best to disregard the agony in his arms and shoulders. He was easily able to ignore his hunger—a lifetime of asceticism meant that he could do without sustenance for great lengths of time—but, try as he might, at daybreak his tight control over his bowels had finally faltered. He lay in his own filth, its stench in the claustrophobic confines overpowering. The day dragged by, punctuated only by his prayers and chants as he kept the hours. With the sound echoing off the stone walls, he could almost pretend that he was at home on Iona with his men. Otherwise, he dozed when he could, losing himself in dreams of lost days of movement and companionship and light. Then into his tomb had come the voice. "Are you that man?"

He squinted at the irregular rectangle of light ringing the slab of stone above him. "That man?" he asked.

At first there was no answer. Just when Columba had begun to fear that the voice had been born of his fevered dreams, it whispered again. "The mage who raised the boy from the dead."

Bred. Columba could see him in his mind: a black cap of hair, a well-worn blanket, a toy chariot clutched in lifeless hands; the beautiful Pictish boy, dead on his pallet in the loch-citadel of Airchartdan. The distraught family, Columba's ineffectual prayers, his despair and then, when he was certain that he had been truly abandoned by his God, the clap like thunder, the light like a bolt from the heavens, and Bred alive.

Bred. How strange to think of the boy here, now, when life seemed no more than a hallucination, a trick conjured up by the mind to distract itself from the stench and the pain and the darkness.

"Yes," he told the voice wonderingly.

"What was his name?"

His name? Didn't the voice already know it?

"Tell me quickly!" the voice spat. "The guards return!"

Ah! The guards. His imprisonment. The voice was testing him. But he knew the answer. Who better? "Bred," he said. "The boy's name was Bred."

"His father's name? His mother's?"

"His father was Emchath, Keeper of the Loch. His mother's I never knew."

There was shouting, a sharp inhalation of breath, then the scurry of feet. The light was momentarily blocked out, there was the stamp of boots, more shouting, sounds of pursuit, and then silence.

Days from their destination, they found shelter in an abandoned Caledonian village in a narrow pass between the steep and desolate mountain ranges of Druim Alban and the Mounth, very near the border with the Miathi. Which is why, when Aedan was awakened in the middle of the night by loud voices and barking outside the flimsy hut he shared with Domelch and Gartnait, he assumed it was the Miathi who had hunted them down.

Clamping a hand over Domelch's mouth, he shook her awake, bringing a finger to his lips to signal for her silence. She nodded briskly, then silently gathered the sleeping Gartnait to her breast. Grabbing both his swords, long and short, Aedan ran outside into the semi-darkness.

But it was an elderly man, stooped in the light of the campfire before an enraged Drust who had taken the second watch. The stranger, trembling with agitation, held himself upright with a weary grip on his horse's bridle. The horse looked little better. Legs splayed, head bowed, it had been ridden to near death.

"My lord! My lord! Please! You must come! They have buried him alive! They have sent for my lord mage Broichan!"

"Buried whom?" Drust demanded, sheathing his blade. The old man posed little threat. Nevertheless Gartnait began to cry in his mother's arms.

"The Great Mage!"

Drust glared at the stranger uncomprehendingly. Aedan fared no better.

The old man jabbed a finger at Aedan. "That one's holy man!" he cried. "The Christian!" Thrusting a hand under his cloak, he pulled forth something strung on a cord about his neck—an amulet in the shape of the crossed sticks of the Christians. "The priest who brought us The Christ!" he cried, shaking it for all to see.

"Columba?" Aedan marveled.

The old man nodded frantically. "He was carrying his *magicks* with him! They threw him into the pit! They are afraid to release him until my lord mage Broichan comes!"

Aedan had seen the fetid holes in the ground which passed for Pictish holding cells. He shuddered to think what prolonged confinement in one of them would do to a man's sanity. And Broichan? Broichan, Bridei's foster-father and chief-mage, bore no love for Columba. If Columba managed to survive the cell, he would not long survive Broichan.

"We have sent for others too—" the man panted, "but hurry, hurry! The mage has been buried now for three days! It will take us two to return to him. Can he live? Can he live?"

In a heartbeat, they were mounted and galloping back towards Glen Mor.

" ... all heaven with its power ... "

The voice echoing thinly off the stone walls was Columba's own. His mind wandered at will now. In the intermittent darkness he felt hardly tethered to life. The pain was fading, which was a relief. His arms had lost feeling. He was speaking aloud simply to fill the darkness. What he uttered was a *caim*, a prayer to surround himself with a protective circle, not of magic but of the comforting presence of his God, the *caim* Patrick had left them before he died.

Heaven with its power. Heaven. He would see it soon, and look his beloved God in the face. He tried to smile at the thought, but his lips cracked painfully. Gingerly, he wet them with his tongue, tasting blood. His stomach clenched in agony, mistaking the brief taste for promise of food.

" ... and the sun with its brightness ... "

He had been entombed for five days. It had grown light and then dark and then light again around that slab five times now. That is how he knew.

" ... and the snow with its whiteness ... "

Snow on Iona. As the wintry image formed in his mind, he caressed it lovingly, rehearsing its shape, finding solace in the memory as he reconstructed it piece by piece: the slate-grey sky; the storm-tossed sea; the frosty hillocks, green grass glowing under a shining blanket of snow. How it crunched when you trod upon it.

" ... and the fire with all the strength it has ... "

The fire burning merrily on the hearth of the refectory. The tang of the peat. He, huddled at his desk, wrapped in a blanket, his breath smoking on his fingers, warming them as they gripped the quill. He loved that part: alone at his desk, writing. This winter, if he were to see it again, he would not begrudge the snow that fell on Iona.

" ... and the lightning with its rapid wrath ... "

Then he was blinded—but not by any remembered vista in his mind. Rather, by full sunlight—real sunlight; no mental construct to ward off the fear. It flooded his cell as, with a deafening scrape, the slab over his hole was abruptly hauled back. He blinked frantically, trying to make sense of the blur of images above him: blue-inked faces peering, spear-points jabbing to see if he was still alive, excited jabbering when he flinched from the pain. And then hands hauling him roughly from the hole.

The world tilted. He had been too-long horizontal. With a jolt, the rope binding his wrists was cut. He cried out, the blood rushing back meanly to his deadened limbs, the agony of it bringing him to his knees. Blinded by the sunlight, he heaved breath, moaning over his hands, upturned and throbbing. Guards encircled him, taunting, pointing at his backside. He did not need to understand their words to know that they mocked him for having soiled himself. Others pawed through his belongings, stripped from him before he was thrown into the hole and now cast rudely on the ground: his portable wooden altar, his chrismatory, his bronze hand bell. Slumped over his knees, he could see neither his staff nor his precious psalter. What had become of them? Had the guards destroyed them?

The ring of guards opened. Through it emerged a figure from Columba's memory—Broichan, the chief-mage of the Caledonii, the foster-father of their king Bridei. Columba would know the elegant white robe, the long, luxurious beard and hair, the hawkish face of swift intelligence, anywhere. The island of Iona had been Broichan's before Bridei had reluctantly given her to Columba. The mage was trailed by retainers and slaves. From just behind, an ashen-faced slave-girl, hair blonder than the sun, stared back at Columba. It took Columba a moment to realize why she had caught his eye: unlike everyone else around her, her face was devoid of tattoos. She gaped back and he realized that she was looking at his tonsure, not with incomprehension but with horror and sympathy. Could she be a Christian, enslaved? Was she one of his own people, a Hibernian?

Broichan loomed over him. Columba tried to get to his feet, but with Columba's own pastoral staff Broichan knocked him back to his knees. Broichan fingered the stolen staff with interest for a moment, grinned maliciously, then bent it over his knee and cracked it in two. The Caledonii jeered encouragingly.

Broichan threw the shattered staff to the ground. "There," he gloated. Columba knew enough of the Caledonian tongue to understand what came next: "I have broken your power. Now there is no escape".

Columba looked wearily at his old adversary. "My power does not reside in a piece of wood," he croaked, his voice sounding to his own ears as if it was coming from very far away. "If you believe it does, then you cannot comprehend my God."

Broichan smiled gleefully. "I should have done this years ago." He snapped his fingers and the guards closed about Columba, whooping in excitement for the kill.

Columba was so beaten down that there was hardly any fear left in him, and no fight: half his mind was already on his God. At the moment of his death, there was, however, a flash of regret. *Dear Lord! Forgive me! I have tried to serve the Light! I pray that I have done enough to atone. Dear Lord. Hold me in the palm of your hand, and I won't be afraid. My men! Dear Lord, tell Baithene: tell him to lead them home again.*

He wondered what dying would feel like, indeed if feeling ended when life ended. Well, he should soon find out. There was only one more thing to do. He searched the crowd until he caught the gaze of the ashen-faced slave-girl. Had he guessed correctly?

Was she Hibernian? "Tell them what happened to me," he said in his own tongue.

She glanced in fear at Broichan and then, reassured that her master was not looking, nodded quickly. "I shall," her lips formed silently in reply.

The guards closed in. Columba shut his eyes.

But then a loud, commanding voice ripped the air. Had it said *Hold!*?

And into the mass of looming weapons and beaten leather burst a young warrior whom, with utter incredulity, Columba recognized. It was Uirolec, the son of Emchath, the Keeper of the Loch. The boy's—Bred's—brother.

Uirolec was shouting at Broichan as he shoved aside swords. Columba looked about wonderingly. Uirolec had brought a handful of soldiers but not nearly enough to overpower Broichan's men. Broichan glowered at Uirolec, swore at the young man violently, waved his men back. As Uirolec was pushed roughly aside Columba saw regret in the young man's eyes.

For a second time, Columba prepared himself for death, but before the swords could end his life, there were hooves of horses thundering and more shouting and another voice cutting in with an authority that would not be brooked. Broichan's soldiers faltered as into the fray burst Drust, the king's son, and Domelch, the king's daughter, and—Columba's heart thumped wildly—the man he sought: Aedan himself.

"Is he dead?" Aedan asked Columba in a whisper.

Aedan hated to ask. He cradled Columba in his arms in the prow of Broichan's ship as it rolled the last few leagues of the great loch of the Ness, a strong wind following. At the head of the loch before them, the river, also called the Ness, narrowed. From that river, they would be spilled out into the firth of Muireb; and from there, they would reach the Fortress of the Bulls. They were all being brought to the king, though Aedan noted with bitter amusement that only he and Columba were being transported there under guard. They had even taken his weapons. He hated to ask, but there was only one reason Aedan could credit for the unexpected appearance of Columba anywhere near the Craig, in fact in Caledonia at all. When he was able to speak again, the abbot would deliver the news that Eogan, his brother, was dead.

Emaciated, shivering, reeking as if he had been submerged in a midden (which, in effect, he had), Columba was gingerly swallowing the water which Aedan poured gently into his mouth. The abbot sipped again, moistened his lips, croaked, "Who?"

Aedan tried to be brave, but he feared to speak Eogan's name lest his suspicions be proved correct, lest that summon the ghosts. He compromised: "My brother," he said.

"No."

"Anyone else dead?"

"Not that I know of."

Training his eyes onto the wind-filled sails, Aedan's stomach righted itself again. When he had recovered himself, he gentled more water into Columba's mouth, could risk humor: "Not Conall?"

"No."

"That's too bad."

"Aye. It is."

"Then why are you here?"

"I missed you?"

Aedan snorted his laughter. Ah! It was good to see his old friend. Taking a loaf of bread from his pack, he funneled tiny morsels into Columba's mouth. When Columba had regained some of his strength, Aedan helped him prop himself against the prow and then rifled through his pack again for one of his own tunics for Columba to wear, carefully helping him dress. When he was finished, there was little to tell Columba from the Picts guarding them, except that a portion of his head was shaved and the rest of his exposed skin was unadorned; and of course his lack of any useable weapon.

"Now that you don't stink quite so badly," Aedan said. "Tell me. Why are you here?"

Hands at rest on bent knees, Columba was taking deep gulps of fresh air, his face tilted to the early-morning sun, wind ruffling his fringe of hair. He turned clear grey eyes on Aedan. "Your brother summons you home," he said.

The message had been delivered very evenly, very diplomatically, but Aedan knew instinctively that urgency underlay it. "Why? Why now? What has happened?"

As the vessel eased from the loch into the fast-flowing river, the either shores tightening, Columba told him, the tightness about his mouth slowly solidifying into deep furrows and his tone taking on a brittle quality until Aedan knew exactly what he needed to know: the message Eogan truly desired conveyed was, *Brother, make haste! Do not delay!*

At last Columba's voice ceased. His thoughts in turmoil, Aedan went to the prow to think about what Columba had told him. Farther down the ship, Drust had hoisted Gartnait in his arms so that his son could peer over the side of the vessel at the water rushing by below. Gartnait exclaimed over this and that, Drust nodded in encouragement, and Aedan felt a rush of gratitude— Drust was distracting Gartnait from the fact that his father was under guard, a sight his young son had never before seen.

He turned to share their view, trying to get some perspective on his own spinning thoughts. The river had narrowed considerably. Wooded slopes rose up from the water's edge. His attention was immediately grabbed by the somber sight of a handful of villagers on the bank across, in the act of burying a shrouded corpse into a hole dug at river's edge. How sad: death. But as they lowered the corpse, the shroud opened unexpectedly and the body of a young man tumbled unceremoniously out. A cry went up from the young man's people. The body had been savaged in the act of swimming.

Its left arm and shoulder were gone, a shriveled lung spilled out from a ragged chest-hole, half its face had been eaten away.

That can't be right, Aedan thought. What creature could cause that kind of damage? Not a bear. Not wolves. The young man had been *chewed*. And then, on the heels of a fleeting memory of another day, another time, but the same body of water, he thought, *Gartnait shouldn't see this*, and was turning to catch Drust's attention when without warning there was a tremendous rolling of the ship. Aedan lost his footing as the vessel listed nearly perpendicularly, he falling through the air to crash into the prow. Only his spasmodic grip on the railing saved him from being pitched into the water. There was screaming, from the Caledonii on board, from the villagers on the shore. A splash, a groan as the vessel thankfully righted itself, but then Drust screaming out in a tone which Aedan had never before heard him use, "*Gartnait!*"

With the vessel's mighty heave, Gartnait had fallen overboard. Aedan was horrified to see the little form of his son struggling in the water. He was not yet a strong swimmer. Aedan vaulted onto the ship's rail to dive in after him, but Drust had been quicker. He was already in the water and, with five powerful strokes, had the boy in his arms.

Gartnait clamped his arms around his uncle's neck, Drust waved to those onboard that all was well, and Aedan was looking for something by which to haul them in when the ship rolled again, though not as severely as the first time—it was as if she were gently lifted on a wave and then softly deposited. It was an odd sensation, but one which Aedan was certain he had felt before: his memory was trying to rush to his aid. Struggling with this, he found some coiled rope and was about to pitch it to Drust when the villagers on the shore began to shriek again, gesticulating wildly at something directly before the boat. He peered over the railing.

There, lying low on the riverbed, was the monster of the loch.

Nessa. Whom the Picts revered as a goddess and who, propitiated by them with human sacrifice, had developed a taste for human flesh.

It was she who had rolled the boat. Drust's body was clearly silhouetted above her dark mass. A big man, rendered even larger by his cloak floating about him and the little boy in his arms, nevertheless his brother-in-law was dwarfed by her.

"*Drust!*" Aedan screamed.

Everyone was screaming. He could hear Domelch's terror. His blue face gone white with fear, one arm clamped around Gartnait, his cloak tangling in his legs, Drust thrashed his way to the safety of the boat.

It was too late. Sensing the water above her stirred by Drust's strenuous agitations, Nessa rose. The wave she created bore Drust and Gartnait up and to the side. Then her head broke the surface of the water.

She was enormous. The impression Columba had formed of the creature all those years ago at the loch-gates of the citadel of Airchartdan had been quite accurate: though her head was small, her neck was as long as two grown men, her body twice that length again, her skin slick and mottled grey.

But what Columba had never before seen were her eyes: large as shields, shark-like and lifeless, with the same watery sheen and dumb spark of life—the simple impulse to feed. Her head swiveled, taking them all in: the villagers on the shore; the people on the ship. When those oily black orbs swept over him, Columba felt a chill of fear slice him to the bone and he realized that he had been mistaken, badly—she was not dumb; far from it: she was not some overgrown mistake of a water-creature but a sentient thing with emotion, and will, and *thought*. Easily he could believe her a goddess.

Her head swung about until, with a wet snuffle, she located Drust and Gartnait. There was a watery snort, and she rushed at them open-mouthed and with a roar, her needle-like teeth long and sharp.

Drust froze in terror. Another great cry went up from the Caledonii. There was only one thing Columba, unarmed and clutching the rail of the ship weakly, could do. He raised his hand. He made a sign of the cross of his Christ in the air, invoking his God, and screamed at the monster, *"Retro me, satane!"*

For a heart's beat, the creature hesitated. She hesitated, but she did not heed: propelling herself on her huge, paddle-like flippers, she rushed Drust. She lunged at him and he and the boy shrieked in terror, her maw closing about their heads when, suddenly, out of the corner of Columba's eye there was a flash of something metallic catching the sunlight and with a wet thud it found her flesh— Aedan had disarmed one of the distracted guards of a sword and had hurled it at the terrible creature with all his might, embedding it to the hilt in one of her great black eyes.

Roaring, she reared back, revealing Drust and the boy—still alive. She screeched mightily in pain, a terrible, massive, inhuman sound. She fell back into the water, writhing and rolling in agony until, with a bump against the stony riverbed, the sword was dislodged from her eye. Through clouds of her blood, Columba could see the blade spinning through the water to settle on the river's bottom. Then, wounded but not, Columba thought, mortally, she fled.

Drust returned to the ship with haste; it was the fastest Columba had ever seen a man swim. And Aedan hauled his son into his shaking arms.

· 6 ·
THE FORTRESS OF THE BULLS

Like the wind buffeting the sails above them, all about the ship
whispers blew: the Caledonii were calling it a miracle. *Columba
had turned back the monster.*

Miracle indeed. Aedan hardly knew what to make of it. It was
later that morning, and they had made landfall on the beach in a
bay to the west of the Fortress of the Bulls, the firth opening wide
before them. Columba was recovered enough to ascend the steep
path to the citadel on his own two feet, which was good since
Aedan could not assist him: after Aedan's escapade with Nessa, for
which no one save Domelch and Drust had even thanked him, the
humiliated guard from whom he had filched the sword had bound
Aedan's hands roughly. His family were being kept from him
by Broichan's guards; Ceo had been muzzled again, poor thing,
and leashed. So he had time to think, but still could not explain
what, at the last possible second, had held back the loch-monster's
headlong rush to consume Drust and his son. For all the Caledonii's

wide-eyed claims, he doubted that divine intervention was the agency. For the briefest of seconds, the monster had hesitated, it was true, just long enough for him to disarm the guard of his sword and to heave it. Luckily, his aim had been true: right to the eye. So, wasn't it his sword and his aim that had thwarted the monster, rather than the abbot and his god?

And why, for the love of all that was precious in this life, had he been the only one on that ship to have the presence of mind to draw a weapon against the creature? The vessel was full of Caledonii; there were villagers on the shore. They had spears and battle-axes, they had bows and arrows and swords. Were they all so cowed by the creature that they thought it impervious to pain? Did they really believe her a goddess, whose will must be their own? Is that what their mages had taught them? Everything within Aedan rose up in furious rebellion against such an idea: the horrifying image of his son struggling in the water, helpless, flashed across his mind. He had no use for such absurd superstition, such *belief*. He loved life too greatly to so effortlessly hand it over, to lay down and die just because a creature—a sentient creature, he was willing to concede: he had recognized intelligence in those slick, greedy eyes—needed to eat. No. When he went, he liked to think that he would go down fighting—hard.

Still, the loch-monster had hesitated. She had. No matter how he turned that particular problem over in his mind, Aedan had to concede that she might have done so because of Columba. The creature was rushing; Columba screamed in his Church-Latin whatever he had screamed; and she had hesitated. Aedan did not know why. He did not know how. It was a mystery he thought himself unlikely ever to solve. If there had been miracle in the event, that second of hesitation, that second which had allowed him to heave the sword, had been it.

Far, far below now, the path steeply rising, waves crashed ever more faintly against the shore, the sound carrying weakly up to his ears. He wrested his thoughts back to the present, for this was a vista which King Bridei had until this moment steadfastly prevented Aedan from seeing. He and Domelch and Gartnait might travel south, they might go east or west, but the Fortress of the Bulls was forbidden them while Aedan was with them. As the bay opened below, it became startlingly clear to Aedan why, and he whistled in wonder. The sheer number of vessels sheltered there was astounding. Easily one-hundred-and-fifty ships bobbed at anchor in the swell—camouflaged scout boats, merchant vessels, hide-covered *curraghs*, logboats. And, dear gods! The ten-bench warships! The number of fighting vessels in just this one bay came close to rivaling Dal Riata's entire fleet. If Bridei could command such a navy, why had he not yet launched it against Dal Riata? Why had he not yet swept down to dislodge Aedan's people from their meager foot-hold in Caledonia? What in the world was holding Bridei back?

And then there was the citadel. On the sea-girt headland above, the fortress loomed; humbling; terribly mighty, the most audacious statement of the Picts' power Aedan had yet been privileged to see. Sea-cliffs fifty-feet high surmounted the bay, and atop these was a slope which rose to a height twice that of the cliffs. Atop that slope was a stone-coursed rampart which was itself surmounted by a wooden citadel, the Fortress of the Bulls. Up and up and up it all went. He had never seen a fortress larger—not in Caledonia, not in Britannia, and certainly nowhere in Dal Riata. Bridei's Fortress of the Bulls was easily eight times the size of Dun Ad, the hillfort-capitol of which his people, the Scots, were so vainly proud. Would that Conall could see it! His cousin's cocky self-importance would melt like butter in the mid-day sun.

The king's inner citadel sat within four massive earthen ramparts, one within the other, cutting off the neck of the headland. They went through these one-by-one until they came to the last, the fortress' landward gate, towering doors of oak. A procession of stone plaques flanked the doors, each bearing the king's symbol: a stocky bull, some at rest, some aroused, others, their shoulders hunched and heads lowered, ready to charge. He knew this image well; saw it recently on his wife: Bridei was the Bull-Lord of the Caledonii.

Domelch. His canny wife. As the gates were opened for them and they filed into the tunnel which cut through the last rampart, he was finally able to sidle up to her. Looking straight ahead, he whispered, using his own language since she understood it but the guards did not, "Can't you get them to untie me? Or cut the ropes yourself? I need my hands free".

She brushed her shoulder against him, keeping her own gaze resolutely forward. "Broichan forbids it," she whispered back. "You are a friend of the priest's, who is in our lands uninvited ..."

"*I* didn't invite him."

"Shhh! He wouldn't be here if it weren't for you. Leave it to me. I shall speak to Father. But first, there is something Broichan has come here to do. Something he wants you and Columba to see—particularly Columba."

Aedan didn't like the sound of that. What did Broichan want them to see? He asked her as much but, coming at last to the far end of the tunnel, they were emerging into the courtyard beyond, full of strong sunlight. To the west, rising up forty-feet or more on a natural rocky outcrop, was Bridei's citadel. Before them, a wide courtyard. But their guards turned, leading the way to an enclosure to their east. They were led through a wooden gate decorated with ever more of Bridei's bulls, then down a dimly lit flight of rock-cut steps, to an underground chamber. It was lined by a stone promenade, below which was a water-filled tank, hewn from the living rock. The room was filling with somber Caledonii. The light which flickered from torches set in iron sockets on the walls barely illuminated the gloomy interior. He seemed to be in some sort of water shrine, sacred to the gods of the deepest past. In the shifting light Aedan could make out rough courses of masonry, the chamber paneled in stone blocks. The big block on the wall on the far side was carved with a vigorous hunting scene: flickering light, and shadows, through which emerged bearded Caledonian huntsmen; archers in the brush on bended knee; hounds and a ten-tined stag, cornered, about to be slain. On the block behind him, a battle: Roman infantry, and Caldonian cavalry, victorious—Roman heads gleefully being severed. The wall at the head of the well, however, was curiously bare of decoration. No self-congratulatory Caledonian victory scenes. Instead, inset in the wall was a crudely sculpted stone head. No neck, no body; just a massive head as large as Aedan's own torso. Its wide, almond-shaped eyes stared dumbly, its drooping mustache framed the gaping hole of its mouth, the stone shelf under the mouth deeply discolored. It had an ugly air, presiding over the well maliciously.

Beside it stood Bridei, the Bull-Lord, *rex potentissimus*, every inch the king: his elaborately curled brown hair, held back by a finely worked silver headband, flowed down his back, the ends of his braided mustache and beard were tipped with beads of silver. Silver also fringed his ankle-length formal robes, and draped over his powerful shoulders and chest was a massive chain of the same metal, each ring the thickness of Aedan's thumb, its front fastening incised with the same bull symbol with which the fortress' ramparts, Bridei's weapons, the iron collars of his slaves, in fact everything the king owned, had been emblazoned.

Bridei's gaze flickered coolly over Aedan and Columba, then lingered an affectionate moment on Gartnait and his son and daughter, but did not come to rest. He nodded at Broichan, attended by a young woman whom, even in the dull light, Aedan could see was exceptionally beautiful. Beside him, Columba twitched, as if he recognized her. Blond hair framed the woman's small face; her skin was milky white and her eyes were blue. When Broichan arranged himself next to the king, the girl ordered his robe with quick, efficient movements; when he flicked behind his shoulders his long mane of hair, she combed it straight with practiced fingers; without being bidden, she fetched Broichan a jewel-encrusted, silver chalice. Though she wore no slave-collar, the absence of tattoos on her creamy skin and her subservient mien told Aedan all he needed to know: *this one is enslaved. And she is not a Pict.*

All the while the chamber had been filling with quiet Caledonii. When every last inch of the promenade was full, Broichan snapped his fingers. Down the rock-cut steps came a pair of mages dragging a tall man by a leash about his neck. He had been bound at the wrists, his head covered with a hood. He wore the heavy silver armlets and expertly woven tunic of a nobleman. At the foot of the steps, on the platform overlooking the well, his hood was ripped off. Brown hair, a distinctive shock of pure white at the temple, tumbled free. His tattoos shifted in the torchlight. He had been gagged. As his eyes adjusted to the light and he saw the well at his feet, his expression, at first defiant, turned horrified. He cried out, but the gag muffled his words.

At Bridei's command, the gag was removed. "My lord!" the captive cried. "You cannot do this! I am your noble hostage!"

"I can do this. Your brother has betrayed me."

"No, my lord! Uurad is true to you!"

Bridei shook his head. The silver beads on his beard-braids tinkled softly, echoing throughout the chamber with incongruent beauty. "Your brother rules the Insi Orc on *my* behalf. He is *my* regulus. Yet he conspires with Galam Cennalath. Why is that?"

"No! I tell you, my brother is true!" the hostage pleaded, his eyes huge. But Aedan saw the truth revealed therein: the man was lying. His brother, this Uurad, the ruler of Insi Orc, the vast group of islands to the north of Caledonia, was indeed conspiring against Bridei with his enemy Galam, overlord of the Miathi.

Bridei shook his head again. "Sadly for you, he is not true. And when your brother receives the gift I am about to send him—your head—he will know that I know it. And that I come for his."

The king nodded at the mages holding the hostage. The man struggled wildly, his piercing screams echoing off the chamber's unheeding stone walls, but in a few short seconds his ankles had also been bound. His remarkable hair was yanked back and the gag smashed against his teeth. Columba yelled, "No! No!", and leapt towards the captive, but was swiftly brought down by the guards, a fist slamming into the back of his skull. Then, as Broichan and the mages chanted ominously, the captive was pushed into the dark, still waters of the well.

He sank, but popped up again to the surface. He jerked spasmodically as he tried to keep his gagged mouth above the water-line, but with hands and feet bound there was little he could do, and he quickly sank again. The plane of his eyes, nose, and lips broke the surface once and then once more, white streak of hair swirling. Gruesome choking sounds filled the chamber but in what seemed like only seconds the man sank for the final time.

The body rose again with a *pop*, the parti-coloured hair streaming, obscuring the death-mask of the hostage, face down in the water. And all the while the assembled Caledonii watched wordlessly as the mages chanted.

His heart in his throat, Aedan looked down at his own bound hands. Was he next? Was Columba? He yanked against the knot but could not loosen it; he frantically gauged the distance to the chamber's rock-cut steps, the door. Too far; the well too close. He searched for clues in his wife's face, Drust's, but, like their fellow Caledonii, they were riveted by the spectacle. He heard the faintest of whispers beside him—under his breath, Columba was offering prayers for the dead man.

But the ritual was not yet complete. The two mages assisting Broichan disrobed. Naked except for their loin cloths, blue skin dark in the low light, they stepped into the water to retrieve the body, towing it back to the platform where they hauled it wetly up. Broichan met them there. Kneeling down, he took a small silver dagger from his belt and slit the corpse's throat from ear to ear. Blood gushed forth which Broichan collected in the ornate chalice provided him by the slave-girl.

Back around the promenade Broichan came, the chalice held high, torch-light glinting dully on the blood pooled within it.

As the mage passed them, he shot Columba a look filled with haughty pride, as if to say, "*That* is how it is done". Then, reaching the stone statue, he poured the blood from the chalice into its waiting mouth. Blood trickled redly over its lips and smeared down its chin, as if it, and not the Caledonian mages, had destroyed the hostage and then drank him dry.

Only then was the body hauled from the chamber feet-first, its skull bumping on the steps, leaving behind a thick smear of blood. Bridei and Broichan and their retainers followed.

When he came alongside Aedan and Columba, the king paused, his expression reserved and grave. Try as he might, Aedan could not read his father-in-law's thoughts.

"You two," Bridei said. "Come with me."

Horrified, Columba forced his legs to shuffle up the uneven stone steps. In the courtyard outside the chamber of the well, a pyre had been erected and on it the body of the hostage now burned. As promised, its head had been hacked off, to be sent as a warning to his brother. This was the three-fold death, sacred to the *druidi*: drowned, decapitated, immolated, the captive's soul was now pure enough for consumption by the stone god of the well. Seeing it, Columba despaired: at the waste; at his own weakness. His Christ needed no such sacrifice. These sorts of propitiations could not control life, could not persuade the gods to alter one's destiny. The mages had it wrong. If he were only allowed, he could show them a better way. A kinder god. A caring god. But instead, he had stood there on the ledge of the well, hardly back to life himself, impotent, mute, while the captive, his only crime a conniving brother, was destroyed.

"Why bother to burn him?" he asked sorrowfully of Aedan, yanked along by the guards. The hostage was dead, his soul long gone; fled this ruinous place. His God wanted that soul, and had taken it. But his young friend had no answer.

The king's hall, a roughly-hewn, round, wooden building, towered over all others in that part of the upper fort. The fire was roaring, but the hall was sparsely furnished, more martial and serviceable than luxurious. Bridei waited for them on his carved bench, Broichan glowering behind.

"Why have you come back?" Bridei demanded of Columba. "Is one island not enough for you?"

In ill-humor, Columba was in no mood to banter. "I have come for *him*," he said of Aedan. "It is time to let him go." All heads turned Aedan's way. Behind the big Scot, his small wife bristled. This surprised Columba. He easily recalled Domelch's fierce intelligence, had respected her for it. Surely she had worked out for herself the reason for Columba's return? Hadn't they all?

"He leaves us when it amuses *me* to let him go," Bridei declared.

Columba dipped his head, not quite as diplomatically as he might have. He found Gartnait, Aedan's son, within the protective embrace of his mother's arms. He was a strong, fine lad, with Aedan's dark coloring. There was much about him which brought to Columba's mind another boy—Artur, Eogan's son, a few years older than the Pictish princeling. And, more surprisingly, of Dunchad, the son of Conall. All three boys shared a clear lineage, the bloodline of the Scots.

"Your grandson, yes?" Columba asked. "The *Ferbasach* foretold by your prophecy? What a fine boy! What prodigious luck! The prophecy turned in your favor. My friend has done well."

No one responded. Columba did not truly expect them to. He waited a beat then said, intentionally misconstruing their silence, "Oh. Is that child *not* Aedan's son?"

Domelch gaped at the insulting implication. Drust bridled. The king arched an eyebrow, saying, "Have you so little care for your life, priest?"

Columba dipped his head. "My mistake. It is as I first thought, then. Aedan *has* had a son by your inestimable daughter. So you no longer have need of him. He has fulfilled his contract. You may let him go."

"How dare you!" Broichan barked. "You speak to the king of the Caledonii!" The old mage was very close, his fist raised.

But Drust was already there, palms to their two chests. "Take care, my lord mage!" the Pict warned. "The priest has power."

"The priest has power! The priest has power!" Broichan taunted with a child's intonation, mocking Drust's words which Columba noted the young warrior had used once before, many years back when they all stood together much as they did now, debating his and Aedan's fate: the Cauldron of Rebirth or life in exile. "He has no such power!" Broichan yelled, his hands flying, his grey beard shaking. "He was buried for five days! His god did not turn back the stone that entombed him. I did!"

"That may be. But what about Nessa?" Drust insisted, again in that low, careful tone. "We all saw him thwart her hunger—*a second time*. He saved me. He saved our Gartnait." His eyes, the horror of the monster of the riverbed sweeping through, grabbed glad hold of the sight of his nephew, safe.

"*Aedan* saved our Gartnait," Broichan corrected savagely.

There was silence, Broichan's face hardening. Columba smiled. Now was the moment to turn them. "My lord," he said to the king, "it is clear that you are a strong king; you protect your people; your enemies cower in fear. You are also wise. You safeguard the Old Ways,"—Columba suppressed his revulsion—"but also consider the New. You gave Iona, a stronghold of your religion, to me—a priest of Christ. Are you not also a man of your word? This man," he pointed at Aedan, "has kept his word. He has fulfilled his contract. He has kept faith with you. Why is he bound like a captive?" Columba proffered his own bound wrists in illustration. "Is he not your son? Has he not given you the grandson you desired? It is time to let him go."

Bridei glared at him for a long, icy moment. Columba stood firm, not so much aggressively as holding to the truth of his words, waiting for the king to find his own truth in them. For how could they be gainsaid? And then Bridei did the last thing Columba expected: he strode over to Aedan, looked his son-in-law long and hard in the face without revealing anything of his thoughts, then drew a silver-hilted dagger from his belt.

Columba gasped and sprang at the king. Domelch rushed, crying, "Father! No!" But with a quick flick of his wrist Bridei only sliced through Aedan's bonds, freeing him.

Then, with a hand on Aedan's shoulder, the king pulled the young man from the room, saying, "Come, son. The roe deer rut in the low hills. Let us hunt".

It always brought Aedan's heart to his throat, the blare of the blast horns, the baying of the lurchers, the men shouting, the horse heaving beneath him over rough ground as wind rushed by; the terror of the creature they pursued, a magnificent six-pointed stag. The hunt was exhilarating.

But not today. Bridei, bare-headed on his fine mount, led the charge after the stag. His retainers followed on foot, carrying spears and targes, easily outpaced by Aedan and the king. In hardly any time, there was a rustle in the underbrush. The bounding deer, flushed, was brought to a stand, and was dispatched by the king's own spear.

Letting their horses choose their pace, Aedan accompanied Bridei back to the citadel, the retainers, bearing the trussed stag on poles, lagging behind. They followed the coastline, which was sheer cliff here. Bridei hummed a lively little tune to himself, as if Aedan were not even there. Aedan was keeping silent for lack of anything useful to say, but all the while his thoughts were darting back and forth. What was Bridei's purpose? What a strange day, how fateful; when all of a sudden there was a roar from the underbrush, and something squat and black and swift, smelling feral, charged them—an enraged boar, tusks lowered for the soft underbelly of the king's horse. It slashed upwards, ripping the horse open. The animal shrieked and reared, throwing the king. The boar turned in a blur as Aedan, steadying his own terrified mount, drew his short sword, kicked his unwilling horse forward, leaned low in the saddle over its side, and punched the blade into the thick ruff at the beast's neck, bringing the animal to its front knees and then, in an agonized topple, over.

Swinging from the saddle, Aedan finished the animal off. He retrieved his sword and looked for Bridei. The king's horse was splayed on its side, grunting in pain, its innards spilled out over the trail, smoking. Aedan rushed to it, but the king was not trapped beneath. A hand over the stallion's terror-filled eyes, he slashed its neck. It snorted once in surprise and lay still.

He could not see Bridei anywhere. He must have been thrown over the cliff. He went to the edge and, on hands and knees, peered over.

Looking back at him, clutching the root of a gnarly pine that itself dangled over nothing but air, was Bridei. "Help me!" the king panted, his feet struggling to find purchase on the rock-face, and failing.

There was shouting behind them on the trail. The retainers were coming at a run, but not quickly enough.

Aedan hesitated, undecided. Bridei's eyes widened. "Help me!" he cried again.

Could he do it, Aedan wondered? Could he allow the king of the Caledonii to die without intervening?

The man who had killed his father?

Who was also his son's grandfather?

Aedan already knew the answer. It was not in his nature to sit by passively and watch death take a man. He either caused death, or he prevented it.

Cursing his own stupidity, he hauled Bridei to safety.

Not long after, there was a knock on the door of the chamber Aedan and Domelch had been given in the citadel. Bridei entered, attired not in his usual kingly splendor, but in a simple, rather anonymous cloak. He was alone. He kissed his daughter on the cheek and lifted Gartnait high into the air, dangling him there until he squealed.

Coming to Aedan, he hauled back his fist and struck Aedan in the chin, holding nothing back. "That's for hesitating, you bastard. You would have let me fall."

Aedan rubbed his aggrieved chin, reset his jaw. "It would have been nothing less than you deserve, you miserable old man."

"You have left me with only one choice."

"What?"

"Domelch, my dear, I need a drink. In fact, you'd better pass it around."

Bridei settled on the bench by the fire, drinking horn in hand. There was a moment of awkward silence, then he pulled a curious little leather-bound book from the pocket of his cloak, a book which could only have come from Columba. "Tell me of this," the king said to him.

Aedan took it. Domelch studied the book from over Aedan's shoulder. A little larger than a man's hand, it was covered in calf-skin, dyed a lovely ochre. Well-thumbed, it fell open, revealing lines of text in a meticulous hand. "It is a book," Aedan told the king. "A psalter, I think it is called. Columba's?"

"My men had no idea what to do with it. It spooked them; thinking it magicked, they gave it to me. *Salter?* Do you mean, from the sea?"

"Not like sea-salt, no. If I remember rightly, a psalter is a collection of their praise-poems to their god, poems they call *psalms*."

"Oh." Bridei took the book back, opened it again at random and pointed to the writing therein, his finger landing on a curly letter, larger than its companions. A curious thing, the letter contained within it both an even-armed cross of the Christ and a fantastic animal, something like a sea-creature, which rushed, open-mouthed, back on the ink which had spawned it. "This language,"

Bridei said. "Is this the Latin with which the Christians record and study their god's truth?"

"Yes. It's what the priests speak. They got it from the Romans."

"Is it like your written language? The ticks and lines?"

"No." This was much more complex, more evolved, than the *ogham* of Aedan's people.

The king was pouring over the pages, his fingers caressing them. "I find this fascinating. Each little black stroke of a creature, each letter and line, contains a truth. Has captured life. I think that with this written language may be said things that have never been said before. That it can capture thoughts, binding them in place and in time, undying, never changing, not so much as a word, ever."

"That is what they claim."

"Can you decipher it?" Bridei's gaze was piercing.

"No. But Columba could, surely."

Bridei paused, considering, then gently shut the book, tucking it back into his pocket. "It is a new power," he said, rising to leave. "It *is* a kind of magick. We would be wise, you and I, to learn how to exploit it."

At the door, he turned. His expression was peaceful, with none of the banked enmity Aedan was accustomed to seeing there. "You may go home now," he told Aedan. "Seek whatever revenge you feel you must against your cousin, Conall. Defeat him if you can; put your brother on the throne of Dal Riata. Do it with my blessing. But I will let you go on the understanding that *you leave us in peace*. I, for one, will vow to leave your particular *cenel* alone. I make no such claim for the other Scots, mind you!, but I owe you this blood-debt. With respect to us, turn your attentions elsewhere. Go bother the Britons. Consolidate your hold over the lands your people still claim in Hibernia. Only do not look northwards again. Your ship leaves on the morrow," he said. "Meet me in my chambers at sunrise."

Aedan was stunned. He asked, stupidly, "What about Columba?"

"He may go. In fact, please take him with you. I tire of Broichan's grumbling."

The king ruffled his grandson's thick brown hair, kissed his daughter on the cheek, and left the chamber.

From a shadow in a crook of the inner citadel's great stone wall, Columba watched the brief play of stars. After his long confinement in the Pictish holding cell, he could not yet abide being indoors. He filled his lungs with air, welcoming the support of the cooling stone against his back. Light filtered from the chambers, snatches of conversations drifting out to him, little of which he could clearly hear. He watched a tall figure steal across the long courtyard alone, recognized it to be King Bridei, saw him pause before Aedan and Domelch's door, gaze up at the stars for a long moment as he absentmindedly patted something in his pocket, then knock on the door and enter. A little while later, he watched the king leave again, his stride now purposeful and sure; Aedan's bemused face framed briefly in the doorway; Domelch behind, her eyes filled with a panic she quickly masked before Aedan turned back to her, the door closing.

Something had happened. He could not tell what, nor did he know what would come on the morrow. For now, he was alive, and Aedan too, and he was glad of it.

"Lord," he prayed, the canopy of stars above brilliant, the air a cool kiss on his skin. "Show me your will. Show me the way."

Aedan really thought he ought to be stupefied. He, promise to leave the Caledonii out of the lands of his future dominion? His future dominion! What a load of blather! Honestly: the things these Caledonii took to be fact. Their extraordinary faith in fancy. Yes, he really ought to be stupefied. Instead he was filled with an unsettling emotion he could not quite define.

He was sitting beside the fire, not on the bench Bridei had just vacated, but on the stone floor, his back against the wall, arms draped over bent knees, the drinking horn, thoughtfully refilled by Domelch who had then left him to his thoughts, in one hand, a long thin stick in the other with which he poked at the burning peat bricks. He took a long gulp of honey ale, his thoughts messy, cluttered, and watched dispassionately as the tip of his poking stick caught fire. It flared up, a bright red flash of flame but then, almost just as quickly, sputtered out. Head resting against the wall, forearm balanced on one knee, stick suspended in air, he watched the smoldering tip send up a thin plume of smoke. A finger-tip's-length from the point, the stream of smoke bifurcated, each trail then twisting quite independently in the air. He followed each ribbon distractedly until he lost them in the rafters, unable to tell where either of the smoke streams ended. How strange, he thought. How oddly beautiful and transporting. Two discreet trails from a single source, and both seemingly without end. As he continued to watch the ever-lengthening wisps, it came to him that the ends of each already existed, were already part of the path, attached to it, conceived at the beginning, before either had become a path, at the stick's red-hot tip. A beginning which he himself had witnessed, just as the tip took spark. A beginning he had created when he stuck the stick in the fire.

This path of his, here, too, had also always been destined to be. From the moment at Dun Ad's forge when he had stupidly agreed to lead Columba to the Craig, when he had traced their impossible route through the Glen on the forge's flag-stoned floor with the sooty tip of the blacksmith's discarded stick—that choice had led him here, to this moment. To this end.

And now, another. He could go home now. All the while he had been waiting for Bridei to let him go, he had very strongly doubted that he would live to see the day of his release. But he had. And just in time: Eogan needed help. Eogan thought to find that help at the Oenach of the Britons. But Aedan was not hopeful: he knew the Britons, at least the Gododdin. They were a chary lot, both distrustful and untrustworthy. He could not speak for the

Britons of Strat Clut: it was Eogan who had been fostered with them, and (his stomach turned over, thinking of her) Ama. Nor could he speak for Rheged. Perhaps these past ties of theirs were strong enough in and of themselves. More likely, the Britons would demand recompense: pay-back, in kind. Who wouldn't? It was the way of things. But he could not for the life of him figure out what he and Eogan could offer the Britons in return for their support.

And then there was Ama, wedded to his brother. Their son might be his own, but he could not claim him for love of that brother. He wondered with a start if that boy, Artur, was the *Ferbasach*, the future savior of the Picts, and not his Gartnait. Was Artur the warrior the Picts awaited? Or Dunchad? For, if Eithne were to be believed, he had not two, but three sons now. How extraordinary! His breath caught. Three sons! Perhaps the *Ferbasach* was one of them. For they were all fools if they truly believed it to be him.

The smoke continued to rise; his thoughts continued to drift. As if summoned by them, Gartnait toddled over to him, sputtering the gibberish that comes to a child before true speech, that pleasing current of words, sound, and melody and, carved wooden toys held in hands outstretched, turned, backed-up, and seated himself in Aedan's lap. Aedan played with his son, a warm, shifting mass, Gartnait's deep brown hair tickling his chin, softly speaking words of encouragement and praise in the boy's ear, avoiding Domelch's questioning eye, all the while thinking to himself, *Perhaps I will not go.* His thoughts spooling out first this way, then that, escaping into the ether without revealing their ends, for the remainder of the evening Aedan let himself consider ignoring Eogan's summons, of staying, instead, on this first path, laid down all those years ago in that smoky forge.

When later they lay down upon their heather pallet, Domelch wanted ever more of him and would not let him rest. There was a desperate quality to their lovemaking, and a pervasive melancholy. When dawn broke, she at last fell into a spent stupor and lay on top of him as if to keep him there in her bed, her ear against his heart. Forearms thrown across the small of her back, he nuzzled her nose under his chin and credited exhaustion for his conflicted heart.

"I will give you one boon for having saved my life."

These were Bridei's words to Aedan as, in the king's hall early the next morning, Bridei and Broichan sat at table playing draughts. The king was intent upon his next move; Broichan, having cornered the king's piece, slouched confidently, his stockinged foot in the hands of his fair-haired slave-girl. Moaning happily, he stretched his foot along the young woman's thigh, his toes digging into her flesh, flattening her linen tunic against the place he planned to visit as soon as the game was done.

The sight disgusted Columba and he made an unintentional, censorious sound. The maid looked up quickly, then down again; she was not to see anything but her master and his needs. But something transferred to Columba with that fleeting glance: some visceral sense of her condition—an intense agitation, just short of panic, commingled with a feeling of immobility, the futile straining against unmovable bonds: imprisonment which, having recently endured it in the holding cell, he could now understand. The pressing weight, the shortness of breath, the scream which went on and on that no one could hear, the immense fear and terror and despair. That you are so insignificant that you are forsaken.

His heart was pounding crazily in his chest, his breath panting. He could not bear the young woman's captivity a moment longer. He simply could not bear it.

Take her then. Take her.

Startled, Columba jumped. The words had been whispered into his right ear. His hair had been blown back by an unseen agency, a puff of breath, encouraging him to take note. But there was no one behind him.

Aedan had not yet answered the king. Seizing the moment, Columba pulled him aside. "What will you ask for?" he asked.

Aedan shrugged. "I want nothing from that man. And besides, I have what I need. My child. My wife. My dog. Bridei has already given me my father's head, which is why I came here to Caledonia in the first place."

"I thought you came here for *his* head." A nod at the king.

"Yes, well: things change."

"They do. Nothing truer! Listen, if your heart does not move you to request anything for yourself, would you request something for me?"

"Another island?"

"No! No. I want the girl." Columba glanced briefly at the blond slave, careful to hide his interest from Broichan.

"*What?*"

"It's not what you think!"

"You have no idea what I am thinking."

"Listen, I have been told to take her."

"By whom?" Aedan looked around: no one.

"The angels. Yes, I know! You scoff!"

"Actually, I don't." Columba could have no idea, but Aedan was thinking of his dead father in the pool, the ethereal hunt.

"I don't know why, or to what it may lead, but I have learned at some cost to obey these promptings when they are given to me," Columba said. "Perhaps she is of some importance? I don't know. But I have been told to take her."

Aedan's head cocked; he considered it. Returning to the draughts table, he seized Broichan's lead piece, held it still, said to the king: "Release the slaves".

Bridei shot back on his bench. "*What?*"

"Release all the Scots you have enslaved over the course of the wars between us."

Bridei's laughter boomed. "You must be joking!"

"I'm not. You have given me a boon. This is it. Is your life not worth a few slaves?"

"A few slaves? We have hundreds!"

Aedan nodded sagely. "Indeed. Well, we don't have quite so many of yours, but let us make a pact, you and I: release our slaves now and, if I am ever able, I shall return the favor and send home to you your lost Caledonian sons and daughters, though this may be many years hence, or never."

Bridei's eyes narrowed as he calculated the cost of such an action. "I can release my own—the Scottish slaves that serve my house. But I cannot freely take another man's property. That is the best I can do."

At that moment, the handmaiden cried out. It was a sound of great longing. She looked around wonderingly. Her hands stopped their expert stroking of Broichan's feet.

The old mage shot upright. "You cannot have *mine*! You cannot have *her*!"

The king's gaze flickered over the handmaiden. "She belongs to this house, foster-father, and serves you only because I tell her to. She is mine to give away."

"She is invaluable to me," the old man declared. "She is my handmaiden. She prepares all my salves and potions. She knows all my needs."

"You can train another in your arts," Bridei suggested.

"No, it must be her."

"Why, foster-father? Why not another?"

"Truth be told, I love her and she loves me." The mage gazed upon the girl hungrily. Columba, attending it all very closely, saw her recoil. It was the tiniest of movements, the faintest of withdrawals, yet he recognized it for what it was: a scream of denial which could not be expressed.

"The love of a slave is never freely given," Columba spat, full of righteous fury on her behalf. "You are a fool if you think it is."

The mage shot him a venomous look. He took the slave-girl by the hand and drew her forward. "Tell him that you love me," he ordered, nudging her.

The girl raised her head. There was no light in her blue eyes, as if she had fled from her situation, from herself, a very long time ago. When she did not immediately obey, Broichan gave her hand another impatient shake. She turned her eyes up to him obediently and she did speak, but she addressed an indeterminate point just beyond his shoulder. "I love my master," she said, but in a rehearsed way and so flatly that all who cared for the truth knew it to be a lie.

"If she loves you as you claim," Columba said, "then you can set her free without fear, for she will make her way back to you."

"Indeed! She would!" Broichan said. "But there is no need to test it. She has no desire to leave me. Do you, my dear?" Another commanding yank on her hand.

"No, my lord," she said. But the word was mouthed hollowly and her blue eyes sought the floor.

Broichan's gaze travelled over the girl's lovely frame. Lust flooded his eyes. She was young and beautiful. "You see? I may own her body—or rather, my foster-son the king may own it—but that is an accident of fate. It is love that binds our souls. There is no master here. No slave. Only partners in trust and affection; equals in the eyes of the gods." Letting go her hand and setting her behind him as if to keep her safe, but in fact simply to keep her, Broichan declared, "I refuse to be parted from her".

The king nodded. "So be it. Aedan, you may have all my Scottish house-slaves but this one."

The handmaiden, so passive, so obedient, came alive. Her face blanched and she beseeched Aedan and Columba with a look of pure panic even as Broichan smiled triumphantly and drew her into his arms. He maneuvered her stiff chin for a long, open-mouthed kiss; released her finally with a pat on her bottom. "Get me a drink, my love," he said.

She obeyed, devastation on her face. But once behind the mage, Columba saw her pause. Her eyes closed, her chin lifted, her fingers convulsed around the wine-filled glass goblet and she took a deep breath. Then she scooped something off the games table and quickly palmed it into the goblet. Handing the goblet to Broichan dutifully, she stepped back, her eyes full of both defiance and resignation.

Broichan smiled at Columba in triumph, saluted him with raised glass, took a long, hearty drink and swallowed.

It was another of those occasions when Columba could have acted but, trusting his God, chose not to.

Horror crossed Broichan's face. The goblet slipped from his fingers to shatter on the clay floor, glass-shards flying. His hands flew to his throat as he struggled to catch breath. Choking, he clutched at the table, the king, the air, then crashed to the floor.

Everyone came running. Broichan bucked on the floor, making watery garbling sounds, his eyes wide, hands clamped around his throat. The king, on his knees beside his foster-father, was bellowing, "Help him! Somebody help him!" Domelch and Drust hovered over the pair, but Aedan held back, looking to Columba for direction. Columba warned him off with a quick shake of his head.

From a distance, the handmaiden watched stoically. *She knows she will be killed for this*, Columba realized. *She doesn't care. She's had enough.*

He walked calmly over to the desperate king and choking mage. Broichan's eyes were bulging from his face, hands clawing for help, heels punching the floor. Columba said coolly, "If you like, I can restore his health".

"*Do it*!" shouted Bridei.

"The handmaiden?"

Bridei face contored with outrage. "*Take her*!"

Hitching up his tunic to his thighs, Columba straddled the mage. With one hand fisted over the other, he stiffened his shoulders, reared back, and punched his weight onto Broichan's chest, just under the old man's breastbone. Nothing happened at first. Under his facial tattoos, the mage's skin had taken on a frightful shade of purple. But when Columba punched his chest a second time, Broichan's ribs cracked with a resounding *crunch*, and something shot out of his mouth with such force that it *pinged* off an iron candle-stand and clattered to the floor.

Columba climbed off Broichan. The mage rolled to his side, knees contracted, heaving in breath. A servant scurried to the king, something in his hand: a white pebble, a marker from the games table, slick with Broichan's spit. The king roared and lunged at the handmaiden, fist drawn back to strike her down. She did not flinch. She was ready to be killed; looked, in fact, that she might welcome it.

But Aedan was already between them, catching the king's fist in his hand. "No. She's ours now," he said.

Bridei growled, teeth bared at Aedan, but he obeyed.

They hurried out of the king's chamber, the handmaiden bustled before them.

Aedan burst in on her. "Domelch! Where is Gartnait? Come! They wait for us."

Taking heed of the tightness about her mouth, the deep shadows under her eyes, he pulled up short. He could tell from her rigid stance that she was deeply unhappy. But the ship was ready; they had to leave before he changed his mind.

"I am not going with you," she said, her arms stiffly folded over her chest, her chin raised defiantly.

This made no sense. He strode to her, took her by the arm. "Come," he said. "I know this is rather sudden. I will help you pack. Where is Gartnait?"

She shrugged off his grip. "I am not going with you."

She was not making this easy for him, yet he understood. He had felt rather the same way when first stranded in this land with a people who wished him dead.

"Domelch. Please. Don't worry. No harm shall come to you."

She sputtered in disbelief.

"I will look after you, as you have me," he insisted. "I would kill any man who tried to hurt you or Gartnait."

She shook her head.

He tugged on her arm again but she held firm, making him fear that she would not be moved without a force he was unwilling to wield. "Please. Tomorrow you will feel differently."

"I will not feel differently. I will not leave. You would do your best to protect me, I know. But I have no wish to live amongst the Scots." She shuddered with distaste.

That smarted. As if he had ever desired to live amongst the Picts! As if he *liked* these Caledonii! His anger flared and he wanted to hurt her in return, but he knew that such a tactic was unlikely to achieve his objective, which was to go home and to have her and Gartnait too. He tried to soothe her instead. "Domelch," he said, pulling her stiff little frame against him.

She threw him off violently. "I said no! Think of our son! They groom him for the kingship!"

He *was* thinking of their son—he was thinking that he could not bear leaving behind yet another son, yet another woman. He threw up his hands. "I must go home. I have no wish to leave you!"

Her mood swifted; her gaze became direct and sad. "That comforts me."

"My brother needs me."

"Yes. And you are loyal to the last."

Why did she say that as if it were a failing of his? "What would you have me do?"

"Come back to me when you can," she shrugged with sorrowful eyes.

Come back to her when he could. Come back here when his work in Dal Riata was done. Leave his own people a second time, this time willingly. Could he do it? Exile himself voluntarily?

A sudden thought: why not? Aside from his brother's need, what was there for him in Dal Riata, really? The things that he wanted there were not his. They never would be.

He left her; he would persuade her later. Went in search of his son.

Gartnait, engrossed in play, did not hear him approach until Aedan had swept him up in his arms. Holding him close, Aedan took one warm little hand in his own; turned it over, brought Gartnait's palm to his lips, blowing hard to make the loud, rasping sound his son loved. Gartnait squealed and giggled, plucking back his hand, tucking it behind his back.

"Gartnait," he said, "Da has to go. Do you understand? Da has to go."

Gartnait was studying his lips as he spoke. He looked up quizzically. "Da go? Da go?"

"Yes. Da has to go. And you are coming with me."

"Don't even think it."

Drust had come up silently; and been trailing Aedan this whole time, to prevent just the sort of thing Aedan had been about to do. Drust's men were with him.

Aedan sized up his chances; they weren't good. The only way this would have worked was with stealth, and he had just lost that. He cursed inwardly, tried another tactic: "If you want him, you will have to take him from me".

"You will lose." A nod at his armed men.

Another: "Coward!"

But Drust refused to be baited. "You cannot take him with you." Drust was very solemn. Almost kind.

The realization that he would have to leave Gartnait nearly brought Aedan to his knees. He tried the truth: "I can't leave him," he said to Drust. "How can I leave him?"

Drust's hand was on his shoulder; not in force, but in comfort. "I know. I know, my friend. Will you trust me? I will look after him until you return."

"Da back?" Gartnait asked.

Aedan devoured the lines of his son's earnest, happy face, his long lashes, his big brown eyes, searing them into his memory. "Da back," was all Aedan could manage; he didn't want to cry in front of Drust's men.

"That's right. He'll be back." Drust ruffled Gartnait's hair. "Now, shall we go find your mother?"

"Look for me in the spring," he told her at the threshold of their chamber, Drust and his men behind to see that it was done. One last kiss for his son, he handed Gartnait to her. With eyes wide-open Domelch pressed her mouth against his in a lingering kiss, and laid her small hand over his heart and said, simply, "Goodbye, husband".

He did not know it but, after he turned his back and headed out of the fortress for the harbor, with proud carriage and high chin she closed the door to their chamber and, sitting down on the stone floor, cradled her face in her hand and rocked Gartnait who called out once or twice "Da?" before he fell silent. And there without making a sound she rocked and she wept.

"Girl," Columba said.

The slave-girl was huddled in the corner, cloak wrapped tightly around her slim frame. She hadn't spoken since the events in the king's chambers, but had been watching Columba warily. When he approached her, she tipped forward onto her knees. He didn't know what to make of it, it was only time to go, until she reached up and began to untie the belt of his tunic. She meant to service him. He lurched back, appalled, hands out to ward off her unwanted ministrations. She flinched, expecting to be struck, her face turned away. But she stayed on her knees.

"No, child! No! You have been ill-used, but no man will ever ... Not while you are under my protection—under Aedan's protection. Come! Please! Get up!"

She looked at him shrewdly, but did not move: she knew better.

"You are free now. Don't you understand?" He searched for her name, realized he didn't know it; Broichan had never used it. "What are you called, child?"

This startled her. "Do you mean my name?"

"Yes. Your name." What else?

It flew out of her violently. "Covna. That was my name once. Covna. He never cared to know it. He called me *pet*."

"Child! Dear child! Covna! You are a slave no more."

Columba and Aedan picked their way down the steep hillside, following the king's road to the bustling harbor below the fortress where the ship waited. As word went out that Bridei had freed the court's Scottish house-slaves, other Caledonii came running, to witness for themselves the unprecedented spectacle, to see what miracle Columba might next perform. As for the house-slaves, now twenty-or-so in number, they cowered in disbelief, not trusting that they were truly free until many leagues had been put between them and their former masters. Covna stayed close.

At the dock, Columba was surprised to see not only Drust waiting for them, but the king himself. Bridei was fingering the white pebble. He tossed it into the air, caught it again.

I should tell him the truth, Columba thought. "I would have attempted to save Broichan," he said, "regardless of the slave-girl."

Bridei made a half-disgusted, half-impressed sound. "You know, they are already saying that this thing is magically restorative. That it can heal. This pebble that would have choked him! You do amaze me, priest! Everything you do becomes miracle."

Columba thought about this; how, here amongst the Picts, that did seem to be true. "I don't know," he said. "I do know that nothing can keep a man from dying when his appointed term of life is finished. However, I suspect that that pebble may indeed come to heal many."

"How so?"

"Faith."

"Faith?"

"Their faith in its miraculous properties will give it power."

Bridei's face screwed up, unconvinced. "What, the power comes from the people themselves? Their faith? Not the pebble?"

"Yes, indeed."

Bridei's mouth turned down as he thought about this. Finally he shrugged, then pocketed the pebble. He turned to Aedan, handed him a leather-wrapped parcel, long and thin and heavy-looking. "Here is something you have earned."

It was Aedan's father's great, two-handed broad sword, a beautiful thing Aedan had not laid eyes on since it had been hacked from Gabran's hand as war-booty in the bloody glen. Aedan said nothing to the king; all he could manage was a nod. He lofted it, slashing the air, testing its weight and balance. Bridei had obviously cared for it; the metal and jewels in the hilt had been polished until they shone.

Then Drust was pressing something else into Aedan's hands, a bulbous parcel under whose leather covering was more metal: a Pictish war-helmet, crested by a figure of a charging bull— somewhat like Bridei's bull, but distinct enough so as not to be mistaken for a mark of the king's ownership—and a flying black mane of coarse horse hair.

"We made this," Drust told Aedan proudly. "So, unlike the ridiculous thing you pass off as a skull-cover, it is very well constructed. It will stay put on your thick head, and when it does, you can thank me. My friend! May your gods go with you!"

Drust drew Aedan into a heart-felt hug, an embrace which, after a moment, Aedan returned. "You keep your promise," Columba heard Aedan say.

Bridei was watching their affectionate farewell with reserve. "The contract between you and my daughter is absolved," he said.

"There is no need," Aedan told the king. "I am coming back."

To that, Bridei merely raised an eyebrow. "When you do, you may wed her again."

· PART TWO·

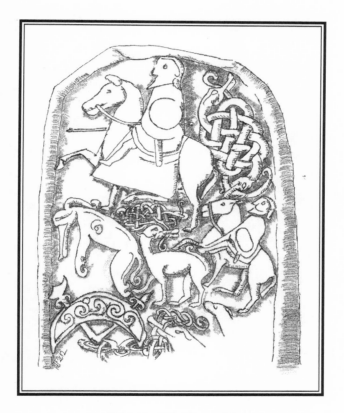

Meigle No. 4 Pictish cross-slab
(Meigle Sculptured Stone Museum, Meigle, Scotland, 800-1000 A.D)

· 7 ·
ALT CLUT

That was how, late one day at the end of July in the year of the Lord 567, a Pictish ship, hull black-tarred, sails furled, a sleek thing meant to quickly transport things of value, pulled into the harbor below the stronghold of the Britons of Alt Clut. Though she was a Pictish vessel, she flew a makeshift Dal Riatic flag, and in this way all who saw her knew the cargo she carried: Aedan, wayward brother of the lord of the Cenel Gabran, returned at last from his exile amongst the heathen Picts. For who else could it be?

Alt Clut, the Rock of the Clut, the chief-seat of the Britons of Strat Clut, a people known in chronicle and legend as the last of the free tribes of Britannia, is a formidable rocky outcrop thrust up from the Clut, a firth, a very wide arm of the sea, some ways to the south and east of Dal Riata. That the Rock has been fortified is no surprise: when times are violent, the people in these northern reaches cluster on high places, the more inaccessible the better. Dun Ad is one such stronghold, Alt Clut another. But Alt Clut is different. Unlike Dun Ad, which emerges moodily from a marshy plain, Alt Clut punches up with defiance from the lively blue rivers around it. Like an island, it rises directly from the water, discreet, self-sufficient. But it is not an island. Rather, hidden from those who come to it first from the sea, friends and foe alike, is a secret: a narrow isthmus connects the Rock to the mainland on its far side, holding Alt Clut to the shore by the most tenuous of threads, passable only at low tide. That little strip of land separates the mighty Clut from the Lemn, rivers which, flowing independently, surge around the Rock to melt in front of it and blend together into the sea.

As fortresses go, Alt Clut is exceedingly formidable; very strongly fortified. But it is beautiful, too, in its way. For the Rock is really two peaks, smashed together. Like twins not fully separated at birth, the peaks share a stony base. They are joined at the hip but their heads cleave apart. The summit to the west, conical in shape, sharper, higher, more precipitous, the first to be seen from the sea, is the fiercer fellow. Teeth gritted and fists clenched, back to its brother, it faces the firth head-on and, with a flinty forbearance, rides out the storms that blow therein from the sea. Atop it lies the king's hall. The summit to the east, with its round form and flat top, is, conversely, gentle and mild. It hunches away from its twin as it reaches hopefully for where the sun rises. Sheltered safely in its brother's lee, it bears the houses and halls of the Britons who claim it.

Happy would these brothers seem, save for the sharp cleft that seeks to divide them. A steep defile runs down between the two, down from their heads, all the way down to their shared feet. Down the long ages of man they have sought to separate, the one pulling away from the other. Yet for all their rending, the two brothers are only yards apart: at its narrowest, the cleft between them is little wider than two men standing side-by-side. This is what makes the

Rock very strong: the only way to reach the crags, and the Britons on them, is to ascend this scar. It is also what makes the Rock so arresting: it is difficult to judge whether the Rock is one contented mass; or two, and those two locked in eternal, impotent struggle to escape the other.

As they sailed up the firth of the Clut on high-tide late on that July day, Columba was thus presented with a sight which has the power to so deeply impress travelers, both before him and well afterwards, that even those not prone to poetry are moved to sing its praises in whatever language they possess: the solid, arrogant mass of the Rock, the blue waters holding it reverently, and all ablaze in the yellow splendor of a sun still sitting fat and high in mid-heaven.

It was fantastic—yet Aedan, beside Columba at the rail, observed its majesty with ambivalence. Looking up at the Rock, familiar to him as the place where his brother had been fostered, he tried his best to dredge up some feeling of excitement or, barring that, anticipation, but to no avail. At best, he felt a modicum of relief that he was not returning home to Tairbert Boitter, to *her*.

The warship backed its sails. A boat was lowered, and Aedan and Columba disembarked. Taking their leave of Uirolec and his crew, bidding them to release the Dal Riatic slaves at some safe place in Cendtire on their homeward journey, they watched the ship unfurl its sails once again and turn back to the north. Then they rowed to the Rock's harbor, crammed with vessels, for boats could go no further upstream than the Rock, guarding as it did the furthest navigable point of the river. There were Strat Clut's mighty warships, lords of all traffic and commerce on the seaway, and the many ships of the Britons who had come to render their tribute to Strat Clut and to others. Eager to take advantage of them all were merchantmen from Gaul laden with Merovingian glass and pottery and finely worked metal and all manner of trinkets such as one might buy at a fair, for such was the Oenach. Working their way through this maze of vessels, they came to the harbor at the edge of the flat grassy plain which stretched to the foot of the Rock, at the moment full to bursting with festive Britons.

Through the crowds on the dock, Aedan spied the little knot of his first family. Eogan seemed grimmer, grey just beginning to fleck his temples, though there was delight on his face at sight of his brother. To a startled Aedan, it was a bit like looking at their dead father. In his arms was a small dark-haired boy. Aedan's heart was in his throat: this was Artur. One arm draped around Eogan's neck, the other tightly grasping the folds of his cloak, the boy squinted to see his celebrated uncle come home at last.

These two were expected. And so very, very welcome. What was not was the woman: Ama. With a hand on her son's back, she shielded her eyes from the sun as she sought him out on the approaching boat. The jolt of longing he felt upon seeing her again was so intense, so painful, it stole away his breath.

And so at last Aedan could begin to understand his feelings: he would have been quite content to stay away from her forever. If he could not have her, he did not want her anywhere near. In his wide rangings, he had somehow managed to blanket his incessant need, how she consumed his thoughts, taking over his better sense. His ambivalence at returning home had been merely a lid to tamp down his anxiety and his dread at having to see her again.

He took a deep breath and he steadied himself. These were heady revelations. They waited for him; he could see their joy. Shoring up his emotions, he leapt onto the dock, Columba and Ceo with him. Eogan set down Artur and rushed to embrace Aedan. As his brother held his face in his hands for a long moment, Aedan was unsurprised to see tears there, for there were tears in his own eyes too.

Words tumbled from Eogan: "By the gods, Brother! It is good to see you! You look well! Well!" To Columba: "You did it! You really did it! Marvelous! I wasn't sure! I had begun to lose hope!" To Aedan again: "Tell us everything! Tell us of the Pictess!"

The Pictess? Ama was looking at him wide-eyed and rather breathlessly.

"Tell me! Do you have a son?" Eogan demanded.

"Yes!" Aedan said, with an afterthought of a smile. Ama stiffened.

"I knew it! I knew it! What have you called him?"

"Gartnait."

"*Gartnait?*" Eogan garbled the Pictish name, laughed at himself, brightened. "Aedan! Look! This is our Artur! Artur! This is your uncle Aedan!"

Artur was taking it all in cautiously, studying the two strange men and the massive hound. At three years of age, he was a handsome little boy, dark like his parents, with even features. He had his mother's eyes: large, long-lashed, deep brown in color; had as many of Eogan's features as Aedan's. Aedan took his hand. Feeling suddenly awkward, he gave Artur a manful shake, then grimaced at the boy's answering grip. Artur giggled shyly.

"I have been waiting a long time to meet you, Artur," Aedan said gently. Unsure whether he should withdraw his hand, Artur smiled tentatively.

Steeling himself, Aedan finally turned to Ama. He took her in: by the gods, she was beautiful! She would insist that she wasn't: at nearly his height, she was tall for a woman, her hair, rich and brown and full, swung in luxurious waves about her face. Her eyes were also a deep, warm brown, her nose long and her mouth full. She was too tall, too angular, for true beauty, but it was as if she had been made for him. Holding himself back, cognizant of Eogan watching closely but permitting himself one very brief, very controlled moment of self-indulgence, he took one of her hands in his own and, moving in close, kissed her cheek, loving the brush of her hair, her breath against his skin, the smell of her. Sunshine and honey.

She was holding herself very still. "Ama," he said, breathing her in, relishing the spark that had always existed between them, the upsurge of vital energy.

Her breath caught. "He didn't say," she said, dazed. "He didn't say that he had called you home."

He let her go. "Let us go do what you've bid me here to do," he said to his brother.

Eogan, who knew the Crag of the Kings well, having been fostered here as a child with Ama, led them unerringly through the crowds to a large guard house on a small rise at the far end of the plain. This was the home of the Steward of the Rock who, after greeting Eogan and Ama as if no time had passed, let them into the guard house through one door and out again through another at its back.

They emerged into a small courtyard which rose on two levels. For such a compact space, it too housed a fair number of buildings, which hugged the side of the Rock, rising sheerly behind them, for protection and shelter. Columba looked around with unabashed interest. After years amongst the Scots, how sophisticated this place appeared! How evident the Rock's civility, its prosperity. And Christian, too! There, a small chapel and a little cemetery; he wondered whose.

Eogan had given him a gift, inviting him here.

At the far end of the crowded courtyard was a long flight of steps carved into the rock, which they climbed to reach a second guard house. This one secured the mouth of the defile running down from the summits. The guard house had, in fact, been constructed inside the cleft so that living rock formed its walls. The Rock above them was so sheer that, even when craning his neck, he could glimpse nothing of the summits. Again, their party was welcomed cordially by the guards and was shown to a door at the back of the hut. However, when this was opened, Columba could see nothing but another set of rough stairs leading upwards. They were so worn by the passing of countless feet over the ages that it proved to be more of a scramble than a climb, the walls of the cleft closing in, cool to the touch but suffocating. Trudging up step after step after step, thigh muscles straining with the straight vertical climb, Columba longed to stop and take in the view, but Eogan, leading the way, did not slacken his pace until they came to a point where the cleft between the two summits was at its narrowest. Overhead, a slender rope bridge swayed, swung across the abyss.

Passing underneath it, they reached the top of the stairs and moved out upon a small patch of level ground. The sun was setting. Here the Rock separated into its two summits, the crags towering on either side. The flat shoulder of land in between the peaks, thrown now into shadow, was taken up by a number of buildings, including many temporary dwellings and tents erected by the visiting Britons. Rising higher than the rest was a sturdy wooden hall, the Chamber between the Crags, which protected Alt Clut's spring, the existence of which ensured that the fortress was invulnerable to anything but the longest siege.

A narrow, winding path led off to the right, up to the summit of the eastern peak, known as the Beak. For the duration of the Oenach the grassy plain down below at the Rock's foot would accommodate those lowest in status: the merchants; the common people. This clearing between the crags, here, was reserved for those of middling worth. The Beak was for the lords of men and those who served them. This path was the only way to reach it, the Beak falling to the sea on its other sides.

The ascent to the Crag of the Kings, the western peak to their left, was even more difficult, for the rope bridge swung over the cleft was its only approach. They headed for it. In the slight, early evening breeze, it swayed over the cleft; on gusty days, surely impassable. Columba tested the knotting with a foot before moving out upon it, the abyss yawning beneath him, an easy twenty-foot drop to the stone steps below. But once safely on the other side, he finally came to the prospect he had been longing to see. His breath caught. The ground around them fell precipitously to the sea, the vantage afforded them encompassing. Above, the western crag loomed; at its top the Windy Hall on the Crag of the Kings. Across, the eastern summit, the Beak, crowned by the halls of the Britons of the Rock. Below, way, way below, the plain, crawling with people. At its edge, the harbor. Straining his eyes, Columba could just distinguish the warship of the Cenel Gabran, Eogan's warship, amongst the others crowding there. And all around, the wide blue firth, except for where the thin isthmus connected the Rock to the shore behind. Ahead, the low hills of the northern hinterland; across the firth, more hills to the south. From where he stood, Columba could easily believe that, though coveted, and rightly so, by men who did not wish her well, the Rock had never fallen to her enemies.

The path to the Crag of the Kings had been carved out of the very cliff-edge. If he were to trip, nothing would impede his fall until he slammed into the firth itself. Eogan resumed the lead cautiously, his son tucked in carefully behind. Climbing steadily, the party at last reached the heady summit. They arrived just as a huge bonfire in the Crag's central clearing was ignited. With a tremendous *whoosh*! logs, piled to the height of three men, burst into flame. Elsewhere, other bonfires were ignited so that all three levels of the Rock blazed with light. And there, behind the bonfire, stood the Windy Hall, home, feasting house, and judgment seat of Tudwal Tutclyt, son of Clinoch, king of the Britons of Strat Clut. Its doors were thrown open to the feast inside.

They entered those doors just as a boisterous party of Britons was on its way out, their lord in the lead. He was a striking man, with pale-blue eyes, a thin, beaked, nose which had been broken at least once, high cheekbones, and curly hair the color of rust, balding at the top. His cheeks were permanently flushed, and fine, red spider veins had begun to web the sides of his nose. Having seen them often enough before, Columba knew the signs: only years of committed dissipation could so sour a face. Yet the lord was muscular and able, and handsome in a sharp way, although Columba sensed what he could only describe as unspecified malice emanating from him.

In the doorframe of the Windy Hall, the lords collided. "Ah! Aedan!" the strange lord said in a voice Columba found curiously high and light.

With a precipitous, protective, motion, Aedan swept Artur and Ama behind his back.

"Who is this?" Eogan demanded, his hand moving to the hilt of his sword.

"Morcant." Aedan's answer was so low that Columba had to strain to hear it. It was as if it disgusted him to even utter the man's name.

Eogan's eyes narrowed. "Morcant of the Votadini? Lord of the Gododdin? Your foster-brother?"

Aedan nodded curtly, his black eyes so constricted they were mere slits.

Morcant's gaze swept Aedan up and down, lingering for a long moment on his face. The look was almost tender. Then an oily smile slicked up the sides of his bitter mouth. "Ah! Foster-brother! How I have missed you!" he said, his voice a caress.

Aedan stiffened. Then, with a movement so lightning-quick that it was completed before Columba had fully registered that it had begun, Aedan drew his sword from over his shoulder and rammed its point into Morcant's breastplate, directly over his heart.

There was a moment full of the rasping of blades: Morcant drew his sword; Eogan felt he had to draw his; and then all the men of the Gododdin armed themselves to defend Morcant. The only thing protecting the small party of Scots from the wrath of the Britons was the constriction of the doorframe which bottled up the Gododdin behind their lord.

"What are you doing?" Eogan cried at his brother. "This is a man we have come here to see!"

"I am going to kill him," Aedan snarled, lunging at Morcant.

Shoving Artur into Columba's arms, pushing them both safely out of the way, Ama plunged right in, crying out: "Morcant! Cease! If you harm them, you harm Rheged!"

Remarkably, it worked. Perhaps it was the shock of a woman, any woman, forbidding the actions of a lord, any lord, especially one so great as Morcant of the Gododdin, but there was a moment of inaction which gave her just enough time to ram herself between the three, right between Aedan's broad chest—the flat of his sword held laterally against Morcant's breastplate skimmed the top of her hair—and the other two. With a strength borne more of fear for Aedan's and Eogan's lives than anything remotely resembling commonsense, she shoved them apart with all her might. She was not a small woman, and she was strong, and the men were pushed apart just enough so that their skewering by one blade or another was no longer imminent.

But it was like trying to put a stop to the ocean's waves. Within seconds, there was snarling and the men had surged back again. She was trying to break them apart a second time, knowing that her strength and her resolve would not be enough, when a voice, terrible and absolute, bellowed: "Who draws swords? There is truce at the Oenach! Who draws swords in my hall?" and the sea of men was sundered apart by Tudwal Tutclyt, king of the Britons of Strat Clut, and all twenty-eight of his house-guard. There was pushing and shoving and grunting as, as one, the Scots and the Gododdin were forced out the doorway, spilling willy-nilly into the courtyard. The Gododdin quickly surrounded them; Ama was jostled against Eogan; against Aedan, and his arm was around her, somehow protecting her in the fracas; and then there was Tudwal, his fancy silks and furs askew on his corpulent form, his balding pate glistening from the exertion, fuming with righteous indignation.

The king stomped to the knot of them, shoved them backwards. Ama would have fallen save for Aedan's firm hand on her back. Tudwal loomed, bulky, glaring without really seeing any of them; rounded on Morcant, barked "Enough!"; swung back, barked at the brothers "Enough, I say! Enough!"

One ferocious inhalation, and he was roaring again. "Morcant! I expect better from the lord of the Gododdin! Cousins! I should have known! Where is Conall? Where is the king?"

"I make render for Dal Riata," Eogan ground out.

"*You*?" The king gaped, revealing a large gap between his front teeth. "Have you been reduced to steward *again*, cousin?" Tudwal emphasized the title with a sneering disdain. "How can Conall expect the lot of the Scots to rise in this world when he behaves like a common *toiseach*?"

Aedan and Eogan flushed angrily. Enjoying their disgrace, Morcant snickered.

That did it; Ama's loyalty won out. She sprang forward, a stinging rebuke on her lips, but was held back by Eogan. "Through me, our *ruiri* renders tribute for Dal Riata," he bit out, ice in his voice. His back ramrod-straight, he was the epitome of lordly outrage. "However, if our cattle are offensive to you, cousin, I will find another lord to take them."

Eogan let his eyes wander the rapt crowd. He did it in a theatrical way so that the effect carried through to even those furthest away. He paused to admire the lords of Aeron who had come to see for themselves the cause of the commotion. Then the fractious lords of Galloway: Gwenddolau ap Ceidaw and his enemies, Gurci and Peretur, the sons of Elifer of the Great Retinue. He tilted his head in Ama's direction, a silent reminder to the others of Rheged, of which she was lady, easily the most powerful of the British kingdoms come together in that company.

"Which lord would be least offended by our tribute, do you think?" he asked Tudwal, all innocence. "You decide: who gets the cows?"

Tudwal heaved a sigh. "Enough, cousin," he said. "Enough. Stay away from him." He pointed at Morcant. "And you," to Morcant. "Come with me!"

The crowd began to dissipate, grumbling: there would be no blood-letting here, today, no sport for their amusement. But Aedan was still fuming. He stalked away, his shoulders stiff. Ama watched him with mounting alarm. Ceo padded to her master's side and whined; Aedan ignored her. Eogan, too, was waiting to see if Aedan could manage his fury. Because Aedan in fury was elemental, just at the edge of control.

She had only ever witnessed it the one other time, but it had scared her then too. It was that summer when she had first met Aedan, when he had been cast out by his foster-father, Leudonus, the old lord of the Gododdin, and sent to Alt Clut in disgrace. Oddly enough, Tudwal had been there then too.

She and Eogan and Aedan had returned from one of their much-loved jaunts through the gentle glens to the north of Alt Clut, she in nearly a state of bliss for, under Aedan's tutelage, she was finally mastering the riding of horses. Full of good cheer, they had drawn up to the stables, down below them, there on the plain at the foot of the Rock, had dismounted, and had led their ponies inside.

She remembered it all so vividly. Late-afternoon sunlight shafted through cracks in the stable's planked walls. Dust and bits of golden hay floated in the air, the cozy scent of which she loved; it made her want to lay down and daydream for a while, especially when the sun was shining, as it had been then. Usually, all was quiet when they returned to the stables; quiet, that is, save for the snort and snuffle of horses welcoming home their stable-mates. But that afternoon there had been an intense, strange sound that in her innocence she could not identify.

But Aedan knew. His face blanched and he made to draw his dagger even though he wasn't wearing one. His fist came up empty as he located the source of the sound: his own pony's stall at the far end of the stable. With a roar he threw himself towards it. After a moment of shock, she and Eogan raced after him. They were just in time to see Tudwal, their cousin, the son of the lord of Strat Clut, who had just returned home to Alt Clut at the end of his own fosterage, with his breeches down around his ankles, heaving himself in and out of a female form underneath. There were squelching noises and quite a lot grunting, but whether from pleasure or pain it was, frankly, impossible to tell.

She did not know quite what to make of it, but Aedan did. A strangled sound emerged from him. His face contorted; his eyes narrowed; and he hissed—he actually hissed—before he launched himself upon his cousin. She had never seen anything like it. Aedan was twelve years old. Admittedly, he was strong and fit for his age, but he set upon his seventeen-year-old cousin with such a frenzy it was as if he had the strength of five boys.

He threw Tudwal to the side and they all got a good look at the girl underneath. Ama did not know her. She had fuzzy brown hair and enormous, fleshy breasts that spilled out over the bodice of her tunic. Their tips were peaked and slick with spit where, Ama supposed, Tudwal's mouth must have been. This was a revelation to Ama and, in addition to the frightening transformation of Aedan into such a pitiless force of vengeance, was one of the reasons she remembered the event so clearly: she had had no idea that boys would want to do such things to girls and that girls would welcome them.

For, even though she had had no experience with these matters, it was clear to Ama that there was no way that the girl was not enjoying whatever it was that was being done to her. She was just as lusty as Tudwal. Eogan saw this too, but Aedan did not. He began to pummel Tudwal who was crying out "What's this? Stop it!" But Aedan ignored Tudwal, and Eogan's own command to let go his cousin, and then her own pleas. It was quickly evident, in fact, that Aedan was so lost in his fury that he could not hear a single word that was being said to him.

To Tudwal's credit, he held himself back: for all Aedan's unnatural strength, Ama was certain the older boy could have beaten Aedan senseless with very little effort if he had so desired. But there was something extremely odd about Aedan's reaction, and Tudwal sensed it too. Grasping the opportunity that Tudwal was giving him, Eogan jumped right in to haul Aedan off Tudwal. But Aedan would not be budged. So she, too, threw herself onto the mass of writhing boys. Together, she and Eogan managed to pry Aedan off his cousin.

Aedan easily shook them off. He looked around wildly. Then he turned to flee. But he had backed himself into the corner of the stall. Eogan was yelling, "Aedan! Aedan! Stop! It's me!" but Aedan's black eyes were wide-open and unfocussed as if he were no longer in the stable with them, but somewhere else, some other very unfriendly place in his mind. He was muttering under his breath. He sounded afraid.

That frightened her more than anything else. Aedan, afraid? Before she knew what she was about, she sprang at him and slapped him across the face as hard as she could. The sound rang out in the stable and his head snapped to the side. Horrified at herself, her hand flew to cover her mouth.

But her unexpected assault did the trick: Aedan's pupils focused and he saw them, saw Tudwal, the outraged, half-naked, gaping girl. He crumpled to the ground. There, with the dust and the sweet hay floating in the sunshafts about him, he cradled his head in his hands and sobbed like a little boy. Wanting to comfort him but unsure what to do, she and Eogan had simply sat next to him in the hay, not looking at him, not touching him or talking to him, until his crying stopped. Later, they had pressed him for an explanation, but he would not divulge what it was about Tudwal and the girl that had so unhinged him. He never did.

Looking at Aedan now, at his broad back to them and his hound, unloved, at his feet, Ama wondered wildly if she had the courage to slap him again. But then Aedan's elbow lifted and over his shoulder he sheathed his broad-sword in its back-slung leather scabbard. And his hand came down to ruffle his hound's ears. And she knew that everything was going to be alright.

Aedan turned. "Brother, forgive me," he said. His hands were braced tensely on his hips, and with his generous mouth he mouthed the words—he was a magnificent creature, even in his most awkward moments—but it was clear from the rebellion on his face that he felt no remorse at all for having drawn his sword on his foster-brother Morcant. On the contrary, he looked as if his only regret was having been thwarted from completing the deed.

Eogan took in Aedan warily, then dipped his head, his black hair swinging down, obscuring the fine lines of his face. He kneaded the tension at the bridge of his nose, a gesture he was making too often these days, then pushed his hair back over his brow. Expelling a deep breath, he nodded.

"Eogan, I won't treat with that man," Aedan said, again with not an ounce of remorse that Ama could discern. "I know you brought me here to do it. But I won't."

"Why not?" Eogan demanded, his anger returned. "We can't afford to antagonize him. Not him."

Aedan ignored his brother; took her by the arm, his face hard. "Under no circumstances are you to leave Artur alone with that man. Do you hear me? Swear it!"

She nodded. He was bruising her.

"And keep well clear of him yourself."

· 8 ·
THE CRAG OF THE KINGS

Aedan was not surprised that it did not go well. In a richly-appointed tent, larger than any other on the summit, they found the Coeling, the men of the house of Rheged, with their king, Kynfarch the Old. Bronze flagon in hand, the aged king was deep in conversation with the eager young men who jostled for his ear. Aedan studied them, found the ones worth noting, the ones who held their own counsel and did not pester the old man, anxious for an approving glance, for advancement. There were two. The young warrior at Kynfarch's side, with striking blond hair and a height and a look equal to the king's: Urien, Ama's step-brother, who was young enough to be Kynfarch's grandson rather than his son. And another lord of more advanced age, older than Aedan, but younger than Kynfarch. He, that new lord, was tall, with a barrel-chest; he looked strong, pugnacious. I bet his sword can make men listen, Aedan thought. He was accompanied by a young woman and a boy, his children. The maid was a small thing, with round eyes, dun-colored hair braided long down her back, and neat features; not more than seventeen. She had her father's nondescript hair and hazel eyes. The boy was about seven. Though unknown to Aedan, there was no doubt that these three were noble: a lordly retinue with an unknown emblem—a rampant red dragon—held guard outside the tent. Britons, of a tribe unknown to him, but powerful enough to stand in the company of the king of Rheged without any discernable need to curry his favor.

At sight of Ama, Kynfarch and Urien ceased their talk. There were tears in Ama's eyes as she went to them and was embraced. In a way, she had been as much an exile in Dal Riata as Aedan had been in Caledonia, seeing none of her family since her marriage to his brother, enduring all changes in her fortune, welcome and unwelcome, alone. His inclination to approve of her family vanished, however, or at least of Kynfarch, when Ama brought forth Artur who had been holding back, in awe of the strange company. Without comment, Kynfarch looked him over, Artur squirming under his grandfather's cold, unrelenting gaze. "*Hmmm*," Kynfarch finally said, snapping his fingers for more wine.

"Conall leads our people to war ... " Eogan began.

"So?"

"Civil war," Eogan clarified.

"Is there a distinction?"

"It is a war we wish to avoid. It would end in a stalemate between our two houses; the Cenel Oengussa, the third house, being unlikely to survive."

"The Cenel who?"

"Oengussa. They inhabit one of our islands. They are the weakest of our peoples." Not the highest praise, but Aedan had to concur: that was about all that could be said of them at the moment.

"If they are weak, they do not deserve to survive," Kynfarch shrugged. "You should ally with Conall. Turn on this other *cenel*. Split the spoils. Thus was Rheged made mighty and strong." He included his son Urien in his assessment of their success.

"Father," Ama tried, "we should like Tudwal to take us on as his direct client. Will you speak with him?"

Kynfarch was astonished; Urien frowned. Then, realizing that Ama was sincere, Kynfarch snorted bluntly. "Tudwal? Why? He already gets tribute from your cousin—why else are you here but to render it for him?" Another cutting snort. "It is your cousin Conall who is *ruiri* of Dal Riata, not you. You may not like him, you may wish to supplant him, but he is an overking. You? You are—". Kynfarch's hands flung out, holding between them nothing but air. Lower lip jutting, old eyes squinting, he searched for the just right word to describe the totality of his son-in-law's insignificance, finally settling upon, "What? You are what, precisely?"

Ama's face twisted with shock. Aedan, his heart roaring with indignation, was about to intervene—no one spoke to his brother this way, not even the king of Rheged—when Eogan, eyes flashing but his expression tightly controlled, thrust up a hand to warn his companions that he desired no defense. And Aedan realized he was right: to defend himself in any way, to respond to the old king with anything but cold reason, would be to undermine their purpose. Because then the discussion would become one about Eogan's merits, or lack thereof (when looked at from a Rhegedian perspective), rather than the matter at hand.

"Besides," Kynfarch added, unchallenged, "what have you done to encourage Tudwal to consider you as anything but Conall's underling? What can you give him? How have you distinguished yourself? The most notable thing you've ever done is to take my daughter to wife." A fond look at Ama. "And that only because I permitted it."

He's right, there, Aedan gave the old king, unwillingly. *About all of it.*

There was heated silence, heavy glances back and forth. Suddenly, a new voice: "*He* has befriended the Picts".

It was the tall, barrel-chested lord. He was appraising Aedan. Tucked in behind him, his children's faces were alive with awe, especially the maid's. As Urien gave belated introductions, Aedan caught her eye; she blushed, dipped her head. "This is Beli ap Rhun ap Maelgwyn, son of the overlord of Guined, and two of his children, Afrella and Iago."

Aedan suppressed a whistle of surprise—a prince of Guined! Why would a lord from such a distant, powerful, British kingdom bother to attend this Oenach festival at Strat Clut? And why bring up the Picts? Which led swiftly to a rather surprising, even troubling, answer: this lord was the nephew of King Bridei whose father, Aedan had discovered from the source himself, had been Maelgwyn of Guined; or Maelchon, in the Pictish tongue. In a strange, convoluted way, this lord Beli and his children were Aedan's relations. Not directly, but enough to be noteworthy, when introduced in this context.

Everybody had swiveled to take Aedan in. Aedan ignored them, looking pointedly at his brother and Ama, directing the conversation back to where it rightly belonged. "Father," Ama implored. "If you could just speak with Tudwal on our behalf ... "

Kynfarch's expression softened with affection; his decision did not. "And say what, daughter? No words of mine, however winning, can long hide the fact that your husband has nothing to offer him. Speaking does nothing for men like Tudwal. I cannot help you."

There was a shout from behind. It was young, blond-headed Urien, waving for them to wait. "Sister! Please! You know Father. It is just his way."

Ama was near to crying. She had set this in motion, had failed. Aedan hated her crestfallen look. He waited for Eogan to respond, to soothe her, but Eogan was lost in his own thoughts; so Aedan did it, in his way: "It's not the first time your father has disregarded your wishes, Ama," he said to her gently. She shot him a startled look rich with private meaning.

"He knows only worldly power," Columba, who had been trailing silently, added. "He will not see Eogan's worth: Eogan's worth is incalculable by the measure a man like your stepfather applies to it. Your husband is a rare man: a man who values peace, concord; who sacrifices his own pride to foster it in others. That is a kind of value your stepfather cannot see."

Aedan felt ever more respect for the abbot. They agreed on the matter: the worth of his brother.

"But we have come here to seek allies. And there are none higher here than Father."

Urien was springing eagerly from foot to foot. "Sister: you must show your worth, to the entire company. That is why we are all here, at this Oenach, is it not? To prove ourselves? To distinguish ourselves? To make them see." There was a mischievous gleam in his eye. "Do you by any chance play *baire?*" he asked Eogan and Aedan.

Aedan shared a knowing look with his brother, saw some of the anger and hurt pride draining from his face. They did. They most certainly did.

Everywhere on the Beak, Britons were making merry: propped up sloppily between fellow inebriates, bellowing hearty, half-forgotten songs; staggering home to their tents, unhappily alone; losing consciousness wherever they happened to be sitting, half-full-flagons still in hand. The mass of bodies around the huge bonfire in the Beak's clearing was so entwined that it was difficult to tell where the limbs of one ended and the other began. Others had paired off to couple in the shadows. In the sound of flesh mating and their cries, Aedan heard their heartfelt ardor.

This was the Oenach and all this was excused, even encouraged in its way. The Britons celebrated the start of the harvest, a good one, this year in Strat Clut. The coming winter, though long and dark as always, would lose some of its terror; most here would survive it. This particular festival was for drinking and eating, a lot; for finding mates; and for proving one's worth in the contests of strength and skill which would begin on the morrow.

Normally, Aedan would hardly have noticed; would, in fact, have joined in. Tonight, however, the enthusiastic revelry, the liberality of emotion, embarrassed him. He felt off, unsure of himself; an interloper in his family's accustomed affairs. His odd mood he understood: he had been away from them for so long. His physical discomfort he subscribed to Ama's nearness, and we wouldn't let himself look at her for too long, because it hurt.

Their tent was at the summit's far side, facing southwards towards the wide-open prospect of the firth. Aedan accompanied them as far as the tent's flap, tied open to capture the breeze and the last of the sunlight, but halted at its aperture. Inside, a brazier blazed, lighting its simple furnishings with a golden glow. Sleeping pallets had been laid out, there was food on low tables. It beckoned to him, soft and warm and inviting.

Eogan's invitation: Brother. Please come in. Would he? Yes, but only on the pretext of delivering the gifts he had brought them, pulling them from his pack. For his brother, an armlet of pure silver, a beautifully wrought piece, heavy and smooth. Fit for a king. Aedan told him that amongst the Picts such ornaments are an emblem of high office, but Eogan only smiled dubiously. For Artur, a round Pictish shield, sized for a small boy. Artur took it straight away to test it out, the beginning of affection for his uncle on his sweet little face. For their mothers, later, at home, exuberantly embellished bone combs and brightly polished mirrors, and didn't they all marvel at the artifice. For Ama, not the fine silver figurine of the Pictish goddess who ruled over home and hearth, as he had initially planned, but a deadly little iron dagger, which he himself had sharpened to lethality. He wanted it right in her belt, as near to her hand as it could be.

And saved for last, their father's sword. When he put it back into his brother's hands, his own trembled. "Oh. Oh," Eogan said, his tears streaming.

"Will you stay with us tonight?" Ama asked nervously at the end, not quite meeting his gaze.

"No!"

She recoiled. He felt badly, but he would not stay in the tent with them that night were the hounds of dark Arawn himself on his heels. It was proving hard enough to be near her again. To see her sleeping by Eogan's side was more than he cared to endure.

Still, she had been ill-used by her family this evening. He did not wish to add to her sorrow. "I am used to sleeping outside now," he said awkwardly, to lessen the sting.

She nodded miserably.

He went in search of a flagon.

"My lord!" It was the young maid of Guined, Afrella, the daughter of Beli, running quickly to catch up to Columba. "My lord! I feel I must inform. Your distress! It is so evident to me. But relief is available to you!"

"Relief?" Columba asked her, surprised that it should be he that she would seek out, and not any of the others.

"The company of your kind. A fellow Christian."

"Do you mean yourself?"

"Well, yes. My father and brother, too. In Guined, we keep the faith. Though few at first, we are increasing, thanks to our great-grandfather, Maelgwyn. He endowed many holy men with little places for their worship." This was said very proudly. "But what I meant is the other holy man, here, on Alt Clut." She spoke with true enthusiasm, her hazel eyes shining. "A very devout young man, highly ascetic. They say he sleeps on a stone shaped like a sarcophagus with no pillow for his head; that he fasts and prays standing naked in the freezing rivers—the *burns*, I think they are called here. Such devotion as I myself would aspire to! Were I not a maid and meant to be married, for the sake of Guined. His name is Mungo."

"Mungo. *Hound?*"

"Yes. *Little-Hound*. It is an endearment given to him by the people here, who love him exceedingly. It is not his given name. His given one is something grander, but I can't recall what: *Hound-something*. He is usually to be found in the chapel down below, in the courtyard at the Rock's foot." Her words tumbling out, she turned herself around, orienting herself. "It is dedicated to Patrick. Patrick! Surely that impresses you! But not tonight. Tonight Mungo will be in his cell." She spun about until she faced the Rock's western peak. "There," she pointed. "His cell is carved into the sea-side of the crag, below the Windy Hall, because it is said he likes to look out over the water, it being purifying." Her little nose scrunched as she breathed in deeply of the evening's air. "In fact, he is assured to be there. Rain is on the way. Can't you smell it?"

He could: a salty freshening, banishing smoke.

She smiled at Columba, almost too brightly. "It will be a soggy night, altogether miserable. Yes, that is where he will be. You will thank me, I am sure. I don't know how you have managed it this long—to be amongst the unbelieving without the benefit of the company of our kind."

The unbelieving. The company of his kind. Funny: but he never thought of the Scots this way, or the Picts; never thought to separate them into this kind of person, and that; to make such exacting, damning distinction. They were all the same to him: his people, whom he now loved. Some of them knew his God, most did not. He didn't see that it mattered much. His God loved them all. And his job was only to show the way. To be the way.

Taking his leave of her, Columba edged over the rope-bridge, careful of his footing in the dim light, then followed the narrow path which wound around the shoulder of the summit. The celebration was raucous behind him but as he moved out upon the path he could also now hear the river below sloshing against the base of the Rock rhythmically. Gradually, the sound of rioting dimmed. The wind felt wonderfully cleansing on his face; it stirred his cloak, his hair. The moon was high. It was all purifying, just as the maid had said.

Ahead of him in the gloom, there was a noise. There, a little below the path, a faint glow emanated from the nearly pitch-black rock-face. It was a cave, its entrance obscured by a thick fur, so mangy that it was no longer possible to identify what kind of animal had sacrificed it. Calling out to make his presence known, he pushed aside the door-covering and squinted into the cave's confines.

Peering back at him was a young man, the hollows of his face thrown into deep shadow by the candle in his hands. In the light of the flame, whipped up by the wind coming off the sea behind Columba, Mungo was an otherworldly vision: slender as a reed, with sunken, bony features and bulbous blue eyes. Columba knew the signs: the results of a too rigorously ascetic lifestyle, an almost non-existent diet. A spirit bordering on, perhaps already taken over by, zealotry? Mungo's sandy-colored, curly hair had not been tonsured, though, so he had not entered the Life. Rather, the young man wore floor-length priest's robes, the natural color of the wool, which he clutched reflexively about his throat with stick-like fingers. With very little meat on his bones, Mungo was feeling the chill. Columba guessed that he was about eighteen years of age, exceptionally young to have been ordained a priest. This, however, was not surprising. Christians were so rare on the ground here that eligible candidates for the priesthood must be few in number.

"Christ's blessing on you, my brother," Columba said to reassure him. "You must be Mungo."

"I am."

"I am Columba—Colum Cille of Hibernia; lately of Iona."

"Columba! Of Hibernia! Now Iona! Yes! Yes! Of course! Do come in! Come in!" Mungo slapped his free hand joyfully against a stringy thigh. Letting the fur-drape fall behind him, Columba eased his way into the cave.

Mungo studied him, his welcoming smile broad at first, but then rapidly chased away by a look Columba could only interpret as disappointment. "Oh, that's too bad," Mungo said.

"Too bad?" Columba asked.

The young man nodded. "Yes. You are too young."

"For what?"

"To have known Patrick."

To have known Patrick? *Patrick?* It took all Columba's effort to mask his astonishment: he did not wish to rush to judgment, having only just met the man, but was Mungo a simpleton? "Yes," Columba finally replied. "But Patrick taught my first teachers, the ones I had when I was a novice."

Mungo looked at him blankly. "Patrick died a long time ago," Columba explained carefully. "There are none now left who knew him. I certainly did not. But I am his heir, as are those brothers who studied with me."

Mungo was struggling with the chronology of it. Finally, he seemed to have it. "Oh!" he said. "Yes, of course! How foolish of me."

The conversation skidded to an awkward halt. The fur door-flap ruffled in the wind.

"And who, pray tell, is your companion?" Columba asked Mungo.

If they thought to trick him, they were mistaken, for Columba's quick senses had known, almost immediately upon entering the cave, that he and the young man were not its only inhabitants. Someone hid in the dark recesses at the back of the cave.

At his question, an old man in thread-bare monk's clothes scuttled from the shadows, eyeing Columba suspiciously. Unkempt hair of a brilliant white floated airily about his face. A stringy white beard, equally airborne, sickly-looking skin, wild, light-blue eyes and thin lips added to the sourness of his face.

Columba's breath caught. He took a wild guess, asking with rising excitement, "Gildas? Gildas of the Britons?"

The reply was surprise, a gruff nod, and a squint of watery eyes.

Columba grinned his joy. Gildas! What a blessing! Gildas of the Britons! This monk before him was the celebrated author of some of the most influential Christian texts of their time: *De excidio Britonum! De Poenitentia!* Columba had long studied them. They had all studied them; by their precepts many of his brethren aspired to live. Not for nothing was Gildas of the Britons famous.

Gildas started forward, his thick white eyebrows beetling. "Is it true?" he demanded, his voice a scratch.

Columba hesitated. Had word of his excommunication and exile to Dal Riata preceded him here to Alt Clut, he wondered? Did they know of the battle? That he had killed a man?

"That you commune with *the Picts?*"

Ah. The Picts.

Gildas hissed, drawing back into the shadows. "A savage nation of naked plunderers! Dirty heathens! Idolators!"

Such damning words. Images flew through Columba's mind, memories. First and foremost, the mage Broichan, the triple-sacrifice of the royal hostage in the Fortress of the Bulls. Columba's own entombment. Other atrocities, from before. But Gildas's vehement attack had encouraged Columba's own temper, and he was in no mood to pander to the old man, or even to explain. Instead, he felt quite contrary. He said, blandly, "I suppose some are, much as any nation. But many lead lives of natural goodness". Because he was also thinking of Emchath, the Keeper of the Loch at Airtchartdan who had converted to the Faith just before he died and now waited for his resurrection in a grave surmounted by a standing stone engraved with both his people's symbols and a cross of the Christ. And of Uirolec, that good man's good son. And of fierce Drust, brought to his knees by his love for his nephew.

"But the sin! The sin! It is foul! Dirty! They sin with anything that moves! Sisters! Slaves! Animals! I can hear them sinning!"

"Your hearing is remarkable."

"He means the Britons, my lord," Mungo whispered, with an affectionate glance at the old monk. "He is old now, easily confused. He means the Britons making ... *merry* tonight, here on the Rock. To him, they are one and the same."

"They are readier to cover their villainous faces with hair than their private parts and neighboring regions with clothes!" Gildas grumbled.

"Indeed, yes," Mungo said. "Yes, my friend. But please! Don't excite yourself. You see, Gildas and I are resolved to avoid the lure of the ... *festivities*, to remain apart. Pure. You can see how they upset him."

Gildas grumbled some more, saying something about copulation, another thing about animals. Mungo's sunken cheeks flushed delicately.

I can see how they upset you.

"Will you stay long with us?" Mungo asked.

"That depends upon the will of my hosts."

"You have hosts?" Mungo was wide-eyed. "I should like for hosts! Mighty hosts! Tudwal suffers me to live here—his Christians, not many! Not many! Clamored for a priest again—"

Suddenly the young priest's voice dropped to a whisper. He looked around worriedly, as if someone might overhear. "You know that he threw out Ninian? Ninian!"

"Riches, power and honour excite him to pride!" Gildas was shivering with indignation, his hair fluttering.

"Surely not Ninian," Columba said. The British bishop and scholar with whom many of his teachers had studied here in Britain was a learned, kind man, they had said; not a man of overweening conceit.

"No. Tudwal, the king," Mungo corrected.

"Tudwal! Yes, Tudwal!" Gildas cried. "Lust of the flesh and lust of the eye and the wealth of the world so ministers to his haughtiness that he presumes himself to be able to do as much as anyone, and that what anyone can do is both possible and lawful for him also!"

"Yes. Yes. In any case, Tudwal hasn't had a priest here since he threw Ninian out," Mungo explained. "Not until me. I hope to impress him, but I think he has done it for show; taken on our faith, or at least the trappings of it, because his people want it so. Do you see my meaning?"

"I do," Columba said, thinking of Conall and his brand-new bishop Budic, installed even though he would minister to no one in Dal Riata, not a single Christian soul. But then of Eogan. For a heathen, he was a much more peaceable ruler, more Christian in temperament, than many who shouted about their conversion.

"Who hosts you?" Mungo asked eagerly.

"The Cenel Gabran."

Gildas shot forward, eyes beading. "Not the Cenel Loarn?"

Columba took new stock of the old monk: beneath that handy veneer of madness, he was remarkably sharp. "No," Columba replied, deliberately answering only the question at hand. "But the Cenel Loarn did give me my island." This wasn't exactly untrue.

"Foul savage pirates, all of them!"

"My hosts?"

"All of them! All the Scots! But especially that be-cursed brother, newly spat back from Caledonia! What is his name, that evil fornicator? That brother? Cohort of the Picts, amongst whom sin is rife, openly, grievously, and shamelessly!"

"You can't possibly compare ... "

"The Scots to the Picts? Oh, yes I can. I grant you that they are to some extent different in their customs, but they are in perfect accord in their greed for bloodshed! You cavort with either of them on penalty of your own soul, Columba! Your own soul! Beware! I tell you this for your own good! Ninian would have agreed! It is a monk's mortal obligation to remain chaste in body and in soul! Yet you—you ... *commune*! And, and, and ... *abide*! You cannot have read my *Penitential*! You cannot have read Ninian's! What do they teach you, there, in Hibernia? Do you impart this rubbish to your people on Iona, too?"

Columba's ire was fit to burst. "Both yours and his do say ... "

Mungo interjected. "You have read them! You have! What luck!" but was himself cut off by Gildas, who scathed, "Then why do you not heed? Why do you persist in your fraternization?"

"With whom? The Scots? Or the Picts?"

"Either. Both. As I have said, there is no difference."

"Answer me this: how can one care for them, Scot or Pict, how minister to them, save to be amongst them, to *abide*? Shall I send missives by pigeon? Shout at them over my wall? Commit injunctures to a skin-bag and float it on the tide? All these might, in time, work to get my meaning across to them, but how should they facilitate my reception of their message, to me?"

Gildas hurumphed. "Their message to you? Whatever can you mean? Heathens have no message to be imparted; none, in any case, that a God-fearing monk should care to hear."

"*A wise man recognizes the gleam of truth whoever utters it*," Columba shot back. "Or so a man I had deemed wise once said. And, as others have taken pains to point out: *we are obliged to serve; to have pity on all who are in need. To receive pilgrims into our houses, as the Lord has commanded; to visit the infirm; to minister to those in chains. From the least unto the greatest.*"

Gildas's expression immediately soured. Mungo's brightened with astonishment. "Now, that is true learning!" the young priest exclaimed. "To be able to quote so without the books themselves before you! And to quote from both, quoting our Gildas here—to himself! To quote Gildas to himself!—and then to quote Ninian, and then back again! I am moved nearly to tears. Especially since I myself can make no sense of any of Gildas's works, or Ninian's little *Penitential*. I can make no sense of them, and Gildas here says that if I am so unlearned as to be unable to read them myself, he certainly will not deign to help me."

Mungo had said this with not a stitch of self-consciousness or embarrassment that Columba could discern. Looking at the young priest, his face pure and open, Columba could begin to see why Mungo was loved by his people: he had absolutely no pride whatsoever in admitting any of his difficulties, and even perceived them to be a result of his own shortcomings rather than his betters'; and Columba felt a growing measure of fondness for him.

Columba's feelings for Gildas, however, were decidedly more mixed. While it was true that Gildas's many learned writings were held in the highest regard by Columba's colleagues, Columba was disappointed to discover that in the flesh Gildas was as full of pomposities and obfuscations as any of his scholarly stylizations—all of which tended to obscure his meanings rather than to illuminate them. Columba did not like the man.

Gildas had drawn himself up to his full, admittedly still diminutive, height. He was spoiling for a fight. But Columba was suddenly in no mood to bring him one. He sighed. Maybe Mungo's goodness was rubbing off on him; a perfume in the air to be breathed in. Columba took another deep breath in case this was true. He had wanted a peaceful evening. In a way, the young maid of Guined had been correct: Columba had missed the simple ease of the company of his kind, where everyone spoke with a kind of shorthand, all having been brought up in the same language, the language of the Church.

Besides, why make an enemy of the old man? Columba had too few allies here as it was. It seemed they all did.

Columba turned to Mungo. "Indeed, your friends's works are ... complex," he said. "I would be happy to assist you with them. Gildas will correct me if I go astray, as indeed I might." He wouldn't, but the look he gave the old man was level. "Won't you?"

Gildas nodded stiffly, proudly. Mungo smiled, his face open and cheerful. "Thank you! It is my own fault, of course. I know that such great men as our Gildas here take pride in outdoing other men. And they should, for they have skills which far surpass others. But not you *Abba*, I think."

Columba chuckled. In the face of Mungo's abject lack of sophistication, his purity and naivety, he could not resist saying, "I have no skills?"

"No! No! No *pride*. I meant you have no *pride*."

Columba smiled ruefully. "Son," he said. "I am as proud as they come."

But Mungo was vigorously shaking his head. "No. I cannot believe it! Not of you! You too are a great man. I cannot believe it of our Gildas, here, either; not really. Rather, you are both just learned and wise. And I am too unschooled to understand."

Deep into the night the three men conversed, finding their way with one another, testing the ground, thrown together as they were in a dank cave on a high rock at the edge of the world on account of the scarcity of their kind; until the sole candle sputtered and, with a puff, went out.

The sun was already high when, the next morning, Aedan and Eogan made their way down the Beak to the clearing between the crags, then all the way down the stone steps to the Rock's floor. *Baire*, the ball-game that was such a favorite of the tribes, British and Hibernian alike, was about to begin.

They assembled on the grassy plain, crowds already five-feet-deep rimming the field, the plain awash with their vibrant checkered clothing, their happy shouts ringing in the air. All around, vendors hawked food and goods from laden stalls. The wares on offer, representing the best of the trade then available in Britannia, had found their way to Alt Clut on that first day of August along innumerable trade-routes, from the smallest dirt tracks to the widest sea-lanes, all over the known world; much of it on the move for months, funneling inexorably to that bright plain. If he had had the time or the inclination for such things, Aedan could have sampled roast mutton on sticks, a delicacy from the fens of Cant; or cured herring from the Baltic lands, or even dried figs from Italia. He could have purchased little trinkets and other wares: bone combs; bronze and tin brooches; pottery from western Gaul, finer than the rough wooden vessels made locally; cloth from the looms of the Franks; Christian relics in bone, wood, or metal, as well as of materials more rare—the severed tip of St Odhran's steering finger, miraculously pliable and uncorrupt, guaranteed to keep its wearer safe from pestilence and disease; fragments of St Martin's cape (not of the lower half which he gave to the beggarman at the gates of Ambianum, but of the upper half which he continued to wear until his soul at last departed to his Christ); even wood splinters from the True Cross of the Christians.

There were four companies brought together to compete, in sleeveless short tunics: regal gold for Tudwal, king of Strat Clut; crimson for his son Rhydderch, a noble lad of sixteen, his nose and brow straight, lips and face long, brown hair falling in gentle curls to his shoulders, streaked with red and gold. Azure for the men of Galloway and Aeron. Mighty Rheged in deepest black, which company the brothers joined, Urien, his shock of blond hair held away from his face by a leather band, sprinting to them, panting, "Come! Help bring honor to Rheged!"

Eogan loped to the field, a fierce wild grin on his face, taking the center of the line of men there, Aedan and Urien to either side. Rheged's opponent was King Tudwal's company: great glory would be had with a win. The leather ball was tossed high into the air, Rheged's mighty swing, a resounding *crack*!, and the ball batted forward to Eogan who deflected it to the ground with his stick and scooped it up again, taking off at a run. The crowd erupted with a roar. Aedan, keeping pace with Eogan, admired his brother's skill as he sprinted, the ball balanced on the flat-end of his stick—no easy feat at a dead run. Nimbly, Eogan dodged the first man who came at him and, at the last minute, ducked below the swinging stick of the second. When he came to three men at once he tossed the ball, seemingly without looking, laterally to his right where Aedan caught it.

Now was the time to set the play, to find their weakness. Slowing his pace to allow his companions to regain their positions, Aedan balanced the ball on his stick, dodging the men of Strat Clut who sought to steal it from him. At last, spying an opening through the crush of bodies, he tossed the ball up into the air, swung fully at it on its way down, and sent it flying sweetly over everyone's heads. Urien, deep within Strat Clut's territory, caught it, pivoted, and batted it to Eogan who, with a swiftness which no man on that field could match, had taken up position directly before Strat Clut's goal. There, he came face to face with the man who guarded it: Tudwal, their cousin, the king.

Tudwal glared, expanding his body; he would not let the ball pass. Eogan swung at the descending ball and in mid-fall redirected it squarely at the king's head.

It was duck or die, so duck Tudwal did.

The ball sailed into the goal; Rheged had earned a point, rather quickly and with an undeniable grace, and the crowd roared its approval and delight.

The rest of the match was much the same. While each man played his part, the contest was Eogan's to win, with Aedan crafting the plays and Eogan the beneficiary of his cunning. And win it they did as Rheged soundly routed the king's side. "By game's end our cousin was ducking even when I wasn't aiming at him," Eogan said, a wicked grin splitting his face.

"Excellent! Can't fail to see our worth when it's coming straight at his head."

They watched as Rhydderch's company overcame the men of Galloway and Aeron, an impatient swirl of azure tunics. As he had been the night before, Aedan was excruciatingly aware of Ama's presence; without having to look, he knew when she left them to visit one of the vendor's stalls and when she returned. When she stood beside him it was as if that half of his body was somehow more awake than the other; when she offered them mutton on a stick he read deep meaning into the gesture. After an hour in her company he felt replete with a sad joy, loving and hating it at the same time. Unable to express it, he redirected that thwarted energy into the game.

And indeed, when Rheged met Rhydderch's company on the field in the deciding match of the contest, Aedan was certain that he had miraculously absorbed some of his brother's fleetness. He seemed to run more swiftly than before. No opponent could reach him. Most wonderfully, as the ball weaved between the men and the men flowed around each other, he saw it all with great clarity as if he were viewing it from some impossibly high vantage point, the field spread flat beneath his adjudicating eye. He knew precisely where to hurl the ball so that it would meet the stick just ahead of his companion who, legs pumping furiously, had pounded into a free space. He knew how to direct his companions to their best defense and, calling out clipped commands, he did so with greater and greater authority even as his lungs were on fire and his muscles screamed in pain and he willingly pushed his body to the limits of its abilities.

But the companies were well-matched. Half-way through play the score was even until, with a sickening crunch, one of Rheged's men blocked an enthusiastic swing with his stick-arm. Lurching, he fell to his knees, his forearm broken, grimacing in pain.

"That's it, then," Urien said bitterly. "We're short a man."

"I am the best in Gododdin," a voice cut in. Aedan recognized it without having to turn—it was high and light and disgusting to him—and he was elbowed roughly aside by the one person sure to leech any joy which might be had from this contest: his foster-brother, Morcant, Lord of the Gododdin.

"Ah, Morcant!" Urien said. "What luck! Can you can take his place: middle line, right-hand side—there? Good! Good! Let us be swift: victory is near!"

The ball was passed up the field from man to man until Aedan, a suspicious eye ever on Morcant, had it. He delayed; looked for the opening; saw Urien hovering before the goal. Aedan swung, the ball lofted high, and was batted down—by Morcant who, racing from behind, had interfered with the pass. The ball skittered to the ground; sticks cracked; there was a tussle of bodies; and when the ball reappeared it was in the hands of Strat Clut. Channeling it rapidly down the field, they scored.

The crowd roared. Urien and Eogan looked to Aedan for explanation, incredulity etched plainly on their faces. Aedan could only shrug in apology, though what he felt for Morcant was pure venom.

Slowly, carefully, Aedan's companions passed the ball back up the field. Again, Aedan had it. Again, Urien and Eogan flew back and forth before the goal, waiting for the ball. Suddenly, Morcant sprinted through an opening and joined them. Aedan weaved and ducked, he spun and pivoted, he kept the Strat Clut men at bay while Urien, Eogan and Morcant wove their own dance before the goal, Morcant being the first free.

There was nothing for it: with a curse, Aedan lofted the ball at him. Morcant caught it; spun; hurled the ball towards the goal. And missed.

Cheated, the crowd groaned. Somehow Urien got hold of the ball and batted it back to Aedan. Again the men sprinted, dodging opponents, looking for that unobstructed shot. Then the blare of horns, once, twice; the contest soon to end. The crowd began to chant rhythmically. The sound was enormous, energizing. Strat Clut brought all its men back, to thwart Rheged. Madly, Aedan's companions sprinted back and forth but none of them could shake this new increase in bodies.

The horns blared again, once, the crowd screaming feverishly. The blood in Aedan's head pounded in time with their chanting, his heaving breath deafening his ears. He stalled for time, balancing the ball on the end of his stick while he waited for his companions to somehow find the way to score.

Suddenly, Eogan was alone before the goal. Aedan saw him spin wildly, a black blur, looking for the ball. Their eyes met. With seconds remaining, Aedan hurled the ball to his brother with all his might. Leaping high, arm outstretched, stick raised, Eogan nabbed the ball as it sailed overhead. In mid-air his body pivoted—how he accomplished it Aedan had no idea, he would not have thought it physically possible, but it was breathtaking to see—and Eogan was redirecting the ball towards the goal. The man there was rushing at him in a desperate attempt to knock it away, but Aedan could see that the angle was wrong: the ball would sail over the man's shoulder. When out of nowhere a stick swiped at Eogan's legs, tangling him up and, just as the horns trumpeted the contest's end, Eogan's shot went wide, missing its goal by inches.

Eogan, entangled with the other man and unable to break his own fall, thudded heavily to the ground. With a resounding *crack!*, his face crunched into the blunt end of the interfering stick. He grunted loudly in pain. Aedan could hear the heartfelt surprise of it from where he stood aghast. Then, limbs lifeless like a discarded doll, Eogan did not move again.

Aedan rushed to his brother. Others were there first. He could not see Eogan. He tore through them in time to hear a high-pitched voice say flatly, "He was in the way. The ball was mine". And then the crush of men opened and Aedan saw Urien bent over Eogan's form, unnaturally still where it lay sprawled on the grass, limbs bent at grotesque angles, his face grey. Morcant stood by, hands on hips. The grin on his foster-brother's face was almost nonexistent, just the barest twitch of lips, but Aedan knew: this had been no accident, no exuberant play gone awry. Morcant had intentionally injured his brother—by the looks of it, mortally.

Aedan's flash of rage was so intense that he simply went with it. He charged Morcant and slammed him to the ground, pinning him beneath him, his foster-brother's pale-blue eyes wide-open in alarm, his mouth gaping, the breath knocked from him by the sheer violence of the assault. Aedan was just drawing back his fist for the first blow—he aimed for the hated face; he could hardly wait to break it, the need to hurt Morcant was all-consuming—when a voice, weak but deadly calm, said, "Brother: don't. I live".

With monumental effort Aedan stilled his hand. He was pulled off Morcant, a thing for which he was profoundly grateful since he felt that he could not be in physical contact with the man for another moment without becoming ill. Eogan had managed to sit up. He cradled his cheek. Aedan pulled his hand away, gently probed for broken bones. Eogan yelped and the abused cheek was beginning to swell like an engorged sheep's bladder, yet as he hauled Eogan to his feet Aedan was relieved to be able to report, "It's not broken, I think".

Aedan looked for Morcant in the throng, but his foster-brother had spirited himself away.

That's alright, Aedan thought: one day I will kill him. Today has just provided me one more reason.

"Did it do the trick?" Eogan said, for Aedan's and Ama's ears only. "Can you tell?"

"Maybe. Look." Eyes were watching them as they moved through the Windy Hall. The leading families of the Gwyr Y Gogledd, The Men of the North, crowded. Tudwal presided, swathed in silks and furs despite the heat and the press, his balding pate glistening in the dancing light of the lamps as he tucked into a food-laden trencher with relish. The Britons of Aeron and of Galloway drank heavily, still smarting from their loss at *baire*; the rival factions of Galloway bickering.

"There, certainly; though I question why." Aedan indicated Beli, the prince of Guined, who was greeting them amiably, inviting them to join him.

"But for the uncertain help you received from the Gododdin, you would have had Strat Clut today," Beli said.

His boy, young Iago, nodded. "My lords," the sister added shyly, wincing at sight of Eogan's heavily bruised face. "You were magnificent."

"Please, sit. Eat," Beli said. "You are just in time to help me with a puzzle my children and I have been turning over with varying degrees of success. Let me understand correctly. Tudwal is your cousin, is he not?"

This was directed squarely at Aedan. "Yes," Aedan allowed, even though he did not at all like the way the three were looking at him. Was he some exotic animal on view at a fair, a delicacy one might buy at one of the stalls, down below on the plain? He lobbed the conversation back to Eogan. "And *his* foster-brother."

"But *your* cousin. How so?"

Aedan waved for ale. Eogan broke in: "A puzzle indeed. Prepare yourself to be baffled by the complexity of it all".

He's not baffled, Brother, Aedan thought. *He already knows it.*

But Eogan was enjoying the stage given him. "The old queen, Iulita there, is my brother's aunt. The sister of his mother Luan." He pointed out the woman sharing the feast with Tudwal. At fifty years of age, the lines which had only begun to crease Aedan's mother's face had burrowed firmly in Iulita's brow. The sisters shared a coloring—reddish-brown hair, grey eyes—but Iulita was tall and regal in a way which Luan, with her mild and approachable manner, was not. "To be precise, Iulita is Aedan's half-aunt," Eogan clarified. "His grandfather, Brychan ... Sorry. Would you like some counters, to help you follow? Shall I draw it out for you here, on the table? It's all very twisted, bound up like a bunch of ivy 'round a tree."

"No. I follow. You mean Brychan of Berneich. The last true lord of Berneich, master of Lothian," Beli proved.

"Yes," Eogan confirmed. "Amazing. You've got it."

Don't be too impressed, brother. By the looks of it, Beli had his bards untangle our particular portion of the vine long before he ever got here. And I question why.

"Well, Brychan had three wives and, by them, one son, Outigern, and three daughters. Iulita, there. One called Nevyn, one of Kynfarch of Rheged's wives. And Luan, Aedan's mother. See? Convoluted."

"It is the same everywhere. Many wives yield many children— especially if the wives are young and the man puts any effort into it," Beli said with a heartfelt laugh. "My own, very pleasurable effort has yielded me seven sons and one daughter. More than enough to leave all the eldest at home to take care of affairs, and to bring the youngest two with me for company." He nodded affectionately at Afrella and Iago.

"Indeed. Well, Iulita, the eldest of Brychan's three daughters, was given to Clinoch, the old king of Strat Clut. Tudwal is their son and is, hence, Aedan's cousin. His *half*-cousin. Nevyn, the middle daughter, was given to Kynfarch of Rheged. Urien is her son."

"So Aedan's cousin too," Beli said. "That is—*half*-cousin."

This was all clearly of some importance to Beli, though Aedan could not credit why. It was not as if Aedan had had anything to do with it. Nor did his tenuous connection with Rheged benefit him now in any way. Hadn't Kynfarch just rebuffed Ama, their whole *cenel*? Kynfarch did not care to remember or to honor the relation. Why should Aedan? Why should Beli, who had stood there unprotesting while the old king made plain the extent of his disdain?

"*Hmmm*," Beli said, fingering the fine silver flagon on the table before him, filled to the brim with wine he had yet to touch. When he looked at Aedan again, his gaze was direct and piercing. "And you have since become the son-in-law of Bridei, king of the Caledonii."

Ah! He comes to it at last.

"You do realize that he is my uncle?" Beli asked. "My father's brother."

"If I didn't, I do now."

"How do you find him?"

"Much as any king."

"The Caledonii," Beli said. "What are their intentions towards us, do you think?"

"Who? Guined?"

Beli nodded curtly.

"Do you fear them?"

Beli shrugged, neither confirming nor denying.

"You should," Aedan said. "They would be happy to see all of us gone."

"Not you, surely."

Aedan laughed bitterly. "Yes: me. I am beloved by very, very few of them. Two. Possibly three."

Beli lifted his flagon and took his first swig of wine. It was a long one. Wiping his mouth on his rich sleeve, he fixed Aedan with another intense stare, his words clipped, pointed. "Strat Clut and Rheged through blood. The Gododdin, through fosterage. Even the Picts, through marriage. How fortunate you are in your relations. All this, in one man!"

Another sharp laugh; Aedan couldn't help it. It just burst out. Fortunate? Try difficult, frustrating; the way it complicated matters. Related to all of them, he was beholden to all of them, while the two things he wanted for himself were kept entirely out of his reach: one, Ama, a table's length away, sadness in her eyes; the other, leagues hence, in Caledonia.

Maybe it was the rush of wine, but Aedan suddenly felt a savage ill-humor. "Ties like mine, they do bind," he told the king and his children, all ears. They leaned in close, expecting to be entertained, misreading his mood. "But do they bind for good or for ill? Let us reason this through. Let us consider the case of my grandfather— Brychan, the esteemed Lord of Berneich. He had three daughters. Three fine daughters, whom he may also have cared for. Needing new relations, new *powerful* relations, he sold them. Did he care for their happiness? We do not know. Did they manage to make their own happiness? Our sources disagree. One did at least, thank the gods. This I can confirm. But: back to my grandfather. Did his daughters' new, powerful British husbands help him when he needed it? Did they help his one son, Outigern: his heir, his pride? When Ida, the Saxon wolf, came skulking around Berneich, sniffing, sniffing for spoils, did Clinoch of Strat Clut ride to their aid, as he had promised, the price he had agreed to for the first use of the flesh of Brychan's young daughter? Did Kynfarch of Rheged? Did they break the siege that strangled Din Guoaroy?"

"Aedan ... " Eogan cautioned with a worried glance around the table.

An angry glare at Eogan; an assessing one for Beli. This was *his* history, and Aedan would be damned if he would keep quiet simply to spare the prince of Guined and his fine offspring digestive distress, a meal ruined. They had asked: he would tell them. "Gabran did," he said. "Our father—the Scot who was so despised that he was sold the least important of Brychan's daughters: my mother. The least best flesh. He honored the contract. He kept his word and sent men. But as he was in the midst of the round of fighting that was to take his own life, they were not many. They were not nearly enough."

"They fought nobly though," the young maid Afrella piped in, her face flushed. "The bards sing that your grandfather and your uncle fought bravely! How they sing of them in Guined! Their deeds are remembered, those noble warriors! They have earned their place in song!" Her eyes shone with fervor.

Her unjaded admiration, Beli's continued careful scrutiny, Eogan's disgust at his uncivil behavior, all conspired to silence his next remarks. Aedan opted instead for a long, pensive mouthful of wine. Beli's motives were becoming clear. The maid's? The maid was such a naïve little thing to think that the securing of one's lasting fame was worth the sacrifice of one's life. What did she know of any of it?

"Oh, aye!" Aedan finally said. He was rewarded with Afrella's bright smile. "They did fight bravely. Alas, it was also futilely. They are gone, all of them. The kingdom of Berneich is no more."

· 9 ·
CERNUNNOS

Bent low over the straining necks of their mounts, reins in hand, cloaks snapping in the wind, spirits high, the riders raced the incoming tide. It had been timed this way, for as long as anyone could remember, Lughnasadh after Lughnasadh, harvest after harvest, year after year: they raced to beat the tide before it swallowed the tongue of land that tied this mighty Rock, Alt Clut, to the shore.

Like the ball game *baire*, this race too had its origins in war. The Britons of Strat Clut were secure on their Rock; no enemy could reach them. On the Rock was safety. They would taunt them from the heights. But booty and wealth and glory lay off the Rock, with those enemies, and neighbors, who lived in the hills and glens and moors of the mainland. So off the Rock the Britons would go, in raiding parties on ponies or on foot, to reive and to have fun and to plunder. But they had to make it back to the Rock before the advancing tide swallowed the isthmus. Those who missed it had either to swim or to stand and face the foes chasing furiously behind, swords in hand. Amongst the Britons it had become a game of sorts—the rashest warriors on the best-trained mounts chest-deep in surge, fearless, laughing—until at some point in the distant past they had made a game of it in fact.

The course of the race followed that fraught path home, a path that wove through difficult terrain as it wound alongside the twisting river Lemn. At the outflow of the river from its source, the great loch Lemn, lay a secondary stronghold of Strat Clut, a palisaded fort. Within its walls, the thirty-or-so riders readied themselves, their horses rearing, hating the commotion and the fort's narrow confines until, at horn-blast, the gates of the fort crashed open and out the mounted riders bounded.

It was just the sort of thing Ama loved. The speed, the movement, the freedom of it, this path in paticular; how chaotic, how liberating; especially with Aedan and Eogan alongside, bent low over the necks of their mounts, their black hair flying. But not today. Today the race had high stakes and her customary joy was overshadowed by the need for the Cenel Gabran to acquit themselves nobly against each of the British factions who fought to succeed, to also distinguish themselves. So it was with a focused determination that they kept to the rough dirt track skirting the eastern bank of the river as it flowed southwards to the isthmus. And didn't they recognize it now? As children, she and Eogan and Aedan had followed this particular river-path many times; they knew its dips and bends, the secrets of its hidden glens, its challenges and dangers. Over that rocky path, through wooded glens, the horses pounded, clodded earth spraying from under hoof, at first in a tight bunch, then more dispersed as horses balked or stumbled and riders fell.

They soon found themselves at the front. One moment her step-brother Urien was with them; the next, in a jumbled heap but mercifully free of his downed horse, he was on the ground. She would have stopped to aid him but, with an impatient, imperious wave, he bade her continue: there was a race to be won, for her, for her husband. And in this way she found herself in the lead on her eager grey mare.

They were less than a league from the isthmus, not far, almost home, when she came around a sharp bend in the path to a turn she knew well, a place she had ridden a hundred times. Here the river bent sharply to the west, then made a wide loop before doubling back on itself eastward again. In the embrace of the river lay a cool forest dell; not large, but secretive and, since it lay off the path, little visited. Up ahead she could hear the river reappearing from its meander to right itself again on its southerly course.

The other riders were close behind, the men of Galloway and Aeron, a raucous pack vying to catch her; then Aedan, and Eogan, for the moment out of sight. The men of Galloway came abreast, its king shouting for her to give way. She kicked her mount and it surged forward. But then a flash of metal—a dagger in the hand of the lord they called Gwenddolau—and her horse reared suddenly, screaming in pain. Gwenddolau sped on ahead. Riders surged around her and she was nearly thrown. Using all of her hard-won skills, she kept her seat, but in the tussle her mount was forced down the ravine. Down it crashed through the thick-set trees and shrubs. She held on, shielding her face as it bolted through a small natural archway in the tree cover. Reining hard, she careened to the bottom of the hollow.

She caught her breath, quieting her disturbed mare. Thankfully, the wound Gwenddolau had given it was not deep. She looked around for a way out, adjusting to the change in the level of light. She was in a little grove of oak trees. She could hear the riders on the path yelling, the horses thundering, but then the sound seemed to dim and retreat. Under the dense canopy of leaves the sunlight slanted in thick shafts to the loam of the forest floor. It was still in the dell, secretive and cool; green and grey and lulling. A thick carpet of moss and leaves lay underfoot, the air pungent with the fecund scent of loam.

She felt as if she had entered a sacred *nemeton*. There were Old Gods here.

Her mare seemed to sense it too, for it quieted almost too quickly. Ama did not immediately urge it back up the other side of the dell: she felt suddenly as if she were waiting for something, but for what she did not know. She wasn't frightened. Aware, yes, almost preternaturally so; but not scared. Then there was a loud noise behind her, branches snapping. A figure came into view. It was Aedan, hurtling on his horse down the ravine after her.

He had come after her. His continued concern, well-hidden when in polite company, made her want to weep.

Seeing her unhurt, he checked his stallion's pace, letting it find its way judiciously down until he was abreast of her. He moved to speak. This was the first time they had been truly alone since his return. But as breathless as she was to have him there with her, she had no desire to shatter the stillness of the dell with any sound. She held up her hand, silencing him: *Do you feel it?*

He looked at her quizzically, then looked about the dell, really listening. He nodded almost immediately. He could feel it as well. It was not difficult: the air was heavy with expectancy. They were not alone in the hollow. He scanned the dell for the source of their unease, unsheathing a long knife from his boot.

Then, abruptly, all sound seemed to stop: gone were the bird calls, the ever-present industry of insects, even the rushing song of the river. Its cacophonous chorus, their companion all during the race, was mute. The hair on the back of Ama's neck stood straight in alarm. Aedan's knife was at the ready. It was close.

They heard it before they saw it: crunching footfalls on the forest floor, deliberate, unhurried, approaching. Then through a break in the trees emerged a creature, a magnificent stag, so large that it stood easily as high as she, atop her mare. Each antler-rack was twelve-pointed. Its great barrel chest heaved as it snorted breath. But it was unlike any stag she had ever before seen, for its wild eyes were red, bright like blood. And its coat was pure white, luminous in the gloam.

She knew it for the stuff of myth, of legend. Regally, primordially, it stood there, legs planted stoutly in the loam, its tail flicking, its broad chest heaving, regarding not her, but Aedan. Only Aedan. For a long timeless moment the white stag simply regarded Aedan with its blood-red eyes.

Spooked, Aedan's horse shied. He steadied it with a tug on its reins. He lowered his knife. But he never took his eyes off the stag, even as it lowered its head briefly in his direction.

Was she mistaken? Had the noble creature bowed?

Then it turned and, delicately for such a large creature, leaned back on its haunches, snorted, and bounded back the way it had come.

She let out a breath she hadn't realized she'd been holding. As if on her cue, sound returned to the dell: birds called; bees buzzed; the river rushed again. She heard shouting as the rest of the riders came to the far bend in the river enclosing the dell. There was still time for she and Aedan to regain the lead. They could get back on the path, up the other side of the dell, ahead of the riders. But they would have to hurry.

However, she had no desire to move. Aedan's eyes were large and dark: stunned, which was exactly how she felt. He had yet to say a word. Sheathing his knife in his boot, he held out his hand as if to take hers. Then he seemed to think better of the impulse and withdrew it again.

He nodded for her to lead their way out. Without hurry, she climbed the far side of the dell until she reached the lip of the ravine. Ahead through the trees lay the river-path. At its edge she stopped.

The men of Galloway raced down the track towards them, Eogan alongside, their horses spitting foam.

With a resounding crash, Ama returned to the world, the day, the race, her place. The otherworldly interlude was over. Nudging her mare forward onto the path just ahead of the oncoming riders, kicking it with a cry again to gallop, she found that she grieved for it.

"I agree, Galloway is a problem with which we must deal," old Kynfarch was saying to Tudwal, their heads bent closely together in counsel as they walked to the Beak's far landing, there to overlook the tidal isthmus all those precipitous feet below and the horse-race which would end there. "Of course I agree. And I will help you. I have said I would, and I will; I don't know why you press so. But what about Manau? Who do the Dal Fiatach think they are?"

"They think they are lords of Manau, too, clearly," Tudwal was saying. "But let us see if Morcant agrees ... "

The Dal Fiatach of Hibernia? Manau? Columba, who had been walking with Mungo, felt his interest peak even as Mungo, catching sight of the lords, called out happily, "My lords!"

A strategic discussion about the Britons' long-term plans for the isle of Manau was one Columba would gladly overhear, even at the temporary postponement of his own ambitions, but his hand on Mungo's sleeve was too late to stop the young man from plowing through the kings' retinues. "My lords! My lords! Wait!"

They stopped. Tudwal righted his rich fur cloak, glaring. Kynfarch's brow was raised in aggravated query.

"My lords! My lords! Let me introduce you to my new-found friend! A friend I know you will also wish to have for your own! This is Colum Cille, my lords! Columba from Hibernia! He is the abbot of Iona now! Iona of the Isles! You might not know of it yet, but you will! You will! But he is also a prince! Did you know that? Of the Cenel ... Well, of a *cenel*. Of Hibernia. The same family as the current high-king! Isn't that so, Columba? He is a great man! Columba that is; Columba, here. Not the high-king. Though I warrant he too is a great man. The things he could do here in Strat Clut!" Mungo shook off the quelling hand Columba had placed on his sleeve. "Columba, I mean, again, of course. In Rheged, even!" he enthused. "His mission ... "

Forcibly, Columba put the young priest behind him, kept him there. He smiled, donned his most amiable manner. This was in no way how he would have chosen to go about this most important audience with these kings, but there was nothing for it now. "My lords," he began.

"Your mission?" Tudwal growled. "Your mission? What do you mean, your mission? Here? In Strat Clut? We have our priest. That imbecile behind you. We have no need of another."

"But his cousin!" Mungo squeaked from over Columba's shoulder.

The two kings shared an incredulous look. "He thinks that having such a relation, a *Hibernian* relation, is incentive for us to aid him!" Kynfarch laughed, an old, jaded rattle in his throat.

Misplayed! Badly misplayed. And humbling: had Columba been speaking with almost any Hibernian king at the moment, that king would now be offering him the pick of his lands for any number of monasteries, and thanking him for taking them as he did so. But there was something else afoot here which, in Mungo's innocent desire to help him, Columba had been forced to stumble into; something which, come so newly to this land of the Britons, he did not yet understand.

"Typical!" Tudwal spat. "Just like a Hibernian." He glowered at Columba. "Not surprisingly, you have gotten it wrong—quite spectacularly wrong. Your people are one of the last we would ever willingly aid. Be content with your present friends, abbot, and look to rise no farther here."

Kingly cloaks whipping, they pushed past.

As they thundered around the last bend of the course and from its solid seat in the firth the imposing bulk of Alt Clut reared up before them, the isthmus in sight, in places already under a foot of water, Ama did not risk a glance behind. Over the lip of the isthmus and down to the shelf of sand she galloped, salt-water splashing about her in huge arcs, drenching her legs, her face against her mare's mane encouraging it with impassioned cries, Aedan and the men of Galloway close on her flanks.

Half-way over the isthmus, and there was the banner which signaled the course's end. Blood-red, it snapped in the wind. But she could not shake the other riders. They clung to her, pounding through the surf. Aedan was there somewhere. The crowds were cheering. A good race. Close, its outcome still uncertain. Bets were on. Who would win? Not the woman, surely.

Then, with a furtive motion, that same metallic flash— Gwenddolau's little dagger. He tried to hide it, but Ama caught it out of the corner of her eye, swiping. Rising up in the saddle, hunching over her horse's neck, she drew back her foot and kicked the dagger out of his hand. The blade flew through the air, splashed into the surf. A silver glint, gone.

Gwenddolau cursed, murder in his eyes; reached down—another hidden blade? Longer? To be aimed at her this time, not her horse?—when out of nowhere, Aedan, shortening his stallion's reins, the powerful animal's lower lip jutting, its protesting snort, slammed his horse into Gwenddolau's, sending man and horse careening.

Just in time. Driving her mount furiously, she crossed the finish line inches ahead of them all.

Ama paid the closing crowds no heed. Her mare dancing on its hind legs, she sought out Aedan in the pack of riders. There he was: his beautiful, ferocious grin.

And then Eogan. "Ama!" he cried, throwing himself from his horse. "We did it! We did it!"

We?

But their sweaty mounts were being taken from them and they were being swept along with the crowd towards the king's tent where the prizes would be awarded. She looked again for Aedan but could not find him until she spied him with Columba, and an unknown priest.

Something Aedan was saying to that young cleric caught her attention.

"You are Kentigern? *Kentigern?*" Aedan couldn't believe it. "Didn't Columba just call you Mungo?"

"Yes: *Mungo*," the young priest replied, all courtesy. "I am called Mungo. That is the name my beloved master, the sainted Serf, gave me. And it is as Mungo that I am known here. But I was given the name Kentigern at birth."

"*What is your age?*"

"Eighteen, my lord. Yes, I know! Quite too young to be a priest, but please believe me that I am certain of my calling, resolute; because of Serf, you see, my sainted master ... "

Sick with apprehension, Aedan ground out, "*Your mother: is she Teneu? Of the Gododdin?*" Aedan had to be sure. Though it really could be none other.

"Yes." Mungo, finally catching on to the urgency in Aedan's tone, drew himself up with a look of befuddlement and the beginnings of unease.

They were all looking to Aedan for explanation. He would not give it. *Kentigern!*

He had to warn the young man. Protect him. "Kentigern ... Mungo ... You need to leave. *Now*." He took his arm.

Kentigern shook him off. "*Leave? Why? Do you know my* mother? Do you know my father? You do! Is he *here?*"

Kentigern's head whipped around, searching the crowds. "Which one? Which one is he?"

Aedan's stomach was in a roil, his blood seething in his veins. He grabbed the young man again, was hauling him away, but Kentigern, looking avidly over his shoulder at the assembled lords entering the king's tent, had already settled on a curly-haired, dissolute man in a red-checkered cloak, a man who all could plainly see he eerily resembled.

Morcant of the Gododdin.

Kentigern's eager expression turned wistful at the sight of Morcant's finery, his noble mien and lavish accoutrements, how he shouldered aside lesser lords who stood in his way. "It is true, then," Kentigern sighed. "He is a great lord."

"No!"

Kentigern's shoulders squared and he said softly, "What have I to fear from him? I think he will be pleased with what I have made of myself". And twisting out of Aedan's grip he quickly made for the tent.

They all rushed to follow, Aedan whipping open the tent flaps to find Kentigern standing in mute fascination before a group of great lords, Morcant holding court. Flagons of ale in hand, the lords conversed good-naturedly, none of them noting the young priest enter—Kentigern was a slight, unassuming figure at best. But when the Dal Riatans barged in, Morcant called out in a carrying fashion full of unspecified criticism, "Ah! All hail the conquering Scots!"

"My lord ..." Kentigern stammered, his bony fingers clutching the neck of his threadbare robes. He cleared his throat, tried again. "My lord. Long have I desired to meet you! I am Mungo. But I was Kentigern at birth."

Morcant had been appraising the priest. But at his greeting, a look of confusion swept across his sharp face. *"Ken ..."* His voice trailed off. His face twisted with unwanted comprehension. *"No. It cannot be."*

"God has willed it, Father, even so," Kentigern replied.

Father and son studied each other for a long moment. Morcant was leaning so close to Kentigern that it looked as if he might kiss him. Then some unnamable horror contorted Morcant's face. He shuddered and lurched back. Thrusting a shaking finger at Kentigern, he cried out, *"This is no child of God!"*

Kentigern, blue eyes bulging, mouth agape, sucked in breath as if he had been struck. Aedan sprang forward. "Morcant! Shut your mouth!"

"No!" Morcant cried.

"Shut it, or I'll shut it for you!"

Morcant's finger was still shuddering in his son's face. "This is ... this is ... *an abomination!*"

Kentigern's face whitened with shock.

"If he is an abomination," Aedan snarled, "—and I cannot believe it of your God; I cannot—*then it is you who made him so.*"

"How so?" King Tudwal demanded. His great saucer-shaped eyes were wide with interest as he sought out the secret which would give him purchase over his uncertain ally, the lord of the Gododdin.

Tudwal's demand, and Aedan's menace, seemed to break the sickly hold the young priest had over Morcant. With one last searching look at Kentigern, a look of fascinated revulsion, Morcant pushed past them all and left the tent. In the rapt silence that followed, Kentigern turned and aimlessly wandered out.

Aedan was right behind.

If the afternoon's humiliating encounter with the father he had never known had unhinged Kentigern, Aedan could see no sign of it as, sun setting, the young priest, magisterial in his flowing white robes, flanked by Columba and the elderly, unkempt Gildas, led a handful of Britons through a Christian mass in celebration of the year's harvest. Before Kentigern, on a long wooden altar that had been erected at the head of the plain, lay the first loaf of bread baked from the season's first grain harvest. Emaciated face composed, bony hands steady, Kentigern broke the bread and blessed it.

Although he had shadowed the young priest for the remainder of the afternoon, it was quickly clear to Aedan that Kentigern, who had subsumed himself again in his priestly mantle, was in no imminent danger: Morcant had let him be. Nevertheless, only when Kentigern, duties over, had begun to ascend the steep dirt path up Alt Clut's western crag with Columba and Gildas in tow in the direction of Kentigern's sea-bound cell, there to spend the night, did Aedan let himself relax his anonymous guard.

Then, Aedan avoided his brother and Ama for the better part of the evening. It was not difficult to do: duties of the mass over, the Britons had resumed their liberal, pagan celebrations. Aedan had simply lost himself amongst them. Having no desire to be on high with the lords that night, he was sitting by the big bonfire down on the plain at the foot of the Rock, drinking; a lot, and quickly. With tin-whistles and drums and triple pipes the players had just begun the tunes of the common people, easy and boisterous and rousing, with none of the studied solemnity and worthiness of the harpists presently entertaining his cousins high in the Windy Hall. It suited his mood. The infectious melodies encouraged him to lose himself, but he had not yet drunk enough to shake off the depression that had shrouded the end of his day; so he would continue to try. Let it not be said that he was a man who shirked his responsibilities. Thoughts of Gartnait and Domelch came and went; he wondered how they were passing this last evening of this harvest celebration; to where they would go next; if they missed him. Thoughts of Ama and Artur; here with him, but as far away as ever. He felt a consuming loneliness, a teeming anger, and quite a bit of contempt.

Then there was Eogan before him, hands on hips. And Ama. They had tracked him down at last.

"Confess," his brother demanded.

"Alright," Aedan said. "I confess: I do intend to get royally drunk tonight. I most heartily do."

"Come now, brother! The air is pregnant with what you—and Mungo ... *Kentigern*, rather—are not saying. What hold have you over Morcant? He did your bidding: he let the young priest be! Had I not seen it, I would never have believed it!"

Aedan studiously avoided his brother's gaze. Eogan motioned to a servant to bring them more ale and sat beside him. Ama took her place at his other side. He felt her against his arm, his thigh. Stealing some of her heat, he began to feel a little better.

At last, ale was brought. Aedan helped himself to more; handed some to Ama. Eogan proceeded, "So Mungo—*Kentigern*— is Morcant's son. That is plain to see: their faces are two sides of a coin. So? Many a child is born out of wedlock. There is no shame in it. There are laws to protect such innocents and to provide for them. I have no doubt that many will be conceived here tonight in fact." He waved at the festive Britons. "They'll have just as many April babies as we always do."

However reasonable Eogan's tone, Aedan had no desire to betray a confidence, especially one so horrendous. Still, over the past few hours he had come to the conclusion that it was best to enlist his brother's aid. And Ama ... well, it was in Ama's nature to do no harm. So he said, praying for the gods' forgiveness as he did so, "Kentigern is a child of rape. A child of incest".

Ama gasped. Eogan's lips thinned into a grimace. Peering inside his drinking horn, sloshing around the ale, Eogan tipped it back and drank it dry. He held up the horn and it was taken by a servant to be refilled. "How so?" he asked.

"Morcant raped his sister. Worse: he raped his twin."

"No!" Ama cried. "Surely you are mistaken!"

"I am not."

"How can you know?" Eogan asked.

"I witnessed it—the end of it. Unfortunately, I was too late to prevent it."

It was a day when he had taken refuge from Morcant in his usual place: a small cave in a rocky outcrop in a forest glen not very different from the glen he and Ama had stumbled upon during the horse race that very afternoon. Over the years of his unwanted fosterage in Gododdin he had made it a comfortable haven: a pallet of heather bracken and grasses, a little cooking pit, the belongings he wanted to keep safe from his foster-brother.

Afterwards, as he looked back on his time at Din Eidyn, he was never sure how he had consistently managed it—to avoid being alone with Morcant; to be ever-so-slightly quicker so that, when the older boy came at him with fist or cudgel or whip, he always slipped away. Never quite sure how he managed to be always one step ahead of him, Aedan had developed over those years a deep-seated certainty that, despite the incessant claims of Gododdin's white-robed priests, there was no such thing as a compassionate god. Had there been, that god would have kept him safe from Morcant's malice. He was a boy. A boy! But no, Aedan had had to hone his own innate skill for self-preservation, and his intelligence, and his physical gifts, pronounced even then and the root, he suspected, of some of Morcant's envy. Because, day after day, he was the one who managed to save himself. No god could be thanked for it.

It was tricky, for Morcant was sly. It was the essential feature of his sadism, Aedan realized when he was safely home and had time to ponder it—he was sly in such a way that he was always successful in keeping his true intentions hidden from his elders. Though he stalked Aedan for years, Morcant was never caught at it. Blind to his base desires, the adults at court thought Morcant a noble prince, a paragon of youth, a worthy subject of verse and song.

But Morcant was not. From the first day he had met him, Aedan had sensed something dark in his foster-brother that had tied his stomach in knots. He was petrified of the older boy for no reason that he could define. Until, that is, the day, not a month after his arrival in Din Eidyn, when Morcant found him alone in his father's hall, admiring its beautiful trappings. Aedan had stolen in to gape at them. The hall was the most sumptuous that Aedan had ever seen; it made Dun Ad, his beloved home, seem rather like a hovel. Morcant approached him and spoke with him, pointing out one of the more finely woven tapestries which adorned the walls. To see it, to understand his foster-brother's explanation of its making and its significance, its woven art, Aedan had to turn his back to Morcant.

That was when he felt Morcant's hand on the back of his neck, forcing his head down. And Morcant's hand where no man's hand had ever been, fondling him. And then Morcant untying the knot which held up Aedan's breeches.

Aedan had shouted, and he had struggled, to no avail. Morcant had only forced his head down farther until he was bent over a bench which, too late, Aedan realized had been in front of him the whole time, as if Morcant had planned the entire thing.

With all of his might, Aedan struggled against Morcant's hold, he panicked, clawing and kicking, but Morcant simply held him imprisoned until he had spent his strength. With his cheek smashed against the splintery wood of the bench, Aedan's gorge rose. He gagged and began to cry.

But then, unbidden, an image of one of the birds which haunted the slopes about his home came to his mind—the bird which, feigning injury with bent wing, lures the predator away from the egg-filled nest. So, even as his trews were being yanked down over his buttocks, Aedan forced himself to relax. And Morcant, registering what he deemed to be Aedan's acquiescence, let go of the back of Aedan's head. With a gentleness that nearly caused Aedan to vomit, Morcant caressed his backside. Aedan even heard him croon a little, as if to soothe him for what was to come next.

With all his might, Aedan slammed his head back into Morcant's face. Morcant's nose crunched, broken. Morcant howled and blood spewed, but Aedan, trews in hand, was already out the door of the king's hall.

Aedan never let himself be caught alone again. He had had to learn cunning, and forethought; to plan a route of escape before he needed it, certain that he would; and to defend himself with whatever tools he had to hand, meager though they might be. Anything could be a weapon. And this is what he would practice day after day, alone in his forest refuge, until he had taught himself all he could. Then he had sought out the sword-master of the citadel to beg for more lessons, more training, more practice, practice, practice. And it had seemed to Aedan that that grisly old veteran of many tribal skirmishes had seen the desperation in his eyes because he took Aedan under his wing and passed on all his knowledge day after day until at last he held up his hands, defeated, saying, "There is no more. You are the best I have taught. Perhaps the best I will ever teach. I do not know what drives you—no! I do not care to know!—but you should offer it thanks, for your fear of it has made you a master".

That was the day it had happened: the thing that had caused his lasting fear of his foster-brother to mutate into an unquenchable hatred. With a shake of hands, Aedan had left the sword-master. He felt safer that afternoon, safer than any day since he had come to Din Eidyn. For some reason he no longer felt the fear. In his mind he played with the idea of confronting Morcant. He thought that he was finally ready to face him; was certain that he could handle himself even if Morcant came not alone but with the pack of familiars with which he liked to hunt.

He was just upon his refuge when he heard the whimpering. It was coming from inside his hideaway. He ran in on the end of the rape: a young man pumping into a girl. With a cry Aedan pulled him off. It was Morcant, his face twisted with lust and anger. Then Aedan saw the girl's stricken face: it was Teneu, Morcant's own sister. Morcant's twin.

Sprawled on the cave's floor, trews tangled about his ankles and his engorged member jutting obscenely, Morcant still managed to look lordly as he wiped spittle from his chin with the back of his hand. There was blood in it. "Whore," he sneered. "She came out here for you."

She had. Lately Teneu had begun to visit him, innocently. She seemed to find comfort in the refuge he had made, as if she too had reason to fear the court. Now he knew why.

"Took a bit of prodding, brother," Morcant said with a rude jut of his member, "but I broke her in. Your turn."

Then Morcant giggled.

It was the closest Aedan had ever come to taking a life in anger. All the years of bullying; Aedan's fear for his own safety; the certain knowledge that if Morcant and his lads had ever managed to discover Aedan alone they would have violated him this way too—Aedan gladly submitted to the purely animal urge and with a howl set upon Morcant with fury. That the boy was two years older did not on that day seem to matter. Aedan's fear had at last boiled over into rage. It had an elemental quality to it. Powered by an almost inhuman strength, he punched, kicked and pummeled, he clawed and bit Morcant until his foster-brother—a boy who by rights should have been closer to him than Eogan, but who had been instead the terror of his childhood—lay unconscious at his feet.

A voice was crying out. *"Aedan! Aedan! Stop!* You must stop! You mustn't kill him! You will be killed for it ... my father ... my father won't care ..."* Cloak clutched protectively about her, Teneu was standing there, disheveled, shaking, beseeching him.

About you, Aedan's heart had cried, not doubting the truth of her words. *About what his son has done. All he sees; all that bastard has ever seen, is Morcant.*

There was no hiding the fact that she had been treated savagely. Her face was soundly beaten, her eyes blackened, her lower lip raw where Morcant had bitten it nearly through. Later that day she told her father, King Leudonus, that she had been set upon by brigands. That she could not identify the attackers. That Aedan had saved her. Morcant grasped the lie eagerly, claiming that they had beaten him too. The king sent a warband to hunt down the brigands but of course no trace of them was ever found.

And then, more horrifying, Teneu discovering that she was pregnant. As it was, Leudonus, unable to avenge his daughter's rape since she could not or, as he had begun to suspect, would not, identify her attackers, blamed the girl instead.

Aedan had approached the old king, begging to be allowed to marry Teneu. He did not love her, but he was moved by a deep pity and a sense of responsibility. In his young-man's mind, not yet used to the treacheries of men, he was certain that if Teneu had not been in the habit of visiting him she never would have fallen prey to her brother. He had not yet discovered that evil will always find an out.

He had always had cause to despise the decrepit old king. He had little respect for a man who refused to see, and name, what lay plainly before him. That day it had turned to hate for, in front of his retinue in his sumptuous, rich, lordly hall, Leudonus opened a mouth full of yellow, rotting teeth and jeered, "You must be joking! Even sullied and torn as she is by some low-life, my daughter is vastly your superior. You call yourself her friend, yet you dishonor her by imagining yourself her equal. Against my better judgment I have fostered you here: I fail to see what fostering you, a Scot, has ever done for me. I should kick you right back to your father. Today. You are a disgrace. Marry my daughter! The shame of it!" The king guffawed, spitting ale.

Aedan fled the hall. But he told Teneu what he had done nevertheless. He begged that she reveal her brother. He offered to take her away. But she was lost inside herself in the self-absorbed way of expectant mothers, already in love with the life she carried and certain that her family would grow to love her babe as she did, and she would not listen. That was the day she had told Aedan that she would name the child *Kentigern* if it lived.

But her family did not love the babe as she had so desperately wished, even though, almost preternaturally, as if it knew for its own safety that it should endear itself quickly to its caretakers, it hardly ever cried but would coo and gurgle in delight; a gentle soul. Aedan had begged again that she reveal Morcant, or he would gladly do it; but Teneu was convinced that her father would kill the babe if he knew that it was his own grandson by incest, and Aedan did not doubt her.

Rather, King Leudonus punished Teneu, in the most publicly humiliating, permanent way that he could devise. He set her and the babe adrift in a tiny boat. Without food, without water, without provisions of any kind save the cloaks they were wrapped in, it was the last Aedan had seen of her: her slight form huddled protectively around the small bundle of her son, consoling the babe as the tide of the mighty Muir nGiudan carried them out to sea.

Aedan was banished. Not home, but to Alt Clut—a brief, glorious, well-needed month full of Eogan's and Ama's company. But then, just when Aedan had begun to let himself hope that Leudonus might make good on his threat to terminate Aedan's fosterage and send him home at last, the king recalled Aedan to Din Eidyn. Aedan knew why: Aedan's father Gabran held the Picts from Gododdin's western door. He was not an ally to anger.

When Aedan's fosterage was at last at an end and he was free to go home, he went in search of Teneu and the babe. For weeks he searched until at last he, too, came to the shore of the grey sea, but they were lost, unrecoverable, as if the sea had swallowed them whole. The first balm he had ever received for that horror had happened this day: Kentigern—Mungo—was miraculously alive; and he had been taken in by a good man, a priest he had named Serf, who must have treated him well to have earned his respect and esteem. It helped Aedan somewhat to know this. The lad had known care. And love.

What had become of Teneu, Aedan did not know.

Ama broke the hard silence. "Nothing we can do tonight can lessen that evil deed," she said quietly. "Columba and Gildas are with Kentigern. Surely their Lord succors them all."

He sighed. She was correct. Still, there was one last matter. "Brother," he asked. "Kentigern may need my … *our* … protection. Does he have it?"

"Aye," Eogan answered somberly.

More ale arrived and they sat in companionable silence for a while, drinking, the Britons dancing about the bonfire, until the clouds opened and rain began to fall in light sheets, soaking them as they ascended the steps back to the Beak.

"Will you come in?" Ama asked tentatively at the flap of their tent. "At least for tonight?"

An eye on the sky, full of drink, cold and sad and sorry, he did. But he kept himself as far from her as he could. And although Aedan dreamt that night of white stags and ravens—hearing in the pounding of the rain on the roof of the tent the white stag's hooves in the forest glen; in the wind's howl the ravens' martial rasp, a girl's cry—when he awoke in the morning he remembered nothing of it.

· 10 ·
GWALLAWG OF ELMET

❦

Aedan was thinking about how the smallest choices can turn a life: his father's decision to foster him upon the unkind Gododdin and not, say, upon his kin in Berneich; to linger to talk more with his sword master rather than to be off home with a wave; to send Teneu away before she ever knew of his hideaway rather than to permit himself a first, simple friendship: all the myriad little choices that brought him home to a raping and not to its escalation (when it might have been prevented) or its aftermath (when it might have been ignored). Instead, thanks to innumerable, often infinitesimal, choices, and to happenstance, in this case cruel, and to the capriciousness of the gods, he had been forced to take on responsibility for an act of violence that was in no way his.

Aedan was thinking about these things the following morning as, head down, hood thrown up and cloak wrapped tightly to ward off the drenching rain, he crossed the rope-bridge behind Eogan and climbed the cliff-path to the Windy Hall on the Crag of the

Kings. It was the morning of the assembly. The lords would finally make good the contracts they had been negotiating at length and in secret over the course of the Oenach. He and Eogan and Ama had done what they could. They had certainly distinguished themselves amongst the company. With judicious action, this was the day Eogan might finally improve the lot of their family, the Cenel Gabran. Or, given how lords vacillated, it might not.

Slipping through the doors of the Windy Hall, they interrupted an argument. A young lord from yet another unrecognized kingdom stood ramrod straight before the lords of Strat Clut, Rheged, Gododdin, Guined, eyes flashing. In his early twenties, he was of average height and weight, with long, straight hair that hung past his shoulders, streaked with a grey come much too soon for one so young, and a long mustache bracketing a wide mouth. Wisps of wet hair had escaped their tie to hang forlornly about his nondescript, careworn face. His fine blue cloak was stained, as were his brown tunic and boots. Haggard and exhausted, nevertheless he radiated authority and command. Easily he held his place among the older lords. "We have come a long way to meet with you here," he was saying. "Our journey was arduous and full of danger. You are a noble people, as are we. We share your language. We share your lineage. We deserve your respect."

It was Kynfarch of Rheged who answered him. The old man said in his most placating tone, "Yes. And you have it, of course. But I repeat: show me evidence of this 'relentless Saxon advance' before which you quake in terror, Gwallawg. I see none. On the contrary. The Deirans are content with their colony in the Vale of Cair Ebrauc, as my sources report. There are rich farmlands there, yes? The Deiran women and children are fat and happy. They fornicate and multiply and farm. While I am sorry that the Deiran dogs are your neighbors, they are not mine. Blame your old Roman masters. It has nothing to do with Rheged".

The lord was Gwallawg of Elmet, a British kingdom so far to the south and east that Aedan had no hope of ever seeing it with his own eyes—a kingdom which presently had some very unwelcome neighbors camped permanently on its borders: Saxons. Saxons who called themselves Deirans.

"Elmet was a mighty kingdom," Gwallawg declared. "Now, rock and water—the Pennines and the Usa—hem us in. I tell you that, while the Deirans may be content with the farmland by which the Romans long ago bought them off, their king, Yffi, is not: he takes more. He takes *ours*. This Yffi, this *king* of Deira, is our concern. He is Elmet's concern. And we shall deal with him." His eyes flashed. Cloak and hair dripping wet, nonetheless Gwallawg cut a noble figure. "However, your concern is that he eyes the Vale. Mark my words: the Deirans aim for Catraeth. For Rheged. They aim for your royal estate there, Kynfarch. I would, if I were they. Not only is it lovely, but with Catreath they secure the lowlands about Cair Ebrauc. From there they will make their way up Dere Street. The Roman road is still passable. They will drive a wedge between you, Kynfarch, content in your Vale of Eden in the west, and you, Morcant, in the east. There will be no more ... *happy* gatherings like this one, no more merry Oenachs. There will be no more mighty block of British kingdoms, but instead scattered and disparate tribes cowering in their mountain fastnesses from the ravenous wolves that stalk the plains below. Mark my words. They want Catreath. And they will take it. But that is not the worst of it. Have you given any thought to what might happen should the Deirans make peace with the Saxons who have seized Din Guoaroy?"

Morcant spat, his sharp face a sneer. "You cannot mean that pirate Ida?"

"Yes, Ida! Who else? Whore's son! Why is he still there? Why haven't you driven him out?" Gwallawg demanded. "Do you know that he is calling his 'kingdom' *Bernicia*? That should tell you everything you need to know! Bernicia! After the Britons! After the Britons he enslaved! Does he think that lends his actions credence? That those of us keeping watch might not notice the difference? The filthy, profligate pagans speak a tongue unfit for the

171

mouths of Christians, but that's alright, not to worry, their name is the same! Mark my words: Ida does not intend to leave the place. Have your ... *sources* told you that he is propagating like mad? That he takes any woman he can get? Saxon or British? Willing or not? That he has seven sons already, and that two of his concubines will disgorge more by snow fall? He is infesting Din Guoaroy with his spawn! He calls his eldest by-blow 'Theodoric'. Pretentious swine! What kind of man calls his son 'King-king'? I'll tell you what kind: an arrogant one! A dangerous one! One with plans, who thirsts for more glory. One to be watched. Carefully. If nothing else, you should clear Ida out of Din Guoaroy while you still can."

Aedan could tell that Gwallawg wanted to pace. His energy, his anxiety, sprouted from him like bristles. But the young lord held himself still. "Why did you not go to their aid?" Gwallawg asked. "They were British. They were our cousins. They paid you tribute. Outigern was a brave man—he did not deserve such an end. They say he screamed for hours before his blood ran out. And Brychan! Longer. Much longer. They kept at it; put all their skill to it. Would not let him die. Not because he withheld something they needed. No. But because they enjoyed his pain. Because he had thought to deny them his kingdom. They, who will be denied nothing." Gwallawg sucked in breath. "Will you abandon us as you abandoned them?"

Aedan's uncle. Aedan's grandfather. Aedan sucked in his own breath, thankful that his sword had been taken from him at the door. That none of them there were armed. Had there not been truce, he was quite certain they'd already be on their way to bloodshed. By his hand.

How would the lords respond? Aedan desperately needed to know. Though his mother had been full of suspicion, she had never had proof. *Please, let her have been wrong*, he found himself praying. *Please, let it be falsehood. A misunderstanding. Let this be a simple matter*.

And Kynfarch did reply simply. "The time of the house of Berneich was at an end."

"You mean you desired that it end," Gwallawg said.

Shrugging, Morcant offered, as if in explanation, "Those who are not strong perish," with Tudwal nodding sagely.

Only Eogan's vice-like grip on Aedan's arm kept Aedan from leaping from his chair. Bastards! All three of them! His mother had been right. Her own brothers-in-law had betrayed her father and brother. They had abandoned their kin in the hour of their greatest need. The shame of it should have driven them mad with self-loathing—they had betrayed their most sacred bonds—yet the lords sat there, gloating, blithely; happy in their conspiracy. Aedan could discern not an ounce of shame between them.

His mother would never know, he vowed. But now he knew. That was enough.

Gwallawg's faced had paled. Aedan felt a sudden empathy for the young lord: like Eogan, Gwallawg sought the aid of, and alliance with, the strong. Yet he was looking in the wrong place if he sought charity here. The mighty give aid only when they also have need. Especially these mighty. And Elmet was a tiny kingdom. What could it offer in return?

"Though I needn't sit here and prove it to you," Morcant said to Gwallawg, "I will tell you that we have Ida in check. He is useful to us where he is. Yes, he trawls up and down the coastline with his raiding parties. He is only the last in a long line of foreign pirates to do so,"—Morcant cast a scathing look in Aedan's and Eogan's direction—"but it's the Miathi he bothers more than us. Which is fine. As long as he passes us by on his way north, he's no bother. And he's no friend of Deira, I can tell you that. Doesn't matter if they're both Saxon dogs. They're rival houses. They'll never unite."

"Perhaps not willingly," Gwallawg countered. "But alliance isn't the only way to build kingdoms. One can eat the other up. And when one of them—I'll wager on Deira—swells to twice its size, it'll look for larger prey. It must. It'll be hungry. It is the way of things. And when it does, who else but us Britons? Don't be fools! It's in the lay of the land. On their borders not already held by other Saxons, Britons beckon. All of *us*. When the Saxons wake in the morning and consider over their gruel where to get farmland for their no-good stay-at-home third son who will finally marry, they look due west and see us: Elmet. They look north-west and see you, Kynfarch, there in mighty Rheged. North is you, Morcant: Gododdin. If they are especially far-sighted they squint and spy Strat Clut on the far horizon. You are so lofty on this Rock, Tudwal, how could they not? Where they no longer look is east. They do not look back towards the sea: they will not leave in their little boats as once they came. And they cannot look south except to see other Saxons, Lindsey and Mercia, whom they may not, nay will not, supplant." He held out his hands. "So I ask you: who else but us?"

"Strat Clut is impregnable," Tudwal growled, wrapping himself more tightly in his fur cloak and straightening in his chair. "He can't get by our ships. We bottle up the sea-lanes. Tight as a virgin's glory. The water is no way in. Neither is the land! The mountains! Honestly! Even if you manage not to get lost in them, you die. Consider how difficult it was for you, our friend, to make it here today—and Elmet knows the way! Why else would the Romans have abandoned that frontier? They couldn't hold it either. The mountains will keep us safe from the threat you imply. No. Our enemies come from the west, the north. Our enemies are the Scots. Not these here." He spared a crisp nod in Eogan's direction. "But the damned Hibernians. They want Manau. Right, Kynfarch?"

"Yes. It is an insufferable situation," Kynfarch sniffed.

"And the Picts. They are our enemies too. The Scots and Picts are what concern us. Not your Saxons. It is a simple thing, which history has borne out: if Rome could not subdue us, the Saxons will not."

Gwallawg shook his head violently. "The wilderness which you claim keeps you safe can also be your undoing. The fortress which safeguards the maiden may be a prison to those under siege within it. When the Saxons have you holed up here on your Rock, to where will you escape? North? Into the arms of the Picts? Will the Scots succor you?" Gwallawg snickered derisively, his control slipping. "Besides, no fortress, even a natural one crafted in His wisdom to shelter so fine and worthy a people as yours, no fortress is without its weakness. The mountains you so admire are not without their gaps. It's true that the Romans did not settle them—I'll give you that. But they did fortify them. Against your murderous rage. They built their roads, their coastal forts and fortlets, their signal stations, for fear of you. And yet it was not enough. So, between little Berneich and you, mighty Rheged, they built their Great Wall. We are all still in awe of it, though much of it crumbles or is mined for our needs, for masterful and wondrous it seems to us, we who rarely harness stone: its length and its grandeur a testament to the power of our former masters.

"And then, even that was not enough to keep you subjected. So they built the other wall, the turf one, between the great arms of the sea, the mighty Clut and the mighty Muir nGuidan, formidable defenses in their own right, upon which sit you, Strat Clut, and you, Gododdin. And still it was not enough. Even with these fortifications Rome could not contain you. You harassed and tormented and plagued them until you drove them away, back home to Italia, tail between their legs. If there is a lesson, this is it: Rome was great. You are greater. But mark my words, the Saxons will be greater still ... "

"How can you say ... "

"It is simple. Where you only steal—sorry, *stole*—in order to redistribute amongst yourselves (for who does not want wealth?), the Saxons annihilate. They burn. They maim. They torture, leaving nothing in their wake. Not a single life, except those they might enslave. Do you see? You are greater than Rome, but are you so great that you will be able to keep the Saxons at bay? Mark my words: what has swarmed south through your fine mountain fastnesses may also swarm north. None of us is invulnerable. None. We must act. We must move against them now. Together."

There was a considered silence as Gwallawg waited anxiously for the lords' decision. Apprehension crossed faces, what might have been doubt. Was Gwallawg correct? Would they have to rise from the gaming tables? Give up the goblet? Couple with their women one last ferocious time and ride out to war? Don sword and shield, raise host against the enemy and bring him low? Show him his gods?

Be shown their own?

Rain battered the roof. Wind gusted back through the smoke-hole, had its way with the fire. Spat ash into the air, veiling their sight. No one could see.

It cleared. All the lords, content in their chairs. "Gwallawg," Tudwal said. "You have not heard us." The lords sat back with a sigh. There would be no movement; no admission. No swifting the race to death. "I am not a rude lord, and you are a friend, so I shall repeat myself: *the Saxons are not our enemies.*"

"Not yet!" Gwallawg cried. But Tudwal had shored up his back imperiously.

Mutely, Gwallawg searched for another way to reach them. He rounded on a new target: Eogan. "This is your fault! You have been welcomed into this hall as a friend and ally, yet we have you to thank for this!"

"Me? Me personally?"

"If it weren't for you damned Scots, we would never have had to invite the Saxons here in the first place!"

"As you say, *you* invited them here."

"To drive *you* out! You pirates! We paid the Saxons to keep you Scots at bay. When they threatened to bring in more of their kind, reinforcements, they said, you proving so bloody difficult to get rid of, we had to buy them off! With land. To settle! Now they no longer accept our bribes. They laugh in our faces! They think of our island as their own. We shall never be rid of them!"

Hands raised in a conciliatory fashion but his face flushed with anger, Eogan was about to speak, when Tudwal stepped in: "Just as the Scots were paid by us to keep the Picts at bay. It is a matter of perspective. And, I suppose, geography. But that was a long time ago, Gwallawg. You speak of old grievances".

"I speak of today. The Saxons are on my doorstep as we speak. Just because he,"—he cast a venomous look at Eogan—"has managed to aggrandize himself with you does not mean that I would ever stoop to foster a Saxon by-blow at my court, as did your father with this Scot, or, God forbid!, sell them one of my daughters. Pagan bastards!"

Eogan a by-blow! Ama, chattel! Fists clenched, Aedan thought he might just go teach Gwallawg better courtesy when Eogan cast him a quelling look, and Aedan managed, how he knew not, to hold his tongue.

"I will not treat with the Saxons," Gwallawg declared. "I appeal to you all to join with me. I appeal to your sense of nobility and camaraderie. Are we not cousins? Do we not share a language? A God? Does not the blood of the first Britons run also through my veins?"

"What would you have us do, Gwallawg?" Morcant asked with a reasonableness Aedan knew was feigned. Morcant was never reasonable; only self-serving. "We are no Arturs."

Kynfarch growled in warning. Morcant had just misstepped. Kynfarch's father had served under Artur. The Pendragon's exhilarating last stand against the Saxons at Mount Badon was Kynfarch's own first taste of Saxon blood. Ah! The Pendragon. The great warlord for whom Ama had named their son. Seventy years ago, when their grandfathers (or fathers, as in the case of Kynfarch) were much as they themselves were now, Artur had been faced with a desperate choice: mount a defense against the Saxons who beat like a storm-tide at full moon against the shores of Britannia, or be swept away. Many fled that flood, in desperate little skin-boats, south across the treacherous Muir Nicht to Armorica. But Artur held. By means of twelve great battles over many years he beat them back. With the last battle, at Mount Badon, the golden age he muscled in flowered for the remainder of his life. Would that it had been longer! No one had yet replaced him; not for a generation; not in the thirty years since he had been taken from them. He had kept the Saxons to their colonies; had made them respect the boundaries of the British kingdoms. Until Gwallawg had spoken today, Aedan had thought they kept there still.

"I repeat—with no insult to you, Kynfarch, since I speak of our incentive (or lack thereof), and not of our abilities: we are no Arturs," said Morcant.

"We have no need to be Arturs," Tudwal concurred. "I see no sea of Saxons. Where is the storm-tide? Where the relentless advance? We see none because there is none. The peace that Artur ushered in resounds around you. Look, here, and you will see stability, and security, and orderly government. The Saxons are happy with their lot. As are we. I repeat: I am sorry that the Saxons are your neighbors and enemies. They are not mine."

"Nor mine," said Kynfarch.

"Nor mine," said Morcant.

"You will do nothing?" Gwallawg's voice betrayed his incredulity. Underneath it was the tenor of fear, and Aedan could almost forgive him his fall in civility. This was a man at his last defense.

"What would you have us do?" Tudwal asked. "Show me the enemy and I will fight him." When Gwallawg moved to speak again, Tudwal silenced him. "I have spoken. I believe I speak for all here. You have come a long way. Enjoy the hospitality of my hall, if you can. Take comfort. Let the merriment of the Oenach ease your worry and drive the shadow of fear from your heart."

Gwallawg stood there helplessly for a long moment, the muscles of his face twitching, his hands clenching spasmodically at his sides. But he made no more appeals. Then he bowed stiffly, turned on his heel, and left the Windy Hall.

The second the great doors had closed behind him, anger erupted. "Idiot! Whiner! Warmonger!" Tudwal slammed his fist on the arm of his chair. "Hasn't he learned never to hold the sour memory of Rome over the head of a *combrogi*? He speaks as if we should have welcomed the yoke of slavery and never have thrown it off! Idiot! His soul was bought and paid for with Rome's silver *denarii*." He spat violently.

"His great-grandfather's soul," Kynfarch pointed out. "And it was gold coin, not silver."

The lords fell silent as they ruminated over Gwallawg's words. Finally, Kynfarch said, "I shall send out spies. To see what, if anything, Deira is up to".

"Father," Urien spoke up. "Let me put the Saxon dogs to the sword. I'll drive Ida from Din Guoaroy."

"And let Gwenddolau take Galloway?" Kynfarch asked. "The Hibernians, Manau? No, son. I cannot spare you."

"I'll keep a closer eye on Ida," Morcant added. "If ... *Bernicia* ... has plans for expansion, I shall know it in a fortnight."

"Your informants are shite, Morcant, if Ida's changed the name of his whole bloody kingdom and this is the first you've heard of it," Tudwal said.

There was more rumination until Kynfarch observed, "If it is true, it is nothing new, you know. For whom do you think the Deirans named themselves? The tribes they put under the yoke: the Deur, the people of the Deorwente Valley—*Britons*".

"Oh," said Tudwal.

More silence, then Tudwal said, "It is not so much the thing he asked for, as how he asked for it".

"Yes," said Morcant. "I only wish there were legitimate provocation. In Gododdin we love a good fight almost as much as we love a good piss-up."

The lords' mood lightened. "Speaking of piss-ups ... " Kynfarch asked hopefully.

"Yes," said Tudwal in such a way that everyone knew that the assembly was now over. "Let us get to it. The revel currently underway just outside this hall has cost me dearly. I intend to enjoy

179

what's left of it. And the *fili* in Gwallawg's company—a young poet from Pouis; have you heard of him, Beli? Taliesin is his name—is by all accounts excellent: perhaps the best of our generation. Lucky, that. Makes me almost glad Gwallawg showed up ... almost."

"Indeed!" Beli enthused. "I have heard Taliesin sing! Astonishing! But you must also hear Aneirin, the lad Taliesin has apprenticed. Extraordinary promise! He may yet outpace his master."

"You don't say?" Kynfarch asked eagerly. "That is something I should like to see."

That was when Eogan spied his opening. "My lords," he said, capturing their attention with his most winning smile. "A quick word, if you would ... "

Tudwal started, almost as if he had forgotten that Eogan was there. "With whom?" he asked.

"What I have to say concerns all of you."

Tudwal sat back down with a nod. "Speak then."

But Morcant shot out of his chair. "*No.*"

"*No?*" Tudwal asked. "He is my foster-brother. I cannot refuse him. Besides, none here can deny that he has comported himself admirably in these contests—he and his family."

"What I mean is, I will treat with him," Morcant said, pointing at Eogan. "But not with *him.*" He thrust the same finger at Aedan but with much more force. If the finger could have skewered him, it would have.

Aedan could only smile. "My lords." And sparing his brother an encouraging nod, he happily left the Windy Hall to the kings and their endless machinations.

· 11 ·
AFRELLA OF GUINED

Rain. Great sheets of it, coming off the sea. The warship rocking underfoot, the rigging cumbersome in Aedan's cold, wet hands. But it looked as if the skies would clear, the heavy grey cloud giving way to blue, rendering their voyage home to Tairbert Boitter easy and, with luck, uneventful.

There they were, Ama and Artur and Columba, Eogan and his retinue, making their way across the plain, the Rock glowering overhead as if happy to see the last of the Scots. Good; Aedan was more than ready to go; could not wait to put a better distance between himself and Morcant. Even from afar, and through the veil of rain, Aedan could see that his brother was smiling. His step was light, as if he had been relieved of a terrible burden. His audience with the kings in the Windy Hall must have gone to his advantage—perhaps Strat Clut had taken their *cenel* on as a direct client, perhaps Rheged too. By the looks of it, their work here was done, and far more quickly and expeditiously than Aedan had dared to hope. He could go home now, back to Gartnait and Domelch.

Home. How odd. When had he begun to think of Caledonia as home?

At the railing, Ama met his gaze bravely, but he could not read her thoughts as she handed him Artur to lift into the boat. He did so easily. The boy was light in his arms, not much heavier than Gartnait. He would be leaving them both. Could he do it? Then he was surprised to see Afrella, the maid of Guined, at the rear of his brother's company, asking for his helping hand, blushing as he complied. Were they to transport her homeward, a favor to her father Beli? In truth, Guined was not far. Her hand was so slight in his own, a fledgling's fragile wing.

Within the hood of her wet cloak, she was beaming. "My lord, you are too good," she said to him.

"Too good for what? For lending you a hand?"

The maid curtsied deeply. "For consenting to take me to wife."

Robbed of speech, Aedan stared at her stupidly, his mouth agape. As soon as his senses returned, he rounded on his brother and barked, "Eogan. A word?"; not as a request, but as a command. Leaping back over the rail onto the dock, Aedan grabbed Eogan by the elbow and dragged him all the way back to the plain until they were well out of earshot of their family and the maid. *"What have you done?"* he hissed.

Eogan wrested back his elbow, but held firm in the face of Aedan's outrage. "Calm yourself! It is awkward, I grant you, and rather complicated. And perhaps unpardonable, to have let Afrella believe that you were privy to the arrangements and had consented to them. But this is a scheme cooked up by Beli."

"Is it, now?" Aedan ground out. *"Beli?* All by himself?"

"He suggested the union. Before I knew what he was truly about, he had her bundled up to come with us to Dal Riata. Once she had joined our company, with such expectations, I could hardly turn her away. She is a young, easily broken, I think. And it is clear that she is fond of you, poor thing."

"Nothing happens to our family without your consent," Aedan snapped. "You had no right!"

"On the contrary. I am your *ri*. I have every right."

It was a mistake. Aedan growled. "Brother, I answered your summons. I came home. I would come *any time* you had need of me. But we are done here. You have what you need from the lords, I take it?"

"Well, yes ... "

"Yes or no?"

"Yes. Yes. We have what we need—"

"Do we? They will help you? What have they agreed to? What are their terms?"

There was a pause during which Eogan rubbed the rain from his face. "Tudwal has agreed to send men if we need them, and Kynfarch too, in exchange for ... "

"And Morcant?"

"No. He would not treat with me."

"Good! Then we are done here. Conall can no longer force your hand at home. He cannot force you to act without drawing in the Britons, who will grossly interfere, I guarantee it, and thwart him, because that is just the sort of thing they like to do most. That is what you needed, what you asked me here to help you achieve. You and Ama and Artur and our mothers—our people—are safe. You have no more need of me. I am going home."

"*Home*? Do you mean *Caledonia*?" Eogan's face twisted with derision. "You prefer the Picts to us? Aedan! Do you hear yourself? What has happened to you? You will return as our *fennid—our* champion. Not the Picts'. *Ours*. How could you think such a thing? Because Conall has always feared you. I don't pretend to understand why, but let us profit from it. He needs to see proof that we are strong, that we have powerful allies who stand behind us now: Strat Clut and Rheged and—" He looked back at the maid clutching the rail of the ship, watching them apprehensively. "And Guined, with this maid Afrella. Think of it! *Guined*! It will give

Conall pause to see how wide a net we have been casting. As far as alliances go, it is an extremely advantageous marriage. I can think of none higher, besides mine to Ama."

An eager light was filling Eogan's face. He grabbed Aedan. "Aedan, we are on the brink of something big! With cunning and a bit of luck—with everyone playing their role and doing their part for the family—we will move up in the world!" Eogan shook him hard. "But first we must forestall the war which Conall seeks to draw down upon us. And you must consent to take the maid to wife."

Eogan's grip was unbearable. Aedan shook him off violently. "*You* wed her," he bit out. "Surely Beli would rather her wed to a king than to me."

Eogan shook his head. "On the contrary: Beli is well-pleased that she wed the son-in-law of the king of the Picts. Bridei greatly outranks me. And as I said, this was his plan, not mine."

"No. You can have no idea, Eogan, but this is a very twisted affair. I don't know what game Beli is playing, but a game there is. And you have been foolish enough to fall into the trap."

"There is no game. Don't you see your commodity? For years now, you are the only one to have gotten close to the Picts and to have come back to tell the tale. Seeing you here, at the Oenach, was a shocking thing for everyone—Beli has only had the uncommon good sense to be the first to seize upon what you can offer. You, alone of men. Guined would like to secure good relations with the Picts. As would we all."

"I will not do it. *You* wed her."

"I cannot," Eogan said, his chin lifting in defiance. "I promised Ama that I would have no other wife."

"*You promised Ama?*" Aedan could not voice the fact that had he been fortunate enough to be Ama's husband he would have made her the same promise; he, too, had never wanted any other wife but her. Instead, he said, "Don't be a fool! What king limits himself to only one wife? Did our father? No! Indeed, had he, I would not now have the uncertain good fortune of having you for my brother—and king! Eogan, this is poorly thought-out: it is poor statesmanship, and you will hurt yourself by it, and our *cenel*. Besides, what of my promise to my own wife, Domelch?"

"Did you make such a promise?" Eogan probed. "Is she to be the only one?"

When Aedan took too long to answer, Eogan said with a hint of triumph, "I thought not. Aedan, your wife is a Pict. A *Pict!* Good Lord!"

"*Good Lord?* What, are you Christian now?"

A shadowy pause, then, "Your contract with her was of a temporary nature. Your duty to her was discharged once your son was born. You are free to leave them".

He would have defended Domelch, were he not so angry—she was the equal, nay the better, of any woman he had ever met, save Ama. "A minute ago, you courted my relationship with my wife's father Bridei. Now my Pictish relations disgust you?"

Eogan only harrumphed.

"I did not want to leave them. I only came back because *you* asked me to," Aedan said. He felt some surprise as he realized that this was true. "I promised her—them—that I would return. They wait for me."

"We have humored you your absence amongst the heathens these past three years ... "

"*Heathens?* You are a 'heathen'. So am I."

"You had no right to make such a promise to her, if indeed you did. Such contracts must be approved by me, and I certainly never approved such a thing," Eogan said. "Aedan. Brother: your duty is to your family."

"They are my family."

"*This* family. Your duty lies with *us*."

"Could you leave Ama? Or Artur?"

"So you do love the Pictess?"

Aedan stared at his brother, taken aback by the bald question. Then he looked away. He could not lie. His son of course he loved, but he did not love Domelch. Not in that way. *It is your wife that I love*, Aedan almost shouted, just to be cruel. But a quick thought for Ama and he did not.

Eogan nodded. "You don't, then. Still, you are loyal to a fault. So bring them here. Bring your wife and child to Dal Riata. We will make them welcome and care for them. I will personally guarantee their safety."

Aedan almost laughed at the absurdity of it. Wasn't his brother's vulnerability the reason they were all in this position to begin with? "Domelch will not leave her people. They groom our son for the kingship."

"Indeed?" Eogan's eyes took on a far-away look as he considered what it would mean to have Aedan's son on the throne of Caledonia. "Wouldn't that be something?" he mused. "Still, this is a problem. Your wife will not leave her family; and you should not leave yours. I can say it no more bluntly, Brother: if you leave us now—if you return to the Picts before this is done—there may be no family for you to return to. Come home with me. At least to Tairbert. Together we can convince the Cenel Oengussa that we are strong enough to stand against Conall. That with our allies we now outnumber him and that he may not act without first securing our consent."

Rain spitting in his face, Aedan glared at Eogan for a very long time. Tairbert was a day's sail. The Cenel Oengussa on their island of Ile, not far hence. What would it add to his journey, to go, speak with them? A week?

He could give them another week. He would do it for Eogan, and for their mothers, and of course for Ama and Artur. He would do it to secure peace for those he loved. And then he would return to Caledonia.

He nodded. Eogan heaved a sigh. "Thank you. And I am sorry. I thought you might welcome all of this."

"Is that so?"

Eogan squeezed the bridge of his nose wearily. "No," he admitted. "To be honest, I suspected you would not. *I* welcomed it." Another heavy sigh, and Eogan looked at him sheepishly. "I hate to be so heavy-handed with you. You, of all people! You know ... you must know that I love you. It has always been you and me, against the world. But I don't know what else to do. You are so strong! Who else do I have? You take everything the world throws at you and make it somehow more beautiful, stronger. Think what you can do! Who you are related to, who you know. Who you *are*."

Aedan had no answer. He had not known that his brother thought of him this way. What could he do, except to help? He turned towards the dock, and Eogan followed.

"Perhaps ... " Eogan added timidly, "perhaps, once we are done with the Cenel Oengussa, you might change your mind and marry the maid? To bring us Guined?"

Aedan spun around, glared at Eogan. "As soon as you are safely home, and Conall is made to understand that he no longer has free rein to terrorize everyone, I am leaving."

"But what am I to do with her? I can't very well send her back now. Beli would never forgive the insult."

"Frankly, I could not care less. You overreached. By your own admission, we had Strat Clut. We had Rheged. They would have been enough. We had no need of Guined, except that it appealed to your vanity to tie yourself to them too. That's fine. You are a king. Do as you wish. Other kings certainly do."

Aedan stomped ahead, his boots squelching in mud, his words thrown as much to the unremitting rain as to his brother. "But to attempt to do it through *me*? That is unforgiveable. The maid is your problem. You solve it. Because I won't."

The silence in which they sailed was so strained it was nearly painful. Columba had never seen Aedan angrier, Eogan more defensive; he had never, in fact, seen the brothers argue. Not once. Ama was watching them both worriedly. The maid Afrella had withdrawn into her cloak at the rear of the ship. There were snuffling sounds emerging from her hood, but no one made any attempt to comfort her.

Aedan and Eogan were ignoring him completely, which gave Columba ample time to order his thoughts. Having retrieved Aedan from Caledonia and hauled him to this parlay with the Britons, Columba had helped to set this particular chain of events in motion. But whether or not any of them were better off for the exercise, he could not say. He doubted that he was. He had made no inroads with the British lords, had rather seemed to earn their enmity and contempt. While it was true that he now had certain allies in Kentigern and even Gildas, it remained unclear how that might help his brothers on Iona. He was not sure that it would, that it could. Both men were near outcasts, such as Columba was himself. They were all still adrift, still at the mercy of brutal, mercurial men.

His brothers. Iona. He longed for them. Their company. The simplicity and familiarity of life on Iona, the order and the ease. How close he was again, at last. After weeks away, he would be home by nightfall three days' hence. Home, to his men, his work, his study, steady prayer; his beautiful island. The life he had come to love.

But, finally, the brothers were speaking again. "Let us regroup at Tairbert," Eogan was saying to a tight-faced Aedan, "and then sail for Ile immediately. We'll meet with Forindan ... "

"Forindan is maimed," Aedan said testily. "Conall took his hand off. How can he still be king?"

"He's not. Not technically. His son Feradach was acclaimed ... "

"The gods help us! *Feradach?*"

Eogan shrugged. "It wasn't up to me. In any case, it hardly matters: the father still makes all the decisions. The son merely carries them out: Feradach's the muscle. It's Forindan we have to convince ... What the hell is *that?*" Eogan gasped, racing for the prow of the ship.

They had rounded a headland which hid a small sea-loch, the eastern approach to the stronghold of Tairbert Boitter, the chief-seat of the Cenel Gabran. The citadel sat on a rocky knoll above the round little loch. Ships which were not the Cenel Gabran's lay at anchor in the harbor—five of them; warships; seven-benchers. A long, snaking line of horses and carts lined the steep path to the stronghold. It was Conall.

They anchored, disembarked, raced to the fort, and were met by two older women at the stronghold's outer gates, Eogan's and Aedan's mothers. The Hibernian, Eogan's mother, was tall and elegant. The Briton, Aedan's, shorter, rounder. Columba could only credit the father, Gabran, for the brothers' dark beauty, the women being as unlike as two with such similar sons could be.

"Are you alright?" Eogan demanded.

They didn't like the sight of Columba, eyed him with suspicion. "Oh. It's alright," Eogan said. "You can speak freely."

Failend, the elegant Hibernian, nodded in apology. "We didn't know; we can't trust the other one."

Luan, grey eyes direct, agreed. "Conall came two days ago, demanding hospitality. He has made free with everything! We tried to stop him ... "

"No! You could not refuse." Eogan looked over the women's shoulders. An air of gloom hung over the Great Hall higher up the hill, eerily quiet. "Where is everyone?"

"We sent the women into the hills. It wasn't safe," Luan scowled.

"Are you both alright?"

"Let him try," Luan said, a hand on the dagger at her belt.

Failend tossed her red hair haughtily. "He is a coward! He threatens from his chair, then demands more wine. I wager his ... *sword* hasn't been ... *raised* in ages."

"What do you mean, 'unwelcome company'? Who is with him?"

"A Hibernian. A Christian—who claims to be a bishop. 'Our' bishop, though I didn't know we had one." Luan looked to Columba. Did he know the answer to this riddle?

189

Unfortunately, he did. *"Budic?"* At Luan's nod, Columba swore under his breath. He had seen neither hide nor tail of Budic since the Great Hall at Dun Ad, Cobthach's murder.

"Did Conall say why he has come?" Eogan demanded.

"He claims it is to verify that you have rendered Dal Riata's tribute to Strat Clut as you were sent to do. But clearly it is to intimidate us."

"We think there may be another reason," Luan added. "He seems to be waiting for something, but we haven't been able to figure out what it is."

Eogan made to push past them, but Failend grabbed his arm. "Be careful, son. He is very moody. Very volatile."

"He starts like an unbroken colt at any sudden noise," Luan said. "He hears insults when none have been spoken—in fact, when no one has been speaking at all."

Eogan shared a grim grin with Aedan. "Don't worry. He's in for a surprise."

They found the king slumped in Eogan's chair before the big fire, sweating, his sumptuous red robes thrown open, his retinue milling around drunk. Servants, only male ones, cowered in the corners. Budic, having taken up position behind the king, gaped when he saw Columba, but quickly masked his surprise. The queen, Eithne, who had been keeping her distance on the far side of the hall, jumped up when the party entered. But it was the sight of Aedan which made her normally cold face come alive, a hand flying to her mouth to cover her gasp.

The look Aedan gave back to her was reserved but not, Columba thought, without some measure of warmth, especially when he laid eyes on young Dunchad. With black hair and eyes, tall for his age and lean, the boy could have been young Artur's brother. But Artur had a sweetness to him. Dunchad, with his pained, pensive expression, looked as if he had eaten something rotten and that that foul taste still lingered in his mouth. The boy was staring right back at Aedan, returned after many years lost, with fascination, perhaps obsession— or could it be *guilt*? Columba was taken aback for a moment, but then realized that of course the boy would be intrigued. Aedan was a rarity. He had lived with the Picts; he had taken one to wife; he had a half-Pictish child: these were surely powerful stimulants for the boy's imagination, in fact apt fodder for anyone's dark dreams. Hadn't Columba himself been kept awake many a night by worry, and also wonder, about how Aedan fared in his life amongst the Picts?

The king's reaction was the most severe. "You!" he cried. "You!"

Eogan made straight for him. "What right have you to invade my hall?" he demanded of Conall.

"You left Dun Ad with a great many of my cattle. I have come to make sure you haven't kept them for yourself."

"Tudwal has them, right and sure. And you know what? When he took them from me, he called you a *toiseach*. That you should have been at the Oenach; not sent me to do your work."

Umbrage crossed Conall's red face. There was a rumble from his men.

"So you can go now."

"I came for my summer food-gift."

"You've already had that."

"I need more." The king waved his drinking horn, the wine slopping out.

"By all accounts, you've taken it. Time to go."

"When I go, you'll go with me. I came to call you to host. We go to war."

Eogan became very still. One of the women—little Afrella, Columba thought—gasped. "Unless you have decided to invade Caledonia while I was away, there is no war, cousin."

"There is, when I make it. And I have a yen to make it against the Cenel Oengussa."

Columba bristled. It was Conall's responsibility to preserve order in time of peace. That was the justice of the ruler. But, as far as Columba had seen, nothing but self-interested destruction emanated from this particular king. He radiated discord. He wrought instability. In fact, the only achievement that had any hope of redeeming what would be the rank memory of Conall once he was dead and gone was this son of his, Dunchad, and, possibly, his wife. An uncharitable thought, Columba admitted. Certainly unchristian. But not untrue.

"Why?" Eogan asked. "On what grounds?"

"They withhold render."

"They withhold render in order to force you to arbitrate."

"I will not submit to arbitration. I have not acted unjustly." Conall's chin lifted dismissively, and he sniffed. "They can carry out their claim against a whipping boy."

"One of yours?"

Conall laughed. "If whipping someone will make them feel better, they can use one of their own boys. But don't be a fool—they won't consent to a stand-in. They plan to distrain my cattle. And I won't have it. They will get what is coming to them and I, for one, look forward to it. They bring this raid upon themselves."

"That is your choice, of course." Eogan paused long enough that the king took notice. Then, "As it is my choice to abstain from this particular raid".

"Your *choice*? To *abstain*? What? You can't abstain ... "

"The Oenach was rather eventful, cousin. You really ought to have attended. You are no longer my only overlord."

"*Your only overlord?*"

"We—that is the Cenel Gabran—also pay tribute to Strat Clut now."

"To *Strat Clut*?"

"And to Rheged too, of course," Eogan said with a brief glance at his wife. "Did I forget to mention Rheged?"

Conall roared, flinging down his drinking horn. He was rising from his chair, sputtering angrily, when Eogan forestalled him with, "And may I introduce you to Afrella?" He pushed the small maid forward to cower before the bellicose king. "Her grandfather is Rhun, the overking of Guined. Her father, Beli. She is to marry into our house. Which gives us Guined too."

"*Guined*?" Conall was shaking in fury. His men were roaring. "You! You!" the king shouted.

"You may wish to rethink your plans, cousin. We will not be waging war with you."

There was a murderous look in the king's eyes. He growled and his men shifted, eyes glinting, but even Columba was shocked when Conall, at last standing, drew his sword and lurched at Eogan. The king was drunk, but was he also mad? Afrella shrieked in fear. But Aedan, drawing his own sword as quick as wind, was between the king and all the other members of his family.

Columba did not know how it might have gone (he had visions of a hall red with blood, his included) if, at just that moment, as if preordained by some god which, because of the way things were to turn out, he doubted was his own, a servant had not run into the hall shouting, "My lord Eogan! My lord! Ships approach! Ships from Hibernia!" to Conall's smile, "Oh, wonderful! Wonderful! Here they are".

You can tell almost everything you need to know about a man by having a look at what rules him, or so Columba often thought. To whom has he pledged his oath? To whom his fealty? And if not to whom, than to what? What faith? What ideology? Or, as is more often the case, we being base, carnal creatures, what passion, what pleasure? And so it was that afternoon, as the Cenel Gabran, and Conall, sorted out for themselves these overriding principles: each one to his own particular ruler. And, as two strange Hibernian lords and their full retinues marched into the hall and took it over as if it were a cowshed and not Eogan's ancestral stronghold, the sorting did not go well. Eogan, shouting, was entirely ignored. Aedan's sword could do nothing against so many men, and he wisely sheathed it, though his hand stayed on its hilt. Columba watched with growing alarm as Budic, hithertofore silent, assumed control of the audience as if he had orchestrated it, which in fact he had.

With a start, Columba realized he knew the shorter of the two Hibernian lords, the one with the blunt, square-rigged features and the pugnacious manner. It was Colman Bec, king of Uisnech; the son of the former *ard-ri* of Hibernia, Dermot mac Cerball, the man who had brought about Columba's exile to Dal Riata.

"And Demman mac Carell," Budic added importantly. Wondrously fair was this second king, with almond-shaped hazel eyes, long lashes, flowing auburn locks and a languid manner. Demman was the king of the Dal Fiatach, *ri Ulaid*. He overruled the province of UIaid in Hibernia. He overruled Conall.

"And Demman's brother and chief advisor, Baetan," Budic said, a hand on the shoulder of the fair king's companion, a man nondescript in all ways in which Demman was outstanding. With thinning hair, watery eyes of such a pale color blue that they were almost white, and pallid, sharp features, Baetan's manner bespoke both cruelty and banked ambition.

"How many men?" asked Conall of the two kings. "How many of the Airgialla have you brought to help me?"

It was Baetan who replied, Columba noted—the fair king's cruel brother, not the king himself. "Forty-two," the advisor said.

Conall whistled happily. It was a heady number. A slow, wicked smile overtook his face as he considered what this new force would mean to his prospects for success against the Cenel Oengussa.

"And I have twenty-eight ... " Colman Bec chimed in. "Sorry! Allow me to rephrase: *I and my personal retinue of twenty-eight seasoned warriors* have come to help you put down your rebellion."

"You have?" Conall asked, wary. He had expected the first, but not the second.

Columba paid very close heed: curt though the question was, it was not a foolish thing to ask. Conall had a right to be chary. He had clearly been expecting help from the Dal Fiatach. But why would the king of a noble, wealthy *tuath* such as Uisnech also seek to join a raid (a *minor* raid, for all Conall's posturing) against the poorest people of a backwater colony on the far side of the sea? Why would Colman come, with his men, unasked?

"Why not come?" Colman replied. "You know that my father was *ard-ri* before the shit who sits on the throne of Temair now—Ainmire." He gave Columba a rancorous glare, looking to say more, to speak of old grievances, but was brought back by Baetan who coughed pointedly. "Right," Colman resumed. "Right. Well, my father's ... *untimely assassination* ... *has caused an* ... *upswell of popular support* ... " He growled in frustration, his words trailing off. "Oh, hang it all! How did you put it, Baetan? How did it go? I don't have your skill with words. They confuse me. I am a man of action." He pounded his chest with a meaty fist. "Let me put it this way. The people love me. So, Ainmire wants me dead. How he tries! But always cowardly-like, behind my back. Won't meet me in a fair fight—not, not him! Not sword-to-sword, man-to-man, king-to-king, to decide it. He's craven. Instead, I keep turning up would-be assassins at my court, eager for the bounty he has promised them. Senses as sharp as a hound, I've got, make no mistake. A couple of the buggers got close, but I am too good to be caught unawares like that. They, not! It was not my head taken, but theirs!" He chortled wolfishly. "Still, why not leave Hibernia for a while? And the other reason is that it would be good practice for my men here. Always keen to find new killing-ground. They have no one to blunt their swords on, and they grow testy. Don't you, boys?" His men grumbled their agreement. "Believe me! Twenty-eight cranky men with no one to beat up is a chancy thing! But to have a *fortuath*, like this Cenel Oengussa you plan to raid? Ah! A beautiful thing! You don't have to check your sword-swing! You can really let go! They can't come back a week later and sue you for damages! Not like your neighbors can. No. And you can have your way with their women, too." His eyes shone. "Just scive 'em and leave 'em. Or take them with you to have again later when

195

there aren't so many other men waiting around for their turn. The men like that. Don't you, boys?" More lurid rumbles. "Who could ask for more? Plus, there is booty to be had in these isles you want raided, right? Oh, I guess that makes three reasons. So I'll take thirty percent. For my twenty-eight men."

Conall considered. "Ten percent."

"Twenty."

"Fifteen. Since he's getting twenty-five." This for Demman.

There were happy grunts and nods back and forth which, Columba noted, the advisor Baetan let continue for just the right amount of time. Then Baetan took over, saying smoothly, "And we've been thinking, my brother and I, that you will need cattle. Provender for the hosting. We have brought quite a few". He hitched his thumb in the direction of the warships in the harbor. "Happy to give them all to you. You'll have plenty. The men will be well fed. It promises to be a most successful raid! One for the songs! It cannot fail! So, just give us your oath ... "

"Oath? Oath? For what?" Conall demanded, asking it of Baetan, the advisor, not of Demman, the king; because the comely king of the Dal Fiatach had already stepped back, deferring to his brother.

Baetan nodded, said importantly, "This concerns the *ard-ri*. This concerns Ainmire".

Conall bristled. "The true *ard-ri* is dead. Dermot mac Cerball—that one's father—is dead," he shot a look at Colman Bec, of some sympathy, "and with him died all the contracts he held with his underkings. Ainmire is a usurper whom I do not recognize. He must renegotiate the terms of my clientship. He summons me to Hibernia to submit, but I am a busy man."

"Aren't we all? And for what it is worth, we agree with you. We, the Dal Fiatach, have also never recognized the overlordship of the Northern Ui Neill. Why would we? We are of ancient stock. The first men of Erainn. As are you. We prevailed over our Hibernian lands long before the Ui Neill were ever misbegotten. Our Ulaid was the most powerful realm in Hibernia. Our stories are the stuff of the sagas. When a countryman of ours, be he king or slave, recounts the sagas by the fire on a winter's night, it is *our* story he tells. Cu Chulainn was our champion. Emain Macha our holiest shrine. Until, that is, Niall Noigallach enslaved us. Invaded our farmlands to gain sword-land for himself. Destroyed Emain Macha. Our citadel, our holiest site, our beloved shrine." Although Baetan's words had turned venomous, they were delivered without any heat, as if he were telling the kind of tale about which he spoke. "The Ui Neill stole our honor. Crushing the Airgialla against us, we had no choice but to hem you, the Dal Riatans, against the unyielding wall of the sea. Where else could you go but to here, to Caledonia? What choice but to take to boat? The division of your kingdom that remains in Hibernia is but a remnant, a distant echo, of your former glory. Your people in Hibernia, the Dal Riatans there, are leaderless, for you, their good and noble king, is here, across the water." Baetan gave Conall a courteous nod. "Who rules from your ancient fortress of Dun Sobairche? A steward. A steward only. We remain, however. With our allies, the Dal nAraide, we fight on. Will we willingly submit to Ainmire? Will we—the protectors of Patrick; the guardians of his great church at Dun da lath glas—ever submit to the Northern Ui Neill? Never! Never!"

"My kingdom too is beyond their orbit," Conall added, in a grandiose tone which mimicked Baetan's.

"Ainmire wants your submission, and he will have it by whatever means."

"How? I am here. He is there."

"Has not his prince come amongst you?"

"Prince?"

"Do you think that that man is here with you by chance?"

Columba felt the eyes of the entire hall turn his way. It was not a welcome sensation.

"Think it through," said Baetan. "Whom has he befriended? Are his friends your friends?" He took in Eogan, Aedan; the king again. "It is very simple: together we can withstand Ainmire.

Together the federation of Ulaid can regain its former preeminence, first in our province of Ulaid, then in Hibernia as a whole."

Baetan was offering Conall the solution he so desperately needed, Columba knew, and the king, no fool, took it. "I like that. I do like that," Conall said.

"Good! Then renew your oath to us for your Hibernian lands and men ... "

"*What?*"

"Renew your oath for your Hibernian lands and men and together will we overthrow Ainmire," Baetan said.

"Your claims of suzerainty over Dal Riata are theoretical only! Whichever the division, here or there!"

Baetan's eyes flashed, but he said mildly, "We, the Dal Fiatach, are the mightiest of the three peoples of the federation of Ulaid. We look after you and we look after the Dal nAraide. We are strong, only together."

"It has been many generations since your people could make good your claims of suzerainty," said Conall. "Once we, the Dal Riata, left Hibernia, there was no king left for you to claim to rule. A steward runs Dun Sobairche for us, as you say. A steward cannot bind the people he serves with his oath."

"You misunderstand me," Baetan soothed Conall. "We do not wish to *rule* you. Have no fear: we have no designs on your lands in Hibernia; or on those here in Caledonia."

"Then why do you need my oath of submission? Since I seek to rid myself of one lord, Ainmire, why would I willingly take on another?"

Carefully now, carefully, Baetan gave the speech which Columba suspected the advisor had rehearsed many times before this meeting, perfecting it, making it unassailable. He said with wonderful simplicity, "You face war here, against your own people. You seek allies. You also hope to find a way to resist Ainmire. Well, here we are. The Airgialla, waiting anxiously on the ships outside, eager to help you, owe us submission. It is to us, the Dal Fiatach, that they owe their military service. We wish to give some of that service to you, to use in quashing your rebellion. Why else are we here? And Colman too. The men of Airgialla, and Colman's men, have boarded their boats and have crossed the sea with us in hopes of raiding. Indeed, they are most eager: chomping at the bit to be at it. But I cannot compel them to take up arms in a hosting for a king with whom they have no formal relationship. I cannot commit them to help you *if there is no relationship between you and me.* They will refuse to do it, and rightly so".

Was he the only one present who noticed that Baetan was no longer troubling to hide himself behind the façade of his brother's office, Columba wondered with awe? *Take care, Demman! There is a serpent in your house! A snake out in plain sight, so often passed safely by that its venom has been forgotten, until the killing strike.*

Baetan's trap was finally drawing in the prey, for Conall's eyes narrowed. "My own private army? Ainmire will not like it."

"Not in the least," Baetan agreed. "So, just give us your oath—a small matter, really, when you consider what you will be gaining; and the oath is theoretical only, as you have said—and this is your son, yes?" He sought out Dunchad, watching the men worriedly. "A fine lad. Not fostered yet? No? Well, of course not—who here is your equal, to raise him for you? No one. No one. You are peerless. Well, we would be honored if you would let us keep him safe for you while you put your affairs in order. We will take the lad under our wing and teach him."

And then Demman, the rightful king of the Dal Fiatach, was there mouthing the proper words and Conall was giving his oath in a rote way. And his submission was given. And Conall was saying to Dunchad, "It is true: it will not be safe for you here at home for a while," and, since the lad had clearly taken offense at the suggestion that he could not look after himself, with a swift change of tactics Conall was amending, "For love of you, I have kept you with me too long. You should have been fostered these past two years, not kept at home like some babe still on the teat of its wet nurse. You are a young

man now—a fine young man; none finer; able, smart and strong—
and you are the son of a king. The Dal Fiatach—noble people, of the
best blood—will teach you everything you need to know to take my
place". And this pleased the lad, but not the queen, Eithne, whose
face had turned quite ashen. And all the while Conall had a dazed
look as if that half-forgotten snake had finally struck.

Conall called for more wine in the hopes that it would steady
his addled nerves. As another amphora of Eogan's dwindling wine
stores was opened and the lords made good their newfound alliance
with hearty toasts, Conall turned his attention back to Eogan. "Let
us make war on the Western World. Glorious war! On Soil. On
Ile. The time is ripe for hosting."

"I will not ... "

Columba had to admire his young friend's courage. Eogan's hall
had been taken over by his enemies. His king had just saddled all
of Dal Riata with yet another unwanted overlord, the price of which
Columba was sure would be the people's to pay. But it was a useless
courage. Slamming his fist against the arm of his chair with so
much force that it was certain to raise a bruise, the king bellowed,
"*Enough of this!*" He made to rise again. He did not succeed. He
settled for propping himself upright in his chair. Out came a finger,
and it jabbed menacingly at Eogan. "Know this, cousin," he said.
"If you fail to muster when we leave for the raid on the morrow—if
you fail to bring your host; and him too, as *fennid*," he glowered at
Aedan, "then I shall forfeit your hostage."

It was then that Columba realized that control of the situation
had slipped from Eogan's grasp—or more to the point, that for all
the young king's care and restraint and strategy, he had never had
control here.

"What hostage?" Eogan asked with bewilderment. "We have
given you no hostage."

Conall said, "Oh, did my message fail to reach you before you
left for the Oenach?" in such a way that Columba knew that no
message had ever been sent.

"You have now," the king added with a mean smile.

The king sought out Ama with malice. He took in Artur with an interest so prurient Columba's stomach turned.

"Lady, make him ready," Conall said. "We take the boy."

Ama raced to their chamber. Eogan was at the window, absent-mindedly rubbing the heavy Pictish armlet now girdling the swell of his bicep. In the late evening light, the thick silver shone. Hearing her enter, Eogan, still transfixed by some troubling internal landscape, said without turning, "Dear God! What has Conall done? He will marry her now, I dare say."

She drew up short. "Who? *Aedan*? The maid?"

"Aye. And he will have to stay. He won't leave us now. It will get very ugly before it is done. He won't leave me here to do it all by myself. It's not his way. It never was. He's always behind you, taking care of things, often even before you've realized you've gotten yourself into a scrape." He rubbed the armlet again, as if it gave him comfort this evening, proof that in the capable presence of his brother he was not alone this time either.

"Husband! He is taking Artur!"

He turned. He looked so weary. "We must take him away," she said when she had his attention, trying to keep the panic from her voice but failing. "I shall take him to Rheged. Kynfarch will keep him safe."

"Ama, we must submit to this," he said.

"Submit? Give him Artur?" The resignation in his eyes filled her with fear.

"At least he'll be fostered with a king."

"He is too young to be fostered!"

"You had thought not to foster him? Ama, my parents did it. So did yours."

"You were miserable at Alt Clut! So was I!" She shook her head to clear it; he was confusing her, the conversation veering to unhelpful places. "I hadn't much thought of it at all yet! *He is three year's old*! But that's beside the point. Conall is using him, to force your hand!"

"Of course he is. And since Conall has played his hand this way, we must play ours in kind."

"Eogan!"

"No! I will speak no more of this. He will have been fostered in due time anyway, perhaps even with Conall. It is sooner than you should have liked, and for that I am sorry. My concern now is how to get our men through the hosting which Conall has demanded of us."

Eogan sighed heavily and turned back to the window, his hand back on the armlet, the light growing dim. "I wish to spare life, but I do not know if I shall be able to do it."

Aedan found her by the outermost curtain-wall of the fort, where the view of the entrance to the sea-loch below was widest, a prospect he usually loved to take in and one he had not had the opportunity to enjoy for some years now. With nightfall on the low hills, and the vessels clanking on the tide, it was a peaceful scene, save for the foreign warriors milling about the ships' decks, their drunken songs and guttural laughter ringing out harshly over the water. As foreboding as it was to have the king's fleet bottling up their own home-port, Aedan felt a far worse chill, almost a premonition. They had been deftly outmaneuvered, back there in the hall. None of this would end well.

Ama was weeping, one arm wrapped around her stomach, the other to her mouth, knuckles smashed against her lips in a vain attempt to stifle her sobs. He stood quietly beside her. He dared not put an arm around her in comfort, though he wanted to.

"Do you think Conall will hurt him?" she asked through tears. "I couldn't bear it! Oh dear gods, if something were to happen to him, if Conall hurts him in any way. I would go mad!"

The anguish in her face haunted him. Because of Gartnait, he knew what it felt like now: the huge, terrible love of a parent for their child. He also knew what he would do to any person who injured Gartnait in any way. An occasion to cause death; no question.

"He is a good boy," she said. "I know you don't know him very well at all yet, but he is a kind soul. He is gentle and trusting. Like sunlight. Perhaps too trusting! I worry for him. He reminds me of you in so many ways; it has been a comfort to me, to see you in him. And Eogan won't help!"

"Ama, I am sorry, this is not what you want to hear: but I don't think Eogan can."

Tears leaked from her eyes. She bit her lip and turned away, her hair-fall shielding her face.

"You need to enlist Eithne's aid," he said.

She shot him a startled look.

"She too is kind, in her way. Kind, at least, to her own son. And with that son now to be taken from her by the Dal Fiatach ... well, perhaps, as his foster-mother, she will grow to love Artur, and to protect him. Yours did you, I think." A nod. Aedan's own foster-mother, the queen of Gododdin had not, being long dead. But this fact he did not add, not knowing if that lady's presence would have mitigated her husband's and son's malice, softened it in any way.

The desolation in Ama's face was slowly being replaced by a sense of hope; he could see it flare in her beautiful brown eyes. He continued: "And you yourself will need to keep to Dun Ad as much as possible. Keep your eye on Artur. Let him know that he is not alone. In the long run, that is all Artur, that any child, really needs. Let him do as much for himself as he can. He is capable. He is strong and smart. But let him also know that you stand behind him, ready to protect him if he cannot protect himself. It will mean everything to him. And it is the least Eogan can do—allow you to be there. That, at least, he will make happen".

"I hate it there," she ground out. "I know that you loved Dun Ad once, loved it when your father ruled from there, those happy days. But with Conall in your father's stead ... " She shuddered. "It is a cold place, entirely without love. Full of shadow."

He nodded. She was correct. He didn't know how to respond; then he did: "You must fill it with love, Ama. Your strength? Marshal it for Artur. Marshal it for yourself."

Aedan looked down upon the Hibernian vessels in the harbor. Tomorrow they were to sail for Soil, then Ile, then the gods alone knew where—Conall had said "The Western World". There were scores of islands they could raid, if Conall so wished. The prospect sickened him.

How he longed simply to leave! Once he was over the border into Caledonia, they would never find him. He need never come back. Dal Riata's woes would be far behind him. He could forget them all; he could forget his own self. But she was crying beside him.

He turned, gazed upon her face, so dear to him, warmed by the flush of the setting sun, its light revealing not more beauty, as it should have done, but the lingering traces of her fear.

"I don't know how else to help," he said. "I could marry her."

"The maid? What? No!"

She grabbed him. Her touch seared him, but he did not pull away. Sad though the occasion was, it felt wonderful.

"You musn't! You will be miserable!"

He shrugged.

"No! I wouldn't ask it of you!"

"I know," he said. "You are the one person who wouldn't."

Aedan slumped against the door to the maid Afrella's bed-chamber. Fingers toying idly with the tie to his trews, his thoughts leagues away, he idled, wasting time. He had to bed the maid tonight to make the contract legal, to put pressure on Conall before they

204

departed by lessening the gross disparity between the number of Conall's forces and their own. The maid seemed eager, relieved in fact to have the deed done at last, but for the life of him he could not muster the stomach for the job.

In the midst of his misery, Ama came upon him. She turned the corner, found him, marched straight to him. "I forbid this!" she hissed angrily, glancing back over her shoulder to make certain they were alone. They were. "You are not doing this! I forbid it!"

Her face was inches from his, torchlight on her skin. Her rich brown eyes, which carried far more sadness than they used to, were furious. Her sumptuous fall of hair swirled angrily about her face. Her generous mouth was pulled back in anger. Her nearness took away his breath.

So much better to see her feeling fierce again, than rent by fear.

"Ama." He said her name sadly.

"Don't you dare do this for me!"

"It's for Artur, too ... "

"Don't you dare! Just—just continue to hate me, as you do! Hate me and go away and go back to them and—"

"I don't hate you!" He grabbed her. He had shouted. Had they been caught out? No. No one came running.

"You do!" she insisted, pulling away but failing to break his hold. "I can feel it! You can't stand to be near me! So, good! Go away! Don't do this!"

"I don't hate you!" he groaned, shaking her. He couldn't bear it that she thought he did. "I don't. If I avoid you ... It's just ... being near you is too hard. It's too hard."

That took the fight right out of her. Her mouth parted in a shocked little *oh*. He couldn't look away from her mouth. His hands were on her wrists so tightly that he could feel her shiver.

Knowing he shouldn't but doing it anyway, he pulled her to him and fit his mouth to hers. He should have kissed her slowly and thoroughly, but he didn't. He was ravenous. So was she. She moaned into his mouth, moving into the embrace of his body,

205

wrapping her arms around his neck, her hands in his hair. He fit her between his thighs where she belonged. The weight, the warmth of her, her curves; her desire and need. By the gods, he craved it.

It took him a moment to realize that she was struggling in his arms, speaking into his mouth. He released her. She pummeled his chest, pushing and pulling him and crying, "Don't do it! Don't do it!"

To shut her up, he pulled her back to him and kissed her again. She gave herself to him, his greedy hands all over her.

He stopped when he realized that she had begun to cry. There were tears on his lips. She was still kissing him, but had collapsed against his chest, no longer struggling.

Her tears. He kissed them from her cheeks, then kissed her forehead, then her mouth one last time. Then he let her go.

The only way he managed it was to think of that embrace. He felt no remorse, either for kissing Ama or for thinking solely of it when he took from Afrella what she was only too eager to give him.

She was dressed head-to-toe in a voluminous white tunic of a scratchy linen which all but obscured her tiny frame. She was even veiled, a Christian custom which made no sense to him lest she was to represent a sacred gift he was about to open, which was not at all how it felt to him at the moment.

Lifting the veil, she stood on tiptoe to kiss him timidly, a little peck. "Do you like that, my lord?" she asked, her eyes demurely downcast.

"Yes," he lied.

She lay down stiffly on the pallet. Closing her eyes, she crossed her arms over her chest. The gods help him, she looked like a corpse. "I am ready, my lord," she said.

He could tell that she meant it. The little thing was quivering. Shutting his mind and his heart, he thought of Ama and did what he had to do, but no more.

· 12 ·
THE WESTERN WORLD

It was mayhem, just as bad as Aedan had feared. The woman was crying, her hysterical screams coming muffled from the other side of the door of the cowshed into which she had been dragged. As Aedan raced to the shed, her scream was cut short. Cursing, he threw open the flimsy wattle door, but was nearly overrun by a frightened heifer which, seeing means of escape, charged past him through the open doorway, lowing with terror. He let the beast lumber pass, the bell around its neck clanking crazily, then stormed inside. Four warriors from the Airgialla loomed over the woman. They were laughing, egging on the man who had positioned himself, trews down around his ankles, between her thighs. One man held down each leg, the abused flesh of her thighs bulging between thick fingers, a third had clamped a dirty hand over her mouth to shut up her wails. Her tunic had been ripped asunder, breasts spilling out. There were reddened semi-circles where she had been bitten there, blood spots oozing from the teeth-pricks. The one at her head grabbed a breast, squeezed as hard as he could. She jerked off the floor in pain, clawing at him, but he got hold of her wrists and yanked her arms over her head. Giggling, he imprisoned her hands between his knees. She continued to struggle but the men simply laughed, their faces stained lasciviously as they watched the man on top pump away furiously, grunting.

They never saw Aedan. They were dead within seconds, all of them. For the briefest of moments he considered sparing their lives, but then that second was gone. He took off the head of the one between her legs with a two-handed swing of his great sword, the severed head falling to be caught in the juncture of her belly and bloody thigh. With the return swing of the blade he felled the two at her sides, his fury propelling it in an easy upward arc through the first one's torso and then the second's neck. When the man at her head reared back with a shout, Aedan's dagger found the sweet spot in the dirty hollow of his throat. The man toppled backwards, his arms thrown out, his mouth a rictus of surprise.

Glee surged through Aedan as he mowed them down: *fortuath* indeed! If they could venture across the water to ravage his people with impunity, then so might he ravage them. Giving no mercy, they deserved none. And he was glad of it.

Yanking the headless corpse from between her legs, Aedan heaved it to the side, freeing her. He grabbed the head by its stringy, filthy beard and flung it against the wall of the shed with all his might. It thudded, blood splattered, it fell to the floor. She drew her legs to her chest and rolled to the side, her face turned away. Pulling a cow blanket from the wall, he covered her. Feeling its weight, she drew it to her chin with shaking fingers, whimpering, but she never looked at him.

Ripping his dagger from the dead warrior's neck, he used the man's own sleeve to wipe it clean of blood, then sheathed it again. With a last cold appraisal of the carnage, Aedan charged from the cowshed, almost directly into his brother's arms.

His glee faded. By the look on Eogan's face when they fell against each other in the crush, by his horror, Aedan knew that there were other women in other sheds and no one to come to the door.

It was pandemonium. With his son Artur firmly in Conall's grasp, Eogan had had no choice but to assemble the Cenel Gabran for Conall's hosting. Their one hope was the sheer size of Conall's army, the daunting numbers. Although Demman mac Carell and his brother Baetan had left at first light, their ship peeling away south as the main fleet held course for the isles to the west, the Airgialla remained, bidden to obey Conall, as did the men of Uisnech under their leader, the dog-like Colman Bec. Conall led so many men that the Cenel Gabran were hardly needed at all, or so they hoped, and Eogan had specifically instructed their men to draw no blood. With luck, they could be present for the raid, as was required, yet take no active part in it.

It was a sound plan, and Aedan was bent on enacting it as best he could. So, when Conall and Colman Bec swept through the first village on the island of Ile, herding up cattle, intimidating the *cenel*, with soft words and raised hands the men of the Cenel Gabran had kept the villagers from intervening. In fairness, the villagers had seemed to need very little encouragement to stand aside: the mood amongst the king's combined forces was decidedly ugly. And the cattle that Conall had demanded in payment for his wounded pride were herded up, and the two kings left the village having harmed no one.

Miraculously, Eogan's strategy worked in the second village too. By the third, Aedan had begun to entertain the hope that the entire raid might pass without bloodshed.

But the third village was the one that surrounded Dun Nosbridge, the hillfort where the *ri* of the Cenel Oengussa resided, their chief citadel. Here, the Cenel Oengussa remembered how their former lord had been maimed by the one who stood before them now, demanding their cattle with impunity. Here, the Cenel

Oengussa had long memories, and pride. Here, the kings' forces met resistance. When Eogan's retinue moved to intervene once again, the villagers pushed them aside. Angry words followed, and jeers, and taunts about Conall's virility. And then a sword was drawn. Aedan sprang to disarm the man, but too late. That was all the provocation Conall's forces needed. They fell on the proud, foolish protestor and, when he resisted, they slew him. He fell to the ground, dead.

In horror, the man's wife began screaming. Others followed. And before either Aedan or Eogan could do anything to arrest it, violence erupted.

Colman Bec's men ransacked the place. Their goal was the cattle, of course, but when the cattle, spooked, stampeded, cutting a swathe of destruction through the village, the men took advantage of the mayhem to make free with the villagers. There was no mistaking it. It shouldn't have been happening—this was a legal dispute, not a war—but it was. Through the crush of crazed bovine flesh, Aedan had spied the woman being dragged, kicking and screaming, into the cowshed by four of Colman's men. It seemed to go on for an eternity. Eogan and Aedan and their men raced about wildly, breaking up fights, arresting rapes, sweeping children from beneath the hoofs of cattle. But the damage was done. When the cattle were finally rounded up and the kings' forces made ready to quit the place, it was to the weeping of the villagers, men and women alike. Aedan would never forget the shock on their faces, the sense of betrayal there, for it flooded his own heart as well. He would never forget the two children, the little boy and the little girl, standing in mute incomprehension over their dead father.

Nor would he forget what Conall had required of him next. Because into the village—finally! Where had he been this whole time?—the young king of the Cenel Oengussa, Feradach, roared. His old father, maimed at the right wrist, sword in his left hand, sprinted strongly alongside. The retinue was too late to protect their people, but not to avenge them, and they fell upon Conall's men with a terrible fury, hacking and screaming their rage.

In the first wave of the assault men fell from both sides and the villagers heartened. But it was quickly clear that Feradach's company was woefully outnumbered and, once Conall's forces regrouped, they were easily surrounded. Feradach was disarmed and thrown to the ground and set upon by Conall's men. Groaning with pain, a pitiable sound, Feradach tried his best to crawl away through the falling blows.

"Stop!" cried the maimed lord Forindan, Feradach's father. "Stop!"

"You raise swords against me!" Conall bellowed. "Traitor! His life is mine to take!"

"It was not he who gave the order, but I," Forindan countered bravely. His son Feradach had got his legs under him. Given distraction, he might in fact get away. So, shoving the stump of his handless arm into Conall's face, Forindan ground the knob, grown over with mottled tissue, against the king's lips. Conall recoiled and slapped the stump away. Momentarily forgotten, Feradach rose to his feet.

"Well then," Conall roared, wiping at his fouled mouth, "*you* die!"

The old man showed only a moment's surprise before his weathered face hardened with acceptance. His son Feradach, hands on knees to gulp in breath, howled in protest.

Spinning around, Conall found Aedan. "You! Get over here!"

Aedan held his ground.

Conall tensed with rage. "Are you *fennid*, or not?"

Everything within Aedan rebelled against his cousin's order, his cousin's rule—his cousin in general; the whole wretched day. "Not, I thought. Isn't he *fennid* now?" From the crowd he picked out his old adversary Murchad.

Murchad stepped forward, but Conall shoved him back. "Is there nothing you honor?" the king roared at Aedan, teeth bared. "Nothing you hold sacred? Not even the life of *his son*?"

Eogan's face blanched. He did not order Aedan to comply; he did not need to. Aedan went to Forindan. On unsteady legs, Feradach rushed at the men who held his father's arms, the one whole, the other not, but was jerked back. A block of wood was kicked forward and set at Forindan's feet. An axe was put into Aedan's hand. He barely registered it, so focused was he on the old man's face, and his cousin's, and the options available to him at that moment, which seemed inadequate at best.

"Take off his head," Conall said when all was made ready.

Aedan palmed the pommel of the axe, but did not take it up. Instead, he offered the king the big axe and said as blandly as he could, "You do it".

Conall hissed.

"They should see the justice of their king," Aedan suggested loudly. Every single aggrieved person there could hear. Old Forindan made a strangled noise. Aedan couldn't determine if it was derision directed at Conall, a plea for mercy directed at himself, or some other thing, some dark and despairing emotion.

"Do it!" Conall bellowed.

Aedan sought out Eogan. His brother was standing stiffly, his gaze flickering over his men, Conall's, Colman Bec's. Their thought was the same. They had been holding themselves back, asking their men only to defend. But what if they were to rise up against Conall here and now, the Cenel Gabran and the Cenel Oengussa together? Could they prevail? Looking over the assembled men, assessing their chance of success, the size of Conall's combined forces, Aedan doubted it. But still he might risk it, if it gave him the opportunity to get to Conall in the ensuing melee, wound him, maim him—perhaps kill him.

But would Eogan risk it? No. A surreptitious shake of his brother's head, regret in his eyes. They would have to wait for a different day.

Forindan saw this, nodded grimly. "Do it," he said to Aedan. "He will have somebody's head today, just for spite. This way it won't be my son's."

Aedan felt a blinding respect for the old man, so proud, so noble. He pulled Forindan close, put his mouth to his ear. "I would help you if I could. How do I help you?"

"Help my son when this is over."

"Are you certain? I don't wish to do this."

Forindan nodded.

Aedan dipped his chin in acquiescence, but this was not what Forindan wanted. "Promise me!" he implored, an old man facing his death. "Swear it! Give me your oath!"

What else could he do? Aedan held the old man's gaze, said, "I swear it".

Calmness descended over Forindan. He straightened his stooped shoulders, glared proudly at Conall, then said to his rapt people, his voice crying out clearly, "Let this king's injustice be known! I curse him! I curse his *cenel* and his reign! Foul king! Wretched reign! Let it be known far and wide what has happened here today! Let the people know! But do not resist him further! Do not attempt to avenge me! You will have your vengeance—" a bold glance at Aedan, then his son, struggling in the arms of the guards, "but not here, not now. Obey Feradach, my good son, your true and rightful lord!"

Forindan sank to his knees in the trampled ground, turning calm eyes up to Aedan and his axe.

"Forgive me," Aedan said.

"I do," the old man replied. "Now do it."

Forindan laid his cheek upon the block, trained his dying sight upon his weeping son. Aedan shuddered. *Pray do not let my last sight be a weeping son!* With one prayer for the old man's noble soul and another for himself, Aedan raised the axe high overhead and with one sure blow took his head off cleanly at the neck.

The old man's blood was still flowing freely when Aedan felt a hard hand on his shoulder, Conall enraged, spinning him around, his dagger at Aedan's throat. "If you ever … If you ever … "

Conall's dagger against his jugular? Perfect. Wonderful. Just the thing. Full of a rage that felt nearly alive, Aedan clenched the axe he still carried, leaned into Conall's dagger. "Ever *what?*" he spat.

"Mock me! Disobey me! In front of the men like that!"

Aedan laughed, his eyes, scathing, on the hand that gripped the dagger. "What will you do? It has been so long, cousin—do you even remember how to use that thing?"

Conall bellowed, pressed hard with the sharp little blade. But it swiped only air—Aedan had already danced away, the axe now up between them. He did not go far: he craved this long-postponed altercation with this hated cousin; wanted another head, this particular red-topped, useless visage, lolling in the mud at his feet. Wanted it with a desperate, vicious longing; Eogan be damned.

Conall, roaring, threw down his dagger and drew his sword, a blade a good deal longer than Aedan's blunt-headed axe. Conall lunged, the sword slashing down across the space where, seconds earlier, Aedan's stomach had been. Aedan, having jerked backwards, blocked the blade with his axe, thrust it downwards, trying to force it from Conall's hand. It was a move that should have disarmed Conall, but Conall held on grimly, staggering to the side.

Against his will, Aedan was impressed. Conall had been a wonderful swordsman as a boy. Strong, quick (though not, to Conall's abiding disgust, as quick as he). But he hadn't seen Conall wield any weapon but a wineglass in a very long time. He had his warband to do the hack work; Aedan, anything close and clinical. Truth was, Aedan had begun to think his cousin incapable of any gross physical action, indeed quite dissolute.

Not so, it seemed. His cousin's thick-set frame hid real strength, real skill. This required more deliberation, more care. With Conall still off-kilter, Aedan charged, axe up, targeting Conall's foolishly unhelmeted head. He wanted that head off. Now. Conall spun around, righting himself in time, his reactions swift again, and met the axe-thrust with sword high in both hands. He held firm against the axe's downward force and vector, grunting, his heels dug in, and pushed back, pushed back, surprising Aedan again, until their faces were inches apart, teeth bared, furious noises, weapons-metal scraping ...

A sound Aedan had no wish to hear: Eogan, frantic. "Aedan! Stop! Stop it!" Aedan ignored him, ignored the flash of glee in Conall's eyes, so close; disengaged from the standoff, whirled, avoiding the tip of Conall's sword which, freed, slashed. Looked for his own opening. Saw it ... Conall not yet fully turned to meet Aedan's next attack. The back of his thigh exposed, just below his costly and expertly-made chain-mail tunic. The axe would imbed deeply there, beautifully, mortally; Aedan would ensure it. He could take the leg near clean off, just above the knee. That's the beauty of the axe.

Lust for his cousin's much-desired death coursing through him, Aedan's smooth, unerring swing ...

"Aedan!" Eogan again.

Damn that irritating shouting! Damn it to hell!

"Artur! Remember Artur!"

Artur! The boy's face a clear, clean image in Aedan's inflamed mind. The face of his own son? His dark, thoughtful eyes. Then Ama's maternal fear, an emotion which was visceral for Aedan, since he loved her so.

Unwanted obligations, with the king within reach. But true ones. Just in time Aedan altered the course of his swing, the axe-head jumping along the stony ground and grinding to a halt, he heaving in frustration and anger—but not before he saw the comprehension in Conall's eyes: *Aedan fears that I will hurt the boy! And now that I know how much he fears it, I will! I will!*

The crowd was roaring. "Do you give?" Conall demanded, out of breath and pacing, sword menacing.

"I do. Today," Aedan ground out. "But I am done being your *fennid*." Another roar of the crowd: what breathtaking insolence! "If Murchad's no good, find another ... " He nearly said, *Whore*. Didn't. "Man."

"There is no other!" Conall bellowed. "There will not be another until your blood runs out in service to me! *Me!* You are not released! Do you hear me? I will never release you! You will do as you are told! You are nothing! Nothing!"

At the moment, Aedan had to agree.

Afterwards, though Eogan's men looked to Eogan for guidance and, it is possible, comfort or reassurance, Eogan did not speak. As they sat morosely around the campfires they had raised on the beach, the warships riding uneasily at anchor on an unsettled swell, dark clouds flitting over the moon's pockmarked face, Eogan said not a word to anyone, not even to Aedan. Conall's forces celebrated riotously some distance away, victory songs bellowing from drunken throats as they danced madly in the moonlight. The reived cattle, an immense herd thirty-strong, was settling down for the night in the grass of the *machair*. Tomorrow the beasts would be loaded onto the ships to be taken hence, some to Dun Ad, some across the waves to Hibernia, payment for Conall's unholy pact with his new, avid overlords. From the village on the hill which also bore aloft the fort of Dun Nosbridge, smoke rose bleakly into the sky. There, no one was singing.

A panicked cry broke Aedan from his sad reverie. "They're dirty! Dirty!" A young man was stumbling about on the far side of the fire, staring at his hands, stained dark with dried blood. Hysteria pitched the lad's voice too high. It was Fraich, the son of Nad, once master of the isle of Hinba, but now dead at the hands of the Picts and the rest of his family enslaved. The young man had begun the day so eagerly, ferociously delighted to have finally been called up to Eogan's elite company of warriors, a worthy outlet for his grief. His stolen mother and siblings had not been among those Scots reclaimed from the Picts by Aedan and Columba. What a heartbreaking thing that had been to witness: Fraich coming running upon seeing the freed slaves, frantically calling "Ma!

Duinsech!", searching the faces for ones known to him. And then, hopes dashed, his dead whisper: "They're not here. They're not here".

It was Fraich now. "It won't come off! I can't get it off!" he wailed, looking around wildly, firelight glinting in his wide, blank eyes.

Eogan should respond. The lad needed guidance—hell, all of the men did. But Eogan only spared the mad figure a shuttered glance before he returned to his private ruminations.

Aedan went to Fraich, gripped him by a thin shoulder and turned him around. "It will, lad," he said, suffusing his words with a confidence he did not feel: the others were watching. "It will."

Fraich stared at him, his shallow breath coming in pants, hands still flailing. But as Aedan held his gaze, the panic slowly began to seep from his face, to be replaced by a blank acceptance from which comprehension still seemed absent.

"Here, I will help you." Aedan drew Fraich to the sea's edge and pulled his hands down into the surf to wash off the blood. He took his time, scrubbing the backs of Fraich's hands with coarse granules of heavy, wet sand, then turning them over and treating his palms to the same rough ablutions. He scrubbed them almost raw knowing that the pain would help to break the hold the lad's tortured recollections had on his ravaged mind. And, indeed, Fraich grew increasingly more calm until Aedan judged that he had returned to himself sufficiently to be released.

"See?" Aedan said, rising from his haunches. "Clean again. Now, come and drink."

Fraich followed him dutifully to the fire where one of the older, more grizzled men, a veteran of many raids, wordlessly handed him a fat wineskin.

Eogan shifted on the log as Aedan joined him. "I don't understand what makes men act so," Eogan at last confided. "I never have. I never will. I hate this game! I hate it. But what choice have we but to play it?"

"You shouldn't have stopped me today. I was well on the way to having his head."

"Yes. And Artur would be dead before we ever returned to Dun Ad."

The purloined cattle lowed. The clouds scuttled, the moon shining out brightly for a moment. The warships' rigging creaked as the ships felt the tide.

"We can play the game," Aedan said so quietly that only his brother could hear him, watching the firelight play across his maddened face. "We can continue to play it. Or we can overthrow him."

A horn blast, once, twice, slightly muffled by the thick-set fog settling over Iona. Squinting against the grey glare, Columba peered across the sound in the direction of the horn's call, his heart sinking. There, on the far shore of Meall, clear for a moment through fog, then wreathed again, were a handful of little figures. They hailed Iona's ferry. Bedraggled, carrying their meager belongings in sacks, their children straggling behind, they were refugees from Conall's continuing raids on the recalcitrant Cenel Oengussa. They sought the haven of Iona, just as the others had; just as others would. And Iona gave sanctuary to all.

In his heart, Columba cursed Bishop Budic, remembering. The day the first refugees had arrived, Budic had also come to Iona, on a warship which was to bear the Dal Fiatach home again. It was the first time Budic had come to the island-monastery he had claimed as his own. Columba had cornered the men on the foreshore. "Do you see what you have done?" he accused, pointing out the makeshift camp sprung up on the near side of the monastery's *vallum*, between that stout earthen rampart and the shore. A handful of inadequate tents, cooking fires, spits of black smoke in the sky, people milling about dispiritedly, an air of despair. "Do you see the price of your avidity?"

Baetan, the cold brother, simply stared at Columba, Columba's personage not meriting direct speech. To Budic, Baetan said: "This is pathetic. You call this a monastery? There's nothing here." Budic made to defend Iona, but, with a snap of his fingers at his retinue, Baeten was already pushing up the beach in the direction of the monastery's high wicker gate. Demman, the comely mac Carell, followed. He had the boy with him—Dunchad, King Conall's son, now the Dal Fiatach's royal hostage, who trotted after the entourage in the manner of a stray dog, hoping to dodge the kicking boot while collecting fallen scraps.

Columba rounded on Budic. "How do you propose we succor these people?"

"If you can't care for them, send them away."

"Where shall they go, if not to here? This is what we do, or have you forgotten? But, tell me: with what, exactly, shall we feed them?"

"If you think to make free with Iona's provisions, you are mistaken. They are not your foodstores now, but mine. And I do not authorize it."

"Good!" Columba yelled. "The blessed day has finally come! You staying here, on Iona! Shouldering your responsibilities! I am glad! Indeed, grateful! We could use the help of *the bishop of Dal Riata*."

Budic laughed. "Indeed not! Once our inventory is complete, I go to Dun Echdach to serve in that household."

"Demman's household? Ah, yes! Of course! Conall is a great king"—a derisive snort—"but Demman mac Carell of the Dal Fiatach is greater! And you chase after power like a hog to slop."

"How little you know, Columba. How little you see. I have been asked to supervise the education of the boy Dunchad in his fosterage. For the son of a king, only a bishop will do. Baeten insisted that it be me." Budic's chest swelled.

"Baetan? Not Demman?"

"Indeed, it was not Demman who courted me, but Baetan! Baetan! What a lord! He is a thing I despaired of ever finding.

And yet! And yet! Here, I have stumbled upon it—a treasure beyond compare: a worthy ally, a man equal to my own talents!"

His hand sweeping across the destitute Cenel Oengussa, Columba said, "This is worthy of your talents. Your ability to manage people, high lords, to help those in need. The boy I knew long ago, my old friend, would have helped, would not now turn his back".

Budic's eyes narrowed. "You lie to achieve your own ends. You never considered me a friend."

"Yes! We were comrades, you and I. Friends. To the end. I did consider you my friend. Indeed, I still could." Columba held out his hand in peace.

An ugly look took over Budic's face. It was not an expression Columba recalled ever having seen there, and its purity and intensity shook him to the core. Hatred, very bitter, very dark. And yet somehow also full of pain. "No! Not to the end!" Budic whispered. "You see? You misremember; I knew you would not remember it correctly. Why would you? In fact, you lie. You never cared for me. We were not friends—not then, not now. My love for you was grossly misplaced. You are evil; black as they come. But now you are mine."

"Mine?"

"Mine to save—mine to destroy." And Budic turned dismissively on his heel and strode up the beach, leaving Columba speechless, sad, and terribly bewildered.

When the Dal Fiatach had emptied Iona of its already meager stores, they left, dragging the petrified boy with them. Columba, who thought it unlikely he would ever warm to Dunchad, nevertheless wanted to steal the boy away, keep him safe from the predations of his new foster family.

And now more refugees today. When would it end?

Columba directed his men to meet the oncoming ferry then, his thoughts in turmoil, made his way to the *magna domus*. His cousin Baithene was inside, scurrying about the large roughly-hewn table which served as many things, at that moment their writing desk.

The prior, who liked to keep busy, especially when his mind fretted over worrisome things, was tidying up. He acknowledged Columba with a nod and then resumed his work, his hands flying over the items scattered across the table's surface, left in confusion when Columba heard the horn's call: cartilaginous quill-tips placed back in their clay pots to dry, feathered edges commingling. Precious vellum rolled up and stored in the tiny compartments of the writing cabinet. Wax tablets wiped smooth of their unschooled scribblings and stacked to the side. Ink pots covered lest the arduously-manufactured ink harden and dry. The book, the precious book, the Gospel, which Columba was having the monks copy as practice, closed reverently with a spoken prayer and put back into the leather satchel which housed it, hung by its long strap on its special peg on the wall.

Baithene's efficient activity helped Columba to order the mayhem of his own thoughts. "Baithene," he asked. "Is the new vellum ready?"

"Yes. It's the last of it though, *Abba*. We'll need to be making more. But where we shall get the calves for it, with so many more mouths to feed now, I hardly know."

Columba sighed. The community's resources, never copious, were now drawn perilously thin. "The solution will present itself in due course, I dare say," he said with little attempt at conviction; he need not dissemble in front of his dear cousin. "In the meantime, can you make note of what I say?"

Taking vellum and quill in hand and dipping the quill in ink, Baithene poised its tip over the roll.

"Not in Latin, though. Do it in Hibernian."

Baithene rasied a thin eyebrow in query.

"I want everyone to be able to understand—everyone: not just us."

As Columba dictated the words savagely, spat out purely from between his clenched jaws, his intention and his thought perfectly formed, needing no revision, Baithene, quill scratching, caught them, nodding as he rendered his abbot's words exactly, quick black ink strokes on the cream-colored calf-skin: "Fect in iardoman la Colman m-becc meic n-Diarmato et Conall meic Comghaill". *A campaign in the Western World was led by Colman Bec, Dermot's son, and Conall, Comgall's son.*

Columba allowed himself a grim smile. He would have his own revenge upon Conall and Colman Bec. The world would know what had happened here, what the two kings had done to his people. It would know, down the ages to the end of man. And it would damn them for it.

The raids of Conall and Colman Bec on the Western World persisted that whole raiding season, and for many seasons thereafter.

·PART THREE·

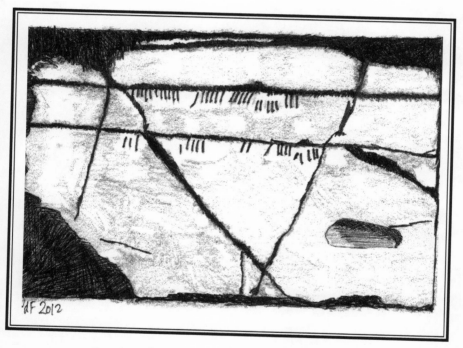

Footprint and ogham inscriptions (Dunadd hillfort, Argyll, Scotland)

· 13 ·
LASREN MAC FERGUS

It was a late March day some years later when the news finally came by way of a fishing vessel from Hibernia, the first of the season to reach Iona. The winter had been interminable; the seas so swelled that passage to or from Iona had been impossible, cutting the island off from the outside world for months on end. In the isolation of those white days, following the comfort of their rituals day in and day out, Columba might pretend that only they twelve, and the little community just outside the gates, existed; that their island was the world. Except that he knew that elsewhere dark things stalked, bringing pain and misery and death, and cut off from them, unable to help or to know, he fretted and worried until the seas allowed mortal interchange once again.

At his desk in the *magna domus*, the vellum-roll containing Iona's burgeoning annals in his hands, Columba's breath smoked in the brisk air; at his orders, young Diarmait had let the peat fire be, and now it dwindled. The men were out working while the day still held. Why waste the turf? There was a sharp light coming in through the open window and a crispness to the air. He breathed deeply, trying to dispel his sense of unease. It would soon snow, if not by the end of the day, then on the morrow. He could smell it. But it would be a half-hearted storming, its hold tenuous, easily shrugged off, the last of the season.

Diarmait would soon sound the bell, summoning the men back in for *sect*. Columba let his eyes roam one last time over the entries he had made to Iona's annal. What had begun with a notice of Conall's and Colman's campaigns in Soil and Ile had, under Baithene's persistent nagging, blossomed into a regular accounting of events both near and far, large and small. He had gone back in time, noting for *Anno Domini* 563 his own sailing to Iona, in the forty-second year of his age. The Great Wind of 567, the year in which his monk Cobthach's murder and Bishop Budic's unforeseen arrival in Dal Riata had propelled Columba north into the Great Glen to bring Aedan back from his captivity. No notes for Pictish raids on Iona or Cendtire in quite some time, *Deo Gratias*!, though some for other places. He and Aedan were being protected, just as King Bridei had promised.

Elsewhere, men were being born and men were dying. In Rheged, Kynfarch the Old was dead. His son, bright Urien, now ruled at Cair Ligualid. And, sad to tell, not four years back, in 570, the repose of Gildas—the British author who had been as perverse in his personal demeanor as he was fierce in his affection for poor, benighted Mungo. Columba had noted his death in his annal far more tersely than Gildas himself might have: *Gildas obiit. Sapientissimus*. The death of Gildas. Wisest of the Britons.

And now, *Anno Domini* 574. With what notation would he fill that empty space?

It had been a tense time, a watchful time. The moment of suspended breath between one strike by a fisted hand and the

226

next. Conall's hostings had continued, stopping only when there was no one left to raid. Next had come a time of waiting and of preparation. But for what? Columba did not know, except that the portents were ominous. There had been the heron which, buffeted by the wind on its long flight from Hibernia, fell from the sky onto the shore. It revived—but only after three days and nights of constant care. And also the dolphins which had beached themselves on the foreshore, though there had been no squall. And, just this morning, the milk pail, left lidded by the door, safe, unaccountably spilt upon his return though no one but he had come in or gone out.

All things linked. All cautioned: *Watch! Attend! Take heed, for soon you must act!*

But how? To do what? He could not discern. He was blind to events in Hibernia. No word for many months now from his cousin Ainmire, the high-king. Little change in Dal Riata, while the raids lasted. Columba had been reduced to marking the hours and the days, to steeling himself, all the while keeping watch for signs that would reveal to him how he might safeguard those he loved, his monks and the desperate Scots—signs of greater specificity that, despite his prayers and attentiveness, had yet to come.

The door opened with a cold creak, breaking him from his reverie. In came Baithene, followed by a young man who peered at Columba from behind Baithene's shoulder, a look of shy awe on his angular face. Something about the young man seemed familiar, a certain air of intellect, but Columba could not place him. He was certainly not a Pict, but neither was he a Scot.

"*Abba*," Baithene said, pushing the young man forward eargerly. "This is Lasren."

Lasren. Lasren. The name rang low bells of recognition in Columba's mind, plaintive echoes of places lost to him; of Hibernia, of home.

"Lasren *mac Fergus*?"

"Aye, my lord," the young man replied.

227

Baithene was beaming, which was a confirmation of sorts. This boy, this Lasren, was Baithene's own nephew, of whom Columba had merely heard rumor and had never met. This was their cousin Fergus's boy. He could now recognize his features in the young man's face: a native intelligence, and the fine, light coloring which bespoke their kin.

His heart suddenly light, Columba rushed to Lasren and gave him the kiss of peace. "Lasren! Lasren! What brings you here? How wonderful! How is your father? Is he well?"

"Aye! He sends his love, my lord, and his high regard."

"Indeed! And how is your mother? And your brother Fiachra?"

"Both well. Both well, my lord. And we have a sister now, too. Lassar is her name."

"Indeed! How wonderful! But why are you here? Have you come alone?"

"He has come as a pilgrim!" Baithene cut in breathlessly. "He wishes to join our community as a novice!"

A *novice*? Columba pulled up short, surprised. A novice? Here on Iona? "You desire to become a monk?"

"I do, *Abba*!" Lasren strained towards Columba in his eagerness. "I do! I have wanted to enter the Life for as long as ... well, for as long as I can remember!"

Baithene was beaming with happiness—too quickly, too presumptively, for Columba's liking. The lad would have to be tested. "You are young, Lasren. Your life may be long; I hope it is. How can you be certain that this is what you desire?"

"I wish to become a monk, my lord. I am certain of it."

"That may be. But I wouldn't advise it. Not for you."

A sour downturn of the lad's mouth. He didn't like that. Good. "You are very well-connected, son. Think of your kin—few are higher. You could do many things, be many things. Things in *Hibernia*. You can be whatever you want to be, have whatever you desire. I could write on your behalf ... "

Lasren was shaking his head vehemently. "No! No, my lord! I have never cared for the things of the world! It is a monk I wish to be."

Columba approved of the firm set of Lasren's chin. It was a good sign. Nevertheless, "Even if we were to take you in, we could change our mind in a year and kick you out again. How would you like that?"

Lasren's brows furrowed. He was unwilling to be thwarted. "Yes! I know! I know! A year of instruction and probation! I don't care! I shall bear it willingly, *Abba*, I promise! Without complaint! I shall! In fact, I shall welcome it! Test me! I am strong, my lord! I will take the monk's vow when winter comes again! I shall prove it to you! You will see!"

You are already being tested, son. "You may—and you may not. The Life may not suit you. Or you, it. You should not be bound to a thing if that tie harms you. You yourself may yet decide that the life of a monk is not your true calling. There are many paths in life that honor God, not just this one."

Finding this particular outcome quite inconceivable, Lasren lifted his chin stubbornly. "You will want me! I promise! You will see!"

Columba smiled, encouraged by the lad's single-minded intention. Hadn't he himself known at an extremely young age how he wished to pass his allotted days, however many they might be? He had known; perhaps Lasren did too.

"I wish you well, lad. And I have the sense that you will indeed succeed in your endeavors. Stay the three days with us. We would be happy of your company, any news you have of home. I shall prepare a letter of introduction for you, for ... Comgall, I think." Columba turned back to the desk, the message already formulated in his mind. "Yes. Comgall of Banchorr. It will be a good fit for you. Comgall's quite rigorous; specializes in the training of missionaries ... "

"No!" Lasren's face had gone quite red. More surprisingly, Baithene was frowning too.

"No *what*, son?" Columba asked carefully.

"No. Not Comgall of Banchorr!"

"Then to Cluan-Erard. My old master Finnian's school." He put some bite in his tone, wanted to see if the lad would budge.

Lasren drew back, pausing. It wasn't long, however, before his chin lifted courageously again. "No! Please! No disrespect to your old master, sir, but not to Cluan-Erard either!" he said. "I wish to be *here*! I wish to be with *you*!"

Columba had to admire the young man's pluck. Still, there were greater considerations. "If loyalty to us, your kin, has made you seek out this place above all others, then it was woefully misplaced," he told him. "Make no mistake: this is a barbarous land. You are far from home, boy. Very far from home. And there are horrors here of which you have never heard."

"No! It isn't loyalty! It is what Gildas said!"

"Gildas? What do you mean?"

"I heard him preach at Magh Bhile! The crowd was enormous but, God forgive me!, I pushed my way forward until I stood at the very front, so close that I could have touched him! I must admit, he was odd, not at all pleasing in his manner, so full of harangue against the Britons, but then as I listened to his words ... exhorting the monks and the people—everyone there, really—to mission! To mission! To bring Christ to the heathens! It moved something in me, something vital. My very heart shifted, fell into place. My friends loved the spectacle of it: Gildas! Preaching! In person! Not through his books! But, for me, it was different. His words stayed with me, long after he had gone. My heart soared as if on a gull's wings across the waves, to this blessed island here, to be with you. It is all I have thought of since, both day and night—for four years now! Four years! You cannot doubt my conviction! Gildas said—nay! He insisted, not once but many times!—that there was naught to be found anywhere in the Western World a more worthy master than you. Indeed, that there may be no worthier master anywhere!"

Columba was so startled that he could not respond. Lasren plowed on, an eager light in his eyes, his voice and manner no longer petulant but brimming with a youthful, passionate zeal. "Word has gone round about what you are doing for the people here, for the Scots. How you care for them in their troubles, how you take them in. And about your wisdom. And your courage! The Picts, my lord! *The Picts*! You are like a warrior of old! And since then, I have thought of nothing else. The desire to join you here on Iona—to be part of your community, to learn from you, to help you in your missionary work, harvesting souls for God, to help the people, here on the world's edge—has consumed me, body and soul. Indeed, I fear my father consented to arrange for my passage here simply to rid our house of my incessant pleading, for no one has been able to sleep with the force of my longing … "

Columba had had no idea that he was garnering such a reputation, that Iona, his Iona … He stared at Baithene, speechless, unable to come to grips with the two halves of himself, the one old, exiled, reviled; the other new. Wasn't he still stained by the sin of Cul Dreimne?

But Lasren's voice had faltered, his face dimming at mention of his father. "Oh," he said, mortified. "I forgot." He dug under his travel cloak, came up with a well-wrapped velum-roll. "I was bid give you this, my lord."

Why was the lad looking at him like that? "By your father?"

"Yes. But I think it was on behalf of Aed."

"Aed?" Baithene cut in sharply. "Not Ainmire?"

Lasren nodded morosely.

Full of foreboding, Columba grabbed the roll. Why not the high-king himself? He recognized the seal stamped into the purple lump of wax which held it shut. It was the seal of the Cenel Conall, Columba's and Baithene's and Lasren's kin, but not of the office of high-king, which Ainmire was.

Columba ripped it open, unrolled it, quickly read the message contained therein. His breath left him. He gazed at the words on the roll for a long time without really seeing them. "What news, *Abba?*" Baithene was demanding. "What news?"

With a crackle, the vellum rerolled in Columba's limp fingers. Through his sorrow, Columba found his voice. "Ainmire is dead. Our cousin, the high-king, is dead."

The grief on Lasren's face confirmed the truth of it. Ainmire, their beloved cousin, high-king for only eight seasons, was gone. Gone. His head taken. His soul fled. This explained Ainmire's silence this past season. Only in death would Ainmire have forsaken him. His cousin had gone beyond the veil and could not pass back through again, even for love of him.

"How so?" Baithene demanded.

"Colman Bec slew him."

"Colman? *Our* Colman? The Butcher of the West?"

Columba closed his eyes in sorrow. It was as accurate an epithet as had ever been bestowed. How well they knew Colman's savage legacy, his penchant for needless violence, here in the Western World. How the Scots had suffered because Conall, their own king, had allied himself with such a reiver. And now this!

"Colman wanted Temair back—his father Dermot's old throne. Colman brought force of arms against Ainmire. He slew him."

"But how?" Baithene demanded. "Ainmire was a mighty lord!"

Indeed, how? "Lasren," Columba asked, "your father doesn't say: how did Colman manage it? Do you know?"

"Father says that Colman grew rich on his spoils from the west."

Under his breath, Baithene cursed. Lasren, realizing what this meant to the two men before him, added, wincing, "Spoils from 'round here, I guess. He was able to hire mercenaries. Many mercenaries. His forces were swollen with them."

"Who rules now?" Baithene demanded.

"It seems that no one does," Columba said, the scroll held out for Baithene to consult for himself. "All is uncertain. Hibernia is headless. Lasren, when was this message written? When did your father write it?"

"A few days ago, my lord. As I prepared to leave."

Baithene shot Columba a heavy, knowing look. Columba nodded. "Yes. Prepare the boat." He had to go to Tairbert immediately. Eogan had to be told that Aed and Colman vied for Temair; that Colman had fled, with Aed in pursuit. The outcome would affect them all. And the king, Conall, must be kept in the dark, were that at all possible.

Baithene turned to go, bustling Lasren out before him, but the young man caught hold of the doorframe and held on stubbornly, his expression plaintive. "What about me, *Abba*?" he asked. "Will you take me in?"

Columba growled. The young man fled. Baithene, however, remained poised in the doorway a moment longer. "Forgive me, *Abba*," he said, "but I think you should take him in."

Columba sighed heavily. "Baithene! Dear cousin! I know what you would say: 'Look what Iona becomes! Our Iona! A beacon for the Life!' And in my proud heart I am ashamed to confess that I concur, that I long to boast from the mountaintops to those who exiled me: 'Look at me! Look at me now!'. But what of Lasren? Can we truly care for him? Keep him safe? What of the men who might come after, if I accept him now? This is a bad place, cousin; a rude, pitiless, hard land. You cannot claim that this is not so."

Baithene nodded sagely, also sighing. "I cannot. Of course I cannot. But, cousin, is Hibernia truly less rude? It seems to me equal in savagery, now, to our Dal Riata. Its civility a memory, false; a memory of ours, we who will always long for home."

Baithene left. His heart heavy with sorrow, Columba made ready to go to Tairbert. Before he departed, however, he returned to the desk one last time. Taking hold of the scroll which held Iona's annals, he dipped his quill in the ink-pot and, with a sigh and a prayer on his lips that the Lord receive the soul of his most beloved, faithfully departed cousin, Ainmire mac Setna, *ri ruirech* of Ulaid, *ard-ri* of Hibernia, he added one more sad note, the latest to an increasingly long line of men and women he had known, now left this earth.

Ainmire mac Setna obiit.

> *Femen, when there was a king, was not a spot that was not brave;*
> *today its color is bright red by the hand of Ainmire mac Setna.*
> *Femen, as long as Ainmire led, nowhere was valor wanted;*
> *today its hue is crimson red, by Ainmire undaunted.*

This is the song they sang of him, in Grianan, his Citadel of the Sun.

Look for me in the spring, Aedan had told Domelch. And he had meant it. Yet many springs had come and gone since uttering those words to her, with him as much a hostage here now, to his family's fate and to Afrella, his very young, very untried wife, as he had ever been then, those years of exile in Caledonia with his Pictish wife and son. As one spring had turned to many, he feared that they were slipping irretrievably into the realm of dream.

He and Domelch had been able to exchange only one message in all that time. It had been in that first spring away from her, when the time had come for him to honor his promise to return to her and Gartnait. Unable to long bear watching a blissful Afrella grow round with their first child, Aedan had taken to pacing the icy fields around Tairbert, roaming out even after the snows had begun to fall and the winds to howl rather than to be holed up in the hillfort with all of them. The thought that Domelch would find him fickle should he not return sickened him. Was he fickle? He could not say. And what of Gartnait? He had made a promise to his son. So when in April the gorse in the fields had begun to yellow with flower and travel north was possible again, he had made what arrangements he could.

Afrella was heartily displeased when he told her that he would be gone for some time. He did not blame her—she was soon due with the child conceived by them on that first night. He knew this because he had not lain with her since. At the news, she had cried rather quietly and then withdrawn into herself, saying nothing and bearing it all with a fallen and disappointed air, an air which he hated. Neither was Eogan pleased, but Aedan did not care. His brother owed him. So Eogan had lent him a small fishing boat.

Since he could not send a messenger via one of their *cenel's* vessels, the ship being unlikely to survive the Pictish pirates, Aedan had to trust his message to a courier. And it had to be conveyed by word since he had never thought to teach the *ogham* to his wife. With few options, he hoped to find a Pict friendly to the Scots who would be willing to travel to the Craig. If there was any such Pict to be found, he reasoned, it would be on the island of Meall. After existing these last years in proximity to the Hibernian community on Iona, the Picts there had learned that, unlike other Scots, these strange, bare-headed, peaceable holy men were not so much enemies as a means by which to make a profitable and stable living.

With Columba accompanying him as his go-between, Aedan went to the village which had grown up near the shore directly opposite Iona's main beach and found its elder. He and his family guarded the boat which Iona kept berthed there, and ferried the very occasional visitor back and forth to the island, or gave them food and shelter when their passage to Iona was delayed by the frequently horrible weather—all for a fee.

But the elder would not consent to undertake such an arduous, uncertain journey, for who would care for his family and his business in his absence? But his oldest son, a lively, adventurous sort ill-suited for quiet village life but very eager to be given excuse to travel to the Craig, fabled court of the king, might, for the right price. And that price was the bull-crested helmet which Drust, son of Bridei, king of the Picts, had given Aedan, for by it Domelch would know that the message truly came from him. Through the merchant's son, Aedan sent his regrets to Domelch. He was unable to come to them any time soon. Would they come to him, in Dal Riata? And then he sailed back to Tairbert where in due course Afrella was delivered of two fine boys, the first of whom, so light was his hair and sweet his disposition, so like his mother, they named Finn; the second, being dark and thoughtful like his father, they named Bran.

Some months later, long after Aedan had given up hope of ever receiving reply, certain that he had been duped by the merchant's son who was now sporting the bull-crested helmet on some fine escapade in Caledonia, the young man abruptly returned. Aedan was in the yard at Tairbert, giving the young men of their *cenel* their daily lesson, the boys hacking one other with wooden swords left and right, when he heard the cry. Finding the Pict lurking in the hinterlands about the fort alone, Eogan's men were bearing him to the hall, trussed up like a captive. Aedan freed him and begged him for news. His face screwed up, his eyes shut tight with the effort to relay faithfully what he had been entrusted to convey, he told Aedan in Caledonian:

Husband:

It gladdens my heart that you still consider me. Though I long for you, I cannot do as you ask. I will not come to Dal Riata, nor can I release Gartnait to you. You would care for him well, I trust, but I am unwilling to be parted from him.

He is a son of whom you would be proud. He has his father's strength and courage and heart. He will be a fine man. We teach him, both our customs and (this I do in secret) yours. In time, he will be a worthy king for both our nations.

There are things of which you must know. My father Bridei fights a war on two horizons: to the north, Uurad, the regulus of Insi Orc, seeks revenge for the sacrifice of his royal hostage brother at the Fortress of the Bulls, the sacred three-fold death which you witnessed. It is said that his heart is broken and nothing but my father's blood will ease it. To the east, Galam Cennalath incites the Miathi against us. For my own reasons, I wish that man dead.

Now is the time for your brother to secure your people's throne; now, while my father looks to his other borders. Once your brother does and you have fulfilled your promise to him, I will look for your shadow to cross the threshold of my door.

Know that my love for you is undimmed, by either time or distance. Or, sad to contemplate, death, should it take us before we meet again in this life. If it does, look for me in the next. I shall look for you.

Until then, be well, and try to be happy. The Gods guide us to the paths we are meant to follow. All we need do is listen, and obey.

With disgust, Drust sends back the helmet.

Your wife.

To ensure the young Pict's safety, Aedan escorted him back to Meall himself, with a costly Dal Riatan blade as thanks and payment for his service. Upon his own return to Tairbert, he went straight to the hall and got drunk, the bull-crested helmet cradled on his knees. Afrella, hearing that his efforts to contact his first wife had been successful, hunted him down, Finn and Bran wailing in the arms of her servant girl, the Hibernian he and Columba had rescued from slavery to Broichan the mage. Covna was her name. Aedan took in Afrella's brittle little form, the condemnation in her eyes, and he could not help but compare her to his wild Pictish wife; and to fiercely loyal Ama, now mostly at Dun Ad with the king's household, to be close to her son. Both women were so protective of the ones they loved—even of him when, try as he might, he still got things wrong. Either of those women would have joined him in his cups, so he held out his drinking horn to Afrella hopefully, motioning for her to join him.

But Afrella was not Domelch, nor was she Ama. Aedan was certain that she had her strengths, but he had yet to discover what they were. She did pray well to her Christian god—he could give her that. And she loved the boys; no question. But her mind? Her heart? Her capacity to imagine another's situation, any save her own? Her imagination in general? Sadly, all small. And unlikely to be increasing.

Afrella had recoiled in disgust and wounded pride, stomping away in a huff, complaining bitterly to Covna as she went, the wails of his sons trailing away. That night, he preferred the hard floor of the hall and the company of the men to her chilly chamber.

In the morning, Afrella came to him again, her skin mottled from crying, her tone strident, saying in front of all the men: "You are not welcome back to my chamber until you make amends". The men sat forward, taking in the exchange wolfishly.

"Amends?" he asked wearily. His head hurt. His heart, worse. "How so, Afrella?"

"I will not share my chamber with another woman! Especially a *Pictess*! I am a princess of *Guined*!" She tossed her head haughtily and stomped her little foot.

The men waited to see his response. He sighed, rubbed the tight knot of tension between his eyes. These matters were so simple for her, so absolute; the causes as easily comprehended as they were to be resolved. Would they were for him!

"I see no Picts here, wife," he finally replied.

All this time later, he had not yet been invited back to her bed, which suited him. It was not a place he had any care to be.

· 14 ·
TAIRBERT BOITTER

Aedan looked up the hill to the hall. A figure descended the winding path, but quick scrutiny told him it was not the one he had hoped to see. It was his mother, who worked her way around the laboring young men until she was at his side.

"Will he come out today?" he asked her.

"No," Luan said.

Aedan let out a deep, frustrated breath. "He should be out here, not holed up inside. It's not good for him and, besides, what do I tell them? He's their *ri*. He ought to start acting like one."

"You are right, of course. I will speak with him again tomorrow."

"Did you ask Failend? What did she say?"

"He won't speak with her about it. To be honest, he is in such a state that I doubt he would even confide in Ama. Only the company of the monk seems to divert him. Thank goodness he has consented to stay for awhile. Thank you for asking him. He is a good friend to you. But the news ... "

It was true. Eogan's weariness, ever-present since the carnage at Dun Nosbridge, had steadily worsened into a kind of despair Aedan did not know how to repair. While Columba's presence at first seemed to cheer Eogan, the news he bore of the high-king's passing had only made him worse.

"She would know how to get it out of him," he said.

"She might, but she's not here, is she?"

He looked over the young men. His own boys, Finn and Bran, almost six now, gleefully whacked each other with the swords and shields he had carved for them, small-scale but precisely fashioned.

"Son?"

"Hmm?"

"Afrella has sent me to beg you—yet again—to cease their training."

"*Mother* ... "

"I know! For what it is worth, I agree with you. But let me beseech you in an official capacity so that I can assure her that I have done as she has asked."

"Alright, if you must. Beseech me."

"Son: please cease this."

"No."

"Will you reconsider?"

"No."

"Then I shall inform her—yet again—that you refuse."

There was some disgust in his mother's eyes, which he had no doubt he deserved. He searched for an explanation. "She sees them as babes still, but they can hold a sword, a shield. Believe me, they seek them out on their own—go after each other with whatever will suit for weapon-play the minute my back is turned. Best get it right, make use of their own inherent interest, because the sooner they can defend themselves the safer they will be."

"I agree and I will try, yet again, to explain that to her. She won't listen, though, despite the merits of your reasoning. Nothing you do pleases her."

He chose not to answer.

"Why is that?"

He sighed heavily. "Not today, Mother."

"I could help you, if you would let me. It would also help if you were to ... treat her as a wife again."

He studied his sword stonily. Some moments passed awkwardly as they watched the boys fight. With a quick jab of his wrist, Finn swiped around Bran's shield and smacked his twin lightly on the ear with the flat of his sword. Startled at what he had done and not quite sure that he liked hurting his brother, Finn stood there, mouth agape. Bran gasped and grabbed his ear, but instead of retaliating he merely grinned good-naturedly.

"Shield up, Bran!" Aedan called. "Especially *after* you've been hit. Finn—don't hesitate! You could have had him there if you had struck a second time!"

"See?" Aedan said to his mother. "Finn is quick. And smart. That is his strength. Bran is strong. Nothing frightens him. He shrugs off injury as if not even feeling it."

"Good. I trust that you will teach them everything you know. I will not sleep soundly again until you assure me that they have surpassed you in skill."

"Nor will I."

"In the meantime, have you given any thought to baptizing them for Christ, as she has asked?"

Aedan turned disbelieving eyes on her. "Yet another thing she has sent you to beg of me?"

"Well, with the monk here, the opportunity does present itself."

"If she still desires such a thing, she can bloody well get down here and ask me herself!"

"Little good it would do her. Be honest, Aedan: you are always so curt with her, closed up tight as a tomb. It is like beseeching a stone for water."

"Mother, she lacks for nothing. In our household, she is accorded the honor she deserves. I willingly consider everything she has to say. I do my best to honor her wishes, when I can."

"I know. It is not that you are ... unreceptive. Or even ungenerous. It is that you are ... not giving of your own affections—save with your boys. They can do no wrong. She, little right. That has got to rankle. She is a good enough girl—not terribly smart, but certainly kind-hearted. And a very loving mother ... "

"Yes. She is. I have always said so."

"Then why can you not love her?"

Yet another thing he would not answer. The silence dragged.

"So will you?"

"What?"

"Give the boys to Christ."

"I fail to see the point."

"It is her faith, son."

"It is not mine."

"The boys are only half yours, Aedan," she gently chided. "Only half yours. Give her that boon, especially as you refuse her this one." A nod at Finn and Bran, hard at their mock-fighting. "Failing to train the boys might hurt them. Baptizing them will not. You like to forget, but I too was raised in the Christian faith."

He hadn't forgotten. "Is that reason enough—that it might not hurt? Rather, will it help? Has Christ helped you, Mother?"

There was a long look away, full of memory. "You know that your father never encouraged me to follow my faith. But neither did he forbid me it. To this day, I keep my faith quietly; I pray."

"And this helps you?"

"It does. I would tell you how, and why, but you do not really desire the answer. You would not hear me. Instead, consider this: would I continue, on my own, here in Dal Riata, alone, if it did not help me?"

He looked at her, looked away, was surprised when she said, "But what about you, son? Were the priests so very bad, in Gododdin?"

The priests so very bad? He almost laughed. What a thing to ask! What a thing to try to answer. How is evil defined? How, good? He had had many years to think about it, and the best he had yet to come up with is that the answer had to do with *action*. A man might humor himself that he was beneficent, his thoughts being good, his intentions for others good, but if, when faced with the opportunity to create, to nurture, encourage good, he did not act, then all his posturing amounted to nothing. I stand on the beach, dawn rising on a new moon, low tide, peering into a rock pool. So much life inside, revealed by the retreating water. Gobies, blennies, stickelbacks; beadlet anemones. More. I find it hard to move away, seeing things I rarely see. Like that young shore crab, poking at a winkle.

But there, behind me! There goes the tide! The water is away! So, up the crab climbs, its thought no longer for the winkle but for the safety of the sea; blessed safety! Not far by a man's stride, not far at all, but leagues for such a little creature; a world of shifting sand away.

Quickly! Quickly it goes! Because, above! The sky! Blackened by a swifting body, a gull, keen-eyed, shrieking for the morning feast.

Now, here I am, standing on the beach, my back to the sea, my mind full of admiration for that crab's single-minded intention, its courage, the sun-glint on carapace, how beautiful it is. Indeed, I wish it well: happiness, success. For I am a good man.

It occurs to me that I am also big. So very big. Easy it would be for me to take it in my hands, bear it to safety to the water. I needn't even move very far: just bend down, scoop, careful of the claws, and fling it over my shoulder into the sea.

But what if I do not save that crab? I am standing between it and the sea. What if I kick it away? What does that say of me?

Surely it says that I am evil.

But what if, as that little crab struggles to go around my interfering boot, I do not kick. What if I do not move at all. And the gull finds the sand, lands, sidles up to us. It squints at me, beady black eye, at the little crab, back at me, at the little crab and then, reading my inaction rightly ... scoops up the crab with its sharp beak. Bears it away with great lifting flaps of its wings. Gobbles it up.

Is something different said of me, if I could have scooped it up before the gull swooped, and did not? Am I not as evil a man as the one who kicked?

I am—as far as Aedan was concerned. For him, this was very clear. And the proof had a face, a name, a profession. The priest in Gododdin. King Leudonus's priest. Who, one dimming autumn evening early into Aedan's fosterage, had come upon the training ground, it occupying the long slope between the high citadel and the field where the priest hoped to construct a fine new church once Leudonus found the necessary funds, to find Aedan being beaten by Morcant and some of his familiars—Aedan wasn't certain of the number; they had attacked from behind as he battled imaginary foes in his mind, practicing his sword-swings on the emptied training field. The priest looked. Saw the newly-arrived, strange Scots boy with his wild, dark, bloodied visage, a pagan, curled up in a ball at the boys' feet; heard his cries. The priest also caught the look which Morcant, foot drawn back for the next kick, threw at him: "Don't interfere, old man. How badly do want that new church from Father?"

The priest had turned away. It was true: he hadn't kicked.

But neither had he scooped.

"The priest there was Leudonus's creature," Aedan told his mother. "He did the king's bidding, afraid to lose his favor ... "

"Because he needed the king's favor to survive?"

Aedan gave her a shrug that did not offer absolution. "He was encouraged to overlook the behavior of the king's son. That is something I cannot forgive."

There was another thing. What about Teneu? That damned priest had stood there on the shore, shoulder-to-shoulder with the haughty Leudonus, offering prayers for Teneu's soul as the skin boat she and the babe had been put in was taken out by the tide. Her soul! The girl had been raped—by her brother, her own twin. Had borne a son! She should have been taken in by that priest, gentled, treated with only kindness for the rest of her life. She was one who should have been scooped. And what of the child, bundled up at her breast? Had the priest a thought for that babe's welfare? Had he prayed for Kentigern's soul? If he had, Aedan had not heard it. Rather he had heard prayers for her lost purity. Her *purity*.

Baptism! There was some fundamental unjustness to a god that valued a girl's *purity* over her honor, ripped from her, ripped from her, ripped from her. No. Aedan had no use for such a god. If he needed gods, he would keep the Old Ones, happily, for they would act as he would act. They would hunt down the men who had harmed Teneu and have their revenge in those men's deaths. As Aedan would Morcant, one day. And in the meantime, his boys would be staying well clear of the One God's priests.

"I am sorry for it," his mother said, reading the deep anger, the desolation, in Aedan's face. "I am so sorry, son. Someday ... someday you must tell me what happened to you there. There is such a shadow in you. I would give anything to have it healed."

He nodded, because he loved her, and it was expected of him. Inwardly, however, was the sure thought: *There is one who can heal it. Until then, the shadow stays.*

Distant movement caught Aedan's eye. Someone was coming down the northern track, a lone figure on a horse, riding hard, cloak whipping, dust trailing in a cloud.

His heart skipped a beat and he was already sprinting to intercept the rider, for it was the very woman.

Just then, in the king's hall high on the hill, Columba was saying to Eogan, "You must not blame yourself any longer for it. You must learn to put it behind you. You did what you could".

"*Abba*, those poor people! I shall go to my grave repenting that our *cenel* has had any part in their ravaging. It sickens me, to think of it. I am glad, so very glad, that Conall's claim on my military service is, for the moment, exhausted. Is that cowardly of me to admit? Is it craven of me, that I cannot stomach any more fighting? It is! I know it is!"

How odd that Eogan did not know how extraordinary this confession made him, how unlike most other men Columba had ever met. "On the contrary," Columba told him. "That is the mark of a good man. Besides, you have no choice—at least not any choice with a price you are willing to pay."

"Not good enough a man. And what of my brother?" Eogan's wild eyes wandered in the direction of the hall's door, the sloping path, the trampled field outside where Aedan labored to train the men. "Conall will not release him as *fennid*. He is made to go on every hosting! Every single one of them!" Eogan shuddered. "And my son is made daily to remember that he is Conall's hostage. Not his foster-son, as Conall claims he is. But his hostage. Though Eithne does her best to shelter Artur from the worst of it. Eithne, of all people! Yet another thing that shames me. To be honest, I have never much cared for that woman—she abandoned Aedan for Conall, did you know that? No? Well, it's true. But now I find that I sympathize with her greatly. And I thank her in my heart for the care she gives my son. But even with both she and Ama looking out for Artur, I am afraid for him. Conall is ever more unhinged. It is never far from my thoughts that one misstep of mine could cost Artur his life. And, I assure you! Conall is keeping a very close eye on all that I do!"

"Is this the cause of your ... anxiety? Your concern for your son?"

"Oh, Columba! I am weak! So weak! This morning I could barely rise from my bed for the fear of it. Such dreams I have. Such terrors at night."

"What is it that frightens you?"

"That the fate of my family lies squarely in my hands! That I am not equal to their care. Artur! Ama! What if ... what if they come to harm, because of me?"

"Oh, my friend! My dear friend!"

"I never suspected that loving in such a way could so weaken me. Before I had them, I was fearless. But now! And Aedan! He would go back to Caledonia if he could. But he cannot. And it is my fault. Afrella ... Afrella is my fault. My brother has borne it as well as he can, but neither are happy. I rely on him too heavily."

"Aedan is good at what he does. You need him here. He will not abandon you."

"Yes," said Eogan sadly. "I knew that when I asked him back. But at what price? Aedan will not like the concessions I have made, when he finds out. If there is a God, a One God, as you claim, he will damn me for what I have done. And there is more. You will not think badly of me, I think, *Abba*, if I confide in you. I believe that with you I may lay bare my deepest fears without reproach. The truth is, I don't know what to do. For the first time in my life, I don't know what I should do next."

"Ah! My friend! Here I may help, because I believe you do know. Your anxiety stems not from indecision, but from fear and disgust for the decision which you know you must make."

"What is your meaning?"

"I shall spell it out. Remember the law. The law says: *Injustice, extortion, and kin-slaying are the three things which cause the overthrow of a king*. It is very clear. It is something you can hold fast to. I know Conall to be guilty of at least two of these evils. In fact, all three. He is unjust in his rulings. Look no further than the cause of the poor Cenel Oengussa. He extorts: he holds a child, your child, to task, to force the father to act. Or, in this case, to not act. And he is a kin-slayer. He slew your father—his own uncle."

Eogan growled to be reminded. Columba continued relentlessly—anything to give Eogan something to hold on to, some shining principle, higher than the morass of his emotions, by which he might obtain some clarity. "What is more, he has violated his truth by falsity and violence and overmight. If that is not enough, he is not sound. He does not distinguish fairly between weak and

247

strong. He is not a man of all sides, full of right; he is not a man inquiring after knowledge; he is neither steady nor patient. This is the law. These are the things we require of a king. Conall is none of them. Your course of action is clear."

"But surely you see!" Eogan cried. "To achieve what you suggest, we must engage in the very activity we seek to end: only more war will bring about the cessation of war."

"Yes. I grant you that it is a conundrum. But so are many of the most difficult decisions we face in life. What choice have you?"

"I would not have believed it of you!" Eogan sputtered. "You? The voice of martial aggression? You? A monk!"

"Eogan, you are an intelligent man. Use your head. Think it through. What is our society's principal interest? War. Not peaceful coexistence, not the steady betterment of our material lives, not the easing of others' pain and hardship, but war. Is that not so? Sadly, it is. Were I to ignore that truth, pretend it did not exist, would I be a better monk? Perhaps. But not, I think, a better man. For would ignoring it help our people?"

"*Our* people?"

"Aye! Your people have become my people. The Cenel Gabran is my *cenel* now too. I want the best for them, I share your ambitions for them, my heart breaks for their suffering; I love them, just as you do. This serves both them and my faith. And what they need now is not Conall. Do you understand? *It is not Conall.*"

Eogan's eyes narrowed. "You advocate war."

"Oh, Eogan! You needn't sound so disappointed. I do love that you seek to perfect the arts not of war but of peace. You are a fine man, a fine king. I know of none better. Indeed, speaking like this with you today only reconfirms this for me. But use your head! Not your heart. Your head. Think it through! There is no contradiction here. Over the centuries, our laws have been developed and matured to help stave off wanton violence—to protect a man and his family, as far as is possible; to give them peace in which to live out and enjoy their short time upon this blessed earth. I have lived long enough—I have seen five decades now, don't forget!—to know that the greatest aspiration of most of us is to see our children outlive us; to see them safe, content and happy. I have no children, but I aspire for these things for my men. Is this not your greatest aspiration too?"

Eogan had no need to nod. Of course it was. His concern for Artur's safety was driving his every decision.

"Our laws—our convoluted; bewildering; exasperating laws—work. They work. *Save when there is no justice at the head. Save when the king knows no justice.* If a man must have a master, let it be a better king than Conall. Let it be you. But to return to your point, do I advocate war? Yes. And no. I advocate the removal of your cousin from the throne of Dal Riata. In the achieving of this, I hope that bloodshed can be avoided. But it must be achieved, one way or another."

Columba's impassioned speech broke off, and he fell silent. And Eogan had no answer for him, no more retort, for Columba had found him out: he had not been able to reconcile himself to the course of action he had already concluded was inevitable. "I know what I must do," Eogan finally admitted. "Of course I know it. The trouble is, I am paralyzed with fear. What if I fail?"

"Why would you fail?"

"I failed before."

"What do you mean, you failed before?"

"When you first returned from Caledonia, when you brought me my ... my father's head in its bag. You told me that it was Conall who had betrayed him. I ... I went straight from the hall that night and I rode hard to Dun Ad and I stole in and found Conall just where I knew I would—drunk in the king's chair, men passed out all around him. And I took out my dagger and I was going to kill him right then and there. Just slay him. Slit his stinking throat from ear to ear."

"What happened?"

"It was the chair."

"The chair?"

"The damned chair. Do you know that when my father was slain and Conall took over, he just moved in? Moved right in to the stronghold. He even took over my father's bed. His bed! Can you believe it? Well, all the furnishings, all the tapestries, everything there, they were my father's. And I was looming over Conall in his chair and I realized, that's my father's chair. My father's! And I remembered how he used to sit in it when he was dispensing justice. This ruling to this man. That ruling to that. And always just. Always just. The people loved him for it. They could count on him to be just. And I thought to myself, what you are about to do, Eogan, is not just. It may be warranted, it will certainly be satisfying, but it will not be just. If you are going to do this, it must be in a just way. So I left."

How extraordinary, Columba thought. How different things would be today if Eogan had acted, slit Conall's throat. But that was not a line of questioning which would be fruitful for the matter at hand, so he asked, "How is that a failure?"

"I have not to this day found a just way to do it. My father is not avenged. And my cousin still lives."

"Ah, my friend! You are not alone in this. We are here to help you. I will stay with you, I won't return to Iona, until your mind is settled on the matter."

"Even if it is settled against outright war?" Eogan probed, a sort of panic in his eyes.

"Yes, even so. If that is your decision, I will disagree. You should know that. But I am foremost your friend, even so. I will support whatever decision you make, and work with you to find a solution that is acceptable to you."

Eogan nodded, momentarily mollified. And then a great sigh escaped him. "I envy you Iona, you know. That island is a place of peace. With none of this ... none of this ... " His hands flailed; failed to find the words.

Iona! "Ah, my friend. My dear friend! You are mistaken," Columba said gently. "Peace is not a *place*. It is in the hearts of men. Or it is not."

Aedan seized the sweaty horse's halter, held it steady as Ama swung down, already talking. "Listen!" She grabbed him. "Listen! I have news! Demman mac Carell is dead! Conall received word yesterday!"

That *was* news. Demman mac Carell, the comely king of the Dal Fiatach and *ri Ulaid*—their suzerain—was dead.

This intelligence eclipsed his joy at seeing her. "Who has taken over? His brother?"

"Aye! It was what Baetan has wanted all along, I am sure. I would not be surprised, in fact, if Demman met his death at Baetan's hand. And now Baetan is demanding that Conall come to Dun Echdach to remake his submission for Dal Riata!"

"Conall was an idiot to have made that oath ... "

"Aye! Conall knows it. He tries to save face; is saying that he never had any intention of honoring it, that he won't ... "

"But Baetan is not the sort of man to brook disobedience. Demman did. But Baetan will not ... "

"Yes! Yes! Of course you see! That is why I have come. Baeten has taken Dunchad, has taken over his fosterage. He says that he will take Dunchad's life if Conall does not obey. Conall must come to Hibernia and give his oath before all and render Baetan tribute, straight away. Baetan is even claiming that he has the right to service from Conall's men!"

"Will Conall go, do you think?"

Ama was grinning. She pulled him closer, hands fisted in his cloak. "He already has! That is why I am here! He set sail this morning, his retinue with him! Dun Ad is empty! And will be for some weeks!"

His own grin burst from him. At last!

But first: "And Artur?"

"He left him here! He is at Dun Ad! Eithne has him! He is safe!"

"How? How could he so miscalculate? It's not like him ... "

"It was Eithne! When the summons came, she could not have been happier. She thought to go with him to Dun Echdach, to see Dunchad. Poor soul! So many years without sight of her son. But Conall refused. Said he would not bring her within a hundred leagues of that stronghold, lest she be taken too. Which I understand, but it broke her heart. How she cried! Then, she took her revenge. When the ships were ready ... "

"How many?"

"Ships? Oh yes, I see. Two. Only two. But he took all of his retinue with him. Yes, it is good. Anyway, he was ready to leave and demanded Artur be brought. 'Oh dear!' Eithne said. 'I had no idea you meant *today*. I have sent him into the hills with Diun ... ' You know, the king's chief huntsman. 'They are not due back for a week at least, husband,' she said. 'Not a week. He must be shown where the brown hares box, where they breed, where the badgers prowl in search of mates ... ' Oh, Aedan! It was masterful. She kept talking while the king fumed and stomped, considering whether or not to strike her; didn't. He stormed off, finally. Left. Without Artur."

It was all Aedan could do not to grab hold of Ama and kiss her. This was good. This was very, very good indeed. They were grinning at one another like idiots, very close.

Made aware of the eyes watching them, she remembered herself first. "I must tell Eogan ... "

"Aye!" he said. Too delighted with this new information to care what might be revealed, he took her face in his hands and kissed her soundly on the cheek. He held her face a bit longer than was wise, still grinning at her, then, "Let us go into the hall.

It will do him good to see you, and not just for the news you bear".

"Upon Conall's return, we meet him—with forces. On the moors, after they've disembarked their ships, but before they can attain the fort. Force him to give up rule." Aedan was pacing furiously, his body in agitated motion, his eyes never leaving his brother's.

"Kill him?" Columba asked pointedly.

Aedan quickly shook his head. "No. Banish, I think."

Columba nodded, satisfied. He cast a knowing look at Eogan. "That's just. Just. But banish to where? He can't be let loose in Hibernia—too many potential allies."

"Caledonia. Most definitely. The Picts would give him a momentous welcome."

"Brother, it won't work. We haven't enough men. Against the Cenel Loarn, our *cenel* is equal, at best."

"We'll have enough with the Cenel Oengussa."

Eogan scoffed. "Not by much. They have been so weakened."

"Then we also build up our own numbers. Revisit our men. Recruit every able man and boy. Let us ride for Cendtire, speak with Sillan and the others. Then sail for Ile."

Eogan was frowning. "If only Ainmire hadn't been slain. That was bad luck! He was our best defense, our most powerful ally."

"His son Aed will support us," Columba insisted. "He is my kin too."

"*If* he manages to attain the high-kingship. At the moment, he chases down Colman Bec. You said yourself that they range across the whole countryside, the outcome uncertain. In order for Aed to be of any help to us, he must first win that contest. And then the high-kingship. That could take months ... "

"Or days," Aedan cut it. "But that is precisely the point! These endless power struggles in Hibernia—they work in our favor. The great men are all distracted, hunting down their enemies, taking heads, securing thrones. Aed and Colman vie. Baetan and Conall vie. No one looks to us, here. No one remembered to lock the back door. We are forgotten. Good! Our numbers are not great, it is true, but they don't need to be great; they just need to be enough. We should bring the fight to Conall when he least expects it, when he is the most vulnerable. That's now."

"Brother, let us imagine that we are victorious. What happens after we remove Conall? When Baetan finds out that we have ousted his man Conall from the throne—a man he summons overseas specifically to secure his oath of submission—he will arrive in force. He will destroy us. He will have to. His mutual oath with Conall will demand it."

"I don't care. We must act now, while Conall is away … "

"We need the Britons," Eogan said. "Strat Clut. Rheged. Guined. They promised their aid … "

"Damn the Britons! Have you ever found them to be trustworthy?"

Afrella gasped, affronted. Even Ama looked a trifle shocked.

"We don't need them," Aedan said, unfazed. "I'd rather we do this ourselves."

Eogan waved a conciliatory hand in the women's direction. "We do need them. It is too risky without them. With them, we can both do this thing properly and hold on to the kingship after it has been done."

Aedan growled, paced, turned, paced again, thought furiously, spat out, "Send word to them then, if you think you must. But do it quickly. We haven't much time. A month at best. Conall told Eithne to look for him when the moon turns again. We'll go to Cendtire in the meantime, to Ile … "

But Eogan had vacillated again. "I don't know. Maybe now is not the time. Maybe it is best to wait. There are too many variables. You are ever hasty, Aedan! What if the Cenel Oengussa do not rise up? What if our own men refuse to host? What if the

Britons ... ? What if they withhold their support, refuse to send men until ... until ... " His voice trailed off vaguely.

"Why would they refuse? Until what?"

Eogan would not meet his gaze, looking around the room, drifting over everyone there, said to himself, "It is no matter, for the moment ... Not until we've received word back ... They may not require ... "

"Require *what?*" Aedan demanded.

"Nothing. It's nothing. Have no fear. All is well. All is well. These are simply ... shadows from the past. Shadows from the past. So much time gone. They cannot matter any longer. We are free. We must be free by now. No. I see now that you are probably right. It is a good plan; good enough, in any case. Yes. This is the way forward. Let us proceed with it until we know otherwise."

· 15 ·
ILE

"**N**ow *is* the time!" Eogan cried, face-to-face with Feradach, son of the old, maimed, murdered lord of the Cenel Oengussa, in a secret parley in a sea-cave on the island of Ile in the dead of night; hiding, for they were there to speak of treason.

"Conall is weak. He has never been weaker. Now is the time to move against him!"

The men who had gathered in the cave at the beachfront said nothing, waiting for Feradach to indicate his intent. In their silence the crashing of the waves on the shore was thunderous. Eogan, his sharp, intense features thrown into harsh contrast by the shifting torchlight, pressed on. "Conall has made many unjust decisions against you. You are a noble people. Free clients. You may choose your own masters. You are entitled to leave him without penalty."

"Without penalty? My father's sword-hand was the penalty for resistance! His life, the penalty!" Feradach cried. "Our women's honor—the children they conceived by rape by the foreigners, the strange little ones we now have among us, who we are forced to care for—their honor is the penalty for resistance!"

"Aye," Eogan said with a deep sound of sympathy. "Aye. But it need not be again. We were in no position to help one other then. Now, we are."

"To whom would we go?" Feradach demanded. "To *you*? Would you become our new masters?"

"Not. Not *to* us. *With* us. An alliance between us would be an alliance of equals."

"Such a thing is not possible."

"It is—if we desire it."

"I won't go with you. *He* killed my father."

"Who?" Eogan looked around incredulously, settled on Aedan. "*Him*? You jest. *Him*?"

"The axe was in his hand." Feradach's face was shuttered, vengeful. But Feradach's men did not agree, and the young king let this pass without further objection, saying instead, "Why should we risk Conall's ire? Why should we join ourselves to you?"

"The alliances enjoyed by the Cenel Gabran make our *cenel* strong. They are powerful allies. Mighty. Martial. And if the Britons are not enough, we have the *Picts*."

A gasp at the hated name. "Thanks to *my brother*, here, our old enemies, the Picts, have not raided us, the Cenel Gabran, in a long time. The Cenel Loarn, Conall's people, yes. You, too, I think?"

"Aye," Feradach ground out through clenched teeth.

"Our *cenel's* protection is thanks to him." A proud look at Aedan. Feradach was quiet for a long moment as he considered it. Finally he withdrew into a dark corner with his men. There was disagreement; gesticulations. Very heated words. When he returned, the young king said with great disgust, being forced to speak against his will, "They want to know what *he* advises," directing this statement at Aedan.

The torchlight flickered across the planes of Eogan's face, but Aedan saw no reaction there. This was not a lack of response on

258

his brother's part, Aedan knew. Rather, it was a sign that Eogan was suppressing emotion. Then, to Eogan's credit, he turned his shoulder to Aedan in such a way that plainly indicated that he included—nay, welcomed; even needed—Aedan's participation, refusing to take Feradach's request as a question of his own authority and command, which it clearly had been.

So to the men around him Aedan gave the truth as he saw it. "It is to the advantage of all Conall's clients that an end be put to his rule. His madness will get us all killed. Now *is* the time. Conall has forfeited his right to rule us. He needs to be removed. We deserve a worthier *ruiri.*"

"And once we have 'removed' him, who will be chosen to replace him?"

"I have no idea," Aedan shrugged. "Whomever the *derbfine* chooses. Just as always."

"Will the *rigdomna* include men from our *cenel?*" Feradach's eyes flickered back and forth. "Will it include *me?*"

You are blind to your own faults if you think it should, Aedan thought. He said, "You are eligible, are you not?"

Feradach nodded curtly, his chest lifting proudly. "Are you certain of the numbers?"

"We have increased our own forces, as you know. Our *cenel* has risen up, greater than before. With you, we will outnumber the Cenel Loarn. With the aid promised by the Britons, success is all but guaranteed. What would so many men be against the Cenel Loarn alone?"

Feradach brooded for a moment, looked around at his men, deciding. "If you are certain of what you say, then we shall do it."

Eogan sighed his relief but, before he could speak, was interrupted by Feradach. The petulant king's next words, however, uttered after some sharp jabs to his ribs by his fellows and with an answering glower of his own, took them all by surprise. "But when all is made ready and the battle comes, it must be Aedan who leads us."

And such was the value to the Cenel Gabran of this particular alliance that all Eogan could do was nod his consent.

They boarded the ship as it rode at anchor under a black sky devoid of light.

"It went well," Aedan said to his brother.

"It did."

"Then what ails you?"

"Ails me? Ails me ... " Eogan shifted his shoulders, looked off, looked back; rubbed at the knot of unresolved tension in his neck. "I don't know. My ... my limbs feel heavy. Worse, my heart—it feels lifeless in my chest: sluggish, grey, dull."

Was Eogan overcome by some sort of malady? "Brother, are you well?"

"I am not taken ill, I don't think. I am merely—I don't know, *sad*, I suppose."

"But you've done it. We gather our forces. After all this waiting, everything is in place. It won't be long now."

"Yes, I suppose. And yet, it somehow feels false to me. That I am somehow a fraud."

"A fraud?"

"I am sorry. It is difficult to explain. I hardly know how to put words to it. Have you ever felt, I don't know, *outside* yourself? That as you act, and speak, you are *watching* yourself act and speak?"

"Never." Or rather, Aedan had never felt that way involuntarily. He regularly donned subterfuge when hiding his feelings for Ama in company, for instance, indeed was quite practiced at it, but this was not what he suspected his brother meant.

"There, with the Cenel Oengussa, it was as if there were two of me. The one, cajoling, encouraging, inciting them to war; the other, watching myself persuade, without feeling that conviction myself; hoping, rather, that it would all simply go away."

This Aedan understood: how he too longed for peace. Still, "It won't go away until we make it go away".

"I know. Of course. But how many men will die for it?"

Aedan did not answer. Unless they could force Conall to abdicate without the drawing of swords, men would likely die. How many? He could not predict. But everything comes at a price. Who knew this better than he?

Eogan turned bleak eyes back to the rippling black sea. "I find the thought of the loss of even one man almost exquisitely unbearable."

Once home, Eogan returned to the small shell beach where it had happened. The event he had yet to reveal to anyone. He sat, the shells beneath his feet crunching, looked out over Long Loch Fine; reached for the memory. It had been early in the year, very early, when they were all still holed up in Tairbert Boitter by the blasted winter snow. Unable to bear his own unhappiness, he had been driven to his feet, down the steep slope of the fort, along the frigid shore, to this small shell beach. He remembered that the day had been quite beautiful, the world inviting him to participate in its icy splendor. Snow hummocked on the hillsides and, falling from the sky, met the loch and melted. Everything was glittery with snow, the tree branches were black, the rock was grey, the water grey, but they failed to move him. He could not feel them at all.

Will I be able to do it? Will I be able to do it, if the time ever comes? His fingers had flexed as if in his palm was the hilt of his sword rather than the folds of his cloak. *Even to help alleviate the suffering of others, will I be able to take any more life?*

This was what was unmanning him. He was afraid he could not. Not any longer. But it was the thing he would have to do, if the events he and Aedan were trying to set in motion were ever to come to pass.

I am a coward.

He contemplated the loch, let himself feel its invitation. Let me wade out into its frigid grey grip, he had thought: it will steal away all thought. The water will be kind. Look how peaceful it looks. I will cease to think; cease to feel pain. Ah! Blessed nothingness. Blessed end. Silence. What he would give for a mind without noise.

And he had got up to do it, to go into the water and not come out again.

That was when it happened. Just then, the beach brightened with a warm light, almost as if the snow falling about him had begun to glow. That was strange enough, but then that lightness seemed to enter him, fill him. He felt quite warm. And filled with a kind of sweetness. His stomach had turned over, as if he had just fallen in love. It was a gorgeous feeling. And, more wondrous to tell, he had felt another thing; something which was neither grey nor anxious. It had been so long since he had felt the emotion, it had taken him a minute to name it for what it was. *Hope.*

Startled by the sense of joy that pervaded, both within him and without, he had looked around, certain that in his misery he was no longer alone on the icy beach. That this beautiful emotion had been given to him by some external agency.

"*Christ?*" he had asked the air.

He smiled, remembering it.

On the near horizon, a small ship passed, loch-bound.

The protesting boys had to be bundled up. Aedan was the one to do it. Their mother was having no luck with them. "But in Guined, dragons live in the hills! Real dragons!" he said, hoping this might persuade Finn and Bran to board the waiting ship.

"Not without you though, Da! Why can't you come with us?" Finn asked. "We don't want to go without you!"

"We don't, Da," Bran added, his dark visage stormy and sullen.

"I wish I could come! I do. I've never had a go at a real dragon. A loch-monster, yes. More than once, in fact! You remember how I told you; how I threw the sword right into her enormous black eye ... "

"To save our brother ... "

"Yes. To save your brother Gartnait, who was about to be gobbled up. Now loch-monsters, great big watery beasties, they have them up north. Just the sort of creature the Picts would have. Suits them. But real dragons, with leathery wings, and whippy tails, dragons that breathe fire? Only in Guined, as far as I've heard. Only Guined. What a place, to have its own dragons! I'd love to come! We'd hunt them down ... "

"Just the three of us ... "

"Yes. Just the three of us. And you both in front, to protect me. You would do that for your Da, right? Go in first? You wouldn't mind? No, I didn't think so. You're brave, the both of you. But before I can come, there is work I must do here first—work that only I can do."

Afrella was watching, her little face pinched with strain. "And Rhun!" she said. "Your great-grandfather Rhun. He is the overking of Guined! The overking! Imagine that. And wait until you see his court! There is none finer. There are gardens there, and stone roads. Not like here. He is a great king, a very great king. With his own poets, to sing to you, to sing to you the tales of our heroes, and beautiful ladies, and valiant warriors, and wise judges, and nobles steeds ... "

But the boys' eyes were glazing over.

"Dragons," Aedan said.

"Yes! The dragons. Your father is quite correct. About the dragons. We have so many, they are like crabs on a beach at low tide. One for every boy to vanquish. Maybe more than one each. In fact, there is a red one and a white one living very close by, deep inside the hills, in underwater caves of purest crystal ... "

"Bran!" Finn shouted happily. "We'll need our swords! And our shields!" Then, remembering himself, he looked guiltily at his mother, down at his feet; up at his father for help.

Aedan left this to Afrella. He was relieved and surprised when she nodded stiffly. Off the boys ran.

The minute they were gone, Afrella rounded on him, hissing. But she didn't say what he expected her to say. Didn't question the coming ambush of Conall, why he must send them on to Guined without him. Taking him completely by surprise, she said, "If she stays, I stay".

Ama.

He fumbled for a response, came up with the truth, which seemed somehow inadequate to the purpose. "She goes with us only so far as Dun Ad. To get Artur. Once we have him, she too will set sail, for Rheged ... "

Afrella wasn't convinced. He didn't know what he might have said if Eogan hadn't come up just then. There was a parchment roll in his hand. News. A response, from Strat Clut? But also a resigned, grey cast to Eogan's face, and no words, not for a good long moment while the sea-wind caught his cloak, his long black hair, whipping it around crazily.

"That was quick," Aedan said. "When do they come?"

"I am very sorry, brother," Eogan said, his voice hollow. "Please try to forgive me. Try to understand. It is as I feared. Tudwal will send help, but first ... first you must take twenty-eight of our men and go to Alt Clut."

"*Twenty-eight*? *Me?*"

"That was the oath that I made. Do you remember? At the Oenach. Gwenddolau ap Ceidaw, who styles himself Lord of the North. He feuds with the brothers, Gurci and Peretur ... "

"I know of no such oath. *Me?*"

"Gwenddolau went too far this time. He stole the lark's nest ... "

"They go to war over a *lark's nest?*"

"It's a ruby. A big one. Nested in gold, with precious stones. The Romans' gift to Coel Hen. The symbol of the lordship of Galloway. Tudwal goes to help Gurci and Peretur get it back, but they are short of men. We help him, then he helps us. First Gwenddolau, he says; then Conall. And not the latter before the former."

Eogan was manfully ignoring Aedan's mounting fury, pressing on, desperate to be heard, to be understood; forgiven. "Five-ships' worth, is what Tudwal has pledged when it is done. Seven-benchers. Seventy men. Our twenty-eight is a small price to pay for such decisive aid."

Aedan's anger exploded. "*Me!* Me! Why must you always, always entangle me?"

There was such sadness in Eogan's eyes, such remorse. "They didn't want my help. I offered, but they didn't want it. They wanted yours."

· 16 ·
THE BATTLE OF ARFDYREDD

❧

And that is how Aedan found himself embroiled in an enterprise so foolish, so far removed from the present concerns of the Cenel Gabran, that he was certain it would be remembered as one of the most frivolous battles of all of Britannia. For the battle was fought—or rather, it would be fought, once they managed to track down the man who had precipitated it—because of a lark's nest.

Down the sea-lane they sailed, following the ships of the Britons of Strat Clut, Aedan and his small band of Scots—twenty-eight men, most from Sillan's dun, and those surrounding; and the young man Fraich too. Then around the Rhinns, and thirty-or-so leagues eastward again where landing was made on Galloway's southern coast. On a low promontory on the north side of the sea-firth, at a great boulder higher than the height of one man and wider in girth than three, the *locus Maponi*, where the god Mabon lived, the Divine Youth, the hosts called up by Tudwal met.

With mounting disbelief, Aedan counted up the hosts. Tudwal, king of Strat Clut, and his son Rhydderch, one-hundred-and-forty men. Gurci and Peretur, the aggrieved lords of Galloway, a force of fifty. Rheged, a company of one-hundred-and-forty men, though not under Urien, who was off raiding the Saxons, but under Owain, Urien's son. And, most surprisingly of all, Beli, prince of Guined, attended by all seven of his sons, with fifty. Aedan's twenty-eight. In this way, the force assembled against Gwenddolau ap Ceidaw, dreaded thief of the lark's nest, usurper of Galloway's honor, was a mighty host over four-hundred strong.

Aedan sized this up, tamped down his anger; tracked down Tudwal in his rich tent which had been erected in the shadow of Mabon's great stone. "Gwenddolau," Aedan asked. "How many men?"

"It's unclear. But it can't be more than I brought, or Rheged." Tudwal laughed meanly.

"You said you needed men," Aedan said. "You don't need men."

"I tire of Gwenddolau's warmongering. I want his head, once and for all."

"Cousin, you know how sorely I am needed at home! You don't need us. What are my twenty-eight to your hundreds?"

"You are twenty-nine. Do your job. Do it well and quickly, and you shall have what you need from me."

Moving rapidly up the valley of the river Annan, hills rolling out to either side, their domes covered densely by the forest of Celyddon, the vast woodland haunt of gods and outlaws and madmen and misfits, they marched on the hill-top complex of Burnswark. They had thought to draw out Gwenddolau from his flat-topped ancestral fortress, but no one was home.

The steward was dragged, screaming, from the empty hillfort. "No, my lord! Have mercy, please! He heard of your coming! Of the great force raised against him! He has taken to the wilds! Down, he went! Down to the safety of the Mosses!"

"How many with him?"

"One hundred, my lord!"

"And the lark's nest?" demanded Gurci.

"With him, my lord! He took it with him!"

"Secure the fortress!"

Once this was done and they had reassembled back in a clearing below the walls of Burnswark, Aedan thought it meet to point out to Tudwal that, in the absence of an enemy to fight, he could have no more need of Aedan's services. "Cousin," he said. "Release me."

"Not until I have Gwenddolau's head on a stick," was Tudwal's terse reply.

The trail led south, back to the shores of the firth and then over the only land-route through the Mosses, a bed of peat and mud and merse so extensive that it stretched for leagues and leagues inland, towards Cair Ligualid, Rheged's main fortress. It was a treacherous place, its river channels ever-shifting, its endless mudflats duplicitous and slow.

"Aedan—take your men and track him," Tudwal commanded. "Twenty-nine may succeed where hundreds fail. Meet us at Cair Ligualid. Flush him out to us there." And off went Strat Clut's vast army to Cair Ligualid by way of the sea in a fleet of four-rigged, sea-ready vessels.

The hunt began. But although Aedan and his men searched the peaty desolation for sign of Gwenddolau, it was as if the man had been taken up by the mists. He was nowhere to be found.

Which was fine by Aedan. "This fulfills our oath to Tudwal," he told Sillan and Fraich, knee-deep in muck, befouled by mud, with moods just as black. "Let us do our work nobly, let us do it properly. At Cair Lugualid he will honor his oath to us and we can return home."

When the Scots straggled out of the mud flats three days later, they were feverish, taken by illness and at the mercy of strange visions and dreams; a gift of the Mosses. On a spur commanding the riverine plain of the firth, two rivers running round it and merse encroaching on all sides save south, Aedan saw fair Cair Ligualid, pride of Rheged: ancient *Luguualium*, beloved of Briton; fortified by Roman as the *ciuitas Caruetiorum*; reclaimed by Briton once Rome had gone.

Urien's stronghold was the old Roman fort, stone-built, substantial, and strong. It needed to be. Above Cair Ligualid lay Galloway, with its endless contentions. Below it lay Cumbria; so mountainous, so ungovernable. To its east stubborn Ceredig, a waning, British kingdom, holding on for dear life in the fastnesses of the high fells, resisting Rheged's dominion. To its west, the sea.

Around the Roman fort, enclosed within a strong wall, was the re-grown town, the houses of the Britons running in orderly lines alongside the old Roman roads. Fraich gaped, his youthful mind expanding: "This is the work of giants!" Aedan marveled too. The size of the encircling wall; the orderly homes, neatly stepped, even, perfect; the evidence of civility and pride in the stone fountain—a fountain of stone!—still running a cold flow; the system of drains which serviced it all. And yet, when he looked closely, there were signs of decay creeping in: walls beginning to crumble; roads to be overrun by unchecked vegetation. Moved beyond words by Cair Ligualid's fading grandeur, Aedan had cause to wonder at the vagaries of fortune that had destroyed so capable a civilization as had created this.

An old man found him, limping, bald, sparse. "Please, my lord. I am the *praepositus* ... "

"I'm sorry: the *what*?"

"The *praepositus*, my lord. The steward. 'Tis a noble title, an old title. My father had it, and his father before him, and so on. From the Romans, sir. From the Romans. You are alone, my lord? Alone? No Gwenddolau? Ah! They will not be pleased. No, they won't. Come this way, my lord. Come with me. They feast in the hall. Can't you hear the music? It is the bard Taliesin! Him as my lord stole from Gwallawg of Elmet with the promise of sweet inducements! And his apprentice, the fine Aneirin!"

What a clean, festive sight, all the men in the hall, gaming, drinking, candles flickering; the fine, hearty feast. What music, what song. The women, beautifully attired and fair to behold. And Aedan's men, tired and sore and fed only on what they could catch these past few trying days—a marsh bird or two, the occasional testy eel.

"Gwenddolau is not in the Mosses," Aedan informed his cousin. Tudwal slammed down his fist. "You are certain of this?"

"Check for yourself if you doubt me, and good luck with it. It is a vile place."

"What say you, Owain?" Tudwal asked the bright young man at his side. "These are your father's lands."

"The Mosses are a skulking place, not quick to give up their secrets. Gwenddolau may yet hide there. Yet, I am sure he did his best." Owain's white-blond head nodded in Aedan's direction. "Perhaps Gwenddolau's steward was more loyal that we thought. Perhaps he lied. Perhaps Gwenddolau went east. Yes. He might well hide out on the Wall and we'd be none the wiser for it. He's at Petrianis, if he's anywhere."

"Yes. I see that it is possible he went east. Aedan, take your men and ... "

Behind Aedan, Sillan growled loudly. Aedan agreed. "Cousin— we have fulfilled our pledge. I mean to return home."

"Gwenddolau is not yet dead. You may return home when he is."

"Cousin ... "

"Do you want my five-ships' worth, or not?"

Aedan held silent a long moment, holding in his anger. He swiftly calculated: how much time had elapsed? How much left before Conall returned to Dun Ad? How far the Wall?

He could risk another day, for such a prize as five-ships' worth. "We'll search the fort at first light."

But Tudwal was shaking his head in disagreement. "Plenty of light left. Why wait? You could get a jump on him if you leave now ... "

"Tomorrow. Tonight we rest, we eat, we sleep. We leave at first light."

"No ... "

"Tomorrow."

While the lords feasted in the bright hall, the strains of music and merriment wafting out late into the night, Aedan and his men spent the night in a barn. He would have laughed at the incongruity of it, save that the barn was huge and made of stone and easily more substantial, more impressive, than most of the huts his people called home. They left at first light, riding for the largest of the old Roman forts along the Wall which terminated here on the west. All that day, they searched the empty halls, halls riddled with the ghosts of soldiers long-dead, their voices in tongues strange to Aedan still muttering in the shadows.

Sillan's foul mood was blackening. "No sign of him, my lord," he said. "No sign that he even sheltered here."

"No."

"This is folly, and you know it! We toil while they feast! They take advantage my lord: they are not kind. They have no concern! They treat us no better than their hunting hounds."

Returning to Cair Ligualid, they found Tudwal and the lords merrily at feast. Indeed, had they even left? "No sign of him," Aedan reported.

"Where could he be, that devil?"

"To be honest, I don't care. We are needed at home—you know we are. Every day is precious. Release me. Honor your oath."

"Have you Gwenddolau's head?" was Tudwal's answer.

So they sent him south, into the forest grown up on the clay and peat below Cair Ligualid, a place which would yield no crops. They searched the length and breadth of the forest fruitlessly for sign or sight of Gwenddolau while the lords took to the woods to hunt boar.

In a hall in a fort on a scarp-top which dominated the tree-covered center of the forest, isolated in every conceivable way from any other site domesticated by man, while the bard Taliesin awed the company with songs of precious cups and hawks and horses, Aedan humbled himself before his cousin Tudwal, saying, "Cousin, please! I beg you! This is a lark! I beg of you: release me! My brother ... my people ... "

But by swift messenger on horseback had come the news: "My lords. Gwenddolau has doubled-back northwards again. He has been spotted in the Mosses. His force is gaining in strength and numbers as it moves through the villages set on the mossy eskers".

"With luck you will find him there," Tudwal told Aedan.

"Are we whores? I won't do it." Sillan was spitting with fury. But Fraich was loyal to the last. "I will go with you, my lord."

"I am not your lord," Aedan said. His thoughts were homeward.

"You are. You are."

"Listen, I don't like this at all, but one last drive; one last hunt. Let us find him and be done with this. Let us do this for our people. For our Dal Riata."

He was like one possessed. With a quarry at last to pursue, he did so with a vengeance, driving northwards, back up the Vale, flushing Gwenddolau from the Mosses, the trail clear now, very fresh, back across the firth, and into the low ground north of Cair Ligualid. Back full-circle, back to the forest below Burnswark, the forest of Celyddon, where weeks ago this lark had begun.

To the Scots was given the task of preventing Gwenddolau from regaining Burnswark, his fortress and the base of his strength; and with a ruthless efficiency driven as much by skill as by disgust that his time should have been so wasted by this man's flight and the lords' folly, prevent him Aedan did. At a place called Arfderydd in the Forest of Celyddon, a lovely clearing full of apple trees awoken from their mantle of spring snow, he drove Gwenddolau to ground. At Arfderydd, three long weeks after it was begun, was battle finally met.

Though the poets were later to remember it grandly, it was a pathetic affair. Gwenddolau's forces were so heavily outnumbered that the battle was, in truth, no more than a blood-fray. And after so many weeks on the chase, Tudwal, peevish, was in no mood for mercy. At the base of a hoary apple tree, its branches pink with flower, they cornered Gwenddolau. On his knees and pleading for his life, he offered in trembling hands the lark's nest, red and gold in his white fingers.

"He is submitting, cousin," Aedan said to Tudwal. "And there is the lark's nest. Spare him, and let's go home. Send him to the Saxon front. I am sure Urien could use him. He'll put him right up front. The first to the Saxons. They'll happily take his head for you."

"I think Rhydderch shall have the honor." Tudwal called for his son. The young man stepped forward and, legs planted firmly on the frozen ground, with a mighty swing of his sword severed the lord's head. With athletic grace, Rhydderch caught the falling lark's nest before it hit the ground. Both were acts performed for the benefit of Gwenddolau's men and they had their desired effect: there were precipitous surrenders and the battle was won.

And so off went the company to Cair Lugualid to feast their victory. Into his father's stone-walled hall went Owain. In went Tudwal and Rhydderch and Gurci and Peretur, finally the rightful, the only, lords of Galloway. In went Beli of Guined and his seven sons. In went the bard Taliesin, and his apprentice Aneirin. In went all the mightiest men save Aedan, the servant of lords.

But before he went, Owain said to Aedan, "Prepare your men. For I do wish to honor my father's oath to you. You have served us well. You leave on the tide. I have already sent word for the ships to be made ready. Six ships of the mighty fleet of Rheged!"

With a slap on the back and a grin of relief, Aedan raced to the barracks. "At last! At last! Six ships from Owain! Five from Tudwal! We will be glad we held our course, when we bring this fleet to Conall!" He helped to ready their things, prepared his men for their sea-journey home, his thoughts speeding to Tairbert Boitter. It would be close, he knew. Close. But there should be enough time—just enough time to make it home before Conall did.

In the midst of his musings, the steward of the fort barged into the barracks. He dragged behind him a withered old man, thin, unkempt, disheveled and in chains. "My lord," said the *praepositus*, "this old man was found hiding in the branches of the apple tree. I didn't know but to bring him to you".

The prisoner lifted his head, blew stray strands of stringy white hair from his eyes, and fixed Aedan with a watery glare. He squinted, sniffed, tilted his head to one side, tilted it to the other, then, as if a decision had been made or tidings had been delivered to him by a means no one else there could discern, he squared his shoulders and stood up straight as if before a great lord. "I drank wine out of a white glass," he informed Aedan. "With lords who were mighty in battle. Myrddin my name, son of Morfryn."

At the old man's proud declaration, the *praepositus* let out a low whistle of wonder. "Myrrdin! Now that's an odd name. An old name. The only Myrddin I know of was the Myrddin who was mage to Artur, to Artur Pendragon. Myrddin was the name of his mage. Now, when the Pendragon was slain ... " The *praepositus* spat in disgust, cursing the name of Medraut, Artur's slayer, Artur's very own son. "When the Pendragon was slain, Myrddin, mad with grief, took to the wilds. Could they have meant *our* wilds, the Forest of Celyddon? Why, they might well have! They might well! I'll be damned! Myrddin! The wild man of the forest! Prophet and seer! The very same as knew our Artur! Won't the lords like to hear of this!"

Aedan had no time for this. "He can't be the same Myrddin. The Pendragon has been dead for nearly forty years." Aedan would know: the stories of the warlord's betrayal and death were one of his earliest memories.

"You are quite right there, you are! Not that I give it any credence, mind you, but they do say that the lives of those who practice the unholy arts are unnaturally long." He spat again, crossed himself. "Perhaps here is our proof."

Throughout the exchange, Myrddin was paying no heed to the marveling *praepostius*, staring at Aedan instead. Indeed, his gaze had taken on a fervent glow which Aedan was finding deeply unnerving. Then, the old man began to speak. "Death takes everyone; why does it not claim me?" he asked. "For years I have suffered agony. I do not sleep easily because of the turbulence of pain that is upon me. My color is pale! Pleasure gives me no satisfaction! No maid visits me!"

Without warning, he surged forward until he was a hair's breath from Aedan. He devoured the features of Aedan's face as if searching for a clue to some ancient mystery. Aedan recoiled from the intensity of the old man's gaze. "I saw Gwenddolau, the king of our region, who had been gathering spoils from all borders, put under red earth. The chief Lord of the North is now still," Myrddin whispered, his fetid breath bathing Aedan's face.

With a yank of the chains, the *praepositus* pulled the old man away. "His reason is gone with the wild men of the mountain," he apologized.

Just then, the lords and the bards, jovial from their feast, entered the barracks. At sight of them, Myrddin lurched back towards Aedan, shouting. He clutched Aedan's cloak convulsively. Pointing at Beli of Guined, and then at the youngest of his seven sons, the slight one whom Aedan knew, fair and sweet, the old man whispered in Aedan's ear: "After Beli, his son Iago. Not him, or him, or him, or him, or him, or him. But him: Iago. Remember: *Iago*".

Spying the bard Taliesin at the back of the pack of lords, Myrddin shouted: "Seven-score noble ones will become mad: their lord perished in the forest of Celyddon! *Seven score!*"

Tudwal's head whipped around. "*Seven score?* Who is this man? What does he mean, *seven score?*" He rounded on Owain. "How many have been accounted for?"

"Gwenddolau's men? Perhaps half that number."

Tudwal swore violently. "More must yet hide in the forest. How did we miss them? They can't be left; take the old man, get him to talk. We must root them out. Aedan, ready your men ... "

Aedan's roared his disbelief. His protest was drowned out by Sillan's. Owain's, too. "My lord!" Owain said. "That is unjust. He has fulfilled his oath."

"I will not rest until each man is accounted for. Would you leave them on your border, Owain? I won't. We have put too much effort into this to leave it undone."

Sillan's face was full of cynical hatred. "*You* have put too much effort?"

"Be quiet, Sillan," Aedan growled.

"But, my lord ... "

Aedan pushed Sillan behind him. He squared on Tudwal, said, "No".

Tudwal gaped at him.

"No," Aedan repeated. "We have fulfilled our oath, over and above our due! You have no more need of us. It is two day's sail to Cendtire! We may already be too late! Make good your promise and give me your men!"

Tudwal's ruddy face contorted. "How dare you? Who are you to speak to me this way? To disobey?" He ground his teeth, spat out, "*Fradawg* ... "

Aedan flinched: it meant *The Treacherous*. Or, *The Wily*. No. Worse than that. That Aedan was an oath-breaker.

As Aedan stared down his cousin, he was dimly aware that beside him the old man Myrddin had begun to chant something over and over in his ear in a low, sing-song voice. Aedan shrugged off the irritant, all his will focused on the task of making his cousin see sense.

"A great slaughter of the allies of the sons of Gabran," came the whisper in Aedan's ear.

Tudwal was seething—no one questioned his commands. The men had gathered round, hands on sword-hilts. Aedan squared his shoulders for a fight, shouting, "You've wasted my time! This is frivolous! My people! Dal Riata!"

But Myrddin, bony fingers claw-like in their hold on his cloak, was holding him back. *"A great slaughter of the allies of the sons of Gabran."*

Aedan swatted away the noise with a flick of his hand. But the whispering would not cease, Myrddin's mouth rounding out the words over and over again. *"A great slaughter of the allies of the sons of Gabran."*

At last the words seeped through. "What say you, old man?" Aedan barked.

"A great slaughter of the allies of the sons of Gabran."

"You speak gibberish. You speak of the past," Aedan yelled, seeking to dismiss the seer's words before dread took hold.

"No." There was no madness now in the old man's eyes. They were clear and bright. "I speak of what comes. *What comes.*"

"This battle you speak of is to come?"

"It comes. Bells toll for the dead."

"When?" Aedan shouted. He shook the old man. Mad Myrddin, the Pendragon's mage, all thin skin and bones, was a limp doll in his urgent hands.

Aedan was hurting him. He did not care. *"When?"* he shouted. *"When?"*

"Why ... *now*, my lord," was the answer.

· 17 ·
BELLUM TELOCHO

Eithne carried the burning taper before her, went to his sleeping chamber, and let herself in, closing the partition behind her with care.

Wan moonlight leaked through the chamber's open window. Wind rattled outside. *Open?* Hadn't she herself secured the window cover earlier, before he was to bed? It must have opened before the wind, blustery and angry, though April was almost over. She moved to close it, quietly, lest she wake him. As she passed his sleeping-pallet, she paused to look down upon his dear face, smooth with sleep. She couldn't help herself. Window forgotten, she bent over him, a smile on her lips. But as she reached to stroke the black hair from his face, there was the slightest movement from the shadows.

She was not alone in the chamber. Someone else watched the young man sleep.

Eithne quickly drew her dagger. The intruder, realizing that they had been caught, stepped out of the shadows and into the light, a hand raised to forestall Eithne's warning cry.

It died in her throat. There stood Ama. In her hand was a cloak—Artur's heavy travel cloak—and his clothing and his boots and his sword. She meant to steal him away.

Every muscle in Eithne's body screamed *No!* This she would not allow. Artur was hers, now, in place of her own son, lost to the statecraft of her husband and his foreign king.

But the desperation in Ama's eyes made Eithne pause just long enough, and she understood. *Yes.* While there was still time, while there was still the illusion of safety. *She should take him. They should leave here. Now.*

Stepping back from Artur's sleeping pallet, Eithne whispered, "You could have asked me".

The shock and relief and gratitude which flooded Ama's eyes struck Eithne to the heart.

Ama woke her son with a hand over his mouth to prevent his crying out. Artur shot up; saw his mother; smiled in surprised welcome. Then the young man saw Eithne and stiffened in confusion. Eithne raised a finger to her lips, bidding him to be silent. Artur looked to his mother for clarification. When she handed him his cloak and craned her neck towards the open window—the means of her entry and, soon, their escape—he nodded in quick comprehension. He threw on the cloak, his boots. He cinched his sword-belt around his slender waist.

But when Ama moved towards the window, Artur hesitated. He came to Eithne. He tenderly kissed her cheek in farewell. Awkwardly, she returned the gesture.

As they clambered out the window and Ama led Artur away into the darkness, Eithne was pressing a palm against her mouth to stifle her sobs.

They picked their way carefully over the causeways through the marsh, using no torches to light their way. Rather, a gaunt marsh-dweller had consented to guide them, loyal as he was to the old king Gabran. He had night-eyes; he knew the bog; he led them rightly over the secret ways through the icy mire. And so they blended into the darkness, mother and son, no more than night-shadows moving slowly through the blighted moor. But not southwards, towards the pass that lay between the hills, towards home, where anyone in pursuit would expect them to go. They went out towards the sea. Behind them, as the stars wheeled and the moon set, Dun Ad shrank away.

They paused at the edge of the marsh, but there were no sounds of pursuit, so they mounted the horses that had been readied for them. Then they rode as quickly as the rough path would allow, on towards the harbor. There a ship waited to take them, not home to Tairbert Boitter, which was no longer safe, but to fair Cair Ligualid, to Rheged, Ama's home, where no war raged.

They never made it. Reaching the head of the loch, they picked their way carefully towards the harbor ... straight into the waiting arms of Conall's warriors.

In the harbor was his fleet, returned. They were bound roughly, watched for a time, then taken to the king. He waited, almost as if at his leisure, in the fortlet at the harbor-mouth. Fires blazed merrily, dispelling the cold. Food lay before him on the table. Across from him sat his beautiful queen, Eithne.

King and queen rose at their entry, all courtesy and grace. "My dear lady," said Conall, genially. "That was a most impressive stunt! Really, quite extraordinary! Dun Ad—noble withstander of the armies of men, never taken—breached by a mother! However did you manage it, I wonder?"

Ama studiously avoided looking anywhere near Eithne. Artur didn't mean to. But he was young, and unschooled in the arts of subterfuge, and his gaze flickered towards his foster-mother.

Conall's eyes narrowed, comprehension swift. He drew back his gloved hand and struck Eithne across the face so hard that she fell to the floor. "You bitch!" he said, murder in his eyes.

The loch lay glassy in the cold morning light, barely a ripple as the fishermen unloaded their herring catch on the quayside. Failend gazed anxiously down at the peaceful scene below the stronghold, her people going about the business of the day, doing her level best to still the fears inside her, fears to which she refused to give voice—that Ama's plan to secure Artur's freedom would not work; that Eogan's plan to secure more aid would be in vain; that Aedan was still absent, still absent; that in her own advanced age she had been unable to help them in any material way—when the waters began to move, rollers washing onto the quays and shore, slowly at first, then ever increasing, pushed inland by something farther out the loch.

She gasped as the first of Conall's warships rounded the headland and entered the loch.

Though she made no sound that she was aware of, Luan, behind her, called out immediately, "What is it?" Then, "Oh," as more and more warships were rowed into the loch and anchored—two; five; ten: Conall's entire navy. "Oh."

"It begins," Failend said. Turning from the sight below her, she donned her cloak and with fingers which she willed to stay steady, to not shake, she drew its hood over her long auburn hair.

"Wait," said Luan with a staying hand on Failend's arm, "I'll get mine."

"No! It must be me, alone. Eogan is my son; it must be me. There is much to do! Send the runners. Do not delay! Gather the *cenel* to us. Oh, if only Eogan and Aedan were here! We have never been more vulnerable! Have the signal fires lit in the west. Summon the Cenel Oengussa from Ile. In the meantime, I shall go down and try to appeal to Conall's good sense."

Luan raised an eyebrow in frightened disbelief.

"Yes. I know that it will not work," Failend admitted. "The best that I can do is stall for time." She grabbed Luan and held her still. "Whatever happens, *do not let Conall into this stronghold*. No matter the tricks he uses to gain entry, *do not let him in*. If he gains

Tairbert, all is lost. We must stall for time. We must hold our home until our sons return."

She kissed Luan on one cheek and then the other, touched Luan's forehead with her own for a moment in farewell. "My dear friend," she said. "That we should have lived to see this day! I shall send a sign by messenger to let you know how I have fared—if I have managed to help the king see reason. If I have not, then strike the bells. Strike the bells. Keep them tolling until help comes. Pray that it comes—for war will be upon us."

"My lord asks that you open the gates."

The messenger that Luan had anxiously awaited stood there belligerently. Not Failend's messenger, as Luan had hoped, but a crimson-clad courier of the king.

She knew the man. "You served with Gabran in the Pictish wars. My husband always spoke well of your skill, and your loyalty. How are your sons?"

"As well as are any of us these days, my lady. Thank you for asking—for remembering. Gabran was ... Gabran was ... He was a good man."

"A true king."

"Yes. Yes." An agonized silence, then, "Please, will you open the gates?"

"I shall not."

"My lady, one-hundred-and-forty men wait below this stronghold. They wait to storm it. And more are on the way."

It was no exaggeration: as the day had worn on and Luan had waited with mounting alarm for word from Failend, Conall's warriors had disembarked their ships one-by-one until the full might of his army was camped on the slopes below the fort. The sight filled her with terror. And more were on the way?

"How many men have you here?" the messenger asked her gently. "Forty?"

Thirty. Only thirty. "Let them try," she said.

He sighed heavily. She found the sound ominous, though she did not know why. Then he held out a leather bag and, after a moment's hesitation, as if he dreaded the act, offered it to her. "My lord offers your ladyship this incentive," he said, the tightness of his words mirroring his expression of extreme dismay.

For all the world, Luan longed to fling the bag away, unopened. If she could have made time stop there, at the moment of unknowing, when all things were still possible, when all courses forward were still open, instead of only the one, she would have. She would have paid any price.

But the time for that was long past. There was nothing to do but open the bag, so she did.

Inside lay Failend's bloody right hand, hacked off at the wrist. On its slender middle finger was the gold ring which Gabran had given Failend at the birth of their son Eogan, its blue sea-glass jewel glazed with blood.

Her stomach heaved. She slowly closed the bag, using the moment to gather herself.

Composed, she raised her head defiantly. "Tell your *lord* that the gates of Tairbert Boitter open only before *a rightful king*. I see none here," she said.

The messenger's expression was pain itself. "My lady ... my lady," he pleaded. "It is madness! I tell you ... I have never seen! There is no reasoning with him! *Her head is next* ... Please! For the love of the gods, open the gates!"

Holding back tears, every muscle in her body screaming *Yes!*, Luan slowly shook her head.

"Then may your God be with you, my lady," he said sadly, and he left.

Luan summoned the guards. She gave the orders. Then, as night fell, as the bells of Tairbert Boitter began tolling all throughout the stronghold, defeaningly loud pleading peals, with

284

great wracking sobs masked by the thunder of the bells, Luan grieved.

Night fell on Iona, spread out below him. Eogan saw it from the summit of the peak of Dun Mor where he and Columba had come to talk of war. He saw the sun as it set in the west.

"So he put Colman in a bog?" Eogan asked the abbot, relishing the image of Colman Bec pinned by stout stakes to the peat, screaming as the tide came in. "Will Aed help us, then?"

Columba had known his cousin—Ainmire mac Setna—well enough to know that he would have. But Ainmire's son Aed, who now held the high-kingship? Columba could not say for certain. Nevertheless, he knew that anything could be bought for a price. The price of his aid would undoubtedly be the submission of the Cenel Gabran.

As Columba was wondering if Eogan would agree to that price, he heard a sound on the wind. He bent his ear quizzically and listened.

Eogan, hearing nothing but the crying of the gulls and the ever-present buffet of the wind, asked, "What is it?"

"I am afraid it is too late to ask Aed for anything," replied Columba.

"What do you mean, *too late?*"

"Bells toll," Columba explained, as he sped down the muddy track to the bottom of the hill.

"I hear nothing," Eogan cried, racing to keep up.

"They toll!" Columba cried, sprinting headlong now. "Make haste! It begins!"

It was all going according to plan. Just as he had devised. At last. Ah, the joy of it! Sweet in his mouth, like red wine from a white glass, ever-flowing, unending.

Even the men of the Cenel Gabran, streaming in little bands towards the stronghold from the countryside both north and south, summoned by runners and smoke and bells to defend their beloved Tairbert Boitter, were of no concern. Their numbers, hardly more than thirty, were simply no match for his host. As quickly as they appeared, waving spears, swords, they were engulfed and mown down. The slopes about the stronghold ran red with blood and rang with the sound of their pain.

His host would have it soon. They would gain Tairbert Boitter. They already held the fort's outer ring. It was only a matter of time before the inner two fell as well.

Conall smiled, pleased beyond words. Try as she might to hold it, the bitch inside would soon see the stronghold breached. For, from what quarter could help now come?

Not from the west. From the west, at sunrise that morning, the second day of battle, the forces of the Dal Fiatach and the Airgialla, led by Baetan mac Carell, one-hundred-and-forty-men strong, had issued over the isthmus between the lochs to join the fray, exactly as planned. It had taken ten ships to transport Baetan's eager forces from Hibernia, and now those ships bottled up the west loch, preventing any other help from reaching the beleaguered Cenel Gabran from the sea at that side.

And from this side? From the east loch?

His ships held it.

Soon, Tairbert Boitter would be his, and then all the lands of the Cenel Gabran: all of Cendtire. Conall laughed. For all their posturing that they were *good men*, Eogan was nowhere to be seen. And nowhere was his brother. The Cenel Gabran's *ri*, and their so-called greatest warrior, had abandoned them in their time of need.

All the better, he thought. More keen would be Eogan's disgrace if Conall were to capture him in flight. And Conall would. As he made his way through the crush of his men to greet his ally Baetan, he luxuriated in the assurance of his success. Events were proceeding exactly as he had planned. But then, pushing through, he saw Baetan; he saw Budic, Baetan's bishop; and, between Baetan and Budic, he saw a young man, attired for battle.

Dunchad! His son! Conall stopped dead in his tracks. They had agreed that Dunchad would stay behind in Hibernia, that his son would not be brought to war. Taken completely off-guard, his confidence ripped away as suddenly and completely as if a veil from a face, all Conall could do was sputter, "What is this?"

Baetan's arm was draped over Dunchad's shoulder. "This is to toughen your resolve, old friend," he said. "And to test his. All boys long for battle. Isn't that so, Dunchad?"

Pleasant words. But Baetan's smile was cold.

Ships lay at anchor, north of the point that protected Tairbert's west loch. Four ships lurking there, bathed in the flat light of the setting sun, but soon to be enveloped by darkness. Not Conall's—he was attacking the stronghold of Tairbert Boitter from the loch at its east side. And still the bells that had summoned Eogan and Columba from Iona tolled plaintively on the air.

Seeing those ships, Columba's heart rose, for they were the ships of the Cenel Oengussa, good to their word.

"Baetan mac Carell's fleet blocks up the west loch," Feradach said, meeting Eogan and Columba on the shore. "He brought the Airgialla with him."

"How many?" demanded Eogan.

"Ten ships'." Feradach's look was grim.

"Was your approach noticed?"

"It doesn't appear so. They don't seem to know we're here."

"What news of Tairbert Boitter?"

Another grim look. "A terrible slaughter. The king came with all his forces; Baetan mac Carell with as many as the king. Two-hundred-and-eighty men, they have! Two-hundred-and-eighty! And we, all together, with the near thirty of your *cenel* who harry them from the hills—and how many inside the fort?"

"I left thirty."

"Then we ... " Feradach's face blanched. "All together, we are only near one-hundred-and-thirty. Only one hundred-and-thirty! They outnumber us by over two-to-one!"

No one spoke. Those were hard odds indeed. It seemed that Conall had left nothing to chance. Then Feradach asked the one question to which Eogan could not even hope to supply an answer: "Where is your brother?"

"I don't know," was all Eogan could offer him.

"How many does he have?"

"Twenty-eight, his own ..."

"Twenty-eight? That's not enough! You promised there would be enough!"

"He'll bring one-hundred-and-fifty-four Britons with him. Which will be enough."

If they still live. If Strat Clut and Rheged honor their oaths. If they make it here on time, Columba thought.

"No one reckoned on the Dal Fiatach and the Airgialla," Eogan added. But Feradach was no longer listening, for a red-faced messenger had come up sprinting. "My lord," he panted, "they have breached Tairbert's second ring!"

"We must reach Tairbert!" Eogan cried. "Feradach, keep a handful of your men here; prepare the rest. You'll come with me. We'll make our way overland, along the northern shore of the loch here, to Tairbert."

"In the dark of night?" Feradach asked incredulously, his eye on the setting sun.

"The way is known to me. It is not far. We can make it long before daybreak. Besides, your men will be setting the diversion. To draw attention away from the fort."

"Diversion?"

"Yes. As we leave, start firing their ships. Burn them all."

Feradach grunted his satisfaction: he had old scores with the Dal Fiatach and the Airgialla, Columba knew, and it was high time that they were settled. And indeed, not long after, in the dead of night, a great conflagration flared up in the west, so brightly that it was as if, the world turning on its head, the sun now rose where once it had set.

It was as if the sun rose in the west.

A strange, wondrous image, which could not help but bring to Columba's mind the prophecy, which all thought pertained to Aedan.

> The sun!—it rises in the west!
> Upon the east a shadow falls.
> It casts in crownless twilight
> All whom its terror calls.
> And ravens feed upon the rest!

Could it mean? Could it mean?
How could it? Aedan was nowhere to be found.

All Aedan could hear were the bells, carried on the wind. As the ships rounded the isles which littered the sound between them and Tairbert, the dawn sky was laced with smoke. The stench of burning wood and flesh tainted the air.

That Aedan had earned from the Britons the epithet *Fradawg* for having refused Tudwal's orders to hunt down Gwenddolau's straggling army in the forests of Celyddon, he cared not a whit. That Tudwal had withheld the ships and the men he had promised Aedan, he could not change. After weeks of his time wasted by a hosting that was not his, he was at last returning home.

But not alone. Alongside his own two ships sailed six of Rheged's, Owain at the helm with eighty-four men. Not what Aedan had hoped, but they best he could do. But, were they in time? Or was he too late? As the fleet rounded the headland and he looked down the east loch—as he saw at last Tairbert Boitter, smoking in dawn, the water of the loch stained red with men's blood—Aedan still wasn't certain.

And then he was. For, as he looked upon the ruin that had been his home, the bells, which had tolled for two nights and a day, tolling terror, tolling need, without ceasing, at last fell silent.

Red and splendorous and untouched by the devastation around him, having had, in all the battle, no occasion to lift his sword, Conall ascended the rough path to Tairbert Boitter. He did so in relative quiet—the blasted bells had at last been silenced. Bodies had been kicked out of his way so that he could take the fort cleanly. All he had to do was throw open the gates, cut down the bitch, Luan, who still professed to hold it, and it would be his.

Then, behind him, a voice he recognized cried out and, surprised, Conall turned on the path to see Eogan sprinting towards him.

At last! Eogan would be destroyed. There was no hesitation on Conall's part, no nostalgia for their shared youth. His cousin was a stranger to him. A hated stranger. He raised his sword to do the deed but before he could do anything more, the bellows of a carnyx rang out, not one carnyx, but many: the great horns of war. The noise was so loud and terrible that it soared above the martial labors of the army and the men stopped in their tracks, stunned. New warships were in the east loch. Fresh warriors were coming ashore, setting Conall's ships there ablaze.

And at the fore, Aedan with his great broad-sword and his great fury.

Seeing Conall on the path, Eogan about to be taken by Conall's blade, Aedan changed course to sprint straight for them.

Damn it!

"I am the *fennid* of the Cenel Gabran!" Aedan was crying. "I am its champion! You must fight *me*!"

The armies heard it.

Damn it!

Men were scrambling to get out of Aedan's way. "If you want Tairbert Boitter, if you want Cendtire, you must fight me!"

Damn it! Damn it! Damn it!

Up the path: the stronghold, its shattered gates tempting, so close. Below: the armies. Conall took a rough counting, realized with utter incredulity that, with the arrival of Aedan and the men of Rheged, the two hosts were now roughly even in number.

"Fight them!" Conall cried to his men. "Fight them!"

But his men had stopped fighting. Both armies had. And, with a sickening in his stomach, Conall realized that none of his men would now look him in the eye. Rather, they were waiting for the outcome of the single combat to which Aedan had challenged him.

Conall had hoped to avoid this, the battle decided in the age-old way of their people. Single combat between champions. For without its king, a *cenel* is headless. No matter what had come before or how close he had been to victory, whoever won this sword-fight would win the battle.

Conall looked at both his cousins. Eogan. Aedan. Sized them up. Sized up his own chances. He took up his sword again. "You're the *ri*, Eogan. I'll fight you," he said.

Eogan hesitated, and then Aedan was there. Shoving Eogan out of the way, he made for the king.

Below them, a young man, the king's son, Dunchad, decided that he had lived enough years—fifteen of them—to know that of all the moments in one's life, now was his moment to act. Budic and Baetan were so caught up in the spectacle on the heights that they were paying him no heed in any case. Taking up his sword and his dagger, Dunchad left the safety of the bishop and his foster-father and made his way up the hill.

With great, heaving, jarring blows, sword against sword, sword against shield, the blows ringing in the air, Aedan and Conall fought for dominion. Aedan held nothing back. He felt no pity, no compassion. No sense of kinship whatsoever for this man before him, his cousin. He saw only Conall's sword; thought only of cleaving him through. He charged, shouting. Swept down his sword, a terrible singing arc. Conall caught the blow with his shield, the metal-clad leather reverberating loudly. Holding on, Conall grunted, pushed back. Aedan fell back, but only as a ruse to bring up his sword again perpendicularly, and down, smashing the pommel onto Conall's helmet. Conall yelled, reeled, tripped, his shield and sword flying up. But Aedan was already on him, roaring his rage. Out of the corner of his eye, Eogan hesitant, his sword lofted. Should he join in, help bring down the king? "No!" Aedan yelled, even as he hacked at Conall's descending shield, forcing it out of the way. Not a lot. He didn't need a lot. Because he had already spun, backwards and around, to get Conall on his other side, his sword a bright flash, cutting through Conall's wrist, severing the hand, his sword knocked loose to fly through the air. Conall was crying out, his stump up, blood jettisoning. Beautiful. But Aedan had spun back around again and, with a mighty two-handed swing, found what he was looking for with a blow that cut deeply into his cousin's side, through the chain-mail, just below his heart.

Conall crumpled, fell to his knees. "Please! Please!" he begged, stunned. Although his ruined hand was up in surrender, with his other hand he had already unsheathed his short sword and was waving it clumsily at Aedan.

Sword raised overhead to cleave him, Aedan considered it. For a blinding moment his treacherous heart was overcome by a desire to be merciful, even to this man.

And in that moment of hesitation, as both armies looked on, Dunchad, unnoticed, slipped to them and, before Aedan even realized that the young man was there, raised his dagger and drove it into the back of the king, at the juncture of shoulder and chain-mail shirt, embedding it to his heart.

It was the killing blow. Conall gasped and, twisting, jerked his sword one last time behind him, catching Dunchad in the stomach and cutting him deeply.

Dunchad tottered. Held his hands, covered in blood, up to his gaze. Looked at them in amazement; and then toppled backwards.

There was silence.

Then there was screaming. Women screaming. Men too. Aedan, who had thought that there could be no more horrors in a day already replete with death, rushed to Dunchad. He cradled Dunchad's head in his lap and sought to stem the flow of blood, but the young man had taken a blow eerily similar to the one with which he had killed the king, and there would be no saving either of them.

Just before he died, Dunchad opened his eyes and gazed up at Aedan. A tender smile crossed his face. "There," he said. "I hoped I have helped you, Father."

And then, with a gentle sigh, life left him.

Aedan surged up. He spun around, eyes unseeing. "Columba!" he screamed. "Columba! Columba!"

Eithne was there first. She ran to her son, skidding to her knees in the mud. She took Dunchad's body in her arms.

Ama and Artur were close behind. Shaking, Eogan gathered his wife and son to him.

Columba came upon them. Seeing him, Aedan shouted, "Do it!" Columba looked at him uncomprehendingly. "Do what you did to that child of the Pict! Do what you did to Emchath's child! Bring him back! Bring Dunchad back!"

Columba nodded, sank to his knees. All eyes were on the abbot and the lifeless young man. Head bowed, hands on Dunchad's limbs, Columba started to pray, mumbled words spilling from his mouth in a language none of them there could understand. There was more prayer, then something like a conversation, with

Columba's questions spoken in that unknown tongue, then gaps in which seemed to be answers, with Columba listening intently, head cocked.

Suddenly, Columba started and cried out, as if in great pain. His hands flew to his eyes to block out the light. "No! No!" he moaned.

Eogan rushed to him, pulled his hands away from his face. Columba was still moaning, very far away. Eogan shook him until Columba returned in mind. Columba drew in deep sobs, but quieted at last. He looked up, his hands palm-up on his thighs. "I am sorry. I am so sorry," he said.

Aedan roared, launched himself on Columba, hauling him to his feet, shaking him. "Do it! Do it now!"

"I am so sorry, my friend. I am so very sorry. It cannot be done. He is no longer in form, but in spirit. He travels paths I cannot follow."

Aedan didn't heed. A horrible sound of hurt was coming from his mouth as he continued to shake Columba.

"Enough, brother!" Eogan was saying. "Enough!"

Hands were on him, pulling him off the abbot, until Aedan mac Gabran, battle-smiter of the Cenel Gabran, savior of Cendtire, staggered away.

· 18 ·
FEIS RI

In sorrow were the bodies of the dead brought home to Dun Ad for burial. For Conall, the king, and his son Dunchad, who slew him and was slain by him, a great burial mound was raised on the plain north of Dun Ad, amongst the many monuments raised there by a people long past to venerate their gods and to honor their dead.

When her son was laid in the mound and the last stone was placed on the cairn, walling him in for eternity, Eithne took her dagger and made to plunge it into her own heart.

Only Aedan's reflexes saved her. He disarmed her easily, flinging the knife to the ground. He took her in his arms where, until late, she had ever longed to be. There, she sobbed, and he did his best to give her comfort.

It was a comfort which he denied himself. When Eithne had at last been led away, Aedan fell to his knees before his son's grave. His family stood around uselessly, unable to comfort him. So deep was Aedan's grief that his seeking of ease from it was instinctual: he reached out for the hem of Ama's tunic and tugged at it and tugged at it until she was brought to her knees beside him in the dirt. He laid his head in her lap. She put her arms around him, and he wept.

For Failend, no mound could be raised, or cist, or grave, for Conall, in his cruelty, when he had had her head, had thrown both head and body into the waters of the loch below Tairbert Boitter, her home; and he had done so with neither ceremony nor care. She could not be retrieved. Rather, Failend's monument lay in the depth of grief felt by those who had loved and honored her in this life.

Baetan mac Carell and his host were allowed to sail home to Hibernia in what warships had survived the battle—for a steep fee of many cattle. Baetan left on the understanding that he did so on the clemency of the people of Dal Riata, for the suzerainty he had claimed over Dal Riata lay in the contract made with the king; and that king was dead; and the people of Dal Riata now owed him nothing.

When these things were done, and the sacrifice made by those who had died for Dal Riata had been honored, it was time again to look to her future health, so the claimants of the *derbfine*, the *rigdomna*, those who were king-worthy, gathered. It was a small host. Many of the most fit men had been taken in battle under Conall's reign. They gathered in the place where the kings of Dal Riata have always been acclaimed: The Plateau of the Kings. This plateau lays in a place which is below the king's Great Hall on the summit of the fort of Dun Ad, to which the man chosen ascends, and from where he rules, but above the living levels of the fort, above the free men, the semi-free, and those enslaved, for such is a king amongst men.

On that plateau are three stones. One has a footprint carved into it, the other a basin carved out of it. The third is a thick, heavy slab of sandstone, the Stone of Destiny. It was carried to Caledonia by Fergus Mor mac Erc when he led his people out of Hibernia. This talisman was brought out of the place where it was kept hidden and safe and was placed in the natural hollow of an outcrop of rock on the edge of the plateau, because this outcrop resembles a throne. And this is the Seat of the Kings. Through the Stone of Destiny is each new king of Dal Riata linked back through the ages to all the kings who have come before him, even to those who lived and ruled and died across the sea in their homeland in times so long past as to be almost forgotten.

Around these three stones gathered the *rigdomna*. The men assembled there could be seen from all the terraces of the fort as well as from the surrounding plains. A great crowd gathered as the people of Dal Riata came to acclaim their choice for king.

Of the Cenel Loarn, chosen by lot to be the first to put forward candidates, there were no claimants. Conall mac Comgall had had a fear of his equals and, through studious and steady effort over the course of his reign had, by various means, ensured that men of high caliber had been expunged from that kin.

Of the Cenel Oengussa, Feradach mac Forindan was put forth as worthy to rule. Full of hope, the young man put himself forward. If he were the people's choice, they would call out their assent, and would strike their swords upon their shields to acclaim him.

Voices called out, but only a few. Feradach was not chosen. He stepped away.

At last, Eogan mac Gabran of the Cenel Gabran stepped out onto the plateau. He turned to all sides and saw the people about him. He heard the wind cry over the plains and the great moss. He saw the sea on the horizon. He thought of all those who had died— Failend! Failend! his mother, and the king, and the king's son, and the men of the Cenel Gabran. Strangely, he thought of Iona with a kind of longing.

His heart was heavy. Yet such was his sense of duty that he resolved that, if chosen, he would rule.

"Aye!" Aedan called out loudly, his sword ringing on his shield.

But, in the acclamation, Aedan was nearly alone.

Eogan was not acclaimed. The people had not chosen their king.

But then Sillan of the Cenel Gabran cried out in a sure, carrying voice: "Aedan! Aedan mac Gabran!"

And then the Cenel Gabran: "Aedan mac Gabran!"

Then the chant was taken up by all: "Aedan mac Gabran! Aedan mac Gabran! Aedan mac Gabran!"

When swords began to clash on shields, melodious was the noise of the acclamation of Aedan mac Gabran. The fort of Dun Ad, the terraces, the plains rang with the voice of the people.

Me? King?

Aedan looked to his brother. It was a farewell, of sorts. Eogan, misunderstanding, said, "Don't you dare ask permission from me!"

Aedan spared him a smile. "No. No, I won't," he replied.

And so, head spinning, heart in his throat, Aedan placed his foot into the footprint cut into the bedrock of Dun Ad. The clash of swords on shields was deafening. The people cried out their joy and their desire.

Aedan looked upon them, and he gazed out upon the kingdom of Dal Riata spread beneath his feet, and he was full of love.

Then he sat upon the Stone of Destiny, his people's throne, and was crowned their king.

"The people require that I honor our ways," Aedan said to the men. "Let us perform the *Feis Ri*."

There was a murmur of assent: the Feast of the King. A sanctification of power. The *Feis Rí* was expected.

By every man there but Columba. "Aedan, don't!" he said.

Aedan looked at the abbot with affectionate bemusement. "Why ever not?" he asked. "When he was acclaimed *ri ruirech* of the Northern Ui Neill, your own great-great-grandfather, Niall Noigallach, slept with a hag. She said that he must, if he wanted to be king. Of course, as soon as he had taken her, the hag revealed herself to be a nubile young woman in disguise, more lovely than the sun—so that was alright. Lucky bastard!" The men laughed. "Niall had to sleep with the goddess to become king. He knew this; the hag knew this. Such are the ways of our people."

"Such *were* the ways of our people."

"No. Dermot mac Cerball held the *Feis Temro* when he was made *ard-ri*—what, fourteen years back? And wasn't he a Christian? No hag for him, poor man: he had to have carnal relations with a horse. A white mare, wasn't it? And then he slew her, and dismembered her, and had her flesh cooked in a cauldron so that he could bathe in it, and then eat and drink his fill."

"Did your cousin Conall lay with a hag?"

"Not unless you can describe Eithne that way."

"Aedan, you can't."

"Yes, I can. But I'll do it in my own way. I shall sleep with neither hag nor horse, as they did, although I wager either experience would be educational." He flashed a wicked grin. "Rather, let a bull be sacrificed, and we'll drink its blood. That should suffice." Around him the men nodded, satisfied.

So a great, fearsome, black bull was led up from the plains bellowing, through the gates of Dun Ad, up through the levels of the fort to the Plateau of the Kings. There, in view of all, it was sacrificed, its blood poured out into a great copper cauldron. And the blood of the bull was ladled into the rock-cut basin. And

Aedan drank from it. And its blood was sprinkled on the rock-cut footprint. And Aedan set his foot in the print again. And these rituals marked the union of Aedan and his land. And then the flesh of the bull was shared out amongst all.

When these rituals were complete, the people began to shout, "Columba! Columba!" seeking the blessing of their holiest holy man too, for their new king.

"Columba," Eogan asked. "Could you bless Aedan? Or annoint him? Or do whatever it is you would do to sanctify his reign?"

"Do you mean *ordain* him?" Colulmba asked.

"Yes, I suppose so. Could you ordain him?" Eogan asked. The word was strange on his tongue. "The people ask for it." It was true: the crowd was crying out Columba's name.

"Eogan. I can't." And Columba walked away.

"That hurt," Aedan said to Eogan. "Was it something I said?"

"Best go after him," Eogan sighed.

"That's hardly kingly."

"I know, but you need him. And he needs you."

Iona. Columba's sleeping hut, Columba inside. For three nights and three days, Columba has refused to come out. Afterwards, this is what they said of it: that inside his sleeping hut, a battle raged. A battle between Columba and an angel of his Lord. That such was Columba's pride that he held out for three nights and three days in the face of the angel's wrath. They said that Columba refused to do his Lord's bidding. In a glass book brought by the angel and shown to Columba whilst he was in a deep trance was a list of the ordination of kings, and Aedan's name was in it. But although Columba saw the name there, writ plain, he shut the book tight with a snap and turned his back to the angel, saying, "I will not do it! I will not do it!"

Quick as lightening, the angel drew forth a whip and struck Columba so violently that Columba's tunic was torn to shreds and his skin was lacerated from shoulder-blade to hip-bone and the wound wept blood. And he carried that scar to his dying day.

But still Columba refused to do his Lord's bidding.

The angel rebuked him, saying, "Do it, or I shall strike you again".

For three successive nights the angel of his Lord appeared to Columba, and bade him read the glass book of the kings, and bade him ordain Aedan. And for three successive nights Columba refused to do it. So the angel scourged him.

Or so they said.

But this is the truth of it. Iona. Columba's sleeping hut, Columba inside. For three nights and three days, Columba has refused to come out. On the third day, there is a knock on the door.

Striding to the door and throwing it open to rebuke whomever he found there, he discovered Bishop Budic. As Columba regarded his one-time friend, now his enemy, he could feel old hatreds swirling in the space between them, the space over the threshold. After the battle at Tairbert Boitter, after the death of his young charge, Dunchad, for whom Budic had developed a sincere affection, he had not returned to Hibernia with Baetan mac Carell. Rather, unable to resist the lure of Columba, he had made his way to Iona. Columba, weakened and perplexed by the events of recent days, stepped back and let Budic in.

As Budic stood before Columba, his need to commune with him was so overpowering that it exceeded his ability to express with language. He gazed hungrily upon the features of his old friend, a friend whom he abhorred with an obsessive passion. In the clear morning light of Iona, he saw how the eleven years of exile had matured Columba, refining his features into an even more pronounced nobility. There was also weariness in the set of his wide mouth, and exhaustion about the eyes, and pride, as ever. Yet there was a transcendence to his gaze, and a shine emanating from his skin, for one cannot be in such close proximity to the divine without being marked by it in some tangible way.

It was more than Budic could bear. It was what he had always wanted. It was who he had always wanted. So Budic took Columba by the shoulders and set his mouth on his and kissed him. Just as a lover would.

"I'm sorry," Columba said. "It is not in my heart."

Budic nodded, released him. "It is in mine. It always has been. I suppose ... I suppose it is why I hate you so."

What could be said? Nothing: nothing that might ease Budic's pain. In the silence that stretched, Columba moved his shoulders gingerly where Budic had embraced him.

"I have hurt you!" Budic cried.

Something made Columba admit it. Budic's own extraordinary confession, perhaps. "No. The angel did that."

"The angel? The *Lord's* Angel?" Budic's gaze swept the modest little hut, found nothing holy in the shadows. "How extraordinary! Here? Why?"

"I am refusing him. He tells me to ordain Aedan, but I will not do it."

"You will not? Why not? I don't understand. Don't you want this? You have been asked to ordain the new king of Scots Dal Riata. *Pagan* Scots Dal Riata. You have converted a nation! And how you did it! There was no coercion. You used no threats. The people simply asked for it. They love you. Your friend, the new king, seems inclined to allow it. Your friend! Isn't he your friend? And the Angel of the Lord! Ah! That the Lord should so choose me! What I would give! Why do you refuse, when all is to the good?"

"You have the right of it. Of all of it. He *is* my friend. And that is the problem. Were you there? Did you see?"

"What?"

"Me fail to bring Dunchad back to life."

"Yes—but that sort of power ... "

"Is not ours to command. Yes. But it was what the Lord showed me while I was praying." Columba shuddered. "I tried to hide it from those who were watching but ... the moment was not without miracle."

Budic was eager, avid. "What? Tell me! What did you see? What did he show you?"

"I wish to spare Aedan pain. If he does not become king, he may yet avoid it. That prophecy. It is real. It is about him. And it will rend the world."

"Can you tell me why? I know you, and there must be a reason," Aedan asked. They walked on the white shell sands of the strand of Iona's northernmost beach. The water offshore shone aquamarine and turquoise in the morning light. The sky was effortlessly blue and the peaks of the mainland rose purple in the distance.

Waves frothed about the hem of Columba's cloak. He struggled to explain himself, mindful of the angel's scourge that still throbbed so painfully under his clothes. The rough linen of his tunic caught and ripped the edges of the wound. It was agony. "It is not that I don't love you, Aedan. I do."

"You think I will make a poor king."

"No. Quite the contrary. You are a man of—a man for—these, our times. Your whole life, you have been called to service."

"Then what is it?"

Columba wouldn't tell him what he had seen. He said, "Eogan should do it". Eogan, who Columba now knew would have no more sons, or daughters. Eogan who, given the chance, would rule chastely, conservatively, even timidly. Eogan, of whom no one had ever uttered any kind of prophecy.

Aedan snorted bemusedly. "Aye! This has all been for him. All this work—all my work. And yet, how odd!" Aedan shook his head, looked at the water, back again. "The people have made their choice. Would you go against them? I find that I cannot. Although it pains me to say it—I have sacrificed much for him—Eogan is ... Eogan is a good choice to be our *ruiri* ... but he is not the *best* choice. Not in these times. I think he knows this too."

This had been proven at such cost that Columba could only nod.

"I think he's rather relieved, in fact, that it's not him," Aedan added.

"Do you desire this?" Columba asked carefully. It would help if maybe, maybe, this was something that Aedan actually wanted.

"I don't. And I do. Part of me wants to flee back to Caledonia. A rather large part of me. But if I do, then ... Who?" A bewildered shrug.

Columba felt a wrenching pity for the man before him, no longer young, who had never been without care, and wondered with awe at the fate the Lord had in store for him: the battles and the bloodshed spreading out endlessly, a promise and a threat. The hair on the back of Columba's neck rose up, remembering the vision given him. There was pain ahead for his old friend. And sorrow. Much sorrow.

But also glory.

He marveled anew at the piteousness of his God.

"I don't need you, you know," Aedan was saying. "Not to be king, that is. The people's acclamation made me king, and the *Feis Ri* gave sanction to their choice. But I should like your support. The people begin to love you, as much for your compassion as for the power which you wield almost without thought. They see you as the 'giver-of-victories', rather like one of our war-gods. They trust that they are protected by your love for them, you being as much a Cu Chulainn as a Christ. They require that I keep faith with you. I *should like* to keep faith with you. I have few friends. I'll have fewer, now. We have been through much together, you and I. I believe that together there is much we might achieve."

Again, Columba felt the chill of premonition. This was the other part of it. The other thing the angel of the Lord had promised: *Ordain him*, the angel had said, *and he shall make you his chief-priest. He will give you new lands for new churches. Many new lands. Your Iona will head a federation. The greatest this land has known, its reach limited only by your imagination.*

"Oh, my friend!" Columba cried.

Aedan was smiling. "You'll do it, won't you? Because your god wills it."

Indeed. *Deus uult.*

At sunset, in the church of the monastery of Iona, before Aedan's host and all who loved him, Columba laid his hands on Aedan's head in ordination and blessed his reign.

But still the extraordinary day was not over. After the ordination, after the company was abed, Aedan quietly left the guest-house and slowly made his way along the rough moon-lit path to the beach on Iona's verdant west coast, to the *machair*, where that night no other soul was roaming. His thoughts were unsettled; everything in flux. Dunchad dead. Conall dead. Failend dead, and the others. He, king! He would send for Domelch and Gartnait on the morrow. Surely they would come now, would no longer refuse him. What a mess it would be when Afrella found out, but if any one event had the capacity to change things, his being acclaimed king of Dal Riata surely was it.

He found his brother Eogan at water's edge, as he had been told he would. But also Ama. Aedan's heart leapt.

"Good," said Eogan. "We are all here."

"Why drag us out here?" Ama demanded. "Why the secrecy?"

"I have come to a decision," Eogan said, "which I thought best shared with the two of you, alone, first." He turned tortured eyes on his wife, then Aedan; swallowed, and said, "I wish to divorce you, Ama ... "

"*Divorce?*" Ama cried.

"Yes. Or, rather, to let you divorce *me*. For I wish that no shame be attached to your name on account of the severing of our relationship."

"*Why?*"

"Is it not obvious?" There was an alarming twist to Eogan's voice, deep pain. He nodded towards Aedan. "To let you marry *him*."

Ama's hand flew to her mouth in shock. Aedan felt as if he had been punched in the gut. "*What?*"

"Stop it! The both of you!" Eogan spat angrily. "Let there be no more false protestations between us! Let us be truthful with one another!"

The silence that fell between them then was heavy. Wind came in off the sea from the west. Waves lapped the sand on the shore. Stars gleamed overhead in the inky sky.

"Brother, will you marry her?" Eogan asked at last.

Marry her? Marry her? Oh, dear gods, how he had longed for this. And yet ... "No," he said heavily, looking at Ama for forgiveness as he did so.

"*No?*"

Aedan's throat tightened convulsively. "No," he said again.

Eogan made a noise of bewilderment. Ama's eyes were wide, her face blanched—she was being utterly betrayed, by the both of them—but Aedan held them off with a beseeching hand. "She cannot be my chief-wife," he said. There was Domelch. And Afrella. "And I will not make her my concubine."

In the face of their confusion, Aedan struggled to explain himself. "Afrella knows that I do not love her—that I cannot love her. She has borne it all these years because ... well, because she loves me, though I little deserve it. She has been a good wife, and a good mother to our sons, and a good lady to my clients. No doubt she will make a good queen. As much as I might like to,"—he looked at Ama, begging her to understand—"I won't divorce her. I won't dishonor her. But neither will I bring you to court as my concubine. For that would dishonor you and her, both."

His gut was twisting with longing. Despite Eogan's extraordinary offer, Aedan might yet lose her. "The only way I will make you my concubine is if, against all reason, you demand it of me—for, the gods help me!, I would give you whatever you desire. Do you demand it? Would you be a concubine? I don't see it. I can't see it. You? No, never."

He was relieved to see that the color had come back to her face. She gazed hungrily at him, her brow creased in fierce, rapid thought. "No," she said, finally, with a sharp shake of her head.

Feeling no sense of relief whatsoever, Aedan pressed on. A disturbing thought had occurred to him. "Do you *wish* to be free of this marriage?" He didn't think that he could bear to look at his brother's face as he asked this, so he did not.

Ama nodded. His heart leapt.

"Once you are free, do you wish to wed another?"

Please say no! Please say no! What if she loved another? It would be no less than he deserved. His stomach lurched again when she firmly shook her head no.

"Do you wish to be alone?" he asked.

Again, a sharp shake of her head.

Then Ama seized her chance: he could see it in the squaring of her shoulders and the lifting of her chin. "I wish to be with you," she said. "If that can be arranged."

To his credit, Aedan could see that Eogan held his head high at her words, though his eyes and mouth were pinched with pain. *He is the most noble of men!* Aedan thought, in awe of his brother, not for the first time.

"It can," Aedan told Ama.

Again, there was a tremendous silence which Aedan for the life of him did not know how to break.

"That's it, then," Eogan finally said. "I am sorry for all of this, Ama. I knew that you didn't love me ... "

"I do love you, Eogan ... " she protested, rushing to comfort him, but he held up his hands to ward her off. "Please. This is difficult enough. Thank you for the years you have given me. No man could have been better served by—and pleased with!—his wife."

"There is only one more thing to do," Eogan said, his expression both haunted and, it seemed to Aedan, full of self-loathing. "I owe you the truth."

"The truth?" Aedan asked, alarmed. He wasn't sure he wanted to hear what his brother would say next.

"I knew it. All those years ago."

"You knew what?"

"I knew that you loved one another."

The world spun. Aedan sucked in breath, but not nearly enough to successfully rearrange his current understanding of his life to include this new, revolutionary fact. *Then why did you take her?*

Eogan shrugged. "I wanted her." He gazed upon Ama with raw emotion. "I wanted you."

Ama nodded, more calmly than Aedan would have.

"Brother. Ama. It is worse," Eogan said, self-disgust writ plainly on his face.

"*Worse?*"

Eogan squared his shoulders and looked at Aedan so directly that there was no way that Aedan could afterwards mistake his meaning. "I took her knowing that you would deny me nothing," he said.

Ama gasped. For the life of him, Aedan longed to strike his brother. In fact, if he didn't love him so much he was quite certain he could kill him on the spot.

But still Eogan was not finished. "There is more: if I had to do it over again, Brother, I would. I would take her from you, and expect you to let me have her."

"*Was it worth it?*" Aedan growled through gritted teeth.

"Aye! Oh, aye!"

To Aedan this made no sense. "Then why release her now?" he demanded, fearful that his control over his fury was not quite as firm as he needed it to be.

"I am weary beyond words. I am weary of this life."

Aedan's stomach plummeted—not Eogan too! Not so soon after Eithne!—and he lunged at his brother as if by strength of arms he could keep him here, alive. *To keep him here, with me.* Ama did the same, grabbing Eogan's hands.

But Eogan shook them both off, explaining, "No. No. I mean that I am beginning to love Columba's God more than anything else. Truth be told, in Him I have found the peace which has eluded me for ... years, now. *In quietam est cor nostrum, donec requiescat in te*: our heart is unsettled until it finds rest in You. Strange to tell! But I find that I desire Him more than I desire you, Ama ... and my love for you is an ache". He laughed shakily. "If He is the sort of God that Columba proclaims He is—if He is *Love*—then my holding you against your will, selfishly, will hardly increase my chances of getting closer to Him. The truth is that I wish to become a monk. And monks, as you may know, may be married only to the Church. I should like to stay on here, at Iona, if Columba will have me."

Aedan was awash with amazement and no small measure of shame: he had had no idea that his brother had been in such pain. He had failed him. And then, following rapidly on the heels of that raw emotion, he felt another: fear. Fear that, in gaining at last the one love—Ama—he was losing the other.

"But I need you, brother," Aedan said. "Now more than ever."

"I shall help you in whatever way I can, Aedan, of course. *But from here.*" With a wave of his hand Eogan swept the night-shrouded island about them.

An eternity passed while Aedan reeled from this last unlooked-for twist of fate in this most remarkable of weeks. Finally, however, Aedan found the strength to nod to his brother, to accept this too. "Will you ... will you consent to be my *tanaise* until my sons reach their majority?" he asked. "I need you. *You.* But before you answer, you should consider that it carries the risk that I may die before the eldest of them ... "

"*Artur?*" Eogan said the young man's name sharply and with a look that Aedan found entirely too shrewd. Beside him, Ama gasped again.

So, this is a day for all truths to be revealed.

So be it.

Aedan nodded. "Before Artur becomes a man," he said. "All I can promise is that I shall try my hardest to remain alive until then."

"It would be my honor, my king."

On the *machair*, away from all prying eyes, at last, after eleven years, alone, and sanctioned in it, Aedan waited only until Eogan was over the ridge and out of sight before he pulled her to him. He wrapped his arms around her and with a groan buried his face in the curve of her neck. She twisted his hair in her hands and would not let go. They held each other that way for a long time, not an inch of space between them, breathing the other in.

"My love," she said. "Please."

He carried her down. They took each other on the *machair*, and it was an outpouring of energy, which was love, and desire, and need, and hope.

On the morrow, Aedan set sail for Dun Ad with his host. And in this way, in the Year of our Lord's Incarnation 574, Aedan mac Gabran mac Domangart mac Fergus Mor mac Erc became king of Dal Riata of the Scots and began his reign.

· CHRONOLOGICAL GUIDE ·

367-68 A.D.   *Conspiratio Barbarica*: Picts, Attacotti, Scots, Saxons and Franks overwhelm Roman outposts in Britain and Gaul

381   Magnus Maximus drives back the Picts and the Scots

397   General Stilicho repulses Picts, Scots and Saxons

406   A confederate force of barbarians breaches the Rhine and lays waste to Gaul and Spain, breaking contact between Rome and Britain

407   Constantine III withdraws remaining Roman legion from Britain

408   Devastating attacks by Picts, Scots and Saxons

409	Britons expel remaining Roman officials and fight for themselves
410	Rome abandons Britain
c. 432-61	*Floruit* of St Patrick
450s	Pictish invasions; civil war and famine in Britain
c. 500	Traditional settlement of Dál Riáta Battle of Mount Badon
c. 521-97	*Floruit* of St Columba
c. 534-608	*Floruit* of Áedán mac nGabráin
c. 537	Battle of Camlann in which Artur and Medraut fell
538-58	Gabran mac Domangairt rules Dál Riáta
c. 540-70	*Floruit* of the British monk and writer Gildas
c. 556	Bridei, son of Maelchon, rules the Northern Picts
560-65	Diarmait mac Cerbaill rules the Southern Uí Néill from Tara
561	Battle of Cúl Dreimne
562	Council of Teilte
563	St Columba's exile to Dál Riáta

· GLOSSARY AND PRONUNCIATION GUIDE ·

<u>Aed mac Ainmire</u>: (**Aid** mac **An**-ver-a)

<u>Aedan mac Gabran of the Cenel Gabran</u>: (**Aid**-an mac **Gav**-rine of the **Ken**-el **Gav**-rine)

<u>Ainmire mac Setna</u>: (**An**-ver-a mac **Set**-na)

<u>Anamchara</u>: (**Ah**-nem **Kah**-ruh) Spiritual director; confessor.

<u>Arawn</u>: (**Ar**-oon) Lord of the Underworld.

<u>Ard-ri</u>: (**Ard**-ree) The High-King; the king who ruled over the five provinces of Ireland. The highest grade of Irish kingship.

<u>Baithene</u>: (**Bay**-then-eh)

Belenos: (**Bel**-en-os) The Celtic sun-god, associated with the festival of May Day.

Beltane: (**Bel**-tan-a) The festival associated with the god Belenos, held 1-3 May to celebrate the arrival of summer and the return of livestock to open pastures.

Boaire: (**Bo**-ar-e) A grade of free man, the prosperous farmer, or strong farmer.

Brenhines: (**Bren**-hin-es) Queen

Brenin: (**Bren**-in) King

Bridei son of Maelchon: (**Brith**-ee son of **Mail**-kon)

Broichan: (**Broy**-ken)

Budic: (**Bu**-dic)

Cailleach Bheur: (**Kal**-ex **Ver**) A figure in Irish legend and poetry, a pre-Christian tutelary goddess of the land who celebrated sacred marriage with those who would become king.

Caim: A prayer for protection.

Caledonii: (Kal-eh-**dohne**-ee)

Cenel, Cenela: (**Ken**-el, **Ken**-el-a) Kin-group; extended family; clan. A term used particularly for the kin groups of Scottish Dal Riata.

Cenel Gabran: (**Ken**-el **Gav**-rine)

Cenel Loarn: (**Ken**-el Lorne)

Cenel Oengussa: (**Ken**-el **En**-guss-ah)

Ceo: (**Kee**-oh) Mist, shadow.

Clientship: The Irish system (céilsine, **Kel**-shin-eh) under which a lord or nobleman supplied livestock and sometimes land (the fief or rath) to a farmer in return for goods and services, including military service and labor.

Cobthach: (**Kov**-thuck)

Coeling: The descendants of Coel Hen.

Coibche: (**Kov**-x-e) The "bride-price", the price a husband paid to purchase his wife from her father.

Columba (Colum Cille): Kolumba (**Kol**-um **Kill**-eh)

Comaltae: (**Kov**-al-tie) Foster-brother.

Combrogi: Fellow-countrymen. Used by the British for other Britons.

Comthinchor: (**Kom**-tin-xor) The property brought into a marriage by both husband and wife.

Conall mac Comgall of the Cenel Loarn: (**Kon**-all mac **Kov**-gall of the **Ken**-el Lorne)

Cu Chulainn: (**Koo Hull**-en) The epitome of the superhuman war-hero, closely associated with the gods.

Cul Dreimne: (**Kool Drev**-enee)

Curragh: (**Kur**-agh) A round-bottomed boat covered with animal hide stretched over a wicker or wooden frame.

Cruithni: (**Kruth**-neh) The Irish term for the Picts.

The Daghdha: (**Dach**-thuh) "The Good God", or "The Mighty One of Great Knowledge." The Daghdha was king and father of the Irish gods.

Dal: (**Dahl**) An archaic name element meaning "the share of".

Dal Fiatach: (Dahl **Fee**-ah-tak)

Dal Riata: (Dahl **Ree**-a-ta)

Derbfine, or Fine: (**Derv**-ine, Fine) Kin, family group, kinsman. The kin-group or "certain" family comprising one's conjugal family of parents and siblings but also all those males who had a great-grandfather in common, up to and including second cousins. The derbfine, or fine, was the basic unit for law-enforcement and land ownership in early Irish society. With marriage, women passed into their husband's derbfine.

Dermot mac Cerball: (**Der**-mot mac **Ker**-val)

Din Eidyn: (**Din Eye**-din)

Drust son of Bridei: (**Drust** son of **Brith**-ee)

Domelch: (**Doh**-melck)

<u>Donn</u>: (Don) "The Dark or Brown One." The Irish God of the Dead who presided over the Land of the Dead. He was the dark, somber, aspect of the afterlife. Both benign and terrible, he created storms and shipwrecks, but also protected cattle and crops.

<u>Dun</u>: (Doon) A fortified dwelling or stronghold.

<u>Dun Ad</u>: (**Doon-Ath**)

<u>Dunchad</u>: (**Dun**-chad)

<u>Dun Mor</u>: (**Doon Mor**)

<u>Eireann</u>: (**Air**-in-a) The tribal grouping, to which the Dal Riata belonged, which claimed to be the original tribe of Ireland.

<u>Eithne</u>: (**Eth**-nee)

<u>Enech</u>: (**En**-ech) A person's honor (literally, their "face").

<u>Eogan mac Gabran of the Cenel Gabran</u>: (**Owen** mac **Gav**-rine of the **Ken**-el **Gav**-rine)

<u>Failend</u>: (**Foy**-len)

<u>Fennid</u>: (**Fenn**-id) The champion, or warrior, of a king.

<u>Ferann claidib</u>: (**Fer**-ann **Kla**-div) "Sword-land"

<u>Fidchell</u>: (**Fith**-chel) A board-game.

<u>Filidh</u>: (**Fee**-lee) A poet.

Forindan: (**Fore**-in-din)

Gabran mac Domangart: (**Gav**-rin mac Doh-**man**-gart)

Gododdin: (Guh-**da**-thin)

Gwyr y Gogledd: (**Gweer**-y-Gogleth) The Men of the North; a British term for themselves.

Himbas Forosnai: (**Im**-bas For-**os**-na) A form of divination practiced by the druids; the "Second Sight".

Hinba: (**Een**-ba)

Iona: (Eye-**oh**-na)

Kynfarch the Old of Rheged: (**Kin**-varch the Old of **Reh**-ged)

Luan: (**Loo**-an)

Lughnasadh: (**Loon**-a-sa) The Celtic festival celebrated 1-3 August in honor of the start of the harvest and associated with the god Lugh.

Manannan mac Lir: (Ma-**nan**-nan mac **Llyr**) Celtic god of the sea.

Manau: (**Man**-ow)

Meall: (**Mull**)

Medb: (**Maeve**) The legendary queen of Connaught in Ireland, a quasi-historical figure who led her armies against the Ulstermen in the saga Táin Bó Cuailnge. Of considerable sexual prowess, Medb was also known for her ruthlessness in battle.

<u>Miathi</u>: (Mee-ath-ee)

<u>The Monastic Hours</u>: A system of communal prayer with set services in each daily cycle:

<u>*Matins*</u>: said in the middle of the night
<u>*Lauds*</u>: said immediately after matins
<u>*Prime*</u>: said at dawn
<u>*Terce*</u>: said at the third hour of daylight
<u>*Sect*</u>: said at the sixth hour of daylight
<u>*None*</u>: said at the ninth hour of daylight
<u>*Vespers*</u>: recited before the community retired to bed

<u>Mormaer</u>: (**Mor**-mare) "Great Steward." The king of a Pictish province.

<u>The Morrighan</u>: (**Mor**-ee-thin) The Irish triple-goddess of war, comprised of the <u>Morrighan</u>, the "Phantom Queen"; <u>Badb</u> (**Bayv**), "Crow, Raven of Battle"; and <u>Nemhain</u> (**Nev**-in), "Frenzy", who spread panic amongst fighting men.

<u>Nemeton</u>: "Sacred place", often used of a sacred grove, a sanctuary for druidic ritual and assembly.

<u>Ocaire</u>: (**O**-gar-e) A grade of freeman, the less prosperous farmer, or small farmer.

<u>Oenach</u>: (**Oi**-nech) An annual assembly or fair.

<u>Ogham</u>: (**Oh**-gum) A twenty-character alphabet consisting of grooves or strokes cut at different angles to a vertical line, used especially in inscriptions, primarily those on stone.

Rath: A ring-fort; a circular fortified farmstead consisting of a protective earthen embankment and ditch within which sheltered one or more family homes.

Regulus: The sub-ruler of a Pictish province.

Rheged: (**Reh**-ged)

Rigdomna: (Ree-**dov**-na) A prince of the royal line, eligible for the kingship.

Ri ruirech: (**Ree rur**-ech) Very-King; king of over-kings; the third rank of kings. A ri   ruirech was king of a province.

Ri (pl. rig): (**Ree**) Lord; leader; the lowest grade of king. A ri ruled over only his own tuath or cenel. The Irish system of kingship can be schematized as follows, with each grade of king drawing on the tribute of those below it:

Ard-ri

ri ruirech	ri ruirech	ri ruirech	ri ruirech
ruiri ruiri ruiri	ruiri ruiri ruiri	ruiri ruiri ruiri	ruiri ruiri ruiri
ri ri ri ri ri ri ri ri ri	ri ri ri ri ri ri ri ri ri	ri ri ri ri ri ri ri ri ri	ri ri ri ri ri ri ri ri ri

Rigain: (**Ree**-gan) Lady; queen.

Ruiri (pl. ruirig): (**Rur**-ree) Over-King; great king; the second rank of king. A ruiri ruled over his own tuath or cenel, and at least two others as well.

<u>Samhain</u>: (**Sow**-an) The greatest of the four major Celtic festivals, held from 29 October to 2 November, roughly equivalent to Halloween. It marked the return of livestock from the summer pastures. The start of the Celtic year, it was the Day of the Dead, the juncture between summer and winter, when it was believed that the barrier between worlds was temporarily broken down and that the dead could walk amongst the living and the living amongst the dead.

<u>Tanaise</u>: (**Ta**-naise) Heir-apparent to the kingship.

<u>Tairbert Boitter</u>: (**Tar**-bert **Bot**-ter)

<u>Teilte</u>: (**Tail**-te)

<u>Tir na nOg</u>: (**Teer**-na-nOhg) The Land of the Young. A paradisian world beyond the motal realms where there is no sickness, old age, or death.

<u>Toiseach</u>: (**Tee**-shuck) A leader or chieftan. A grade lower than king.

<u>Tuath</u> (plural <u>Tuatha</u>): (**Tooth**; **Tootha**) "A people"; a petty kingdom; territory; tribe. The most basic unit of governance in early Irish society, the <u>tuath</u> was in essence an extended family group sufficiently large enough to be ruled by a king. Standing amongst kings was assessed by the number of <u>tuatha</u> subordinate to one and the level of subordination. It has been estimated that at any given time between the fifth and the twelfth century there were between 80 and 150 kings in Ireland.

Ui Neill: (**Ee**-nail) The descendants of Niall Noigiallach ("Niall of the Nine Hostages").

Ulaid: (**Oo**-lah)

Urien: (**Yuh**-ri-an)

Uurguost: (**Ur**-gust)

· HISTORICAL NOTES ·

This series takes as its theatre the North Channel (The Straits of Moyle) which lies between the North of Ireland and Scotland, as well as the Irish Sea, that tempestuous body of water between Ireland and Britain. It is helpful to think of it all as a wide lake bounded by land or as a "sea-valley", easily crossed by the sea-going skin-boats, the *curraghs,* of the age—indeed a super highway which allowed significant cross-fertilization of culture, technology, ideology, and peoples. In the 6th century, the lands which adjoined these seas had far more in common than not, sharing a history linked by language, politics and often intricate familial ties.

As to which languages the characters in this series are speaking, Primitive Irish was undergoing a transformation to Old Irish from the 4th to the 7th century. Therefore anyone from Ireland (Hibernia in the book) is speaking a form of Primitive Irish (i.e. Gaelic), as are any of the Scots of Dalriada which was an Irish colony. (Scots Gaelic was a later offshoot of the Gaelic brought to Scotland by these early colonists.) With his brothers on Iona, Columba is speaking Irish, except when he is acting in an official, liturgical, capacity as abbot, in which case he is using medieval Latin, the language of the Church.

325

The Britons of the northern kingdoms are speaking Primitive Welsh which began to diverge from British at this time.

The language of the Picts still defies codification. Based on years of often fruitless analysis of the surviving inscriptions from Pictland, there are four possibilities as to the nature of Pictish: that the Pictish language is older than Celtic or Germanic, and may not be Indo-European at all but more akin to the language of the Basques or Finns; that Pictish is a P-Celtic language akin to British-Celtic (that is akin to Welsh, Cornish and Breton); that Pictish is a mixture of P-Celtic (Welsh-like) and Q-Celtic (akin to Irish, Manx and Scots Gaelic); or that the Pictish inscriptions are in Old Norse, commemorating people of high-status of Norse descent, rendering the Pictish inscriptions far later in time than the stones on which they were written and giving us no indication as to what language the Picts actually spoke. I have chosen to portray the Caledonii as speaking P-Celtic, and a more archaic form of it than the Miathi.

I have provided a glossary of terms which also gives a rudimentary guide to the pronunciation of names and places. There is also a brief chronology to situate the story in place and time.

The map which adorns the front cover is a detail from *Scotiae Tabula*, Theatrum Orbis Terrarum (1592 × 1606) by the cartographer Abraham Ortelius (property of the author). The inset on the hand-drawn map of Hibernia is a detail from the Arrest of Christ on Muiredach's cross at Monasterboice, Co. Louth, Ireland (early-10th century). The map of Dal Riata features a detail from the underside of a pseudopenannular brooch from the Hiberno-Viking period (9th century), found in Killamery, Co. Kilkenny, Ireland, and now in the National Museum of Ireland (R. 165). On the map of Britannia Part, the inset of the Roman riding down barbarians is from the Bridgeness distance slab, Antonine Wall (2nd century), now in the National Museums of Scotland. The inset on the map of Caledonia (the three armed warriors—possibly an Orcadian chief with two of his retinue) is from the Brough of Birsay, Orkney symbol stone (8th century), now in the National Museums of Scotland. The images in the frame of that map are from the corpus of Pictish symbols, clockwise from top left, the water-horse (possibly a porpoise), the Burghead bull, the dog/wolf, and the boar. On the map of Iona, the detail is from the Papil shrine-panel, Shetland (early-8th century). It shows monks processing towards a cross, with the horseman perhaps an abbot or a bishop, and is now in the Shetland Museum in Lerwick. The drawing of the sword on the genealogical tree is that of a short iron sword with bronze hilt and scabbard found in the River Witham but now lost.

The illustration underlying the Part One page is the Selkirkshire *orans* figure (RCAHMS 1957, no. 65, now in the National Museums of Scotland). It depicts a figure praying in the *orans* position, that is dressed in a tunic with arms bent and hands slightly above the shoulders, palms facing outwards, a position classic in early Christian iconography. It dates roughly from the 6th or even 5th centuries and is the earliest vernacular figure-carving in northern Britain. *Orantes* are believed to represent deceased souls already in Paradise who pray for those still here on earth. This stone was discovered near an ancient church in Over Kirkhope in a remote upland valley in the Borders and may have marked the grave of a hermit.

Underlying the Part Two page is a detail from the back of the Meigle No. 4 Pictish cross slab (Meigle Sculptured Stone Museum, Meigle, Scotland). Though fragmented, the cross-slab is a masterpiece of Pictish sculpture, its back tightly packed with carvings of mounted horsemen, interlaced serpents biting each other's tails, a beast resembling the Pictish "water-horse" (probably meant to represent a porpoise), another fantastic creature, and a crescent and V rod symbol (perhaps a shield and broken arrow—as Domelch says, "the sign of the fallen archer"). Most of the Pictish stones at Meigle, an outstanding collection, date from the 9th and 10th centuries.

The image underlying the Part Three page is that of the footprint carved into the rock near the top of the hillfort of Dunadd which may have been used in the inauguration ceremonies of the kings of Dalriada. The poorly preserved *ogham* inscriptions which accompany it (the bundles of straight parallel strokes arranged to either side of the two base-lines) have recently been shown to be Old Irish rather than Pictish but have yet to be satisfactorily interpreted. (Since 1978 the entire carved surface of the rock has been covered over with a protective fiberglass facsimile.) Although the *ogham* inscriptions at Dunadd may date from as early as the 5th or 6th centuries, they more probably date from the 8th-10th (with the late-8th century being the likeliest date if the Old Irish reading is correct). As such, while they appear in the art, they do not appear in the story. The rock-cut footprint may be decidedly older, and therefore does.

All maps and illustrations in this book are by the author.

What follows are brief historical notes organized according to the book's chapters. They are meant to help the reader pick out the story's factual core from its fictional trappings. I have kept the bibliography to a minimum and provided a specific citation only where one is needed, or where the point made in the novel is subject to more than the usual amount of historical debate. I have tried not to duplicate information provided in the historical notes for Book I, *Exile*. The following notes, then, should be read in supplement to those.

Preface:

Columba sails for the hillfort of Dunadd (Dun Ad in the book) from what is now known as Columba's Bay, on the south-east corner of the island of Iona. The beach there is split into two by a rocky outcrop and, unlike other beaches on the island, is pebbly, not sandy.

Erraid is an island located just off the Ross of Mull, opposite Iona. It is a tidal island, accessible across the sands for two hours at low water. According to Life of Columba I.40 (the principal source of information about St Columba, written in the 690s by Adomnán, abbot of Iona until 704, from an earlier work, now lost), the monks had a "little island that is the breeding-place of the seals we reckon as our own". In that passage, Columba has a vision of a thief about to poach seals from the island. He sends two of his monks to intercept the man. Seal meat was eaten at the monastery, with the skin and the oil of the animal being as important as the meat itself (Richard Sharpe, trans. Life of Columba (London, 1995), n. 181, pp. 302-03). Incidentally, Erraid also figures in Robert Louis Stevenson's Kidnapped, which he is said to have written while staying on the island.

Life of Columba II.15 and other early sources tell us that it took half a day to sail from Iona to the nearby island of Tiree, and two days' fair sailing to get to the Faroes from the Northern Isles. It therefore should have been possible to sail from Iona to Dunadd in one long day.

The hymn which Columba composes on his voyage that day is from the 6th or 7th century and is attributed to Columba: "I beg that me, a little man, trembling and most wretched, rowing through the infinite storm of this age, Christ may draw after Him to the lofty, most beautiful haven of life ... an unending holy hymn forever". (T. Clancy and G. Markus, (Latin) text and trans., Iona, the Earliest Poetry of a Celtic Monastery (Edinburgh, 1995), pp. 69-80.)

Chapter 1: The Mounth

Aedan is standing on the slopes above Loch Eil, which feeds into the Great Glen near the town of Fort William.

Stirrups were not in use in Europe at this time. Their use began spreading across Europe in the late-6th or early-7th century, primarily due to invaders from Central Asia such as the Avars, becoming more widely adopted by the 8th century. Without these aids, the legendary horsemanship of the Picts becomes rather more impressive.

It has been suggested that the Gartnait, son of Domelch, who was king of the Picts (dying in 601) was the son of Áedán mac nGabráin.

Chapter 2: Dun Ad

The principle of "overswearing" in early Irish society (indeed in many early societies) is both deeply fascinating and morally questionable to our modern, egalitarian sensibilities. In effect, the oath of a person of a higher rank would have automatically outweighed the oath of a person of a lower rank. Simply put, if a lord and a commoner had a legal disagreement, the lord would win. (Fergus Kelly, A Guide to Early Irish Law, 1991, pp. 199-200.) However, even though Columba is King Conall's client, the two men are of more-or-less equal rank, Columba being who he is, and neither can overswear the other. Instead, Conall cleverly maneuvers Columba into accepting the judgment of a third party, Budic, who has just been made Columba's bishop—in effect, his lord. But Budic must defer to his own lord—Conall.

Each person in early Irish society had an "honor-price" based on his or her rank. The fine for killing someone, or otherwise seriously harming them, was based on their honor-price. If the person was killed, the fine was paid to their kin-group. (Fergus Kelly, A Guide to Early Irish Law, 1991, pp. 7-10.)

Chapter 3: Iona

Images of long-legged wading or marsh birds, cranes or egrets, appear frequently in Celtic iconography and written mythology where they seem to be birds of ill omen. (In the Conquest of Ireland, I.33, written in 1189, the monk and traveler Gerald of Wales tells us, for instance, that in early Ireland it was taboo to eat crane flesh.)

At this point in the story Eogan would not yet know of the Picts' practice of exogamy and that, in addition to his brother Aedan, other foreign princes had fathered royal children on their Pictish wives, including the man some historians have hypothesized was the father of the known Pictish king Bridei mac Maelchon— Maelgwyn, former king of Gywnedd (died about 547).

Chapter 4: Dun Dear Duil

The anonymous, beautiful, quatrain which Aedan quotes as dialogue ("There is one/upon whom I should gladly gaze/to whom I would give the bright world/all of it, all of it, though it be an unequal bargain") is from the Finn Cycle, written in the 9th or 10th century. In it, the legendary Gráinne speaks of her lover Díarmait with whom she has eloped even though she has been promised in marriage to Finn. I have paraphrased from the translation by Gerard Murphy, ed., Early Irish Lyrics (Oxford, 1956; reprinted 1962).

From their encampment near Loch Eil, the party has crossed Loch Linnhe, and is traveling along the northern shore of the River Nevis into beautiful Glen Nevis from the north. There Aedan spies the Iron-Age, now vitrified, fort of Dun Dear Duil (Dun Deardail or Dundbhairdghall). It is there that I have set the battle in which Gabran, Áedán's father, the king of the Scots of Dal Riata, lost his life in 558 or 559. For that year, The Annals of Tigernach and others note two major events which, though not necessarily, are very probably linked: "The death of Gabran, Domangart's son, king of Scotland"; and "Flight of the Scots before Brude, Maelchon's son, king of the Picts".

Chapter 5: Below the Craig

The scene in the abandoned Caledonian village, in a narrow pass between Druim Alban (here, the Monadhliath Mountains) and the Mounth (here, the Cairngorms), is set in the vicinity of the towns of Aviemore and Avielochan.

Medieval commentators erroneously believed that the Picts hid themselves underground. This was an attempt to understand and explain a type of Pictish structure known as a souterrain. Gildas, On the Ruin of Britain, 19.1, writing about 540 A.D., says: "As the Romans went back home, there eagerly emerged from the *curraghs* that had carried them across the sea-valleys the foul hordes of Scots [Irish] and Picts, like dark throngs of worms who wriggle

331

out of narrow fissures in the rock when the sun is high and the weather grows warm". A later, Icelandic text, claims: "[The Picts] did wonders in the mornings and evenings, but at mid-day lost their strength, and hid in holes in the ground" (Historia Norvegiae, 1100 × 1200).

To keep himself sane and to pass the time while imprisoned, Columba sings "St Patrick's Breastplate", a *caim*, or protective charm, traditionally attributed to St Patrick: "Today in this fateful hour/I place all heaven with its power/and the sun with its brightness/ and the snow with its whiteness/and the fire with all the strength it has/and the lightning with its rapid wrath/and the winds with their swiftness/along their path/and the sea with its deepness/and the rocks with their steepness/and the earth with its starkness;/all these I place, by God's almighty help and grace,/between myself and the powers of darkness".

In writing this scene, I had in mind the various preaching aids with which Christian missionary monks would go into the field. Among the relics of St Cuthbert (bishop of Lindisfarne, 685-87) is an oak slab about five inches square inscribed with a cross at each corner and a Latin inscription from the 7th century reading, "In honor of St Peter". This was presumably a portable altar, used to celebrate mass while on tour in remote villages. Missionaries would also have traveled with a chrismatory (a container for the chrism, the consecrated oil used in the sacrament of baptism, amongst other rites), a hand-bell (to call the faithful to prayer), and a copy of the gospel. In this case, I have modeled Columba's prayer-book, which is later marveled over by Bridei, on the *Cathach*, or "Battler", an early-7th-century Irish Psalter, the oldest known Irish manuscript, traditionally associated with Columba (see notes to Chapter 6).

This episode with the Loch Ness monster is modeled on Life of Columba, II.27. In that version, Columba orders his monk Luigne moccu Min into the water to retrieve a boat lost by a man who had been savaged by Nessie while swimming. When Nessie turns on Liugne, Columba saves the monk by praying vigorously.

Chapter 6: The Fortress of the Bulls

The Fortress of the Bulls is the majestic fortified headland of Burghead, the chief Pictish center on the Moray coast of Scotland. The promontory fort had four landward ramparts which were demolished in the early 19th century to create a planned town. The area enclosed within comprised two areas, an upper and a lower fort. In terms of size, Burghead would have dwarfed Dunadd (being 8 times larger). In northern Britain, only the fort of Milfield was larger, but Aedan has not seen this yet (Leslie Alcock, Kings & Warriors, Craftsmen & Priests in Northern Britain AD 550-800 (Edinburgh, 2003), pp. 192-97; and Martin Carver, Surviving in Symbols, A Visit to the Pictish Nation (Edinburgh, 1999), pp. 29-31).

The logboats which Aedan sees in the harbor are like those described by the 4th-century Roman writer Vegetius. Given the proximity of excellent anchorage, Burghead was very likely a major naval base for the Picts, perhaps one from which they launched their famous and terrifying sea-borne attacks against the Romans.

Six stone plaques survive from the fort, the famous Pictish Class I Burghead bulls, which may have been arranged as a processional frieze around the entrance passage through the fort's multiple ramparts. (Only 6 remain from an estimated 25-30 found at the site.)

One of the most evocative structures in the fort is its well, still extant today. In the lower enclosure of the fort, a flight of rock-cut steps leads down to a chamber which contains a smaller tank of water. The tank, hewn from the living rock and surrounded by a promenade, is always full. Over the centuries the well may have served as the focus of a pagan Celtic water cult, a place of execution, a Christian baptistery, or a simple water-cistern. I have modeled the sculpture I have set inside the well on survivors from the fort: the hunting scene from a fragment of a slab-shrine; and the stone-head on one purportedly found in the well (which has a distinctive drooping mustache, a hole in the mouth, and almond-shaped eyes).

Life of Columba, II.42 relates how Columba stayed for a time with King Bridei on the other side of the mountain range of Druim Alban. With Bridei at the time of that visit was the under-king (*regulus*) of the Orkneys, whose hostages Bridei held. Galam Cennalath was a Pictish king (556-557, died about 580) who held a one-year joint-reign with Bridei before Bridei's solo reign.

The three-fold execution was sacred to the *druidi*. (For instance, there is a record of Talorgen son of Drustan, a king of Atholl, being drowned by Angus son of Fergus in 739.)

Bridei admires the enlarged initial G, with cross and animal, from the *Cathach* of Columba, written in Latin in early majuscule with ornamental capitals, which is the oldest extant Irish manuscript of the Psalter and the earliest example of Irish writing (Royal Irish Academy, MS 12 R 33, fol. 48). The *Cathach* contains a Vulgate version of the Psalms and dates from around 600. It may have been written by Columba himself and shows the very beginning of the Irish manuscript art which was to flower in later centuries with masterpieces like The Book of Durrow and The Book of Kells (also from Columban monasteries).

The practice of slave-taking, ubiquitous in Columba's day is, sadly, still present in our own. St Patrick lamented: "I do not know what more to say or to speak concerning those of the sons of God who have departed, whom the sword struck all too hard. For it is written: 'Weep with those who weep'; and again, 'If one member grieves, let all the members share the grief'. Therefore the church mourns and weeps for its sons and daughters who so far have not been put to the sword, but have been carried far off and transported to distant lands, where sin is rife, openly, grievously and shamelessly; and there freeborn men have been sold, Christians reduced to slavery—and what is more, as slaves of the utterly iniquitous, evil

and apostate Picts". (St Patrick, "Letter to Coroticus", 15 (432 ×
461), ed. and trans., A.B.E. Hood, St. Patrick, His Writings and
Muirchu's Life (London, 1978), pp. 37, 57-58.)

The episode of the freeing of the slave-girl is based on Life of
Columba, II.33. In the Life, Columba asks the mage Broichan to
release his slave-girl "having pity on her as a fellow human being".
When Broichan refuses, Columba prophesies that Broichan will fall
ill; indeed he sees this event in a vision as it happens. Picking up
a white pebble from the shore of the River Ness, Columba blesses
it, then sends it up to the fortress where it is used to make a potion
which immediately heals Broichan. We are told that the pebble was
kept thereafter in the royal treasury where it "brought about the
healing of many ailments among the people". My version attempts
to find a rational explanation for the miracle while remaining true
to the spirit of the original story.

Chapter 7: Alt Clut

Alt Clut is, of course, the famed Dumbarton Rock, located in the
Firth of Clyde, outside of Glasgow, Scotland. It was the premier
stronghold of the Britons of Strathclyde.

This is how Bede describes the Rock of the Clyde: "There is a very
wide arm of the sea which originally divided the Britons from the
Picts. It runs far into the land from the west. Here there is to this day
a very strongly fortified British town called Alcluith. The Scots whom
we have mentioned settled to the north of this arm of the sea and made
their home there ... " (Bede, Historia ecclesiastica gentis Anglorum,
i.1 (about 731), ed. and trans., Bertram Colgrave and R.A.B. Mynors,
Bede's Ecclesiastical History, Oxford, 1969, pp. 20-21).

All the characters at the Oenach are based on historical figures
and known relationships. Tudwal (or Tutagual) was the father of
Rhydderch Hen (the Old) or Hael (the Generous), who was king of
the Strathclyde Britons from 580 to 612.

Kynfarch and his son Urien were rulers of Rheged in the 6th
century.

Gwenddolau ap Ceidaw was a Northern British ruler who lived in the 6th century and died at the Battle of Arfderydd/Arthuret in about 573. His traditional rivals were Gurgi and Peretur.

Morcant was a tyrannical 6th-century British ruler from an unidentified Northern British kingdom, probably of the Uotadini. He appears in Joceline of Furness, Life of Saint Kentigern, xxi (1175 × 1199): "A considerable period of time having passed, a tyrant called Morcant ascended to the throne of the Cambrian kingdom whom power, honor, and riches had persuaded to exercise himself in great matters which were too high for him".

In the Welsh genealogies, Beli ap Rhun was the grandson of Maelgwyn, ruler of Gwynedd (who died in a "great mortality", or plague, about 547), a very strong British kingdom in North Wales (called Guined in the book). Beli is said to have had seven sons, the youngest of whom was Iago. Afrella is a fictional creation. Since Bridei, king of the Picts, is also known as Bridei mac Maelchon, historians have hypothesized that he might have been the son of Maelgwyn Gwynedd, perhaps as a result of the Pictish practice of exogamy. If so, this would make Bridei the uncle of Beli—and create interesting complications for Aedan, as I have exploited in the book.

Chapter 8: The Crag of the Kings
St Kentigern, also known as Mungo, was the first bishop of Glasgow and patron saint of the Strathclyde Britons, about 550-612. Kentigern's mother was Teneu, a Northern British princess whose father set her adrift in a boat as punishment for her illegitimate pregnancy. Since one of the only sources to mention Morcant is Joceline of Furness' Life of St Kentigern (see notes to Chapter 7, above), I have posited a relationship between Kentigern and Morcant.

Gildas (died 570) is the famous 6th-century British chronicler and monk, a leading figure in the Church of his day. He is the author of many celebrated works, including De excidio Britonum (On the

Ruin of Britain), and a penitential, De Poenitentia. (These have been assembled in one handy volume by Michael Winterbottom, ed. and trans., Gildas: The Ruin of Britain and other works, London, 1978.)

Ninian (traditionally 4th-5th century; but more probably about 500-550), is the first Christian missionary in Scotland's history who is known to us by name. His see was St Martin's Church in Candida Casa ("The White House"), now Whithorn in Galloway. There is growing consensus amongst scholars that Ninian may be the same man as the Uinniau who authored a penitential, The Penitential of Uinniau. Indeed—to complicate matters further—that both names are in fact scribal errors for the Irish St Finnian of Moville, a historical figure who died about 589, so that Ninian/Uinniau/Finnian are one and the same man.

For this series, I have equated Ninian of Candida Casa with the Uinniau who wrote the Penitential; but have left Finnian of Moville a discreet historical figure.

Finnian of Moville, however, should not be confused with Finnian of Cluan-Erard (Clonard, Co. Meath) with whom it is known Columba also studied. (In other words, there are two Finnians.)

Some of the dialogue between the three clerics is taken from these, and other contemporary, works, as follows: "A savage nation of naked plunderers! Dirty heathens! Idolators!" (Michael Winterbotton, ed. and trans., Gildas, On the Ruin of Britain and other works, (London, 1978) 14, 19.1, 21.1); " ... who lead lives of natural goodness ... " (Richard Sharpe, trans., Life of Columba, (London, 1995), III.14); "They are readier to cover their villainous faces with hair than their private parts and neighboring regions with clothes ... " (Gildas, On the Ruin of Britain, 19.1); "You know he threw out Ninian? Ninian!" (from the late-8th-century Latin poem, Miracles of Bishop Ninian); "Lust of the flesh and lust of the eye and the wealth of the world so ministered to his haughtiness that he presumed himself to be able to do as much as any one, and that what any one could do was both possible and lawful for him also!" (Alexander Forbes, ed. and trans., Lives of St Ninian and

St Kentigern (Edinburgh, 1874), from Ailred of Rievaulx, Life of Ninian, Chapter IV); "Cohort of the Picts, amongst whom sin is rife, openly, grievously, and shamelessly!" (A.B.E. Hood, ed. and trans., St Patrick, His Writings and Muirchu's Life (London, 1978): Letter to Coroticus, 15); " ... but they are in perfect accord in their greed for bloodshed!" (Gildas, On the Ruin of Britain, 19.1); "Then why do you not heed? Why do you persist in your fraternization?" (Gildas, On the Ruin of Britain, 14, 19.1, 21.1); "A wise man recognizes the gleam of truth whoever utters it ... " (Fragments of Lost Letters of Gildas, 8); " ... we are obliged to serve; to have pity on all who are in need. To receive pilgrims into our houses, as the Lord has commanded; to visit the infirm; to minister to those in chains. From the least unto the greatest ... " (J.T. MacNeill, ed. and trans., Penitential of Vinnian, (1922), 33).

Chapter 9: Cernunnos
The ball game played on the first morning of the Oenach is loosely based on the game of *baire* which has come down to us as hurling (Irish) and shinty/*comanachd* (Scottish).

I know of no antecedents for a horse race at Alt Clut, though the course I have set for it along the River Leven, the watershed of Loch Lomond, is geographically possible. A *nemeton* was a sacred grove, or wood shrine, a place of assembly and sacred rites for the Celts. Cernunnos was a pre-Roman, shape-shifting Celtic horned deity, the lord of animals, fertility, abundance and regeneration.

The Irish did have remarkably forward-thinking and compassionate laws with regards to the rights of women and children.

Chapter 10: Gwallawg of Elmet
Gwallawg was a 6th-century ruler of Elmet, a British kingdom in the former West Riding of Yorkshire. This chapter was inspired in part by the following passage in Gildas: "It has always been true of this people (as it is now) that it was weak in beating off the

weapons of the enemy but strong in putting up with civil war and the burden of sin: weak, I repeat, in following the banners of peace and truth but strong for crime and falsehood" (Gildas, <u>On the Ruin of Britain</u>, 21.1).

Saxon mercenaries, descendants of the *foederati* recruited by the British war leader, the *tyrannus superbus* ("proud tyrant") Vortigern to help defend Britain against the Picts and the Scots, had settled a colony on York and the rich farmlands of the Yorkshire Wolds by the mid-5th to the 6th century. This was the beginning of the Saxon kingdom of Deira which proceeded to expand up the rich Vale of York in the second-half of the 6th century.

A rival house of kings established itself on coastal Northumbria, ruling from the old British fort of Din Guoaray, renamed Bebbanburh, the fortress of Bebba (now Bamburgh Castle). This became the kingdom of Bernicia. Neither the name Deira nor Bernicia is English in origin and both presumably were taken from the British tribes whom they subsumed, the *Deur*, the people of the Derwent valley, and the *Bernech*. "Saxons" was the term the British, Picts, and Scots used for these settlers: "Angles" was the term the English used for themselves.

Ida is the first historical king of Bernicia, ruling from Din Guoaroy from 547 until 549. Six rulers succeeded him until the ascension of his grandson Aethelfrith in 592/3. Of these, his son Theodoric (572-79) has come down to us as an inveterate enemy of the Britons. I have eclipsed Ida's reign to 547-72.

The author of the early 9th-century <u>History of the Britons</u> (62) recorded that one Outigern fought bravely against the Saxons, juxtaposing him in time with Ida of Bernicia.

Taliesin and Aneirin were both renowned 6th-century bards. Works ascribed to them comprise much of our knowledge of the period.

<u>Chapter 11</u>: Afrella of Guined

The concept of "the justice of the ruler", *fír flathemon*, was of immense importance in early Irish society. The king had two main tasks: the raising of an army (*slógad*) in times of war and the preservation of law and order in times of peace. The health and welfare of a king's people was dependent on his putting right rule into practice: when he failed, they failed, and so did the land. Pre-Christian in nature, this concept articulates the belief that the king is tied to his people and to his physical kingdom—indeed is joined to the land in the form of a marriage to a goddess of kingship, a personification of "sovereignty". All are linked.

Early Ireland was a society bound by a rich and complex legal system which helped to counterbalance and keep in check the rampant and indiscriminate violence which was a defining feature of this and other early medieval societies. At the heart of this system were the obligations of mutual advantage owed between members of a family, a kin-group, between kin-groups, and between a ruler and his people. The primary means for a person to enforce a claim against another was by means of distraint, that is the formal seizure of property belonging to the defendant in order to force him or her to arbitration. First, the plaintiff would give a formal notice of his or her intent to impound the defendant's property (for instance, the pigs which caused damage to the plaintiff's crops). The defendant might then put matters to right by either paying a fine or otherwise fulfilling his obligations. If he failed to do so, the plaintiff would enter his lands and remove cattle to the value of the amount due, since cattle was the currency of early Irish society. The plaintiff was again given an opportunity to pay the fee or otherwise discharge the debt. If he did not, the distrained cattle would become the property of the plaintiff. (For this, see Gearóid mac Niocaill, Ireland before the Vikings (1972), pp. 52-53, and Fergus Kelly, A Guide to Early Irish Law (1991), pp. 177-82).

The same procedure took on political overtones when carried out between *tuatha*, or petty kingdoms, and many recorded raids were probably the seizure of chattel from recalcitrant kingdoms. A king would raise a hosting, cross into the territory of the offending *tuath*, take as many head of cattle, horses and valuables as he could lay his hands on, and return home. If the *tuath* could raise its own host in time, there would be a battle. If not, then the raided *tuath* would retaliate with its own raid as soon as it was able.

In this case, King Conall knows that the aggrieved Cenel Oengussa are planning to distrain his cattle to force him to arbitration over the act of taking the sword-hand of their king, Forindan (which happened in Book I, *Exile*). Conall decides that he will raid them instead, in effect to distrain *their* cattle for withholding the tribute (render) they owed him to begin with. Knowing that this has as much to do with wounded pride (both Conall's and the Cenel Oengussa's) as any actual offense, Eogan suggests a second, ostensibly more peaceful, option—the use of a whipping boy. The custom of using a (literal) whipping boy was developed in early Irish society in order to prevent the king from sustaining any outrage to his *enech*, his "face", as a man's honor was known. For once a king lost "face" he could lose his mandate to rule.

The vengeance taken out on the back of the unfortunate stand-in also gave the aggrieved party some measure of satisfaction—what little satisfaction they could expect from having been misfortunate enough to have been wronged by a king. In this matter the Cenel Oengussa had been doubly-wronged: by the initial offense of the taking of their lord Forindan's sword-hand; and by the fact that it had been performed by a man who was legally beyond their reach, a man whom no one could "overswear". As the maxim went, *A king's honor is too great to be claimed against.*

Toiseach was a long-lived Celtic/Pictish title for the rank of leader, chief, or chieftan, a grade lower than king.

Dun da lath glas ("Dun of the Two Fetters") is Downpatrick, Co. Down, the locus of the cult of St Patrick and the site of his burial before Armagh took it over.

Chapter 12: The Western World
The hillfort of Dùn Nosebridge is on the island of Islay (Argyll and Bute).

The monastery of Iona is believed to have been the first to begin compiling annals, though that annal is now lost. Entries from this lost, so-called, <u>Iona Chronicle</u> form the core for all later Irish chronicles. It was probably begun in Columba's time, and was certainly being kept by the 7th century. In the 8th century it was brought to Ireland for safe-keeping from the vikings, where it was copied into other sets of annals, including the <u>Annals of Ulster</u> and the <u>Annals of Tigernach</u>.

For the year 568, the <u>Annals of Ulster</u> read: "A campaign in the Western World [was led] by Colman Bec, Diarmait's son, and Conall, Comgall's son".

Chapter 13: Lasren mac Fergus
The death of Gildas is noted in the <u>Annals of Tigernach</u> for the year 570. <u>Life of Columba</u>, I.48 relates the story of a heron which, buffeted by the wind on its long flight from Ireland, fell from the sky onto the shore of Iona. It revived, but only after three days and nights of care by Columba. <u>Life of Columba</u> II.16 and II.38 also recount various miracles regarding milk-pails. Though almost painfully naive to our modern sensibilities, these stories are lovely reminders of how the early Irish saw portents in even the simplest things, the divine being omnipresent and all life linked.

Lasren (or Laisran) was the son of Columba's first cousin, Fergus (or Feradach). He appears frequently in the <u>Life of Columba</u>. Novices were required to undergo a year of instruction and probation before making their vows and being taken on as permanent members of a community (<u>Life of Columba</u>, I.32).

St Comgall founded the monastery of Bangor on the south shore of Belfast Lough, Northern Ireland, in the 550s. St Columbanus, the crusading missionary who brought Christianity to the Franks and Lombards, was one of his students. St Finnian, Columba's old teacher at the great monastic school of Clonard (Cluan-Erard in the book), died in 579.

Ainmire mac Setnai ruled at Tara from 566-569. In 569 he was slain by Fergus, son of Néillíne. There was a period of a multiplicity of kings, then his son Aed became high-king, ruling until 598.

In 573, Colman Bec attempted to take over the leadership of the Uí Neill, but was defeated at the battle of *Feiman* in Brega. By 574, Colman Bec was slain by Aed at the battle of *Belach Dathi*. There are two locations by the name of Femen, one near Tara, the other near Cashel. The battle of *Belach Dathi* is unlocated.

In order to simplify the narrative, I have conflated these reigns, revenges and battles, having Ainmire rule 566-574, and his son Aed succeed him in 574 after slaying Colman Bec.

The verse lamenting Ainmire's death is found in the <u>Annals of Ulster</u>, amongst others, for the year 575: "Femen when there was a king/was not a spot that was not brave;/today its color is bright red/by (the hand of) Ainmire son of Setna. Femen, as long as kings led,/nowhere was valor wanted;/today its hue crimson red/by Ainmire undaunted".

Áedán mac nGabráin had many sons. He had two by the name of Eochaid, a Eochaid Find and a Eochaid Buide. To avoid confusion with the Eochaid who comes later, I have called this first one Finn (the Irish descriptive Find/Finn means "white, light, or shining"); and have made him a twin with another of Áedán's known sons, Bran (Irish for "raven", i.e. black or dark).

<u>Chapter 14</u>: Tairbert Boitter

Maxims from the <u>Críth Gablach</u>, an early-8th-century Irish legal tract, underpin Columba's reasonings here. Among them: "Question—How many things is it proper for a king to bind by pledge on his *tuatha*? Three. What are they? Pledge for hostings, pledge for government, pledge for treaty, for all these things are benefits to a *tuath* ... These are the sustaining means of a true ruler over his *tuatha*, and he cannot violate them by falsity or violence or overmight. Let him be sound, distinguishing [fairly], and upright, between weak and strong. There are also three other things that they require of a king: let him be a man of all sides, full of right; let him be a man inquiring after knowledge; let him be steady and patient ... "; "Injustice, extortion, and kin-slaying are the three things which cause the overthrow of a king ... " (Críth Gablach, xxxvi, xxxix).

Demmán mac Cairell was king of the Dal Fiatach in Ireland and overking of Ulster. Whoever held this position was also nominal suzerain of Dal Riata, both its division in Ulster and its division in Scotland. When Demmán died in 572 he was succeeded by his brother, Báetán mac Cairill.

Chapter 15: Ile
There is a lovely little shell-sand beach on the shore of Loch Fyne, east of the town of Tairbert. It was used as a boat launch. This is where I imagine Eogan had his transformative vision.

Chapter 16: The Battle of Arfderydd
Arfderydd was a dynastic battle between two branches of the same royal family, who were ruling in the Pennines and Borders. The battle appears in the Annales Cambriae (the Welsh Annals) under the year 573, as follows: "The battle of Arterid between the sons of Elifer and Guendoleu, the son of Keidiau. And in this battle Guendoleu fell. Merlin became insane". The armies clashed at a place called Arfderydd (or Arthuret), indentified most plausibly with the "Roman Camp" or "Moat of Liddel", near Carwhinelow/ Carwinley, in the valley of the Liddel, eight miles from Carlisle and within sight of the fort of Burnswark.

According to the Welsh genealogies, Gurci and Peretur were the sons of Elifer of the Great Retinue, the son of Gurgust Letlum, the son of Ceneu, the son of Coel Hen. Gwenddolau, son of Ceidaw, was also a Coeling, that is he was also descended from the great Coel Hen. All the principals of this battle, then, were rival factions of the same house. Gwenddolau was slain in this battle and his bard Myrddin went mad. Gurci and Peretur were later slain by Adda of Bernicia at the battle of Caer Gren in about 580.

The Welsh poem <u>Yr Afallennau</u> (The Appletrees) depicts Rhydderch, son of Tudwal of Strathclyde, as the victor of the Battle of Arfderydd and the tormentor of the mad prophet Myrddin. The Welsh triads refer to the battle as second amongst "the three frivolous battles of the island of Britain" because it was " ... fought because of a lark's nest". Gildas complains bitterly of this meaningless infighting among the Britons, foreshadowing the later battles of Medcaut and even Catraeth.

The stone of the god Mabon where the armies assemble is the Clochmaben Stone, on a low promontory on the north side of the Solway Firth (Dumfries and Galloway). The stone is 8 feet high and 18 feet in girth. Its name recalls the regional cult of the British god Mabon, or Maponus, "The Divine Youth". It has phallic/fertility associations and remained in use as a gathering place well into the Middle Ages. The forge of Gretna Green, where runaway marriages could be performed without license, banns, or priest, is nearby. Also close by is the large Celtic, then Roman, complex of Burnswark, where I have sited the principal stronghold of Gwenddolau.

Cair Ligualid, known to the pre-Roman Britons as *Luguualium*, and to the Romans as *ciuitas Caruetiorum*, is the city of Carlisle. The Flavian fort is thought to have been the location of a British stronghold in the 6th century. St Cuthbert, who is said to have visited the city in 685, was taken by the citizens to see the "walls of the city and a marvelously constructed fountain of Roman workmanship ... " (Bede, <u>Life of St Cuthbert</u>, xxvii). While there, Cuthbert conducted his business with an official who held a post that survived from the Roman period, a *praepositus*. Aedan's wonder at Cair Ligualid's fading grandeur is in part inspired by the Old English Poem from The Exeter Book, <u>The Ruin</u>, a description of a fading Roman city, probably Bath: "Splendid this rampart is, though fate destroyed it,/The city buildings fell apart, the works/ Of giants crumble. Tumbled are the towers,/Ruined the roofs, and broken the barred gate,/Frost in the plaster, all the ceilings gape,/ Torn and collapsed and eaten up by age".

Petrianis is the fort of Stanwix on Hadrian's Wall. The name form is from the <u>Notitia Dignitatum</u>, compiled about 410 (David Breeze and Brian Dobson, <u>Hadrian's Wall</u>, pp. 271-72). The fort on the scarp-top in Inglewood Forest is Dobcross Hall, Dalston.

The Battle of Camlann in which Artur and Medraut fell is thought to have been fought in 537. We know that Aedan was born in about 538. (As I have it, February of that year.) Much of Myrddin's speech/prophecy to Aedan is taken from the poems ascribed to the seer in <u>The Black Book of Carmarthen, Peniarth 3</u>, and <u>The Red Book of Hergest</u>. "I drank wine out of a white glass ... with lords who were mighty in battle ... Myrddin my name, son of Morfryn ... " is from the poem <u>Gwasgargerdd Fyrddin yn y Bedd</u> (<u>Myrddin's Discourse in the Grave</u>). "Death takes everyone; why does it not claim me?" and "Pleasure gives me no satisfaction! No maid visits me!" are from <u>Yr Afallennau</u> (<u>The Appletrees</u>). "For years I have suffered agony. I do not sleep easily because of the turbulence of pain that is upon me. My color is pale!" and "I saw Gwenddolau, the king of our region, who had been gathering spoil from all borders, put under red earth. The chief Lord of the North is now still ... " are from <u>Hoianau</u> (<u>Hails</u>). "His reason is gone with the wild men of the mountain ... " and "After Beli, his son Iago ..." are from <u>Cyfoesi Myrddin a Gwenddydd ei Chisaet</u> (<u>The Discourse of Myrddin and his sister, Gwenddydd</u>). "Seven-score noble ones [became] mad: their lord perished in the forest of Celyddon ... " is from <u>Ymddiddau Myrddin a Thaliesin</u> (<u>The Discourse of Myrddin and Taliesin</u>).

The <u>Welsh Triads</u> mention an expedition of Aedan to Strathclyde, but in what context and when is unclear: "The third [costly plundering of the island of Britain] was that in which Aidan the Traitor went into Alclut to the court of Riderch Hael: after it, there remained neither food nor drink, nor any living thing." The British term applied to Aedan here, *Fradawg*, means "traitor".

Chapter 17: Bellum Telocho

The Annals of Tigernach note for the year 574: "The battle of Delgu [Telocho] in Kintyre; and in it Duncan, son of Conall, son of Comgall, and many others of the allies of the sons of Gabran, fell".

Chapter 18: Feis Ri

Kilmartin Glen, the valley stretching to the north of the hillfort of Dunadd, has the one of the most important concentrations of prehistoric burial monuments in Britain. The density and quality of Neolithic and Bronze Age standing stones, chambered cairns, cist burials, and rock carvings including cup-and-ring clusters is astounding. (There are 350 monuments within a six-mile radius of the village, 150 of which are prehistoric.) There is even a stone circle and the only henge and cursus on the west coast. The landscape of the glen was clearly the focus of ritual for millennia, up to and including the age of the overkings of Dalriada.

The grouping of rock carvings on the exposed plateau of the hillfort of Dunadd (the footprint, stone throne, rock-cut basin, *ogham* inscriptions and carving of a boar) has long been associated with the inauguration of the kings of Dalriada. Other inauguration sites are known in Ireland and Scotland, but within Dalriada the one at Dunadd is clearly the most important. (I have omitted the boar carving and *ogham* inscriptions from my account as they are of a later date.) When the king placed his foot in the footprint, he could look out over his people on the terraces, his land, the peak of the holy mountain of Ben Cruachan in the distance—and this stretch of ancient landscape, sacred to all who had come before.

The Stone of Destiny is the Stone of Scone, a block of Old Red Sandstone, one of the most powerful icons of Scottish nationhood, returned to Scotland in 1996 after lying in Westminster Abbey for 700 years. There are many myths about its origins, including that it was brought from Ireland with the Gaels when they first settled Dalriada.

Life of Columba, III.5 claims that Columba at first refused to ordain Áedán as king of the Scots, holding his brother Éoganán in higher regard. Though an Angel of the Lord rebuked and struck him with a whip, showing him the glass book of the kings in which Áedán's name was present, Columba held out, only relenting after the third night. Columba's ordination of Áedán in 574 A.D. is the first record of an event like this occurring in Europe (which later become the norm)—though this may have had more to do with late-7th century ideals about kingship (when the Life was composed) than about 6th-century reality. In any case, that ordination is said to have taken place on Iona.

Áedán mac nGabráin became king of the Scots of Dalriada in A.D. 574.

And then his and Columba's adventures really began ...

Read on for an excerpt from
ISLAND-PILGRIM
the third book in
THE CHRONICLES OF IONA

Coming in 2013

Dal Riata: Beltane, 574 A.D.

His people had a saying: *heaven lay beyond the ninth wave of the sea.* And he often thought that there might be some truth to this (for the sea was in the blood of every Scot) which he would one day discover for himself—but only after his life was wrested from him and he punched through the veil between the worlds and at last stared his gods in the face.

Today, however, Aedan mac Gabran mac Domangart mac Fergus Mor mac Erc, newly acclaimed king of Dal Riata, had to disagree. Today, that fine first day of May 574 A.D., heaven lay not beyond any wave, eighth or ninth or even tenth, but before him, in the sea-girt land of his people.

Below him spread the valley of Dun Ad, terraced, hummocky and hot, with the sea a tempt on the horizon, the sun riding overhead in an azure sky. He took it all in eagerly: the precipitous outcrop of rock upon which the fort of Dun Ad sat; and the great expanse of marsh about the rock's foot; and the river Ad snaking around the rock, making Dun Ad an inland-island. Enclosed within the fort's sturdy stone walls were the houses and buildings of his people, and the king's Great Hall (now his!). At the rock's foot and extending across the marshy glen and up the valley behind him were more of his people's homesteads.

He loved this place. He loved how the thin river Ad meandered to the sea-loch harbor to drain into the sea to the west. He loved how behind him the hills grew to mountains which grew to stout peaks and thence to fastnesses so forbidding that you crossed them only in the greatest need and at your peril. Those fastnesses kept

351

his people safe from the Picts. Most especially, he loved the gentle peninsula that lay to the south of the valley: Cendtire, the division of his kindred, the Cenel Gabran.

This was heaven. Especially since, against all odds and every reason that he could think of, he had been made its king; he who had only ever been a second son of a slain king, an unwilling warrior, and an exile. Now, for as long as he managed to keep his head attached to his shoulders, these people were his and he was theirs. Looking upon it all again after more than a month away, he felt that he could not be more full of love for it than if his lover lay before him, her ready smile welcoming him home.

Which he very much hoped she soon would be. It had been a long month, this month of his *Crech Rig*, visiting all his people, all three kindreds, to show them that he was strong, and that he deserved their loyalty, and their render, and their fighting men, to fill his new warband. Since it was a circuit Aedan had never imagined he would take, he supposed it had gone as well as could be expected. He had given the people what they wanted, had performed the necessary rituals: two more king-makings, in fact. One on an outcrop near Aberte, his father's old fort at Cendtire's end, in the footprint carved there, the one that pointed back across the water towards Ulaid, their ancestral homeland in Hibernia. That had made him *ri*, the king, of his own kindred, the Cenel Gabran. The second king-making: on a similar rock carving, this time near the royal stronghold of Dun Nosbridge on the island of Ile. That had made him *ruiri*, over-king, of the Cenel Oengussa.

As for the Cenel Loarn, however, so recently at war with his own kindred—so recently at war with everyone, actually—there was little he could do but move amongst their strongly fortified hill-top duns, farmstead to farmstead, doing his best to persuade them of the rightness of his rule. He didn't know yet if it had worked. Their king, Conall, was dead. Whether or not they had liked him while he was alive was no longer the point—it was Aedan who had killed him.

Still, they owed him tribute. And he had taken it, and then had gladly sped towards home. That tribute, those cattle, now made its way to Dun Ad for the Beltane festival. But the cattle and wagon-trains were still half-a-day behind, toiling towards him on Dal Riata's rudimentary trackways.

Which was a mercy. It left him just enough time for something which was in no way kingly. He could see Dun Mor, that modest stronghold not a third-of-a-league southeast from Dun Ad. There it was, rising on its hillock. Flanked by his retinue, some newly recruited, others hand-picked from amongst his very first clients, promoted now with him to high lords, Aedan forded the river Ad, crossed between the standing stones that guarded the fertile plain there, and came to the rise. At the base of the hill, he bade his retinue stay. Dismounting his horse, his companion the wolf-hound Ceo left to lope about as she saw fit, Aedan quickly climbed the path, the sun hot on his back and his spirits rising. At the top, he pushed open the wooden gate of the dun, and entered.

The dun was a simple place: its stone walls, twelve-feet thick, enclosed a circular courtyard. At the far end of the courtyard, a thatched round-house hugged the wall. Chickens scolded him from underfoot; the house-dogs ran to snuff at his hands. The slaves, Colgu and Mogain, were grinding grain on rotary querns in the afternoon sun. He had startled them, they made to rise, but with a finger to his lips he silenced them. With mounting excitement, he crossed the courtyard and, ducking his head under the low wooden lintel of the door, he entered the house.

"Yes?" she said.

Made in the USA
Charleston, SC
27 January 2013